ALYSSA'S RING

ALYSSA'S RING

Book Five of
The Guardian Cycle

JULIA GRAY

orbit

www.orbitbooks.co.uk

An *Orbit* Book

First published in Great Britain by Orbit 2002
Reprinted 2003, 2004

A CIP catalogue record for this book
is available from the British Library.

ISBN 1 84149 146 2

Typeset in Erhardt by M Rules
Printed and bound in Great Britain by
Mackays of Chatham plc, Chatham, Kent

Orbit
An imprint of
Time Warner Book Group UK
Brettenham House
Lancaster Place
London WC2E 7EN

This book is dedicated to the memory of
Betty Shine, who was not only an extraordinary
healer but also a wise and generous spirit who
brought enlightenment and inspiration to our world.

Prologue

It was a night when mountains ground their teeth, when islands moved like ships and the oceans boiled.

The people of Senden knew nothing of the ways of the sea or the fate of islands, but they heard the distant mountains growl and felt the ground shake beneath their feet. This was the night they had been waiting for, and they watched in awe and terror, the words of the Zealot echoing in their ears, as events unfolded in the sky above. The time of fire and darkness was upon them, the time when the moons would fall and the world would end – the time when all their sins would have to be accounted for. It was time to die.

As the four moons moved slowly and inexorably towards their fatal convergence, the Family gathered together for the last time. They abandoned the huts that had cost them so much time and effort to build out there in the wilderness, and left behind their few belongings, knowing that they no longer had any need of personal possessions. They made their way to the open space at the centre of the village – the heart of Senden – where the shape of the dark, five-pointed star had been marked upon the hard, stony ground, each of its points extended in tapering wavy lines that reached out like tentacles to the edges of the arena.

When they were all in place there were more than a hundred people present, two thirds of them women, and they all sat facing inwards, turning their backs on the rest of Nydus, rejecting it. There was a feverish joy on some of their faces, naked fear on others. The youngest of them, infants who could not understand what was going on, could only trust in the adults around them – their parents, the Zealot's servitors – and, most of all, in the Zealot himself. He moved among the group, his voice ringing out in ecstatic promises or whispering words of encouragement to the less brave among his flock.

Nomar Veress sat on the ground beside his mother. She was crying softly and, although he didn't know the reason for her sorrow, her tears distressed him. He knew that something was going to happen this night – something important – but although the prospect had been exciting at first, he wasn't used to being awake so late and he was finding it hard to stay alert. His mother's sadness was the only thing that remained clear to him, and he tried to comfort her, slipping his small hand into hers. But she didn't even seem to notice that he was there, and her red-rimmed eyes stared up at the night sky.

Nomar followed the line of her gaze just in time to see a shooting star streak across the heavens. A collective murmur rose from the Family, and the boy felt his mother grow tense. In the past he had always thought shooting stars were wonderful – so bright and so fast – but recently, since the mountains had begun to shake, everyone seemed to regard any unusual sight in the sky as a possible cause for alarm. His mother mumbled something he couldn't hear, but he knew she wasn't talking to him and so he didn't ask her what it was.

'Don't cry,' he whispered instead, but she gave no sign of having heard him.

'Nomar is right, Lia. You should not be crying.' The

Zealot had appeared before them as if by magic, his feet making no sound on the hard-packed earth. Now, as he squatted before them, his silver-grey eyes shone in the diminishing moonlight and the dark tattoos that marked his face and forearms seemed like living creatures upon his skin.

Lia nodded, wiped her eyes and tried to smile, but Nomar knew that her sadness had not gone away.

'This is our day of release, of our salvation,' the Zealot said. 'You know that, don't you?'

Lia nodded again.

'Then rejoice with the rest of our Family,' he told her earnestly. 'There should be no fear, no unhappiness, in such company.' He paused, then added, 'Paradise is coming.'

That was something he said quite often. For a long time Nomar had waited for a person called Paradise to arrive at the village, but that misunderstanding was behind him now. He still wasn't completely sure what Paradise was, but he knew it was good, and he hoped he and his mother would enjoy it.

Lia glanced around at those nearby, receiving a few encouraging smiles in return, but Nomar could tell that there was still something wrong. There was a kind of emptiness in her eyes now, as if she was looking for something she could not see. He longed to be able to find it for her.

'I wish . . .' she began, then faltered as her gaze returned to the Zealot's face.

'I know what you wish, child,' he said kindly, taking her free hand in his own. Then his voice became a little sterner. 'The Family is like a tree. Each branch, even the smallest twig, is strong because it is part of the whole, linked to the great trunk and the roots that hold it firmly in place. But it can only remain healthy if dead wood, those rotten parts that could spread weakness and disease to the rest, are cut away from time to time. Do you understand me?'

For a few moments Lia's face remained expressionless, but then she nodded, her eyes downcast – and Nomar found that he too knew what she had been wishing for. The boy had not really understood the story about the tree, but he knew it had something to do with his father. His mother had not been looking in vain for something, but for some*one*.

'You have all that you need around you here,' the Zealot went on.

There had been times when Nomar, like all the children of the Family, had been encouraged to think of the Zealot as his father. His real father was a shadowy figure he couldn't even remember properly, and they never talked about him now. When Nomar had first been old enough to notice that their small family was not like most others, he had asked and been told that his father had 'gone away'. He could still remember the funny way the words had been said. At the time he'd asked, 'When is he coming back?' 'Soon,' his mother had replied. But he never had. And not long after that, Lia had announced that their stay with the Family was to become permanent.

'Did you bring your cup?' the Zealot asked.

Lia nodded again. They had all brought them, and she held hers up now.

'And Nomar's?'

She turned to the boy at last, and squeezed her son's hand. Obediently he took out the small wooden bowl he had helped to make soon after they had come to Senden. The crooked black star painted on the side had been his main contribution. He had always known that the cup was special, but he had never been allowed to use it until now.

'Good boy,' the Zealot said approvingly. He picked up a jug that one of the servitors had set down beside him and poured a little liquid into the cup. Nomar thought it looked like watery milk, but the smell was wrong.

'It's for the toast,' the Zealot explained. 'When the moons come together.' He poured a slightly larger portion into Lia's bowl. 'It won't be long now.'

Nomar glanced up at the sky, following the gaze of the adults around him. As he did so, some of the grey liquid spilled from his cup on to his leg. He moved quickly to hide his clumsiness and, much to his relief, no one seemed to notice. When he looked up again – more carefully this time – he saw that the four moons were almost in line now, the Red, Amber and White shrinking to crescents as each was hidden by the one in front of it, while the closest of all, the invisible Dark Moon, slid across, swallowing their light. Soon, when the confluence was complete, the sky-shadow would obliterate them all.

Such a precise alignment of full moons was very rare, happening only once every seventy-five years, and everyone – even someone as young as Nomar – knew that such moments were significant. On Nydus, the aspects of the moons always meant something.

The Zealot had left them now, returning to the centre of the gathering to stand at the midpoint of the dark star. The servitors had all completed their tasks and were sitting with the rest, watching the sky above. The night seemed hushed, unnaturally quiet, and when their leader spoke his voice rang out like a sonorous, deep-toned bell.

'My name is Araguz!' he declared, his arms spread wide.

There were gasps of surprise all around. The Zealot had never told any of them his real name, and the fact that he had chosen to do so now only deepened the significance of the moment.

'The invisible forces of earth and fire, of wind and sky, flow through me. The moons move within the tides of my blood.'

Above them, the lunar crescents grew thinner.

'Rejoice now!' Araguz cried. 'Only after the black night of the darkest star will we all find peace. Welcome to the only true light.'

The moment was upon them. At the exact moment of conjunction, the last vestiges of the moons disappeared. As the sky became a deeper black, the distant stars shone brighter, their dominion for once unchallenged. The whole world seemed to hold its breath, even as the ground beneath them trembled slightly.

'Drink now,' the Zealot intoned. 'Paradise is here.'

The Family obeyed. And darkness claimed them all.

Nomar woke, feeling sick. The sour taste of the liquid was still in his mouth, and every muscle in his body felt as if it had been battered by rocks. When he opened his eyes, the pain that sliced through his head almost made him faint, and when he tried to move, his stomach rebelled and he vomited a thin stream of horrible green bile. He knew that he was more ill than he had ever been in his short life, but he also knew there was no one there to help him. When he was finally able to get his eyes to stay open, and to focus, he saw his mother sprawled on the ground, and reached out to touch her. She was cold, and her skin was pale and hard. He knew that she was dead.

They were *all* dead, except him. As terror and guilt engulfed him, he curled into a ball of misery and self-loathing, waiting – and wanting – to die.

When he next awoke, nothing around him had changed,

but the thoughts ringing inside his head had. He still felt awful, and a raging thirst had now been added to his torments, but as the reality of what had happened became a little clearer, he experienced the first intimations of amazement, then a reluctant curiosity.

The world had not ended. The sun had risen as it always did, and the daylight was warm, but there was no all-consuming fire, no smothering darkness of smoke and dust.

Nomar didn't understand what had happened, but when he heard the faint sound of a nearby stream, his body reacted instinctively. Slowly, agonizingly, he began to crawl towards the water.

After several torturous hours, he reached his goal. The clear liquid was cool and wonderfully refreshing, and he drank eagerly. It was not the Paradise he had expected, but it would do for now.

PART ONE

KENDA

CHAPTER ONE

The last thing Terrel saw before the darkness found him again was the White Moon falling from the sky. Even as the bright disc filled his dream, threatening to crush him beneath the weight of destiny, he saw the moon in all its guises. It hung over the tower of a hilltop fortress, was mirrored by a circle of pale stones in the sand, and floated like a perfect icy sphere above a mist-enshrouded island. Terrel had changed during his years of exile, and his dreams had changed with him, but some things never changed. The eternal moon vanished, extinguished without a trace.

Terrel braced himself for what he knew was coming next. Pain reached out with red fingers . . . but grasped at nothing. The crimson tide ebbed away as the dream ended prematurely, and Terrel struggled to make sense of what was happening. Fingers – real, human fingers – gripped his good arm, shaking it gently but with purpose.

'What is it?' Terrel mumbled, fighting to shake off the cobwebs of sleep.

'My father has one of his headaches,' Taryn replied. 'A bad one.' The boy's voice trembled as he spoke. Although he was only six years old, he was an unusually mature and resilient child, and seemed more than capable of dealing with most of the difficulties that presented themselves during his erratic journey through life. But when his father was in the grip of one of his periodic attacks, Taryn reverted to a helpless, fearful infancy. These were the only times Terrel ever saw him cry.

'I'll go to him,' the healer said, untangling himself from the blanket that was twisted round his legs.

Taryn nodded, and the look on his face made the need for haste all too clear.

The damp chill of the night air wrapped itself around Terrel like a cloak as he stumbled past the dying embers of their campfire, and he was uncomfortably aware that autumn had begun its gradual decline into winter. Sleeping in the open would soon no longer be an option, and the journey ahead of them would become more hazardous as the weather closed in. But those problems lay in the future. Just now, Terrel had more immediate concerns.

With Taryn at his heels, he hurried across to the small, leaf-strewn hollow where the boy's father had chosen to lay their bedrolls. Their fellow travellers were also awake now, obviously aware of the disturbance, but no one spoke, knowing that Terrel needed to concentrate. Above them, as serene as ever, the full White Moon rode across the heavens, looking down on the feverish activity of humankind with a certain disdain. Even as he knelt beside his patient, Terrel couldn't help wondering briefly if the moon's influence had coloured his own dream – or helped to precipitate Nomar's illness.

The man Terrel had come to regard as a friend was a few years older than the healer. His slender build and gaunt face disguised a sinewy strength of both body and mind, and he was normally in excellent health. The only exceptions to this were the vicious headaches that afflicted him every so often, striking without warning and with devastating affect. Apart from the crushing pain that made Nomar claw at his cheeks and temples, the attacks induced a kind of delirium in which he obviously saw and heard things that were imperceptible to anyone else. He muttered and gasped in response, occasionally shouting something aloud, and all the time his face betrayed horror and despair. Terrel believed that it was as if Nomar were trapped in a tortured form of sleep from which it was impossible to wake, a nightmare that could only end when it had run its course. Occasionally Nomar said something intelligible, but neither his son nor the healer had ever been able to make sense of these disjointed utterances – and in the exhausted calm after the storm of pain, Nomar either could not or would not explain his words.

Even as he clasped his friend's hot trembling hand, Terrel knew that his healing efforts would be defeated, just as they had been on every previous occasion. Although he could help Nomar deal with the physical torment of his ailment – Terrel had always understood pain and the ways of controlling it – he could never locate the source of the illness, let alone attempt to heal it. It was too deeply ingrained, hidden within the shifting planes and surfaces of Nomar's waking dream. Terrel could follow its trail only so far, retracing its passage through that ravaged inner world, but he always came to a dead end, or found himself trapped in an endless loop, unable to progress. His healer's instincts made him want to persevere, obstinately hunting for a solution to a problem that, in his heart, he knew to be insoluble. But in the end, all he could do was accompany his friend throughout the ordeal, protecting him where he could, and hoping that in the process he did nothing to prolong the agony. If he could not find a cure, he could at least offer comfort.

'We were never going to use it,' Nomar declared, his eyes glittering as they stared sightlessly up at the night sky. 'I thought . . .' The rest of his words were lost as his voice became an inarticulate mumble, his lips working rapidly but without purpose. A trickle of saliva ran from his mouth, and his tortured body writhed.

'Easy now,' Terrel said softly. 'I'm here.' He had no need to speak aloud – on some level, Nomar was already aware of his presence – but the words seemed to have a soothing effect nonetheless. His patient's limbs grew quieter, the muscles relaxing slowly, and his face lost a little of its terror.

'Will he be all right?' Taryn asked anxiously.

'Eventually,' Terrel whispered. 'We just have to ride this out. Like before.' The pain was still gouging at Nomar's skull, but that was something the healer could deal with. The underlying nightmare went on, shadows within shadows.

'I've never seen him this bad before,' Taryn said.

'He'll be all right,' Terrel reassured the boy. 'Let me concentrate now.'

'Leave the healer to his task.'

The commanding voice came out of the darkness as Terrel closed his eyes, and he knew that Faulk would stay with Taryn for as long as necessary. In the meantime, he had work to do. He let himself sink deeper into the other man's world, and tried to make sense of the chaos around him. He fought a hundred minor battles, pushing back darkness and unnatural pain, restoring equilibrium where he could, though he knew that his strategy was merely defensive. This was a war he could not win.

'Don't cry,' Nomar breathed, his distress obvious. 'I wish . . .'

Terrel tried to follow the patterns of thought, of memory, but failed, as so often before. Although there were different voices here, each linked to a separate set of emotions, they were all intertwined and he couldn't untangle them, no matter how hard he tried.

'It's for the toast,' Nomar stated clearly, then screamed,

the harrowing sound changing slowly into a mirthless laughter that was even more chilling. Terrel caught glimpses of love and hatred, fear and hope, guilt and revulsion; brief flashes of colour, of sounds and smells; a face; drops of liquid sticky on his skin; a dark labyrinth; the sudden shock of cold water. This was the signal that the end was in sight, that the worst was over. Terrel had no idea how much time had passed, but his own legs – especially the one that had been twisted from the time of his birth – were cramped and numb. He opened his eyes to see the first glimpses of dawn along the eastern horizon.

'Paradise,' Nomar mumbled, then added something that Terrel couldn't hear.

'Is it over?'

Terrel looked up to see Faulk's imposing bulk looming over him.

'It's over. He's sleeping now. Is Taryn all right?'

'He fell asleep about an hour ago. Shall I wake him?'

'No. Let him rest a while longer. We're not in any fit state to set off just now.'

Faulk nodded, and offered Terrel his hand. The healer took it and allowed himself to be pulled to his feet, grimacing as needles of pain spiked through his bones and the blood began to flow back into his legs. Faulk eyed him thoughtfully but made no comment. He was not one to use words unnecessarily.

'We'll wait for sunrise at least.' Even as Terrel spoke, he was groaning inwardly at the prospect of starting to walk again. And yet he knew he would. He had no choice. A tiny sliver of hope remained in his heart, and until this was extinguished completely, he would go on.

Terrel had been travelling for so long now that he could scarcely remember a time when he had stayed in any one place for more than a few days. Havenmoon, the madhouse in which he'd spent the first fourteen years of his life, seemed to belong in another realm. More than a decade had passed since he had left the only home he had ever known. During that time he had seen and experienced more than he could ever have imagined when as a child he had sat in his secret library and dreamt of the world outside the asylum's walls. But now his journey was coming full circle. Regardless of whatever else fate had in store for him, Terrel had sworn to return to Havenmoon. The reason for his determination was simple. Whether she was dead or alive, that was where Alyssa was.

'Do you have any brothers or sisters?' Taryn asked.

Terrel hesitated before answering, then nodded. One of the few things he knew about the boy was that he was an only child – and a lonely one.

'I have a twin brother.'

'Really?' Taryn said enviously.

'But I've never met him.'

The boy looked confused.

'Then how do you know . . .'

'I've been told about him,' Terrel said. 'And I dream about him sometimes.' And that's only part of it, he added to himself. The whole story was far too complicated to tell now.

'Does he look like you?'

'No,' Terrel replied, then changed the subject. 'How's your father doing?'

'All right. He's asleep.'

Terrel had called an early halt to their journeying that day. Even though they hadn't gone as far as he would have liked, Nomar had obviously been close to collapse. The healer had been exhausted too after his night's work, and so when they had found a suitable campsite – at the foot of a steep and stony path that led up into the hills – he had decided to leave the climb until the next day.

More from habit than necessity, Faulk had scouted the surrounding area, fixing the lie of the land in his mind and identifying ways to defend their camp from any threat. Lawren had taken advantage of the last of the daylight to do a little hunting, and Roskin had collected the wood for the fire beside which Terrel and the boy now sat.

'Thank you for stopping when you did,' Taryn said quietly. 'I don't think my father could have gone on much longer – and he hates it when we slow you down.'

'I was glad to stop myself,' Terrel replied truthfully, wondering once again at the formal way Taryn referred to Nomar. He always spoke of 'my father', never 'papa' or 'dad'.

'He's scared that one day you'll go on without him,' the boy added softly.

'I'll only do that if I have no choice,' Terrel said, deciding that he deserved an honest answer. 'I'd much rather have the two of you with me.'

'Really?' Taryn exclaimed, looking pleased.

'Really,' Terrel replied.

In the past, Terrel had always resisted travelling in company when his bargain with fate forced him to move on. He had made friends and accepted hospitality in the various places to which he'd been drawn – in Macul, Misrah and on the island of Myvatan – but in between times, since he'd become a seasoned traveller, he had preferred to journey alone, beholden to no one, fearing that other people would slow his progress or interfere with his mission. However, recent events had changed his attitude.

The closer he came to his own homeland – and although he did not know the distances involved, every instinct told him that he must be near now – the more trouble he saw all around him. An atmosphere of uncertainty and suspicion seemed to pervade the whole planet, brought about by the continuing oddities in the sky – the inexplicable changes in the orbits of the moons, the strange coloured lights and clusters of shooting stars – combined with the more immediate problems of frequent earthquakes and unusually violent weather. In such circumstances, the arrival of a stranger, especially one whose appearance was as peculiar as Terrel's, was bound to cause unease, and the fact that he was now part of a group – even such a disreputable-looking, disparate company – meant that he had not been singled out for unwanted attention. Moreover, his fellow travellers provided him with a degree of protection, practical help and companionship. Although Terrel was grateful for all that, in truth he was not entirely comfortable with any of them, and it was impossible for him to trust them completely. He found it hard to accept their sometimes glib explanations as to why they had chosen to go with him – and the suspicion that each of them had obscure reasons of their own for making the journey was inescapable.

The four men and the boy had been with Terrel for some time now, but in spite of this the healer didn't know a great deal about any of them. Each, for his own reasons, had been reticent about their past. Terrel was closest to Nomar, but he knew little of his history, not even what had happened to Taryn's mother. Any questions regarding her – or any other family connections – had either been ignored or deflected in a manner that made clear Nomar's need to keep his secrets. Terrel could respect that. He had a few secrets of his own.

Although the healer was younger than all but one of the adults in the party, there had never been any doubt about his leadership. From the outset, Terrel had made it abundantly clear that he would not allow them to divert him from his purpose. They could travel at his pace or not at all. And they'd go where he decided. They had all accepted these conditions readily enough and, while Terrel had been glad to take their advice on occasions, no one – not even Faulk, who was clearly a man more used to giving orders than obeying them – had ever disagreed with any of the healer's decisions. There were times when Terrel thought of them as his followers, as if he were the leader of some strange pilgrimage – and this was something he found distinctly embarrassing.

The greatest test for each of his companions had come when the healer had chosen to reveal his eventual destination. Here, in the divided land known as Kenda, there were several legends about the Floating Islands – just as there had been in Macul. Most of the tales revolved around the idea that normal life was impossible on land that *moved*, endlessly traversing the great Movaghassi Ocean. Some said that no one could possibly live under such conditions, others that only barbarians could survive that way, while a few claimed that existing in such an inherently unstable environment must render its inhabitants insane. Terrel knew that all these claims were untrue, but he couldn't prove it – and knew better than to try. Although at one time he'd made no secret of his destination, he had learned to be more circumspect with strangers. The varying degrees of surprise shown by his companions had faded as he'd told them something of his homeland and now, while they were still curious, no one questioned the wisdom of his plans.

In spite of his weariness, Terrel lay awake for some time that evening. The air felt damp on his skin, but to his relief the weather remained mild. The night sky was completely blanketed in cloud, so that the darkness was almost total. The passage of the moons was invisible, but Terrel still sensed their presence. He was acutely aware of them constantly now, more than he had ever been before. It was as though something inside him – some internal sensor – was able to detect their phases and relative strengths, 'seeing' their shapes, from crescent to circle, without the need of his eyes. He saw their varying influences not only in the world around him, but also in his own reactions and emotions. And in his dreams.

This was partly why he was finding it hard to fall asleep. The closer he got to Vadanis, and to the completion of his circular voyage, the stranger and more intense his dreams became. And amid all the other bizarre imagery, he constantly found himself trapped within the thunderous swell of the crimson sea, the ocean in which he swam but which he had never seen. Those dreams took him back to a time of terror, when he had first learnt the ways of pain, a time even before his birth. Ordinarily, his only escape from these nightmares was to draw in upon himself, becoming smaller and smaller until he was invisible and then ceased to exist. Taryn's intervention had saved Terrel from that ordeal the night before, but to sleep was to be alone again – and prey to a thousand fears. And yet he desperately needed to rest.

If only Alyssa was here, he thought. She'd be able to explain my dreams. Nomar's too, probably.

But Alyssa was not there, and Terrel knew she was not likely to come any time soon. The last time he had seen her, she had been in the borrowed shape of a gyrfalcon, and the bird's plight had made it clear that she was terribly ill.

Her parting words to him – *I can't help you any more* – still lay like a malignant shadow within his mind, and the memory of her distress always plunged him into despair. That fateful encounter had taken place almost two years ago, and in all that time he had not heard from her at all.

CHAPTER TWO

'It's a fish,' Taryn said, stating the obvious when none of his elders seemed willing to do so.

'Up here?' Nomar queried.

'Perhaps it's a flying fish,' Roskin said with a grin.

'Someone must have carved it into the stone,' Nomar said. 'It can't be real.'

'No one carved that,' Lawren responded. 'Look at the detail.'

'And why would anyone want to carve anything up here?' Roskin asked. 'We're in the middle of nowhere.'

'This part of the rock face was only exposed quite recently,' Faulk said, indicating the jumble of boulders that had blocked their path and forced them to clamber to the ledge where they were standing now.

'He's right,' Lawren said. 'This would have been underground not so long ago.'

'Not too many sculptors work underground,' Roskin commented.

'But fish don't swim in rock!' Nomar objected. 'It *can't* be real.'

'It's real,' Terrel said, entering the debate for the first time. 'Or it was once.' As he stared at the delicate outlines of scales and bones, he was remembering the other occasion when he'd seen remnants of an ancient life transformed into stone.

'But we're halfway up a mountain,' Nomar persisted. 'There aren't any rivers or lakes within miles of this place. There might be a few streams in winter, but nothing big enough for a fish that size.'

The creature was the length of a man's arm, its fins splayed out and its tail flicked up – as though it had been frozen in the act of swimming away from some invisible foe. It was a strangely beautiful and – to Terrel, at least – a rather melancholy sight.

'I've come across something like this before,' he told the others. 'There were some ancient bones and a few huge lizard eggs that had turned into stone. When my friends broke one of the eggs in two, you could see the remains of the tiny bones inside, just like this.' He'd been blind at the time, but had traced the skeletal contours with his fingers – and had been granted a vision of the ancient past through the eyes of the long-dead creature. 'Sometimes there are memories embedded in the stone.'

'Memories?' Roskin queried, his interest quickening.

'Don't get him started,' Lawren groaned.

Roskin ignored the comment.

'How do you find the memories?' he asked.

'Touch it,' Terrel suggested. 'See what happens.'

The younger man hesitated, then stretched out a hand and gently ran his fingers over the surface of the rock. He closed his eyes as he did so, a look of the utmost concentration on his face.

'This still doesn't explain—' Nomar began, but broke off when his son put a hand on his arm, distracting him. Eventually Roskin stepped back and opened his eyes.

'Anything?' Terrel asked.

Roskin shook his head, obviously disappointed.

'Are you going to try?' he asked.

'No. It's the future that concerns me, not the past.'

'But how did it get here?' Nomar burst out. 'You'll be telling me next that there are birds at the bottom of the ocean.'

'Maybe this was the bottom of the ocean once,' Terrel replied. As he spoke, he realized that his decision not to explore the relic for memories had been based not on indifference but on fear. The sort of upheaval necessary to transform the planet's surface to such an extent would have to have been unimaginably violent, and he shuddered inwardly at the idea.

'Now that *is* hard to believe,' Lawren remarked.

'So it remains a mystery,' Faulk concluded with a shrug.

'It's just a fish,' Roskin agreed. 'It's not important.'

'It would have been if you'd felt something through those mystic fingers of yours,' Lawren needled.

'Mock all you like,' Roskin retorted. 'One day I'll get to see *your* future, and you won't be so flippant then, will you?'

'When that day dawns, there *will* be birds at the bottom of the ocean,' the hunter replied.

'We should be moving on,' Faulk stated. 'I'd rather be on the other side of the ridge before that arrives.' He nodded in the direction of an approaching mass of dark cloud.

The company of travellers set off without further ado, but Terrel glanced round and noticed that one of their number had hung back for a few moments. Before he ran to catch up with his father, Taryn reached out a small hand and laid a tentative fingertip on the fish. For a brief instant the boy smiled, then saw Terrel looking at him and quickly moved away.

They crossed the ridge and found shelter just in time. As the first gusts of rain slashed through the air, the travellers wedged themselves into a series of crevices below an overhang of rock. Soon afterwards the sky turned an angry shade of purple, and hail was mixed in with the now torrential rain. Thunder rolled across the hills and valleys, a new peal beginning as the previous one faded. Dozens of small waterfalls cascaded down over the jagged outcrop, but because they were on its leeward side, Terrel and his companions remained reasonably dry and comfortable.

The healer was sharing a cramped space with Lawren Bir. As they had settled in, Lawren had put his fingers to his lips and emitted a shrill whistle. Within moments the hunter's trained falcon had swooped down out of the gathering gloom, alighting on its master's gauntletted wrist and then edging up along his arm to perch on his leather-patched shoulder. It was still there now, keeping quite still, its unblinking black eyes staring into the storm. The bird's name was Kephra. According to Lawren, this meant 'beautiful one' – a singularly apt description – but the falcon could be deadly too, and had proved its worth to the company many times.

'I was told once that the longer a hawk's tail feathers, the better flyer she is,' Terrel said. 'Is that true?'

'It's true,' the hunter replied. 'But Kephra is a tercel – a male.'

'I don't know enough to tell the difference,' the healer admitted. To him the bird looked very like the one he'd seen in Misrah, but Isptar had been female.

'It's enough to know that other falcons can,' Lawren said with a grin.

The hunter, together with his avian partner, had been the second to last to join the group. He was apparently making his way to the coast, where an important falconry tournament was to be held in the spring, and travelling in company would make the rigours of the journey easier to bear. Terrel believed there was more to it than that, but Lawren and his bird had been a welcome addition to the party – not only because their expertise provided a supply of fresh meat, but also because Kephra's constant presence meant that Alyssa would have a suitable host if she were ever able to come to Terrel again. When her spirit wandered, re-entering the world in the shape of an animal, Alyssa would often choose a bird if she had the chance, finding their relatively uncomplicated and uncluttered minds the most amenable to her purpose. Terrel had long since given up any expectation that she would come, but a forlorn hope was better than none.

Beyond their refuge, the storm raged on.

'How long do you think this will last?' Terrel asked, raising his voice above the noise of the storm.

'An hour, no more,' Lawren replied, then reconsidered. 'Who knows these days? The weather's gone mad the last few months. I'm just glad Faulk got us here in time. If it had been up to the Great Londolozi, we'd still have been out there discussing stone fishes and being battered to bits by hailstones.'

Londolozi was the grandiose name Roskin had used when he'd first introduced himself to the company, and Lawren's contemptuous tone made it plain just what he thought of such pretension. At the time he and Nomar had just smiled, while Faulk, stony-faced, had simply asked the newcomer what his real name was. Eventually he had admitted that it was the rather more prosaic Roskin Steyer.

'You shouldn't be too hard on him,' Terrel said.

'He's no more a seer than I am,' the hunter replied. 'And he never will be.'

'You can't be sure of that.' The healer was thinking of others he had known who, against all expectation, had shown talent of that sort. Neither Mlicki nor Kjolur had *looked* like prophets.

'The man's a complete charlatan,' Lawren persisted. 'My guess is he's sticking close to you because if he's with someone with a real gift, he's more likely to be taken seriously himself. By the gullible, at least.'

'But he might genuinely want to learn.'

'I don't think your talent's going to rub off on him. In any case, he doesn't want to be a healer, he wants to be an oracle. Which is all nonsense, whichever way you look at it.'

Terrel chose not to argue the point.

'I don't know why you let him tag along,' Lawren added. 'What help is he to you?'

'None of you are here because of me,' Terrel replied. 'You're all free to come or go as you choose.'

The hunter shrugged, unconvinced.

'Nomar I can understand. With a bit of luck, you might be able to teach him to be a half-decent healer. He's shown us all enough to think that. But Roskin's another story. You surely don't need disciples that badly.'

'I don't need any of you,' Terrel snapped, stung by his companion's choice of words. 'Not even a hunter.'

Lawren glanced at him, then looked away again.

'Sorry,' he said. 'Point taken. You've every right to travel with anyone you choose.'

'I do,' Terrel agreed. 'We all do.'

As originally predicted, the storm passed within the hour, and the travellers were able to set off again. Faulk led them down a narrow trail, heading towards a wooded area that promised at least some shelter for the night ahead. Once they were inside the trees, the others soon realized that their guide must have been to the area before when he led them straight to an old woodcutter's hut. Although the cabin was obviously no longer in use, the structure was still sound, and the prospect of having a roof over their heads ought to have cheered the company. As it was, their mood as they went about their regular evening tasks was surprisingly sombre.

Three days had passed since Nomar's attack, and most of the after-effects were fading now. His eyesight had returned to normal, and the numbness that had affected the left side of his face was retreating, but he was still nauseous occasionally and very tired all the time. He slept at every opportunity, and even when he was awake – especially towards the end of the day – he often seemed not to be fully alert, and the others frequently had to repeat anything they said to him before they got a response. In the circumstances it was remarkable that he'd been able to keep up with his companions. After all his earlier protestations, Terrel could not afford to play favourites and slow the pace for him. Nomar's determination drove him on, but he was paying a heavy price for his efforts. And so was Taryn. The boy's natural concern for his father had made him push himself beyond the boundaries of his own resources, and so he too was exhausted at the end of each day. Terrel did what he could for them both, but there were limits to his powers of restoration.

Of the others, Faulk was his usual undemonstrative self, and even Roskin and Lawren were subdued that night. For all their supposed mutual disdain, these two were the most likely to provoke conversation or laughter among their fellows, but on this occasion, as they worked together to build a fire and prepare a meal, both were unusually quiet, responding to each other with curt monosyllables and impatient gestures. Terrel watched them uneasily, hoping that the tension would not spill over into outright animosity. He didn't need any of these people, but if they were to remain together, the last thing he wanted was any internal dissension within the group.

The healer couldn't help wondering whether Roskin might have overheard any of Lawren's comments during the storm. That seemed unlikely, but it might explain the would-be seer's current sullenness. On the other hand, the two men were so different from each other that it was hardly surprising there was friction between them. Unlike the hunter, who was tall and lean with a matted thatch of coarse black hair and a thick beard, Roskin was short and stocky with long, wispy blond hair that he was forever having to push back out of his eyes. He was about twenty-one years old, but looked much younger, his chin covered in only a fine down. However, the contrast was not only physical. Lawren was a practical, pragmatic man, accepting the world as it was and dealing with it accordingly. Roskin looked for hidden meanings in everything, and although he was willing enough to help with everyday tasks, at heart he was a dreamer. The only thing the pair had in common was a sense of humour, and they could usually be relied upon to recognize the comical aspects of any situation. But tonight even that shared talent seemed to have evaporated.

'Wood's wet,' Lawren muttered as smoke billowed up from the fire.

'You don't say?' Roskin said, once he'd stopped coughing.

The two men glared at each other for a few moments, but before either of them could speak again they were distracted by a strange orange light that flickered through the foliage above them. In common with the rest of the party, they looked up and saw a bright star streaking across the sky. At the same time, the air around them seemed to hum with a sound just beyond hearing. Both phenomena lasted for only a few heartbeats, and left behind an eerie stillness.

'Well, if that wasn't an omen, I don't know what is,' Roskin said eventually.

'Drivel,' Lawren responded, though he did not sound wholly convinced.

A few moments later the ground beneath the travellers' feet vibrated slightly, and a drawn-out rumbling noise filled the air.

'There must be another storm coming,' Nomar muttered.

'No,' Terrel said. 'That wasn't thunder.' He pointed through the trees to the sky on the far side of the ridge they'd crossed earlier. The clouds there were now glowing red, as if lit from below by a great conflagration.

CHAPTER THREE

By the time their meal was finally ready true night had drawn in, and the company sat around their campfire and ate their meal – in silence for the most part, each of them occasionally glancing over to the northern sky. The horizon was still outlined by the reflected glow from the clouds.

'Do you think it's a forest fire?' Roskin asked.

For a few moments no one answered, then Lawren cleared his throat.

'It's not likely at this time of year, now that the rains have set in.'

'Then what is it?'

The hunter shrugged.

'I don't know.'

The eerie radiance reminded Terrel of the red light emitted by a volcanic eruption, something he had witnessed several times on Myvatan, but he saw little point in mentioning this. As far as he knew, there were no volcanoes in Kenda.

'Might it have something to do with the shooting star?' he asked instead.

'I don't see how,' Lawren replied, although his expression made it clear that he had wondered about this too.

'It's quite a coincidence, though, don't you think?' Roskin queried. 'I've never seen one as bright as that before, and the glow didn't start until after it went over.'

'We don't know that,' Lawren countered. 'Whatever it is, it's a long way away, and until we lost the sunlight we wouldn't even have noticed the reflection on the clouds.'

They were quiet again for a while, until Taryn piped up.

'If it was a star,' he said, looking round at the others, 'why was it underneath the clouds?'

Nomar frowned at his son.

'Don't be silly,' he said. 'It can't have been.' But weariness robbed the rebuke of much of its force, and Taryn was not to be put off.

'Yes, it was,' he insisted. 'It lit up the clouds from below.'

'The boy's right,' Lawren said. 'That's how I remember it too.'

'What phase is the Red Moon in?' Roskin demanded abruptly.

'Just over half full and waxing,' Terrel replied. 'Why?'

The would-be seer frowned. This was clearly not the answer he'd been expecting.

'Are you sure?' he asked. 'It's not a crescent?'

'I'm sure. What's this about?'

'I dread to think,' Lawren muttered.

'I thought it might be a fire-scythe.'

'Oh, for—' Lawren began.

'And it makes sense that it's the Red Moon,' Roskin went on, overriding the hunter's obvious scorn. 'It rules the spheres of war and fire, after all. Perhaps the moons are punishing us.'

'How do you work that out?' Lawren demanded before Terrel had a chance to speak.

'This is a time of change,' Roskin stated simply.

Although Terrel had heard this phrase many times during his exile, hearing it now sent a chill down his spine.

'Everyone knows that,' Roskin went on. 'The orbits of all the moons have altered, so we should be doing things differently too.'

'How?' Lawren asked, sounding weary now as well as contemptuous.

'If I knew that, I wouldn't be sitting here with you. I'd be in Vergos, advising Kaeryss.'

'Now that I *would* like to see,' the hunter exclaimed, laughing. 'She eats fools like you for breakfast.'

'Who's Kaeryss?' Terrel asked.

'She's a madwoman who's somehow got the ear of King Gozian,' Lawren answered.

Terrel knew that Gozian was the self-styled monarch of one of the small domains that made up the ungovernable whole of Kenda.

'Don't listen to him,' Roskin said. 'He can't help being so ignorant. Kaeryss is a great prophetess, the greatest Kenda has ever known. She discovered the Raven Cypher.'

'No, she didn't!' Lawren cut in. 'It's been around for centuries. She's just the one who claims to have broken the code. And if you ask me, that was only a ruse to inveigle her way into a position of power. Now she can make up anything she likes and no one's going to contradict her.'

'That's rubbish,' Roskin responded angrily. 'Her translations have been verified. She's proved her worth to all the court elders.'

'Who are probably as easy to fool as you are.'

'What is the Raven Cypher supposed to say?' Terrel asked, wondering if it had any similarities to the Tindaya Code, the ancient prophecy from his homeland which had been a guiding force in his own life.

'Don't encourage him,' Lawren warned.

Roskin ignored this remark.

'There are all sorts of predictions,' he said, 'many of which have already come true.'

Lawren rolled his eyes, but didn't interrupt again.

'And now I think about it,' Roskin said, 'there's a section which talks about fire and darkness coming from the sky, and the moons falling—'

Terrel had become tense, recognizing the parallels between this and the more apocalyptic passages of the Tindaya Code, but his reaction was mild compared to that of Nomar. The man leapt to his feet, his earlier tiredness forgotten, and practically threw himself in front of Roskin. His face was contorted in a snarl of rage as he grabbed the would-be seer's collar with both hands.

'Shut up!' he screamed. 'Shut up!' Then, controlling himself with a visible effort, he added in a venomous undertone, 'Don't you ever spout such vile nonsense. Not ever. Understand?' He broke off to glance at Taryn, and saw his own fear reflected in his son's eyes.

Roskin nodded slightly, so taken aback that he was unable to speak. Nomar shook him again, then was startled when a large hand clasped his shoulder.

'Take it easy,' Faulk said quietly. The big man had risen without appearing to hurry, and his voice was calm. 'I think you've made your point.'

Nomar relaxed, and let go of Roskin's jerkin. Once he had stood up he seemed about to speak, but then he simply turned away and stumbled into the cabin without another word. After a moment's hesitation, Taryn followed.

The silence around the campfire lasted for a while.

'What got into him?' Roskin said eventually, his voice still shaky. 'I was only saying—'

'I think you've said enough for one night, don't you?' Lawren cut in.

*

In spite of the events of the evening, and of everything he had to think about, Terrel slept better that night than he had done for some time. Equally surprising was the fact that everyone else – even Nomar – also rested well. And when the next day dawned bright and almost cloudless, their spirits rose still further.

They were heading southwest now, following a trail that led through the fringes of the forest and then emerged on to the flank of another ridge – one of many that led up into the foothills of the true mountains beyond. The path was wide and well established, but the fact that it was becoming overgrown in places was testament to the little use it had seen recently. The company trudged on at the steady pace set by Faulk. Nomar walked beside him, clearly intent on demonstrating that he was fit again, and Taryn was at the front too, sometimes dashing ahead or making small detours to investigate something that attracted his attention. After the exertions of the last few days, he seemed to have recaptured the apparently endless energy of childhood. Lawren took up his usual place at the rear – Kephra circling effortlessly on the wind above him – leaving Terrel with Roskin. In truth that was an arrangement that suited the healer well enough. He wanted to return to the previous night's discussion without having to involve the others.

'What exactly is a fire-scythe?' he asked.

'No one really knows,' Roskin replied, instinctively glancing round to check that Lawren was out of earshot. 'I'm glad you're broad-minded enough to discuss it, though. Not like that idiot.'

'You said it had something to do with the Red Moon,' Terrel prompted.

'That's what most people think, especially when it's a few days either side of being new.'

'When it's a crescent?'

Roskin nodded. 'Like the blade of a scythe,' he agreed. 'One of the theories is that a bit of the moon breaks off and falls down to Nydus.'

That didn't sound very likely to Terrel, but during his long travels he had learnt not to dismiss anything until he'd got to know as much as he could about it.

'I know it doesn't make a lot of sense,' Roskin went on. 'I mean, if a bit like that can fall down here, then why not the whole moon?'

'There are many invisible forces at work in the world,' Terrel replied. 'And beyond it.'

'So you're a follower of the mysteries of the Dark Moon,' the younger man said thoughtfully. 'Matters of life and death.'

It was a comment that might have been made by one of the seers of the Floating Islands. And Terrel had often come across similar beliefs about the influence of the various moons. He recalled that either Shahan or Muzeni – he couldn't remember which – had told him that, as he came closer to home, he would return to the sphere of the Dark Moon, the invisible presence that had played such an integral role in his life.

'We were talking about the Red Moon,' he reminded his companion.

'The moon of passion and violence,' Roskin said in melodramatic tones. 'Appropriate enough for something that can reduce whole forests to charred splinters.'

'Is that what a fire-scythe does?'

'So I've been told. I've never seen it for myself. And I certainly wouldn't want to be too close when it happened either.'

'Nor would I.' Terrel was thinking back to the inexplicable blaze they had seen in the sky, and was glad that they'd crossed the ridge when they had. He shivered, realizing that he was beginning to take Roskin's theories seriously.

'I feel closer to the Amber Moon myself,' Roskin said. 'And of course Lawren is definitely under the control of the White.' He glanced round again. 'How sad it must be to be so hidebound by logic and practicality.'

'It has its advantages,' Terrel commented.

'Oh, don't be so reasonable,' Roskin said, grinning. 'Anyone would think you really prefer his company to mine.'

'That's true,' the healer said, smiling himself. 'I'm only talking to you now because you might have some information that could be useful to me.' This was uncomfortably close to the truth, but fortunately Roskin took it as a joke – as Terrel had intended.

'So now you want me to tell you about the Raven Cypher?' the young man guessed.

'I'm interested in such things,' the healer admitted.

'Most people are like Lawren. They think it's all nonsense.'

'But you don't?'

'No. At least . . .' Roskin hesitated. 'I've seen things before they've happened. In here.' He tapped the side of his head. 'So I know it's possible to predict the future. Most people don't have that.' He paused again, waiting to see if Terrel was going to respond. When he didn't, he went on. 'The Raven Cypher's different, though. It was written down a long time ago, in a language no one uses any more. No one knows who wrote it, or why. For all we know, the stones in Vergos might be copies of the originals, so they might not even be accurate.'

'It's inscribed on stone?' Terrel queried. This was another resemblance to the Tindaya Code.

'I don't suppose it would have survived any other way,' Roskin said. 'The thing is, many scholars have tried to work out what it all means, and they've come up with plenty of theories, but nothing made much sense until Kaeryss came along. The work is far from complete, but she *has* translated a good part of it, no matter what Lawren says.'

'And it's a prophecy?'

'Yes. Or rather, it's a warning.'

'About what?'

'Oh, all sorts of stuff. Seas drying up and mountains crumbling, cities being consumed by fire or swallowed up by the ground. Moons falling out of the sky. That kind of thing.'

'Not very pleasant reading, then,' Terrel concluded. He still wasn't sure whether he needed to take the Raven Cypher seriously.

'Everyone's heard tales about how the world's supposed to end,' Roskin said. 'Some may even believe them. But no one thinks it's going to happen to them. It's all about some vague, far-off time in the future.'

'But you think that's about to change?'

'I'm beginning to wonder.'

'Why?'

'Because of some specific events predicted in the cypher. For a start, there's the way in which the moons have changed their orbits. And the Dark Moon's getting bigger. Did you know that?'

'Yes, but that's been happening for several years now. Kaeryss could have seen what was happening and arranged the translation to fit the facts.'

'You can be cynical if you want,' Roskin muttered irritably.

'I'm just trying to get to the truth.'

'I'm sure Lawren would say the same thing,' the would-be seer said bitterly. 'Haven't you ever accepted something on faith? Without any proof?'

More than you'll ever know, Terrel thought, but he said nothing. Roskin was quiet too, apparently sulking, and the healer wondered how to coax him into continuing. In the end, there was no need of any further prompting.

'It also predicts all those shooting stars we've been seeing,' the younger man said. 'And they didn't start until recently, *after* Kaeryss had been in Vergos for a while. It's the same with all the strange weather we've been having, and the earthquakes. Those are all supposed to be forerunners of the really unpleasant stuff. When we saw those lights in the sky last night, I remembered some of it. I didn't expect Nomar to react like that, though. Do you know why he went berserk?'

Terrel shook his head. He had the feeling that it was somehow connected to the nightmares that accompanied Nomar's headaches, but he didn't want to speculate aloud. Instead he went back to his probing about the Raven Cypher.

'Everything you've told me so far has been about natural phenomena. Are there any people mentioned in the prophecy?'

'Quite a few, apparently. Heroes, warriors, kings; even a few demons.'

'What sort of demons?' Terrel asked, remembering the various ways the elementals had been described to him in the past. Until he'd seen the amorphous creatures for himself, none of those descriptions had made much sense.

'I don't know,' Roskin said.

Perversely, this admission made the healer feel that he should consider the rest of what he was being told a little more carefully.

'Do any of the heroes have names?'

'I'm sure they do,' Roskin replied, sounding frustrated now, 'but I don't know what they are.'

'Is there anything in the cypher about a four-moon conjunction?'

'How did you know that?'

'Just a guess,' Terrel lied, not sure whether he should be pleased or alarmed by this discovery. In the Tindaya Code, the Guardian – the hero whose actions were meant to avert a massive catastrophe on Nydus – was born on a night when all four moons came together in a multiple eclipse. And it also foretold how the Guardian would fulfil his destiny by the time of the next such confluence. In the past, the confluence had occurred every seventy-five years, but because the moons had changed course it was going to take place much sooner this time – although no one knew exactly when. 'What does the cypher say about it?'

'Just that important events take place at those times. Pretty obvious, really. The last one was a few years before I was born.'

'I was born that night,' Terrel said, without thinking.

'Really?' Roskin exclaimed. 'That's incredible!'

Regretting his hasty words, Terrel remembered what he'd learnt about the night of his birth. He and Jax had been born to Empress Adina at the exact time predicted by the court seers. For some time, this had led to a belief that Jax was the Guardian – and indeed this was still the theory adhered to by many people on Vadanis. At the time of his birth, Terrel had been regarded as an inconvenient aberration – not least because there was no suggestion of twins in the Tindaya Code – and his abnormal appearance had sealed his fate. No one had even been willing to consider the idea that he might be the hero from the prophecy. And it was only years later that anyone had even begun to believe that he might be important after all.

Now even some of Jax's supporters had begun to have their doubts over the prince's role, while Terrel's ghostly allies were certain that neither of the twins was the Guardian. They believed that Terrel's role was that of the Mentor, the person who would help the hero choose between good and evil, and that together the elementals somehow made up the figure of the Guardian. For his own part, the healer had no wish to be a hero. It was bad enough being fate's messenger.

Roskin had been silent for a while, but now he glanced at his companion.

'Is that why . . . ?' he began.

'Why I look like a freak?' the healer completed for him.

'I wouldn't have put it that way,' his companion said with an embarrassed smile, 'but I've heard stories about babies born at such a time.'

Terrel was not surprised. Every culture he'd encountered had similar tales of strange deformities and madness caused by the unusually strong lunar influences. And while his twin brother, Jax, had been physically normal, his own appearance had reinforced the various superstitions – and had led to his abandonment by his parents and, indirectly, to his eventual exile. However, he knew that his twisted leg and withered arm owed more to human intervention than to the power of the moons.

His eyes were another matter. They were almost colour-less, as bright as diamonds, and in sunlight they glittered as though they were formed from crystalline shards rather than human flesh. The only person who had ever been able to look into their unnatural, rainbow-flecked depths without experiencing a certain degree of unease had been Alyssa. On occasions, Terrel had even had to resort to dis-guising his eyes in order to avoid the trouble they sometimes provoked. Once people got to know him they were usually able to put their prejudices aside, but their initial responses varied from astonishment to nervous curiosity, fear and outright enmity.

'I've no way of telling why I was born the way I was,' Terrel said, wishing he'd kept his mouth shut. 'I'm just who I am.'

Roskin nodded.

'It must help in some ways,' he said. 'I mean, you can tell you're special just by looking at you. People must be more willing to take your healing powers seriously.'

'They take my healing seriously because it works,' Terrel said. 'My eyes have nothing to do with it.' He had never thought of his peculiar appearance as an asset before. It had always seemed to him to be a liability, but now he wasn't so sure.

'Why is it called the Raven Cypher?' he asked, changing the subject. He didn't want to talk about himself any more.

'Because each of the stones has a small raven carved into the top left-hand corner,' Roskin replied.

'Do people here think of them as birds of ill omen?'

'Yes. But owls are worse. I don't know why.'

They walked on in silence for a while, Terrel's lopsided gait matching the younger man's pace easily enough. The healer needed a specially made boot to fit his right foot, which was bent back on itself, and that leg would never match the other perfectly, but as he had grown to manhood and gained in size and strength, he had overcome his disability. His movements would never be elegant, but they were generally effective. The constant travelling of the last decade meant that he no longer even thought about it.

'How do you know so much about the cypher?' he asked eventually.

'I'm interested in such things,' Roskin replied, a slight smile on his boyish face.

'Have you ever been to Vergos?'

'No, but I've talked to people who have.'

'Is there anything you can tell me about it?' For some reason, Terrel had the feeling that Roskin hadn't revealed everything he knew about the Raven Cypher.

'I don't think so. But if I think of anything I'll let you know.'

'Have you always been "interested in such things"?'

'Ever since I was a child. I noticed that the different phases of the moon affected my dreams, and then I saw that they affected a lot of other things too. That led to a curiosity about anything the world finds strange, things we can't explain.'

Terrel nodded. The moons of Nydus formed an inescapable backdrop to everything that happened on the planet.

'I think we'll all be watching the skies a little more closely now,' Roskin went on. 'Especially the Red Moon.'

Terrel knew that he would be watching *all* the moons, but he could understand his companion's preoccupation. The prospect of encountering any more fire-scythes – if that was indeed what they'd seen – was unnerving.

'Have you ever been in love?' Roskin asked after a while.

The question took Terrel aback, and it was a few moments before he worked out the train of thought that had led to it. Apart from violence and fire, the Red Moon's other main sphere of influence was love.

'Yes,' he replied belatedly. 'I still am.'

Roskin nodded, looking uncharacteristically thoughtful. Terrel expected him to ask more, but he did not.

'Have you?'

'No. I was married once. Technically, I suppose I still am.'

'So that's what you're running away from,' Lawren remarked. Unnoticed by the other two, the hunter had come up behind them and had evidently overheard Roskin's admission. 'What was the problem?' he asked as he fell into step beside them. 'Did she nag you too much?'

'That's none of your business.'

Lawren grinned.

'Was she ugly?' he asked. 'Frigid? Too demanding?'

Roskin said nothing, staring fixedly ahead.

'Oh, come on,' the hunter said, obviously enjoying himself immensely. 'You've got to tell us something.'

'Actually, she was none of those things,' Roskin answered coldly.

'Then what was wrong with her?'

'She was a stranger.'

Lawren's smile was replaced by a puzzled frown.

'You married a complete stranger?'

'I was given no choice.' Having revealed his secret, Roskin evidently decided to explain fully. 'It was a business arrangement. My father was a rich man and I was his only heir, but he swore to disown me if I didn't marry who he wanted. So I went through with it. It was the biggest mistake I ever made.'

'Can't have been that bad,' Lawren said.

'You don't know anything about it,' Roskin snapped.

'So what happened then?'

'I stood it for as long as I could. Then I left.'

'And became the Great Londolozi? Begging on the streets?'

'There are worse ways of living.'

'Have you ever thought of going back?' Terrel asked.

'No. I'll have been disinherited long ago. My father would probably kill me if I showed my face there now.'

'You have hidden depths,' Lawren remarked. He

sounded almost admiring. 'Do you think you'll ever find a woman you won't need to run away from?'

'I hope so,' Roskin said quietly.

'That's not a part of the future you've managed to see yet then?' Lawren needled.

'Leave him alone,' Terrel said, sensing the pain behind Roskin's impassive expression.

'He's a big boy now,' the hunter replied. 'He can take care of himself.' He grinned. 'Unless there's a woman involved, of course.'

Roskin turned towards his tormentor and fixed him with a measuring stare.

'That's rich, coming from a runaway slave,' he said.

Lawren's smile faltered.

'What are you talking about?' he asked.

'Do you think we don't see the scars under that putrid beard? You were branded, weren't you?'

Lawren's hand had gone up to his face in an unconscious act that betrayed him, and Terrel noticed the irregular patterns of the scars beneath the hair.

'I suppose you'd know about such things because your father was the sort of man to keep slaves,' Lawren growled.

'Yes,' Roskin agreed. 'But I'm not. Does that make you feel any better?'

'I'm not ashamed of my past. And I'm a free man now.'

'As am I.'

The two men looked at each other, and Terrel saw the tension between them slowly ebb away. There was a tenuous bond between them now.

'What about you, Terrel?' Roskin said a little while later. 'You want to tell us about that tattoo on your hand?'

The healer glanced down at the four concentric circles on the back of his left hand. In the past he'd used various explanations for them – including his having been a former slave – but on this occasion he saw no reason to hide the truth.

'I spent the first few years of my life in a madhouse. All the inmates were marked like this.'

'You don't seem insane to me,' Lawren remarked. 'A little eccentric, maybe, but not mad.'

'You were shut away because of the way you looked, weren't you?' Roskin guessed.

'I suppose so,' Terrel replied, surprised by the younger man's perspicacity.

'So we're all running away from something,' Lawren concluded.

The three men exchanged glances.

'I think Faulk needs some help deciding where we're going to run to next,' Roskin said, looking ahead to the others.

Faulk, Nomar and Taryn had come to a halt at a point where the trail divided, and the two adults seemed to be arguing. Terrel watched them as he approached, knowing that he would be the one to decide which fork in the unknown road they should take next.

CHAPTER FOUR

The final leg of Terrel's voyage had already taken much longer than he would have wished. At the beginning he'd had to wait several months – until Myvatan's time of hibernation had ended – before he could arrange passage on a ship. However, once he'd left the island behind he had hoped to move quickly and with purpose. For the first time since the start of his travels he had a clear goal in mind. After all his searching, all he needed now was to go home.

He had come to this conclusion because he'd found what he believed to be the last of the elementals, those strange entities who had no physical shape or substance yet who controlled vast reserves of power. They could make rocks fly and rivers run uphill. They could cause earthquakes and volcanic eruptions and make islands spin on their axes. The creatures were so old that Terrel had named them the Ancients, only to realize that in their own terms they were no more than infants. To them, a human life-span was an insignificant instant in time.

Terrel had looked at the Ancients, had even been *inside* them, and yet he still did not really have the words to describe them properly. The best he could do was to say that they were like a swirling darkness, shadows where there should be light, bright flashes where there should be nothing. With each encounter he had learnt more about the way they thought, from their instinctive hatred and fear of water – which they regarded as an evil, magical substance – to their growing ability to create startlingly realistic images of the human world. At the same time, the elementals had learnt from him, sometimes misinterpreting his thoughts in ways he could barely understand, but always eager for knowledge. In some ways, though, they were still as much of a mystery to him as when he had come across the first of the creatures in the mines of Betancuria. And the last of them had presented the greatest puzzle of all.

The Ancient on Myvatan was not only ill but utterly insane. With the others, Terrel had been able to utilize his healer's instincts to restore the creatures' energy patterns to their proper form – and in doing so had gained a measure of their trust – but he had known from the start that his efforts on the ice-covered island would be in vain. This Ancient's madness was limitless, beyond the scope of his puny talent. With the help of friends he had been able to prevent the creature from turning its malevolent fury upon all the people of Nydus, but he'd had no hope of curing its malaise, or of renewing the bargain he had made – and re-made – with its three 'brothers'. Terrel had left Myvatan knowing that he had done all he could, but also aware of the fact that this might not have been enough.

If the seers' most recent interpretation of the Tindaya Code was correct, and the elementals represented the Guardian of the prophecy, then Terrel's role was that of the Mentor, the go-between linking one form of life to the other. And because he had been unable to communicate properly with the Ancient on Myvatan, he was obviously failing in his duties. His healer's intuition was telling him that some fragile balance had been upset, with the result that the entire planet was now in a state of turmoil – and with the possibility of much worse to come. In addition, because there was a link – one Terrel still did not fully understand – between the sleepers and the Ancients, he was also convinced that the elemental's madness was responsible for Alyssa's illness. In the past, whenever he had been worried about her, about her fragile, vulnerable body lying in a basement of Havenmoon, she had always assured him that she was 'protected'. He had come to realize that this was probably true, because he'd seen other sleepers who had been deeply unconscious for many years and yet who were still alive and apparently unharmed. They had not even aged. For them, time had slowed to a point where its passage was almost imperceptible. However, the source of this protection was almost certainly also the power that had sent them into their long sleep in the first place. And at least part of that power was now ill, and regarded humanity as its enemy. Terrel's greatest fear was that he might not get back to Vadanis before Alyssa died, and so wouldn't have the opportunity to try to heal her – or even to say goodbye. A very long time ago he had sworn to return to her, and he had every intention of keeping that vow. When everything else seemed set against him, it was this thought that drove him on. The fact that she had not come to him for so long now deepened his pessimism but didn't alter his determination.

He had been impatient for the sea voyage from Myvatan to end, and once on land again he'd wanted to move on immediately. However, right from the outset he had been plagued by delays. Unseasonable and sometimes violent weather conditions had often forced him to postpone a journey or to travel by an indirect route. For most of the way he had had to rely on his own instincts to guide his path, because the inhabitants of the mostly sparsely populated lands he was travelling through often treated him with suspicion, and granted him only grudging aid at best. He was not familiar with any of these countries, was ignorant of their laws and customs, and often fell foul of some unexpected pitfall. His healing abilities had frequently been his saving grace. It was a skill that was universally prized, and it usually aided his acceptance into any community. But such work was in itself time-consuming and tiring, and had its own risks. On one occasion he had even been imprisoned for some days when his attempts to cure a young noblewoman of a fever had been misinterpreted by her over-protective father.

At other times, the delays had been of his own making. Sometimes he had been unable to decide where he should go next, and had wasted time in often fruitless enquiries. It was more than a year after leaving Myvatan before he found anyone who had even heard of the Floating Islands and the Movaghassi Ocean, let alone anyone who knew where they were. After that, progress had been easier, though still somewhat erratic. He'd been tempted to linger in the great city of Kian Cerchia when he discovered that it contained an enormous library of ancient carvings, scrolls and books, and which – astonishingly – was free to all. He had met scholars who'd spent their entire adult lives inside its dusty chambers. He'd agonized over whether to accept a ride on a canal barge, recalling the almost disastrous consequences of such a decision in Macul. He'd looked to the skies, searched for omens and signs, consulted sages and listened to meaningless gossip, all in the hope of confirming the route ahead. But in the end, on every occasion, he'd known that he simply had to move on.

This had not changed after he'd been joined first by Nomar and Taryn, then Faulk, Lawren and finally Roskin. And even now that he had access to their local knowledge, and the way ahead – at least as far as the coast – seemed reasonably straightforward, there were still obstacles to be overcome. Apart from the constant search for food and shelter, there was the weather to contend with, especially now that they were heading up into the mountain range they had to cross in order to reach the shore. And the recent spate of earth tremors had altered the terrain in places, making some trails dangerous and others impassable.

Only a few days earlier, the travellers had crossed a vast ravine, looking down from the swaying rope bridge to the river far below. The cables had been strung between parapets on either side – all that was left of a massive stone bridge that had once spanned the chasm but which had been destroyed long ago. From what remained it was possible to imagine the whole structure, and it was clear that the unknown people who had built it – who were now lost in the mists of history – had possessed techniques that the present-day locals could not imagine, let alone duplicate. None of the recent earthquakes had had any effect on the remaining bastions of stone, and it was obvious that the disaster that had caused the bridge's collapse must have been incredibly violent.

It had been Terrel's decision to make the crossing – the alternative being a very long detour – and he had insisted on going first, edging his way carefully across the puny bridge as his weight and the freshening wind made the ropes sway unnervingly. Once on the far side, he'd watched, his heart in his mouth, as the others made the traverse one at a time. Only once they were all safe had his thoughts turned again to the road ahead.

'What's wrong with the western route?' Terrel asked.

Nomar looked flustered.

'There's plague there,' he blurted out.

'How do you know that?' Lawren enquired.

'Because I've been there before.'

'When?'

'That doesn't matter. Neither Taryn nor I will go that way. If you choose to do so,' he added, looking at Terrel, 'this is where we part company.' He was clearly in earnest.

The travellers were still standing at the fork in the trail. Faulk had suggested that they turn west because it offered easier passage than the southern path, which cut closer to the scree-strewn slopes of the mountain that lay directly ahead of them.

'It's the curse, isn't it?' Roskin said.

Everyone except Nomar looked at him.

'The plateau beyond the pass is supposed to be cursed,' he explained. 'That's why Nomar doesn't want to go that way.'

'Is this true?' Terrel asked.

Nomar would not meet the healer's gaze. His son was looking up at him too, but the man stared fixedly at the ground.

'You're not going to let this nonsense influence you, are you?' Lawren said.

'What *is* the curse?' Terrel asked.

When Nomar still did not speak, Roskin supplied the answer.

'It should be a fertile region, but every settlement there has failed. Crops wither and livestock die for no reason. People too, if the rumours are true.'

'We're not planning on settling there,' Lawren pointed out. 'We're just passing through. And it'll be a lot easier than scrambling over half the rocks in Kenda.'

'For you, perhaps,' Nomar mumbled.

The healer turned to Faulk.

'You said the southern way is shorter, more direct?' he asked.

'In terms of distance, yes. In terms of effort, no.'

'And in terms of time?'

'About the same.'

Terrel had been faced with a similar choice in the deserts of Misrah, but then he'd had an oracle to guide him. Here he was on his own.

'We'll go south.'

Nomar glanced up then, and smiled gratefully. Lawren looked disgusted, raising his eyes to the heavens, but said nothing, while Faulk simply accepted the decision with his habitual calm. Only Roskin felt it necessary to comment.

'This way will take us quite close to Vergos,' he said, sounding excited, and turned to Terrel. 'Perhaps we'll get to read the cypher in person!'

Their progress for the rest of that day was as strenuous as Lawren had predicted, but to his credit he did not complain. The rough path also took them higher than they'd been before, and there was a distinct chill in the air now that promised an uncomfortable night. Moreover, the rugged terrain offered few places suitable for a campsite. Terrel was beginning to wonder if he'd made a bad mistake when they came across a wide, low-ceilinged cave just above the trail. There was no need of any consultation before they decided to stay there for the night. Faulk muttered something about checking for bears and disappeared into the deeper recesses, emerging a short time later to report that they were the sole occupants of the cavern.

'Apart from this,' he added, holding up a large snake. The creature was headless and thus obviously not much of a threat, but for once Terrel was glad of his protector's caution. The thought of waking during the night to be faced with an angry serpent was horrifying.

Faulk tossed the corpse down and began to clean the blade of his sword. As always, he reminded Terrel of the soldiers on Myvatan. He had the same dedicated mentality and erect military bearing, and even his clothes – stained though they were from long use and hard travelling – had the look of a uniform. And yet if Faulk *was* a soldier, then he was beholden to no master and to no country. He was part of no army. Terrel had wondered whether he was some kind of mercenary, prepared to fight for anyone who would pay him, but he had asked for nothing from the healer in return for his services. In fact, Terrel still did not know why Faulk had appointed himself as his bodyguard. However, there was no doubt that, in Roskin's terminology, he was a servant of the Red Moon, a man made for war.

'We can roast it when you get the fire going,' Faulk said now, gesturing to the snake. 'There's good meat on that.'

'And Kephra will finish what we don't want,' Lawren added. The tercel had already been eyeing the carcass hungrily, but had made no move towards it.

There was little wood in the barren area they were now crossing, but the travellers had all been collecting whatever they could as they went along, and as a result there was soon a fire in the mouth of the cave. A meal followed shortly. Outside, the clouds had returned and it was raining again, making them even more glad they had found shelter. But the increasing cold of the night could not dampen their spirits, and an almost festive atmosphere filled the refuge now that the rigours of the day were behind them. Even Lawren seemed to have overcome his annoyance at Terrel's decision, and regaled them all with a tall tale about the time he *had* found himself sharing living quarters with a bear.

'I was saved by a mouldy piece of cheese,' he declared to various expressions of disbelief. 'I'm serious. It was in my pack, and the bear was more interested in that than in me.'

'It probably smelt better than you,' Roskin commented.

'While it was rummaging round trying to find the cheese, I was able to sneak out and hide,' the hunter went on. 'The only problem was, I'd been sleeping, and had to leave all my clothes behind. It was hours before the wretched beast went out to hunt and I could slip back inside. That was a cold night, I can tell you.'

The evening ended in laughter, and nothing disturbed their rest that night.

Unusually, it was Terrel who woke first the next morning. There was only the slightest pre-dawn glimmer in the sky outside the cave, and although it was no longer raining, a layer of heavy cloud made the scene even gloomier. He saw no point in rousing the others yet, but he felt restless and knew he wasn't going to be able to go back to sleep. He made his way cautiously to the mouth of the cavern. From there he had a wide view over a series of mist-wreathed valleys and tapering foothills, all drained of colour in the dim light. The air about him felt damp, and it was cold too. His hand instinctively went to the pocket where he kept the red crystal that had given him both light and warmth during the seemingly endless dark of Myvatan's winter. He took it out and studied it anew. The stone no longer glowed when he touched it, but he found it comforting nonetheless.

'That's pretty.'

Taryn's voice startled Terrel. The boy had emerged from the cave without making a sound.

'Is it valuable?'

'Only to me,' Terrel replied.

'Have you got any other treasures?' Taryn asked, sitting down beside the healer and rubbing his eyes sleepily.

It seemed an odd question, but when he thought about it, Terrel realized that in fact he did. He had carried Muzeni's clay pipe through all his travels, having taken it from the skeletal hands of the long-dead heretic. He had also been given a curved dagger and a colourful woven belt by the Toma, as well as a pendant that hung on a leather thong around his neck. It was engraved with an oracular symbol that to the desert nomads meant 'the river in the sky'. Together with the red crystal, these objects formed a sort of record of Terrel's progress. It didn't seem much to show for ten years of his life. And now that the idea had occurred to him, it seemed curious – almost wrong, some-how – that he carried nothing to remind him of his time in Macul. He'd been given a fire-opal there but had sold it in order to repay the family who had saved his life, and the only other gift he could remember from that stage of his journey was the carved staff that had been presented to him by the sharaken. It had been destroyed when the palace in Talazoria had been torn apart by an earthquake.

Terrel pulled his thoughts back to the present and found that Taryn was still looking at him expectantly. However, the healer did not feel like talking about himself and so sought to distract the boy from his interest in treasures.

'I saw you touch the fish in the rock. Did you feel any-thing?'

If Taryn was disconcerted by the sudden change of topic he did not show it.

'I could feel how it moved,' he said. 'When it was alive, I mean.' He made a swimming motion with his hand, smiling as he did so. Then he looked worried. 'That was all right, wasn't it? Me touching it, I mean.'

'Of course.' Terrel was glad the boy had seemed to

enjoy the experience. His own contact with the memories of stone had been rather more traumatic. 'It shows you have talent.'

'I'd like to be a healer like you. And my father. How did you learn to do it?'

'It just happened. I didn't mean it to. Being a healer can be wonderful, but it's also a big responsibility. You'll know if it's right for you when the time comes.'

Taryn nodded solemnly, then – with another of his quicksilver changes of mood – became excited.

'I have my own treasure,' he said. 'Do you want to see it?'

'If you don't mind showing it to me.'

'I don't usually. Father . . .' The boy's voice trailed off as he dug inside his shirt and pulled out something that hung around his neck on a cord. It was a small silver ring.

'That's beautiful.'

'It was my mother's,' Taryn said quietly.

Terrel nodded, waiting to see whether he would volunteer anything more.

'She died when I was born,' the boy added, matter-of-fact.

'Terrel doesn't want to be bothered with your tales,' Nomar said sternly, coming up behind them. 'We should be getting ready to move on.'

Taryn jumped to his feet, looking anxious, but his father smiled and put his arm around the child's shoulders.

'It looks as if—' Nomar began, but got no further.

At that moment they all became aware of a distant humming in the air, a whirring sound that grew in volume with incredible speed. An instant later, a ball of fire burst through the layer of cloud and raced across the sky in front of them, trailing a stream of thick black smoke. As the travellers watched in awe-struck terror, the thunderbolt hurtled over several ridges below them, then vanished into a distant vale of mist. What happened next left them numb with shock.

For a few heartbeats, a fierce red light shone brighter than the sun. As this faded, the area where the fireball had struck the ground was enveloped by an expanding cloud of smoke, and the entire mountainside shook with the reverberations of the impact. Outside the cave, stones and boulders tumbled down in a dozen avalanches and then a sound – like the loudest, most prolonged peal of thunder Terrel had ever heard – rolled over them, making them cower and clap their hands over their ears. At the same time they were buffeted by a series of fierce, capricious winds.

Much later, the sun rose to find that the morning was already stained red. Half the world seemed to be on fire.

CHAPTER FIVE

Daylight revealed the extent of the devastation. A huge area of land had simply disappeared behind an impenetrable pall of smoke. At its edges, everything seemed to have been charred black. Beyond that, a truly gigantic forest fire was burning.

The central column of ash and dust was now rising into the sky like the trunk of some monstrous tree, spreading out as its branches mingled with the layers of cloud. Strong winds made the mixture boil and ripple, while flashes of lightning lit the darkening mass from within. As the travellers watched, gusts of wind scoured the mountainside, bringing a reminder of the destruction below. Even though their position was many miles from the point of impact, the air around them was becoming acrid and warm. The one small point of reassurance was that the earth tremors had subsided, and there no longer seemed to be much danger from further avalanches.

'I told you we'd have been better off going the other way,' Lawren grumbled, breaking the awe-struck silence.

'Oh, I suppose you saw this coming,' Roskin remarked sarcastically.

'*I* don't pretend to be a seer. It's just—'

'We wouldn't have done any better going that way,' Terrel cut in. 'And perhaps we were meant to see this.'

'Because it's an omen?' Lawren queried, unable to keep the scorn from his voice.

'It was a fire-scythe,' Roskin declared. 'What else could it have been?'

Terrel was not about to argue with that. He was remembering the strange rocks he had seen, first in Qomish, then Akurvellir, and the local legends that spoke of them having fallen from the sky. It had seemed ridiculous at the time, but now he was not so sure. *Something* had fallen through the clouds, and if it wasn't a piece of one of the moons, he didn't know what else it could be.

'We should get going,' Faulk said.

'Quite right,' Lawren agreed. 'I won't feel safe till we're a long way from here.'

They set off soon after that, but Terrel couldn't help wondering whether *anywhere* could be considered safe when burning rocks fell from the sky.

The travellers found the going hard that morning. As the trail twisted round the southern flanks of the mountain, it became even narrower than before, and the recent rock falls had either blocked the path or destroyed it completely in several places. This meant they had to scramble over patches of new scree, traverse several small crevasses, and occasionally even double back on themselves in order to rejoin what was left of the track. Because of this their progress was slower than they'd hoped, and their anxiety increased when several stinging showers of rain fell, making conditions underfoot even more treacherous. When the water from the raindrops evaporated, it left a thin film of ash-grey powder over everything it had touched, and this did nothing to improve their mood.

Eventually, however, as the travellers' route swung westward again, and they made their way down into an area that had been less badly affected, the path – while still narrow – became easier. As long as they moved in single file they could walk normally, and the group picked up speed once more. Even the fact that the slopes to either side, going up to their right and falling away to their left, were becoming more and more steep, did not worry them unduly. But then Faulk, who had been in the lead, came to an abrupt halt.

'There's someone on the trail ahead of us,' he reported. He had just reached the top of a small ridge, and the others couldn't yet see what he was talking about. Something in the soldier's tone puzzled Terrel. He couldn't tell whether Faulk was annoyed or amused.

'Do you think they're any threat to us?' he asked.

'No, but they're blocking the path. We may have to do some climbing to get past them.' There was no doubt now that the soldier was finding the scene ahead of him comical in some way.

'What do you mean?' Terrel asked, then came up behind the big man. 'Oh, I see.'

About fifty paces away, at a particularly narrow point on the track, and with precipitous slopes to either side, a mule stood facing them. Someone was sitting on its back while another person, who seemed to be weighed down with a lot of packs, stood behind the animal. Both people were shouting, and waving their arms about, but the mule was ignoring them completely, unmoving apart from an occasional kick with its hind legs when the man at the rear came too close. The voice of the rider was shrill and panic-stricken, and although the figure could not be seen beneath several layers of clothing, Terrel was in no doubt that it was a woman.

'What's going on?' Lawren asked from the rear as the others crowded up behind Terrel.

Faulk did not answer but strode forward again, and the

others hurried to follow, eager to find out what was happening. As they drew closer, Terrel was able to make out what the strangers were saying.

'Move, you vile creature!' the woman shrieked. 'Pieri, do something!'

'What am I supposed to do?' the man replied. 'If he kicks me I'll end up halfway down the mountain, and then you'll be stuck here on your own.'

'You miserable little worm!' the woman shouted. 'How dare you!' It was not immediately clear whether she was addressing her companion or her mount.

'I told you, he doesn't like being ridden. I warned you, but you wouldn't listen. You'll just have to get off.'

'There's no room!' she protested. 'I'll fall. Besides, I'm injured.'

'A blister doesn't count as an injury.'

'Who do you think—' she began, then broke off, having at last noticed that they were not alone. 'Hello there!' she cried. 'Can you help us?'

'We can try,' Faulk called back. 'What seems to be the problem?'

'This wretched creature simply refuses to move. I'm stuck, and my man here is useless.' The woman ignored the choking sound that came from behind her. 'We were going along quite nicely until we got to this point. Now he just won't budge.'

Peering around Faulk, Terrel could see a malevolent intelligence in the animal's eyes that belied its species' reputation for stubborn stupidity. He thought the mule knew exactly what it was doing, and had chosen its stopping place with some care.

'He's probably got a stone stuck in a hoof,' Faulk said, moving forward.

'I wouldn't bet on it,' the man called Pieri responded.

'Jarek was fine when he was just carrying baggage. It was when her ladyship decided she couldn't walk any more that—'

'Are you implying that I weigh more than our supplies?' the woman demanded angrily, twisting round until she almost overbalanced, at which point she thought better of the idea.

Pieri did not reply. His expression was one of disdain bordering on contempt, but Terrel caught a humorous glint in his eyes and realized that the man was probably enjoying the entire episode.

'Throw me the reins,' Faulk said. He had come to a halt in front of the mule, which was now staring at him impassively.

'But I'll have nothing to hold on to then,' she objected. Behind her, Pieri sighed heavily.

'Hold his mane with your free hand,' Faulk suggested.

The woman did as she was told – though her expression made her distaste clear – then tossed the reins to the soldier, who caught them deftly and gave them an experimental tug. He used only a fraction of his strength but the mule reacted quickly, bracing its legs against the ground and pulling its head back violently.

'Oh, be careful!' his rider cried. She now had both hands entwined in the animal's mane.

'I don't think force is going to work,' Faulk decided, turning back to his companions. 'Anyone got any ideas?'

'Can't we just squeeze past?' Lawren asked.

'That's not very chivalrous of you,' Roskin commented.

'I don't think we can anyway,' Faulk said. 'There isn't enough room. One wrong step and Jarek'll push us over the edge.'

'Well, we can't stand here all day,' the hunter said impatiently. 'What about you, Terrel? Can you heal animals as well as men?'

'I can try.' In fact, the earliest indication that he might have some talent had come – inadvertently – when he'd brought a stillborn calf back to life. 'This isn't exactly healing, though, is it?'

'Not unless obstinacy is a disease,' the woman replied. She was obviously intrigued by this development. 'But surely it can't do any harm to try.'

Terrel put his pack down and edged carefully past Faulk. When he patted the mule on its nose, it snorted and jerked away.

'Come on, Jarek,' he whispered in the creature's ear. 'Let me help you.' He laid his fingertips on the side of the mule's neck and this time it did not pull away. Terrel had never made a deliberate attempt to enter an animal's waking dream before. He wasn't even sure that they had one in the same way that humans did. But he tried to let himself fall into the alien realm, using the same technique as he did with any of his patients, and was rewarded by instant results. It was an unnervingly clear and momentarily disorientating experience, and he withdrew almost immediately.

'Faulk was right,' he reported. 'There's pain in the hoof of his right foreleg.' That was not all he had seen, but he didn't know what to say about the rest. He wasn't even sure he could put it into words.

Faulk took a knife from his belt, changed places with Terrel again, and knelt to pick up the animal's leg. It was the work of a few moments to dislodge the sharp stone that had been causing it such discomfort. The soldier stood back, took the reins again and tried to pull the mule forward. The reaction was exactly the same as before.

'Now what?' the woman demanded, gripping the mane so tightly that her knuckles turned white. 'What more do you want, you ungrateful brute?' She kicked the animal's flanks, but it simply ignored her and still did not move.

Then Taryn appeared beside Faulk, having squeezed past his fellow travellers. Before anyone could ask what he was doing, he took the reins from the soldier and then placed his hand on the mule's neck. A moment later, the previously immovable beast took a couple of steps forward. The boy smiled modestly at the various expressions of surprise around him.

'Well done, lad,' Faulk said. 'Lead him on. We'll go back a bit. There's a wider ledge just past that ridge,' he told the woman. 'You can turn around there.'

'Turn around?' she queried. 'No. We're going on.'

'You can try if you want to, but several parts of the trail are impassable now except on foot. You'd have to leave the mule behind, and even then it would be rough going.'

The woman took a few moments to digest this unpalatable information.

'But that's impossible,' she said eventually.

'You'd be better off coming with us,' Faulk added, ignoring her protest. 'If you really need to go on, there has to be a better route. And from what we've seen, half the country on the other side of the mountain is on fire right now.'

'I told you so,' Pieri muttered.

'But I can't go back!' she cried. 'I can't.'

'I don't think you have much choice,' Faulk replied.

Listening to the exchange, Terrel couldn't help but wonder what she was leaving behind – what could be so bad that she was prepared to face such a dangerous trek.

When they reached the small plateau, and the newcomers had been able to see a little more of what lay ahead of them, common sense prevailed and the woman reluctantly agreed to retrace at least part of their journey. Her companion seemed relieved.

'My name is Pieri Archuleta,' he said. 'And this is Yllen Mora.'

'That's not my real name, of course,' the woman put in with a coy smile. 'But it'll do for now.'

'Don't mind her,' Pieri said with a resigned shrug. 'She's always been like this.'

'Like what?' she demanded indignantly.

Her companion ignored her and looked at Faulk, clearly expecting him to introduce the travellers. The big man remained silent, however, leaving it to Terrel to name himself and his companions. That done, the ever-practical Lawren pointed out that time was passing, and that if they wanted to find a suitable camp before dusk then they ought to be on their way.

They set off in single file once more, which did not encourage conversation. Jarek was happily carrying baggage now and seemed to be pleased that they were going down-hill. Yllen was walking, limping when she remembered her blister and moving quite freely at other times. Behind her, Terrel was both amused and intrigued by her behaviour. From what he had seen of her, he guessed she was a few years older than him. She had wispy blonde hair, and pale green eyes that were rarely still. Her smooth-skinned face was pretty and slightly plump, and he suspected that her body – under her bulky clothing – was probably much the same.

By contrast, Pieri seemed to be all sinew and bone. There was hardly a grain of fat on him. He was a small man, with a narrow, pinched face and a permanent gleam in his chestnut-brown eyes. Clearly at ease within his own body, he moved with a natural grace that contrasted with his threadbare garments and his wild mop of black hair. He was leading the mule now, walking directly behind Faulk, and from time to time Terrel could hear the two men exchanging information about the terrain ahead.

On impulse, Terrel turned round to Taryn, who was immediately behind him, and leant down to whisper in the boy's ear.

'What did you say to Jarek to make him move?'

'I didn't *say* anything.'

'You must have done something.'

Taryn looked embarrassed and glanced back at his father.

'I let him know he'd won,' he said quietly. 'That if he let her get off, she'd never try to ride him again.'

'How did you tell him all that?' Terrel asked in amazement.

'In pictures,' the boy replied, then gestured ahead. 'We'd better hurry up. We're getting left behind.'

CHAPTER SIX

They set up camp that night on a small patch of level ground within the curve of a horseshoe-shaped cliff. Pieri was obviously familiar with the place, and the remains of old fires showed that other travellers had taken advantage of the sheltered location. The cove also benefited from a supply of fresh water – a small brook that spilled down over the rock before soaking away into a hollow in the stony soil – and from a good source of firewood provided by a nearby copse.

The weather had become much warmer, which was comforting – until the travellers thought about the possible reason for the rise in temperature. Above them a heavy layer of high cloud, possibly mixed with smoke, still blotted out the sky, but there was no sign of any rain. Once their fire was burning, and the aroma of roasting meat began to fill the air, the general mood became one of contentment – mixed with curiosity. As they gathered round the flames, their chores completed, the group all knew that the time for talking had arrived. However, no one seemed prepared to begin the process, to ask the first of many questions that hung in the air. Terrel sensed his companions' reticence and did not know what to make of it. He wasn't surprised that Faulk and Nomar remained quiet, but he would have expected either Lawren or Roskin to initiate a conversation. Yet they too seemed hesitant. The only explanation he could think of was that one of the newcomers was a woman, the first to infiltrate their exclusively male company – although why that should have left them tongue-tied was a mystery.

In the end it was Yllen herself who began the inevitable exchange.

'Are you really a healer?' she asked Terrel.

'Yes.'

'And just a healer?'

'What do you mean?'

'You have enchanter's eyes.'

It was the first time he had heard this expression since he'd left Vadanis. He was surprised to hear it now, but perhaps it was another indication that he was getting closer to home.

'I'm not an enchanter,' he said. He thought about Jax, but decided not to describe his brother's talents.

'What's an enchanter?' Taryn asked.

'There's no such thing,' Lawren said.

'They're supposed to be able to control other people's minds,' Roskin explained. 'Make them do anything the enchanter wants.'

'But they don't exist,' Lawren told the boy.

'Nothing exists unless it fits into your neat little world, does it?' Roskin exclaimed.

'There's nothing neat about the world,' the hunter replied. 'I just don't pay attention to stupid superstitions.'

'Have you ever met an enchanter?' Taryn asked Roskin.

The would-be seer shook his head.

'For a healer, you don't look very healthy,' Yllen said, returning to the original topic.

Terrel was surprised by her bluntness, but it did not bother him. He'd had to listen to much worse comments about his appearance.

'I can't heal myself,' he explained, glancing at the clawed fingers of his right hand. 'Would you like me to take a look at your foot?'

'I thought you'd never ask,' she replied with a mischievous smile.

Terrel found himself grinning back, reacting to the infectious humour in her eyes.

'Don't encourage her,' Pieri muttered. 'She'll only want to ride again, and then we'll get nowhere.'

'I've learnt that lesson, thank you,' Yllen said tartly. 'As far as I'm concerned, we can chop that vile beast into pieces for tomorrow night's dinner.'

'What? And carry your own pack?'

'That's what you're for,' she told him blithely. 'Besides, if Terrel heals my injury I'll be able to walk better, won't I?'

Wisely, Pieri chose not to respond.

'I can't heal injuries as such,' Terrel warned her. 'You still have to do that yourself. What I *can* do is speed the process up a bit and help you deal with any pain.'

'Fair enough.' She began to unlace her boot.

'Come closer to the fire so I can see better.' Strictly speaking, Terrel had no need to see her foot at all, but he'd learnt from experience that his patients responded more quickly if he first took note of the visible symptoms of their illness or injury. As one of the most important elements in the healing process was a person's belief – both in Terrel's skill and in their own powers of recovery – anything that helped their mind also helped their body. He would trace and combat the problem from inside, but only after looking at it from the outside, like any normal physician.

Yllen moved over and took off her boots. Her feet were surprisingly delicate, and at first glance her skin was smooth and unblemished – but Terrel was horrified to see that all ten toes seemed to have been bleeding. However, on closer examination he discovered that this was not the case. Each toenail had been painted with a dark red substance.

'That's not where I hurt.'

'What is this?' he asked, peering at the unnatural colouring.

'Nesiac polish. Do you like it?'

'What's it for?'

'To look pretty,' she replied, with a touch of impatience. 'I don't always have to wear boots, you know.'

Terrel had come across various kinds of personal adornment before. In Misrah, many of the women had decorated their faces with tattoos, and in other places he knew that they used various powders on their lips and eyelids, but he had never seen anything like this before.

'The problem's at the back,' she said pointedly. 'On the left heel.'

Terrel shook off his bemusement and shifted round so that he could pick up her foot and examine the wound.

'It's just a blister,' he reported, 'but quite a nasty one.'

Yllen glanced at Pieri as if to say 'I told you so'.

'There's no sign of infection, though,' Terrel added.

'It hurts,' his patient complained. Having been vindicated, she was obviously intent on making the most of her ailment.

'I can do something about that. Then we'll clean it and protect it.' He closed his eyes.

'What are you doing?'

'Let him work in peace,' Nomar advised her. 'Terrel knows his business.'

A short time later the healer opened his eyes again to find Yllen staring at him with undisguised admiration.

'That's incredible,' she gasped. 'How did you do that?'

'I just showed your body how to deal with the pain.'

'I can't even feel it any more.'

'You will tomorrow, but it won't be as bad. By the next day you'll be as good as new, as long as you're careful.'

'Thank you.'

Without the need of any bidding, Taryn went to fetch some water and a length of cloth so that Terrel could clean and bind the wound. Yllen flinched when he touched the broken skin, then relaxed when she still felt no pain.

'I think you've made another convert, Terrel,' Lawren remarked.

'You may never get rid of her now,' Pieri added. 'Believe me, I know the feeling.'

'It's your fault I had to run away,' she shot back. 'You admitted as much yourself. You *have* to look after me.'

'It was just a joke. How was I supposed to know it was true?'

'Know what was true?' Lawren asked, sensing a story.

'That's none of your business,' Yllen snapped.

'Sorry, I'm sure,' the hunter said, feigning offence.

The bandaging was finished now, and Yllen flexed her ankle experimentally, then smiled.

'This seems like a miracle,' she said. 'Are you sure you're not an enchanter?'

'I'm sure.'

'I'd like to meet the man who could get you to follow his instructions,' Pieri remarked. 'Enchanter or not.'

'A woman's not supposed to have a mind of her own, of course.'

No one quite knew what to say to that.

'It's getting hot.' Yllen undid the clasp at her neck and took off the cloak that had been wrapped around the upper part of her body. Not satisfied, she untied the belt of her padded grey coat and removed that too, tossing both garments to one side.

The silence around the campfire grew profound.

Underneath the coat Yllen was wearing leggings made of some soft black material and a long tunic that fitted snugly over the curves of her body. And there were a lot of curves to cover. The overall effect was undeniably attractive, and only Pieri – who had presumably seen it all before – was not mesmerized by the sight. As far as Terrel could judge in the firelight, Yllen's tunic was lilac in colour and made of fine-spun cloth. The neckline, which was decorated with a pattern of shiny beads, dipped quite low, exposing an impressive cleavage.

'What's the matter?' she asked. 'Anyone would think none of you have ever seen a woman before.'

Terrel had the feeling that she was perfectly aware of the reactions she was provoking, and that beneath her scornful words she was not displeased.

'You don't see many travellers wearing something as decorative as that,' Roskin commented eventually.

'I didn't have much time to choose my outfit,' she replied. 'Thanks to my friend here.'

'You can't go on saying things like that and not explain them,' Lawren said. 'You'll drive us mad.' He was grinning as he spoke, and Yllen favoured him with a smile.

'You think so?' she asked innocently.

'For the moons' sake, woman, tell them,' Pieri growled.

'*You* tell them,' she replied. 'You're the one who's supposed to make his living by entertaining people. But do it properly. I wouldn't want to upset you by interrupting.'

'You're a storyteller?' Terrel queried, thinking of the times he had spent listening to nomads spinning yarns under the desert moons.

'Among other things,' Pieri admitted.

'Then tell us a story,' Lawren said.

'Very well.'

Pieri sat up, squared his shoulders and took a deep breath. In those few moments an incredible change came over him. His face seemed to fill out and his eyes grew brighter. The firelight now appeared to fall on him alone, leaving the rest of them in shadow. Even his unruly hair took on a new lustre and his clothes no longer seemed so drab.

Terrel had witnessed a similar transformation many years earlier. Babak, a man who was both an apothecary and a swindler by trade, had been able to alter his appearance in the eyes of anyone who looked at him by the use of what he called 'the glamour'. That, Terrel had learnt, was an extension of psinoma, the silent transfer of thoughts between two minds. And Babak had proved to Terrel that he too had the talent to use it effectively. So, it seemed, did Pieri.

When the storyteller spoke, his voice was deeper, more resonant.

'There was once a poor man's son who had a great gift for all kinds of music and song. He could play any instrument within moments of touching it, and only had to hear a tune once before he could repeat it, note perfect and with greater feeling than the original performer.'

'He's exaggerating, of course,' Yllen remarked. 'He's good, but—'

'Shh!' Taryn hissed. 'You said you wouldn't interrupt.'

Pieri stared at them both and they fell silent.

'But because his family were so poor,' he went on, 'he had to beg for the chance to display his skills, leaving his home and travelling to the courts of princes and noblemen. Most spurned him, but the few that allowed him an opportunity to play were entranced. Yet even then they were not satisfied, and insisted that he also entertain them in other ways. So even though his heart longed for the pure beauty of the best music, the young man was forced to indulge the whims of men with greater riches but less taste, singing drinking songs so that his audience could join in the vulgar choruses, telling jokes and repeating foolish tales in order to earn a meal or a few coins. And he became so good at this that the music inside him slowly faded away to almost nothing, until it lay hidden deep within him, beneath the skin and costume of a jester.

'And so he began to travel further and further afield, searching for what he had lost, his only constant companion his mule, who knew nothing of music.'

'That's Jarek,' Taryn informed them.

Pieri glanced at the boy, then smiled, and Terrel guessed that interruptions from Taryn would be tolerated because he was a child. By now Yllen was looking bored, obviously regretting her request to the storyteller, but she knew better than to say anything at that moment. Pieri held the rest of his audience spellbound.

'One day, at the full of the Red Moon, the young man – who was not quite so young any more – came to a town that I will call Hindol. There he was asked to perform for a local lord and his guests, who had gathered to celebrate the nobleman's wife's nameday with a lavish feast.

'Late that evening, when most of the food had been eaten and much wine and beer had been drunk, the not-so-young man began to tell a story. It was about a merchant who discovered his wife had been unfaithful when she received the gift of a silver bowl filled with pink rose petals from her secret admirer. Torn between anger and sorrow, the merchant donned the horns of a cuckold and ran from his home. Now, if the storyteller had been able to finish the tale, he would have related the comical events that occurred when the horned man became embroiled in various misunderstandings involving a local farmer, his daughter and a herd of cattle. But as it turned out he was unable to do so, because one of the guests at the banquet rose unsteadily to his feet and declared that his nameday gift to the hostess had had no such connotations.'

'What are connotations?' Taryn asked.

Lost in his tale, Pieri looked bemused for a moment, then answered the boy's query.

'Hidden meanings,' he explained. 'You see, unknown to the jester, the guest's gift had been a fine vase decorated with the images of roses. This unexpected interruption caused an uproar. The nobleman had often suspected his wife of keeping secrets from him, but until that moment he had never considered the possibility of her infidelity. Now, as several other men also rose to their feet to protest their own innocence, he became certain that he had been betrayed, and his wife – who had indeed been unfaithful, although not with the man who had given her the vase – didn't help her own cause by shouting at her guests to keep quiet before running from the hall.'

'That was you?' Taryn whispered, glancing wide-eyed at Yllen.

She nodded but remained silent, an enigmatic smile on her lips.

'In the confusion, the storyteller made his own exit,' Pieri went on. 'He had no wish to become a victim of the nobleman's wrath, and even though he himself was innocent, it was his words that had sparked off the crisis. But he did not escape so easily. When he hurried to the stables to collect his mule, he found the noblewoman hiding there and, like a fool, let her persuade him that her plight was his responsibility. They've been travelling together ever since.'

As the tale came to an end, and Pieri shrank back into his normal self, the silence around the campfire became deep and thoughtful. The listeners could not resist glancing at Yllen, but no one could meet her gaze for long. She alone seemed perfectly at ease.

'That's quite a story,' Lawren said eventually.

'Does it have a sequel?' Nomar asked.

'What do you mean?'

'Did the storyteller and the noblewoman become lovers?'

'No, no—' Pieri began.

Yllen laughed, a full-throated expression of genuine amusement.

'I may have the morals of an alley-cat,' she declared, 'but I do have *some* standards. I mean, look at him!'

Pieri had slipped into the shadows again, and Terrel couldn't be sure how to interpret the strange expression on his lean face.

CHAPTER SEVEN

'So now you know our story,' Yllen said. 'Are you going to tell us about yourselves?'

Once again, no one was prepared to answer her.

'Such modesty!' she mocked. 'You seem like an interesting group. You must have *some* stories to tell.'

Terrel wondered if she would succeed where he had failed, and persuade his companions to talk about their pasts. For the time being at least it seemed that none of them was willing to start the process.

'Do you think we've fallen in with a band of thieves and murderers, Pieri?' She did not sound unduly worried about the possibility.

'Maybe they're just not so eager to reveal *their* secrets,' her companion suggested mildly.

'Which makes them all the more intriguing,' Yllen said, eyeing each of the company in turn. 'On the other hand, if they *are* criminals, we might find ourselves with our throats cut in the morning.'

Surprisingly, it was Nomar who was the first to respond to her taunts.

'There's enough evil in the world without imagining more,' he said.

'My father would never hurt anyone,' Taryn added indignantly.

Unless they threatened you, Terrel thought. He believed Nomar would be capable of anything then.

'So we're safe here?' Yllen asked, smiling at the boy.

'Yes, you are,' he replied confidently.

'I wish to become a healer,' Nomar said. 'That's why I travel with Terrel.'

'It's a laudable ambition,' she responded. 'What about the rest of you? Do you all want to be healers?'

When no one answered, she turned her attention to Terrel.

'Your followers aren't very forthcoming, are they?'

'They're not my followers. They're my friends.' It was the first time he had ever made such a claim, and he hoped now that it was true.

'Yet you're the one who decides where you go?'

'For the moment, yes,' Terrel conceded. 'But no one here is beholden to me. They can choose their own path.'

'And where is your path leading?'

'To the Movaghassi Ocean.'

'That's wild country. Why do you want to go there?'

'I'm returning to my homeland, Vadanis.'

Yllen frowned, obviously unfamiliar with the name.

'It's in the Floating Islands,' Terrel added.

'I thought only savages lived there,' she said, obviously surprised.

'If that's true, then maybe you *will* get your throat cut tonight,' Lawren put in.

'Terrel's not a savage,' Taryn declared loyally.

'I know that, little one.'

Taryn bristled at her words, but Nomar put a hand on his son's shoulder and the boy subsided.

'So you're going to continue to the west,' Yllen concluded, sounding rather disappointed.

'Yes,' Terrel confirmed, 'and to the south a little when we get the chance.'

'Why don't you come with us?' Lawren suggested. 'We could do with someone to cook and wash our clothes.' His sly grin betrayed the fact that he was trying to provoke her, but Terrel sensed an undercurrent of hope in his words.

'If I ever become a maid,' Yllen replied disdainfully, 'it will be to someone with more style and grace than you.'

'A thousand pardons, m'lady,' the hunter said, tugging at an imaginary forelock.

'Besides, I've set my mind on a new life somewhere.'

'You could still come with us as far as Vergos, at least,' Roskin suggested.

'No one's said we're going that way,' Faulk pointed out before Yllen could respond.

'No, but we could, couldn't we?' Roskin said.

'It would mean turning north.'

'Yes, but only a bit. And there are advantages to going there.'

'Such as?' Lawren asked, then answered his own query. 'You're hoping Terrel's healing will get you into Gozian's court. You really think Kaeryss would let someone like you anywhere near the Raven Cypher?'

'Why not? Besides, Terrel's interested in such things too.' Roskin's defensive tone only encouraged the hunter's scorn.

'Yes, but Terrel doesn't share your delusions. His talent is real.'

'There might be other benefits to such a detour,' Faulk put in.

'I was just going to say that,' Roskin declared.

'There are always opportunities to be taken in any large city,' Lawren admitted. 'For a start, it should be easy enough for you to find work, Terrel. The rest of us too, perhaps.'

'And we could all do with a few nights with a proper roof over our heads,' Roskin added eagerly.

'In a real bed,' Lawren said, warming to his theme.

'And with decent meals.'

'You think we could earn enough to pay for all that?' Terrel asked.

'No harm in trying,' the hunter replied.

'We could do with replenishing our supplies,' Faulk said. 'And we're not thieves, so we'll have to work for it.'

'And what is *your* trade, Faulk?' Yllen asked.

'I can turn my hand to many things.'

'I'll bet you can. Have you ever been to Vergos before?'

'No.'

'None of us have,' Roskin told her. 'What about you?'

'I've never been there,' she replied, 'but I've heard a lot about it.'

'Then you could be our guide,' Lawren proposed.

Yllen shook her head, but before she could say anything Faulk spoke again.

'I've heard there are ships that ply their trade along the Syriel River, between Vergos and the coast. If we're lucky, we could get passage on one of them all the way to the sea.'

'Excellent idea,' Roskin exclaimed.

Terrel was not so sure. Travelling on water always made him nervous. At times it was unavoidable – during his long voyage he had been forced to cross several oceans – but on at least one occasion in the past, the fact that he'd chosen to shorten his journey by going on a boat had almost had disastrous consequences, because it had prevented Alyssa from reaching him. On the other hand, he hadn't seen her in a long time now, and the likelihood of her arriving any time soon was remote. And such a means of transport would make what was left of his journey much easier. What was more, contact with a ship's crew might help him find someone willing to take him to the Floating Islands. He had always known that this would be one of his most difficult tasks. But the idea still made him feel uneasy, and when Yllen spoke again her words only increased his sense of foreboding.

'Do you really want to entrust yourselves to Kenda's Sorrow?' she asked.

'What? What are you talking about?' Lawren said.

'That's what the river's called.'

'Why?'

'Because of its murderous propensities,' Pieri replied.

'Its what?'

'It kills people,' the storyteller explained. 'On quite a regular basis. Ships founder for no reason, whirlpools appear in calm water, and the tidal surges are often violent and unpredictable. People get swept off the banks and drowned.'

'Sounds like you've been listening to too many stories,' Lawren commented.

'Water is a power for good,' Nomar stated forcefully. 'For life, not death.'

'Not this water,' Pieri replied. 'It seems to have a particular liking for children,' he added, glancing at Taryn.

'Hence the name,' Yllen concluded.

'But there's a thriving trade along the river,' Faulk pointed out. 'How is it there are any sailors left alive?'

'Some can read its secrets better than others,' Pieri replied, 'although even the best of them have been having trouble lately, since the moons went crazy. And the rewards for success are great. There's no shortage of volunteers.'

'You sound very knowledgeable,' Terrel commented. 'Have you been to the city?'

'Once. A long time ago.'

'You never told me that,' Yllen exclaimed.

'You never asked.'

'Do *you* think it's worth trying our luck there?' Terrel asked.

'I doubt that luck will have much to do with it,' Pieri answered with a smile. 'If it were up to me, I'd go. In fact, I'd like to come with you.'

'We can't go to Vergos!' Yllen declared fervently.

'Why not?'

'You know very well why not.'

'Oh, come on. Even if Gozian recognized you, he'd think it was funny. There's no love lost between him and your husband.'

'He might send me back.'

'He'd be more likely to add you to his own harem,' Pieri remarked.

For a moment Yllen looked outraged, and then she frowned.

'He's more likely to make an example of me,' she said. 'Gozian's my husband's overlord, after all, and I don't think he'd want to give his own women any ideas.'

'You think adultery's contagious?' Pieri enquired.

Yllen ignored his facetious question.

'I'm not going to the city,' she stated firmly. 'We have to go in the opposite direction.'

'What's out there for us?' Pieri asked, gesturing vaguely to the east. 'It's unknown territory, and in any case, for all we know there's no way through now. I don't fancy walking through a forest fire.'

'That won't last for ever,' she muttered.

'Our supplies won't last for ever either,' he told her.

'We can't go on avoiding people indefinitely. At least in Vergos we'd have a chance to earn some money. And aren't you in the mood for a little comfort?'

'And you can always head on from there,' Lawren put in. 'If you still want to go east, that is.'

Yllen turned to the hunter, staring at him across the dwindling flames of the fire.

'And just why are you so keen for us to come with you?'

'Isn't it obvious? You're a heck of a sight prettier than any of this lot.'

'Do other women actually find that smile charming?' she asked caustically.

'No, they all hate me on sight,' Lawren replied. 'It sometimes takes me *days* to change their minds.'

Despite herself, Yllen laughed.

'Initially, most women seem to go for fresh-faced lads, like Roskin here,' the hunter went on. 'But he wouldn't know what to do with them.'

'And you do?'

'Oh, yes. In any case, I'm sure you have more discerning taste in men.'

'That's certainly true,' she conceded.

'Which is why I'm currently her guardian,' Pieri said, grinning.

'Is *that* what you are?' Yllen exclaimed.

'So are you coming with us, as far as Vergos at least?' Lawren persisted.

'No. I'm sorry to disappoint you,' she said with a patent lack of sincerity, 'but we're going to turn east again the first chance we get.'

Terrel found that he was glad of her decision. Yllen's presence had somehow disturbed the balance of the group, and there were already enough tensions among them. He would be relieved to see them go.

Preoccupied by these thoughts, it was a few moments before he realized something else was amiss.

'I haven't decided if *we're* going to Vergos yet,' he pointed out.

'Well, aren't we?' Roskin asked, his dismay obvious.

'Let me sleep on it,' Terrel replied. 'I'll let you know in the morning.'

The raven kept changing colour. It had been black when it first alighted on top of the engraved stone, but then it turned white, then blood-red. After that its feathers took on a golden amber hue before reverting to black.

'You too,' Terrel said.

The raven did not reply, but simply regarded the healer with its dark, jewelled eyes.

'We always come back to the Dark Moon, don't we.'

The bird croaked loudly, then stooped and scraped its beak over the lichen-encrusted stone. Terrel looked at the inscription there, but he could make no sense of the unfamiliar lettering.

'Am I supposed to know what this means?'

The raven flew away, its wings blurring in a mixture of the four colours, and the stone vanished. Terrel glimpsed a rapid succession of symbols – painted onto a glass dome, carved in smooth blocks of jasper, etched into the desert sand and upon the sloping walls of a wizard's pyramid. He knew – or thought he knew – what some of them meant, but he wasn't sure whether the oracle was trying to tell him something.

Then he saw all four moons reflected in still water. Even the Dark Moon was visible for once, outlined by a silver radiance as if it were a ghost. But when he looked up, the sky was dark and empty. The moons were gone. And the water was no longer still.

Terrel was swept away by the current, helpless within its flow. He was terrified, and yet – far away, at the end of the great river – he recognized the fractured shimmer of the crystal city. He tried to swim towards it, allowing the tidal race to speed him on his way.

Above him, the bright-eyed raven flew in the livery of the moons.

Terrel emerged from his dream knowing that his mind was made up, but with an inexplicable feeling of disquiet. It was still the middle of the night, but the White Moon was riding directly above him, and as it was only a few days past full it gave enough light for him to make out details of the campsite and the cliffs around them. A moment later, as his eyes became more accustomed to the gloom, Terrel realized with a start that someone was crouching next to him. He was about to speak when a large hand was pressed gently over his mouth.

'Don't make a noise,' Faulk whispered. 'And don't make any sudden moves.'

Terrel froze in place, his heart thumping in his chest, wondering what was going on.

'We may not be thieves and murderers,' the big man said quietly, pointing to the open end of the horseshoe, 'but I'm not so sure about them.'

Terrel raised his head slowly, and saw several figures silhouetted against the entrance. They were moving stealthily and in complete silence, but with a menacing sense of purpose. Even from a distance Terrel could see that they were all carrying knives.

CHAPTER EIGHT

'Stay where you are,' Faulk whispered, then got to his feet and drew his sword in a single fluid movement. At the same time he gave vent to a wordless roar of fury, sounding more like a wild animal than a man. Reacting to his lead, the rest of the group rose up as one, each yelling at the top of their voices. After the silence of the night the sheer volume of noise was shocking, and echoes from the surrounding cliffs sustained and amplified their screams. Jarek's braying added an almost demonic note to the cacophony, and Kephra – flying overhead – contributed his own piercing cries to the din. Even though Terrel knew the sound was coming from his friends, he was still thoroughly unnerved by it – and he knew that if the aural assault had been directed at him he would have been terrified.

The healer scarcely had time to sit up before there was movement everywhere, and he realized that the others had all been woken and warned before him – perhaps because Faulk believed Terrel would be the least use in a fight. As his friends moved forward purposefully, the raiders – who had been rooted to the spot for a few startled moments – began to break ranks. While some of them hesitated, not sure who or what they were facing, the others turned tail and fled.

Startled by a fresh bout of screaming to his right, Terrel

glanced round and realized he was not the last to have been woken after all. Yllen had evidently been left to sleep and so had received no warning of what was about to happen. She was sitting up now, her face a mask of terror. As Terrel watched, Taryn appeared beside her and said something to the woman. Her reaction was to reach out and pull the boy down into her arms, even as she screamed again.

The healer had got to his feet by now, but when he looked back at the entrance he saw that the battle was over before it had begun. All the intruders were running away as fast as they could. But Faulk had moved faster. Instead of rushing straight towards his foes he had moved swiftly to one side so that he came at them out of the shadows of the cliff. The last of the thieves had hesitated a moment too long before turning to make his escape, and as he went past Faulk flattened him by diving at his legs. The man screamed as he fell, until the breath was knocked out of him, and his knife clattered away into the night. An instant later he was pinned to the ground by the soldier's weight, with Faulk's left forearm pressing heavily on his throat. The others ran on, giving no thought to their fallen comrade.

'Let me go!'

The indignant cry came from Taryn, who was still clasped tight in Yllen's arms. The boy was struggling, and it was clear that Yllen was the more frightened of the two. When she released him Taryn ran off towards his father, but Yllen stayed where she was.

The others were all gathering around Faulk and his prisoner. Terrel collected a part-burnt stick from the embers of the fire to use as a torch and went to join them. The flickering light illuminated a macabre tableau. Faulk's sword was back in its scabbard but he held a dagger in his right hand, its tip held only fractionally above the captive's left eye. The fallen man looked very young, little more than a boy, and he was clearly terrified, his breath coming in painful, laboured gasps.

'Your friends seem to have left you behind,' Faulk remarked casually. 'No loyalty among thieves?'

The young man tried to speak, but a shove from the warrior's arm cut off the attempt.

'Do you want to tell me what your business was with us?' As Faulk spoke he released a little of the pressure on the man's neck, to allow him to speak.

'Nothing . . .' he rasped, half choking. 'We're just . . . travellers. I swear—'

'At night, with knives drawn? You're lying. I ought to slit your throat right now.'

'No, no. Please. We meant no harm.' It was another transparent lie, but Terrel found it hard to believe that this snivelling wretch had ever represented much of a threat.

'There's no need to kill him,' Nomar said.

'You think he'd have shown *you* any mercy?' Faulk asked, not moving his gaze from the captive. 'Or Taryn? His sort would stab you in your sleep for a few coins.'

Nomar said nothing, his hand resting protectively on his son's shoulder.

'Perhaps we should let Kephra peck his eyes out,' Lawren suggested with a malicious grin. 'He'd think twice about robbing people then.'

The prisoner's gaze flickered to the tercel, which was now perched on its master's shoulder. His eyes grew even wider with terror – then he screwed them shut as if to deny the horror of what was happening.

'And it would save me having to feed him,' the hunter added hopefully.

For a few heartbeats no one moved or said anything.

'Let him go,' Terrel said. 'He's no danger to us now.'

'They could come back,' Lawren argued.

'I don't think so.'

The prisoner shook his head fractionally, his eyes still firmly closed.

'Open your eyes and listen to me,' Faulk ordered.

The young man did as he was told, blinking as he found the blade still poised above him.

'Tell your friends that if they ever come near us again, I'll slit them from gizzard to neck and leave them for the crows to feast on. You got that?'

The captive nodded, a little hope now mixed with his fear. In his place Terrel would have reacted in exactly the same way. The calm certainty in Faulk's voice was chilling, and Terrel was in no doubt that if necessary the warrior would do exactly as he had promised.

'Now get out of my sight,' Faulk spat.

Released from the soldier's grip, the young man got up and hobbled away into the welcoming darkness, moving as fast as he was able.

'You think that was wise?' Yllen asked, her voice trembling. Unnoticed by the others, she had come over to join the rest of the company.

'I don't think we'll have any more trouble,' Faulk replied. 'But we'll set a watch for the rest of the night, just in case.'

'How did you know they were coming?' Terrel asked as they made their way back to the camp.

'I'm a soldier. I've learnt to sense danger before it arrives.'

'Even when you're asleep?' Roskin queried.

'Especially then.'

'That's a useful trick,' Lawren commented.

'You might have warned me,' Yllen complained. 'When you all started shouting I nearly died of shock.'

'Saving your life wasn't enough for you?' Lawren said incredulously. 'You want it done *politely*?'

'I was only saying . . .' She faltered. 'You really think they would have killed us?'

'It's easier to rob someone when they're dead,' the hunter replied. 'They tend not to make such a fuss.'

Yllen's face was now as pale as the White Moon.

'Who's going to take first watch?' Roskin asked.

'I will,' Pieri said. 'I don't think I could get back to sleep now if I tried.'

'Me neither,' Terrel said. 'I'll keep you company.'

Faulk nodded his approval and the rest of the group went back to their beds in silence.

'You know, Faulk's premonition might not have been quite as miraculous as it seemed,' Pieri said.

'What do you mean?'

The two men had wrapped themselves in blankets, and were huddled by the remains of the fire. For a time they had remained silent, straining eyes and ears for any sign that the bandits might be about to return. Neither of them thought that very likely, and eventually – when the rest of the company was asleep again – they had begun to talk quietly.

'Remember when we first got here?' Pieri went on. 'And he paced around, getting the lie of the land?'

Terrel nodded.

'He always does that,' he said.

'I think he was memorizing the noise a boot would make in certain places. And once those sounds were locked in his mind, hearing them would act as a kind of alarm bell in his head.'

'Even when he was asleep?' Terrel asked, echoing Roskin's earlier query.

'I didn't say it wasn't remarkable,' Pieri replied. 'I just don't think it's some kind of supernatural gift. You must have had times when an outside noise affected your dreams, for instance. It's not a big jump from that to it actually waking you up.'

'If you're right, then why wouldn't he have just said so?'

'Everyone likes to keep a few trade secrets.'

'Like the glamour.'

'What?'

'The way you changed when you told your story.'

'I've never heard it called that before.' Pieri gave Terrel an appraising glance before resuming his watch on the entrance to the camp. 'I'm surprised you noticed. Most people don't.'

'But it was so obvious.'

'Only to someone who knows what it is. I take it you have some talent in that area?'

'A little,' Terrel admitted. 'Looking the way I do, it's sometimes useful to make my appearance rather more ordinary.'

Pieri nodded, understanding.

'I generally try to do the opposite,' he said with a rueful smile. 'To make my performance more interesting. It was an old pedlar who first taught me the trick of it.'

Terrel laughed softly.

'What's so funny?' Pieri asked.

'What was the pedlar's name?'

'Cobo. But he always called himself—'

'The King?'

'The King of the Marketplace,' Pieri confirmed. 'Have you met him too?'

'No, but I met someone like him in my own country. I think there must be at least one in every land.'

'I travelled with him for a while,' the storyteller added.

'Playing music to help draw people to his stall. He was a crook, but I couldn't help but like him.'

Terrel nodded, remembering his own sojourn with Babak.

'Do you carry your instrument with you still?' he asked.

'A few whistles,' Pieri replied dismissively. 'Nothing special. A really good lute or viol is expensive, and they don't travel well, so I make do with what I've got and anything I can borrow at the time.'

'I'd like to hear you play.'

'No. These days I only play for money. I wouldn't insult you with the sort of thing I do now.'

It was clearly a painful subject, and Terrel decided to let it drop.

'When you made your escape from Yllen's husband,' he asked, 'were you able to use the glamour to change *her* appearance?'

'How did you know that?'

'Just a guess. Tell me how it works.'

'You can only do it when you're physically touching the other person,' Pieri explained. 'When there's some connection between you. Like your healing, I suppose. I don't really know what happens. I didn't want people to recognize her, so I just made sure they didn't. Once we were able to get her something to cover up with it was a lot easier, but she can't help showing off sometimes – like she did tonight. Daft cow.' He was trying to sound dismissive again, but the indulgent tone of his voice softened the insult.

'She does have quite a lot to show off with.'

Pieri laughed.

'That's true enough,' he said.

'Is that why you've stayed with her?' Terrel probed gently.

'Moons, no! Even if I fancied her, you heard what she thinks of me.'

'So why are you still together?' the healer asked. He knew he was prying, but was unable to stem his curiosity. 'I mean, I can see why you felt responsible for her being forced to leave, but once you'd got away . . .'

'I still feel responsible,' Pieri admitted. 'Despite appearances, in many ways she's just an innocent. I dread to think what would happen if I left her to her own devices.'

Terrel knew that this was not the whole story, but there were limits to just how nosy he could allow himself to be.

'She was terrified by the attack tonight,' he remarked.

'She has more to lose than most.'

'Her "supplies"?' Terrel guessed.

Pieri nodded.

'When she made her hasty exit from her home,' he explained, 'she had the foresight to collect some of her jewellery. We've sold some of it since to buy food and clothes, her boots, and so on – but what's left won't last much longer.'

'You think tonight's raid might make her change her mind about coming with us to Vergos?'

'I hope so,' Pieri replied.

Terrel found that, in spite of his earlier misgivings, he hoped so too.

CHAPTER NINE

'What *is* that?' Roskin exclaimed.

'It's incredible,' Lawren breathed, agreeing with the younger man for once. 'I've never seen anything like it.'

They were all looking up at a cliff that formed one side of a hill. From the other side it had appeared unremarkable, conical in shape and covered with scrub grass. But once they had rounded the slope they'd come to an abrupt halt. The cliff before them was about sixty paces in height, its surface jagged but sheer. For the most part it was made up of a matt black stone that seemed to absorb all light – and which, on closer inspection, proved to be pockmarked with millions of tiny air bubbles. However, embedded into this dull surface were at least a dozen oval-shaped areas of bright green crystal that glittered enticingly in the sunlight. Some of these intricately patterned patches were massive, more than twice the height of a tall man; others were no more than a hand span or two across. But they all shone with an elusive, constantly changing beauty that contrasted starkly with the sombre setting. It was as though the entire hill had been crafted as a giant piece of exotic jewellery.

The lowest of the crystals were out of reach, well above head height, but Lawren had decided that the rough surface of the black rock looked easy enough to climb. He was already testing handholds and looking up when Pieri spoke.

'I wouldn't do that if I were you,' he warned.

'Why not?' Lawren asked, hesitating.

'The rock might look solid enough, but it's treacherous stuff. It'll crumble if you put your weight on it.'

'Don't you want to get a closer look at those crystals?' the hunter asked. 'Wouldn't it be worth a little risk?'

'No, it wouldn't. The green patches are called fool's jade. It's beautiful in places, but if you break it off it'll just turn to powder in a few hours. Like that dust by your feet. It's worthless.'

Lawren glanced down, obviously disappointed.

'I was wondering why there were no prospectors here,' he said.

'How do you know all this?' Roskin asked. 'I thought you said you'd never been on this trail before.'

'I haven't,' Pieri replied. 'I had no idea this was here. But I've seen another cliff just like it.'

The others all knew that the storyteller was more familiar with this area than they were, and had come to regard him as their unofficial guide.

'There's somewhere else like this?' Nomar queried.

'*Exactly* like this,' Pieri confirmed. 'I saw it a long time ago. I don't remember too much about it, but I *do* remember being told that the pattern of the ovals there matches these precisely, like a mirror image. Someone even measured them, apparently. I never quite believed it until now.'

'Where is this other place?' Terrel asked.

'It must be two hundred miles away,' Pieri replied, pointing to the north. 'On the other side of those mountains.'

'Then how can they possibly match exactly?' Lawren queried. 'It doesn't make sense.'

The storyteller shrugged.

'I'm just telling you what I heard.'

'So the hill was sliced in two and one half was dragged two hundred miles north over a mountain range?' Roskin said. 'Even *I* think that's ridiculous. It must be a coincidence.'

'Common sense from the lips of the Great Londolozi?' Lawren gasped. 'Wonders will never cease!'

Is it more ridiculous than finding the remains of a fish halfway up a mountain? Terrel wondered. He had imagined another explanation for the phenomenon – the thought of which made him shudder inwardly. What if the range that now separated the two halves had not been there originally? What if it had somehow *grown*, out of the ground – like the black mountain above Fenduca had grown – and in doing so had split the crystal hill apart? On the face of it this seemed absurd, but it could be another indication of a massive upheaval that had afflicted Nydus in the long-distant past. The thought that something similar might happen again was even more unnerving. Terrel decided he was not willing to share this theory with his companions, who seemed content to dismiss the whole thing as a bizarre accident of nature.

Accident or not, the results were undeniably extraordinary. As the company went on their way again, each of them glanced back occasionally for another glimpse of the jewelled cliff.

Four days had passed since the night they'd foiled the band of thieves. The Dark Moon had grown full and was now waning again, just as the crescent of the Amber had vanished and then started growing once more. Halfway through its own cycle, the White Moon continued to wane, while the Red was still two days short of its full glory. But all this celestial movement had gone unseen, because for three days and nights the sky had been entirely blanketed by cloud. Some rain had fallen, as well as a few stinging showers of hail, and the air was frigid and damp, but it was the unremitting grey gloom that most affected the travellers' mood.

The dismal weather and lack of sunlight had reminded Terrel of his time in Macul's fog valley. The people there had *never* seen the sun or the moons – and yet their lives had still been affected by the lunar influences that controlled so much of what went on on Nydus. The healer's visit had been memorable for a number of reasons, not least his friendship with a pregnant girl named Esera. Thinking of her now, with a fondness tinged with melancholy, Terrel realized that her baby – which had been due shortly after he'd left – must be more than eight years old now. It seemed barely credible, but when he stopped to think about it, he remembered Ysatel Mirana, and an even more incredible possibility from his time in Macul. She'd been expecting the child she and her husband Kerin had yearned for for so long when she had become a sleeper. If she was still alive – and Terrel had no reason to think she was not – then she would have been pregnant now for almost ten years! This thought was almost unbearably sad, and because Terrel had no way of knowing when or if her baby would ever be born, he forced himself to set such memories aside and concentrate on the journey in hand.

The first breaks in the cloud had appeared around noon on the fourth day, and the sun had broken through at last – lifting the travellers' spirits and making the entire landscape seem much less forbidding. By the time they'd reached the crystal hill the sun was sinking towards the western horizon, though it was still shining brightly.

Terrel's decision to head for Vergos had been accepted readily, as had Yllen's decision that she and Pieri would accompany them. They had already talked about what they planned to do when they got there, the opportunities and pitfalls such a city might present, and the reputed nature of its people and its ruler. As yet no one had seen fit to speculate on how long they might stay there or where they would head after that.

They reached the hamlet just before dusk, having seen it some time earlier from higher up the valley. Even though the weather had taken a turn for the better, the prospect of being able to trade their skills for some fresh food and perhaps a roof over their heads had spurred them on. But as they came closer it was clear that all was not as it should be.

'It's too quiet,' Lawren observed.

'No movement anywhere,' Roskin agreed. 'Where is everyone?'

The village looked prosperous enough. The mixture of stone- and wood-built huts seemed to be in good repair and the land around them appeared fertile, but there were no fires and no sign of any livestock. And there were no people to be seen anywhere.

Faulk came to a halt, and although his face remained impassive Terrel knew that he was studying the situation, allowing his permanently suspicious mind to consider various options. The others stopped too, following the soldier's lead, but for a moment no one spoke.

'What do you think?' Terrel asked eventually.

'Either there's no one here, or that's what they want us to think,' Faulk replied.

'It's a bit early for them to have gone inside for the night,' Lawren said.

'Unless they saw us coming?' Pieri countered.

'Do we look that dangerous?'

'We know bandit gangs are operating in the area. Perhaps they're just being cautious.'

'Surely they wouldn't have had time to douse all the fires if they'd gone into hiding as soon as they saw us,' Yllen argued. 'There'd still be some smoke.'

'She's right,' Lawren said. 'This should be a busy time of day, when they'd need fires for cooking and warmth.'

'So there's no one here, then?' Roskin concluded. 'That doesn't make any sense.' He seemed almost pleased, obviously scenting another mystery.

'Wait here,' Faulk said. 'I'll go and find out.'

'Alone?' Terrel queried.

'Yes. One man's not as likely to be seen as a threat.'

'Even when he's carrying a sword?' Lawren asked.

Without a word Faulk unbuckled his belt and gave it to Terrel. Then he strode off, covering the remaining distance to the hamlet at a rapid pace.

'Mind you don't do yourself any mischief with that thing,' Pieri advised Terrel.

'I don't think I could even lift it,' the healer responded. 'It's too heavy.' He was resting the tip of the scabbard on the ground, his left hand covering the pommel. He knew that entrusting someone with his weapon was an honour Faulk did not bestow lightly.

'Faulk carries it easily enough,' Yllen noted admiringly.

'You like a bit of brute strength in a man, do you?' Lawren remarked, flexing the muscles of his right arm.

'In a *man*, yes,' she told him.

'That put me in my place,' the hunter muttered. But he was still grinning, in spite of his supposed chagrin.

They were silent then, and watched as Faulk made his way into the nearest house. After a few moments he emerged and went on to the next. Before long it was obvious that there really was no one in the village, but the soldier did not return until he had checked every last dwelling.

'It's been abandoned,' he reported. 'Several days ago, at a guess.'

'Why?' Yllen asked.

'I've no idea. There are no signs of any violence.'

'Some sort of illness, maybe?' Roskin hazarded.

'No fresh graves.'

'No bodies left to rot?' Lawren asked cheerfully.

'Nothing like that,' Faulk said. 'I don't think they even left in much of a hurry. They just collected everything of value and left.'

'But why?' Yllen repeated. 'We've seen plenty of places far worse than this, with people still living there.'

'It's not high enough to be just a summer camp,' Lawren said. 'Besides, it looks permanent.'

'Perhaps they're coming back,' Terrel suggested.

'People don't just leave their homes and land to the mercy of anyone who happens along,' Pieri said. 'Even if most of them were away at a wedding or something, they'd have left someone behind to guard their property.'

'Anyway, they've taken too much with them for that,' Faulk said.

'Perhaps the place is cursed,' Lawren said. 'Eh, Nomar?'

'No. This is nothing like Senden,' Nomar replied seriously, ignoring the hunter's mocking tone.

'Where's Senden?' Taryn asked, looking at his father.

When Nomar did not respond, it was Roskin who supplied the answer.

'That's the place we went south to avoid.'

'When we ended up in a cave instead,' Lawren added. 'Not one of our better moves.'

'Oh, I don't know,' Yllen said. 'You wouldn't have met us if you hadn't gone that way.'

'You're right!' the hunter exclaimed. 'So Nomar's superstitions have their advantages.'

'Don't mock things you don't understand,' Terrel said, rather more sharply than he had intended.

'Sorry,' Lawren muttered, looking genuinely offended for once.

'So what are we going to do?' Pieri asked hurriedly. 'Just stand around here all night?'

'I can't see any reason not to make the most of the shelter here,' Terrel said.

'We'd be stupid not to,' Lawren growled.

'It'd be better than another night in the open,' Roskin agreed.

'Then let's go and choose our sleeping quarters,' Terrel said.

'We could all have a place of our own,' Yllen declared.

The travellers had confirmed for themselves that any of the huts would provide a comfortable resting place for the night. Indeed, compared to many of their recent accommodations, the village seemed almost luxurious.

'It would be better if we kept together,' Faulk said.

'Couldn't I have some privacy, just for once?' Yllen asked.

'I'm only concerned for our safety,' he told her.

She was about to protest further, but then smiled suddenly.

'Perhaps you'd like to keep me safe personally,' she suggested.

Faulk looked as close to uncomfortable as Terrel had ever seen him.

'I'll do it,' Lawren volunteered before the soldier had a chance to respond.

'I'd have to be truly desperate before I'd accept an offer like that,' Yllen replied.

'Oh, well.' Lawren shrugged. 'You can't blame a man for trying.'

'Have you no shame?' Nomar demanded, glaring at Yllen.

She looked stunned by the sudden outburst, which left her speechless for once.

'You make a mockery of love, of marriage, of—'

'Leave her alone,' Pieri cut in sharply. 'None of us is faultless, not even you.'

'No, I'm not,' Nomar admitted. 'But at least I have the decency not to flaunt the fact.'

Terrel felt that Nomar had been on an emotional knife-edge ever since the mention of Senden, but this verbal assault seemed uncharacteristically cruel.

'Who made you the judge of what's right or wrong?' Yllen demanded, becoming angry now as she recovered her poise. 'The way I live my life is none of your business.'

'It is when you parade your harlotry in front of my son—'

'That's enough!' Terrel stated forcefully. He'd had all he could take of their bickering, and Taryn was already looking frightened and confused.

Everyone obeyed the healer's edict. After a few moments Nomar turned away and went into one of the huts, followed almost immediately by his son.

'Who put a burr under his saddle?' Lawren wondered aloud.

'It was only a bit of fun,' Yllen said quietly. She seemed genuinely upset now.

'It's all right,' Pieri consoled her. 'He didn't mean what he said.'

Yllen glanced at her long-term companion. Although she

was obviously grateful for his support, it was equally clear that she did not believe him.

'Perhaps it would be better if we all had a bit of privacy tonight,' Terrel said.

There was a curious air of detachment about Terrel's dreams that night – almost as though he was seeing them through someone else's eyes. At first he was moving – without apparent effort – through a series of doorways that linked a seemingly endless succession of rooms. The rooms were all empty and windowless and, apart from the black ones, they were all bright. The floor, walls and ceiling of each was a uniform colour – white, red, amber or black – until he came to one made of crystal, where a white-faced owl flew in endless circles above a small fountain that bubbled up from the translucent floor.

Alyssa? he called hopefully.

There was no response, but even so he couldn't help wondering if there were any messages here. But if there were, he had no idea how to interpret them.

Without warning, the scene changed abruptly to a more realistic setting – although the sense of remoteness remained. A woman was falling to the ground while a man stood over her, his brutal face contorted in a snarl of rage. Terrel didn't recognize either of them, but he was almost overwhelmed by anger at the man's cruelty. The images blurred then and he saw the woman again, alone – with him? – as they fled through unfamiliar streets. Her shy smile caused such a rush of tenderness that he felt as though he were lighter than air. This was followed by a surge of happiness so pure and so heartwrenching that it made him gasp. He sensed the rebirth of a love – no, of a *capacity* to love – that had seemed long dead. In the light of that sunrise, after an interminable night, he glimpsed a flash of silver, a delicate hand. But then the darkness closed in again, in blood and sorrow, and he found his only consolation in the eyes of a child.

Terrel awoke to find himself looking into those same eyes.

'Will you tell me what it means?' Taryn whispered.

'What?' The healer was still half lost in the labyrinths of sleep.

'The dream.'

Which one? Terrel wondered. He was aware now of the light touch of the boy's hand resting on his own. He had no idea how long Taryn had been there, but he was beginning to see what might have happened.

'*You* showed me that?' he asked hoarsely.

'The pictures, yes.'

Terrel considered this for a few moments.

'Was it your dream?' he asked eventually. 'Don't you know what it means?'

'No, it was my father's. I share them sometimes, when he lets me.'

Terrel felt his grasp of the situation slipping away again.

'Was that my mother, do you think? Taryn asked. 'I think it was. But who was that other man? The horrid one?'

'I don't know,' the healer replied. 'Why don't we go and ask your father?'

'I can't do that.' The boy was looking frightened now.

'But I can,' Terrel said, getting up from his bed. He could tell that this was desperately important to Taryn, and it seemed unfair of Nomar to share his vision and then not explain it. 'Come on.'

They left Terrel's hut and passed by the fire, where Roskin was sitting. A watch had been arranged – to appease Faulk – when it had become clear that the group was going to split up for the night. If the villagers returned, or anyone else approached the settlement, there would at least be someone to raise the alarm.

'Is everything all right?' the lookout asked.

'Nothing to worry about,' Terrel replied.

He followed Taryn into the boy's hut – and knew immediately that there *was* something to worry about. Nomar was sitting up, his eyes wide and staring at nothing. As the healer watched, he raked his fingernails across his temples and down his cheeks, leaving dark weals on the skin, and a low moan escaped his lips. Any dreams he'd had earlier were gone now, replaced by horrors that only Nomar could see. He was in the throes of another attack, and Terrel knew they would get no answers from him that night.

CHAPTER TEN

Terrel stayed with Nomar for the rest of the night, helping him through his ordeal. The healer's subsequent decision that they would stay in the village for another day was greeted with universal approval. Everyone could see that Terrel had been exhausted by his efforts, and it was obvious that Nomar was in no fit state to travel. Although he was no longer in pain, his torment had left him weak and in desperate need of rest. Terrel and Taryn also spent much of the morning asleep. It was only when the boy had finally been convinced that his father was over the worst that he had given in to his fatigue, and he was now dead to the world. The others were simply glad of a day of relative ease in comfortable surroundings – and the longer they stayed, the more advantages they discovered.

Closer inspection of the various cabins revealed some welcome food supplies – strips of dried, salted meat, two sealed earthenware jars packed with honeycomb, a tray of wizened apples, some grain and a few bunches of herbs. There were also plenty of winter vegetables that had simply been left in the fields.

'They'd have rotted soon,' Roskin reported when he returned, happily covered in mud, carrying the results of his harvesting endeavours. 'What a waste.'

Terrel, who had just woken up, looked at the bedraggled figure and had a sudden flash of memory. He instinctively glanced up at the sky, running through the current phases of the moons. Two were waxing, two on the wane.

Roskin noted the direction of his gaze and looked worried.

'There isn't going to be another fire-scythe, is there?'

'No,' Terrel replied, hoping this was true. 'I was just checking on the moons.'

'Why?'

'In Vadanis we had laws about when crops could be sown and harvested.'

'I've heard of such ideas,' Roskin said, glancing down at the vegetables he'd collected. 'Did I break any of the laws?'

'No, but if you'd waited another two days you would have done.'

'Because the Red Moon would be waning then?'

'Yes, but we're not in Vadanis, and I never thought those rules made sense anyway.'

'I wouldn't want to do anything to offend the moons,' Roskin assured him. 'This place is almost too good to be true.'

'Don't worry. Even if you *had* broken any of the laws, no one's going to punish you.'

Roskin eyed the healer thoughtfully, aware of the undercurrent of bitterness in his words.

'It sounds as though you've had first-hand experience of such punishment.'

'I had a friend once who was declared insane and imprisoned just because he tried to steal some potatoes at the wrong time.'

Although Elam's family had been on the brink of starvation, in the eyes of the law that had been no reason to excuse his crime.

'Is he still in the asylum?' Roskin asked.

'No. He's dead.'

'I'm sorry.'

'It was a long time ago,' Terrel said, determinedly push-ing aside the memory of Elam's murder. 'We should eat well tonight.'

'Even better if Lawren manages to get us some fresh meat.'

'It feels odd, though, just helping ourselves to other people's provisions,' the healer added.

'If they left the stuff here, they obviously didn't want it. It's not stealing.'

'This is no time for delicate sensibilities, Terrel,' Pieri said as he joined them. The storyteller was carrying a jug in one hand and a beaker in the other. 'Look what I've found.' He passed the cup to Terrel, who saw that it was half full of a frothy brown liquid. The strong smell was enough to tell him what it was – and that he didn't want any.

'Try some,' Pieri urged.

'No, thanks.'

'What is it?' Roskin asked.

'Beer. It's good stuff too. And there's a whole cask of it back there.' Pieri gestured towards one of the huts. 'You don't know what you're missing,' he told the healer.

'Alcohol doesn't agree with me.'

'All the more for us then.' He offered the beaker to Roskin, who accepted it and drank readily enough.

'This place *is* too good to be true,' the would-be seer commented.

'Odd, isn't it?' Pieri said. 'It looks as if they just took what they could carry and left everything else behind.'

'And not just food,' Roskin added. 'They don't seem to have taken any of their tools or cooking pots, all sorts of things.'

'There's plenty of firewood too. And water's not a problem,

with the spring over there. Why would anyone have wanted to leave all this?'

By the middle of the afternoon they were no closer to solving the mystery of why the hamlet had been abandoned, but because there was still no sign of any of the inhabitants, even Terrel had overcome his qualms about taking food that did not belong to them. As Lawren pointed out – when he returned with two rabbits that Kephra had killed – most of the provisions would either have rotted or been eaten by animals sooner or later. And there was no doubt that the enormous stew cooked that afternoon was the best meal they'd had for a long time. For those that wanted it, the beer made the occasion even more enjoyable.

Terrel ate his food sitting on the doorstep of Nomar's cabin. His patient had woken briefly on several occasions during the day, and the healer had been able to get him to eat and drink a little before he relapsed into what was now a thankfully dreamless sleep. In some ways Terrel was now more worried about Taryn. The boy was clearly fretting, and alternated between feverish bouts of activity and morose languor. Terrel had tried to get him to talk, but never managed to gain his attention for more than a few moments. Taryn would run off to check on his father, or stare at what someone else was doing, or simply curl up and fall asleep.

Just at that moment the boy was inside the hut. He was quiet, having been given strict instructions not to disturb his father, and Terrel thought he was probably napping again. So it came as something of a surprise when the boy slipped out of the cabin and came to sit next to him on the step.

'Do you want some?' Terrel asked, offering his bowl of stew.

'I'm not hungry.'

'You should eat. To keep your strength up.'

'It does smell good,' Taryn conceded.

Terrel looked over to where the cauldron was still bubbling over the fire, and saw that Yllen was already ladling out another portion. She brought it and a spoon over to the doorway, and handed them to Taryn.

'Be careful,' she warned him. 'It's very hot. Don't burn your tongue.'

'Thank you,' the boy whispered, his eyes downcast.

'How is your father?'

'He's sleeping.' Taryn's voice was barely audible.

Terrel could see that Yllen wanted to say something more, but didn't know how to put it, so she left them alone. Taryn glanced up to watch her, then looked down again and began blowing on his stew to cool it.

Terrel went on eating. He knew that Taryn was thinking about the previous night's argument and he wanted to distract him if possible. After a moment's thought, he decided to try to persuade the boy to talk about Nomar's illness and the dreams that had preceded it. It was better than pretending it hadn't happened.

'Will you tell me more about the pictures?' he began tentatively. 'The ones you showed me?'

'What about them?' Taryn asked between mouthfuls.

'What you showed me was amazing. It almost felt as if it was my own dream.'

'I suppose it was, in a way. Dreams are just what we imagine when we're asleep, aren't they?'

Terrel had the feeling the boy was repeating something that had been said to him.

'Yes,' he replied. 'But most people can't see what someone else imagines. Or shape those images into pictures for another person to see. How do you do that?'

'I don't know. They're just there.'

'Could you show me a picture now?'

'What of?'

'Whatever you like,' Terrel replied. Then, as the boy hesitated, he added, 'It doesn't have to be anything special.'

'I couldn't do that again.'

It took the healer a few moments to work out that Taryn was referring to Nomar's dream. Because the boy had not mentioned this again, Terrel had begun to wonder if he'd forgotten about it. Even though, for most people, dreams had a habit of slipping away after they'd woken up, in Taryn's case it seemed more likely that he simply did not want his father to be bothered with any questions.

'Why not?'

'It was private,' the boy explained, looking ashamed now. 'I shouldn't have shown it to you.'

'Don't worry,' Terrel told him. 'I think it might have something to do with your father's headaches, so telling a healer was a good thing to do.'

'You really think so?' Taryn asked hopefully.

'Why else would you have chosen me rather than any of the others?'

'Because I know you're our friend.'

Terrel was touched by this simple pronouncement. It made him all the more determined to try to help Nomar.

'Not everyone can see what I show them,' Taryn added unexpectedly. 'But I knew you would.'

'*How* did you know?'

'I just did. Do you still want me to show you something?'

Terrel nodded.

'What should I do?' he asked.

'It usually helps if you close your eyes.'

Terrel did as he was told, and felt a small hand slip into his own. A moment later he found himself gazing at the most incredible building he had ever seen. It was perched on the summit of a great mountain, and its stone-built towers seemed to reach up to the stars. Every column, parapet and archway was carved with symbols and signs, and yet the overall design gave the impression of stability and grace. Although it might be intricate, this enormous temple had been built to outlast a hundred generations of men. The whole thing was breathtakingly beautiful, and the setting could not have been more spectacular – with other mountains in the distance and a silver river snaking away across a wide plain.

All too soon it vanished, leaving Terrel speechless.

'You didn't say it had to be something real,' Taryn said with a shy smile.

The healer found himself feeling unreasonably disappointed. He had been about to ask Taryn where he had seen this wonderful sight, but then realized that such an extraordinary place could not exist in the real world.

'You have a vivid imagination,' he said instead, feeling that this was a considerable understatement.

'I saw it in a dream first,' the boy told him, 'but now I can picture it whenever I want. I keep hoping I'll find the real mountain one day, but I don't suppose I will.'

'I've never seen anything like it,' Terrel admitted, but even as he spoke a vague memory nagged at the back of his mind. Something about the temple had been familiar – but he just couldn't think what it might have been.

They were interrupted then as Pieri strolled over to join them.

'What are you two up to?' he asked.

'Nothing really,' Taryn answered.

Terrel realized the boy didn't want to discuss his 'pictures' with anyone else.

'Are you sure you won't have any beer?' the storyteller asked. 'It really is very good.'

'No, thanks.'

All the others had joined Pieri in a drink, though Terrel had noticed that Faulk drank only sparingly.

'Beer's horrible,' Taryn declared, making a face.

'Ah, the innocence of youth,' Pieri said, grinning. 'You'll learn, my lad.'

'And it makes you do silly things,' Taryn stated firmly.

'That's the point,' Pieri said, laughing now. 'If you ask me, the world could do with a bit more silliness.'

Taryn paused, obviously considering this idea.

'Does Jarek like beer?' he asked.

'I shouldn't think so.' The mule's owner looked puzzled. 'Anyway, I wouldn't waste it on him.'

'Give me some.'

'I don't think—' Terrel began.

'It's not for me,' Taryn explained hurriedly.

Pieri passed his cup over, his lean face betraying a mixture of perplexity and amusement. Taryn took his prize and trotted over to where Jarek stood, unmoving, a little way from the fire. Everyone watched as he put a hand on the mule's neck and then held the beaker under his nose. The animal's nostrils twitched, but he did not react in any other way, until Taryn took back the cup and looked round at his expectant audience.

'Time to be silly,' he announced. 'Jarek, stamp your right foot. The front one, I mean.'

To the astonishment of all the spectators, the mule raised his right foreleg and brought the hoof down with a thud.

'Now the left. Three times.'

Once more Jarek obeyed, prompting both laughter and applause from the onlookers.

'Now kick both back legs in the air at once,' Taryn commanded. 'And sing at the same time.'

The mule did as he was told, bouncing his hindquarters up into the air and braying wildly. The movement was so unnatural and the sound so ridiculous that it reduced the audience to helpless laughter.

'More!' Lawren cried when he was finally able to speak. 'Make him do something else.'

'No,' Taryn replied firmly. 'He's done enough to earn his beer. I need a bowl.'

Yllen brought a dish to him and he poured the remains of Pieri's drink into it.

'He won't touch it,' the storyteller predicted as the boy set the bowl down on the ground.

Taryn did not reply, but he did not need to. Jarek bowed his grizzled head and slurped the beer down with every sign of enjoyment.

It was only then that Terrel realized someone was standing behind him in the doorway, and he felt a moment's unease – but then looked up and saw that Nomar was smiling. It was the first smile that had crossed his face in a long time.

Several hours later, long after darkness had fallen, the adults were all still awake. Roskin kept adding logs to the fire, and the beer jug was passed round every so often. Although conversation was intermittent, no one seemed to want the evening to end.

At one point Pieri disappeared into a hut, and returned with a board and pieces that looked to Terrel very like those used for a game called chaikra, which he had played on the Floating Islands. Lawren immediately challenged the storyteller to a match and Roskin, Yllen and Faulk gathered round to watch, making tactical suggestions of variable worth from time to time. Terrel found himself able to talk privately with Nomar for the first time since he'd got up.

'Taryn showed me the dream you had before you became ill last night,' he said quietly.

Nomar did not respond immediately, and Terrel wondered anxiously if he had been too blunt.

'He shouldn't have done that,' Nomar said at last.

'He knows that now,' the healer replied, 'and he's sorry for it, but your son has a remarkable talent and what he saw was obviously important to him. I'll understand completely if you don't want to talk to me about it, but I really think you should talk to *him*. He deserves that at least.'

When Nomar did not respond, Terrel told himself that it was possible his patient might not even be able to recall the dream now. Given all that had happened since – and given the quicksilver nature of dreams – this was a distinct possibility. He could only hope that his clumsy intervention would not get Taryn into trouble with his father. Nomar seemed calm enough, but the man was full of contradictions, and Terrel had already seen how his emotions could explode without warning. The healer was about to speak again when Nomar beat him to it.

'When I first met Taryn's mother, she was another man's wife.' The quiet, even tone of his voice contrasted with the surprising import of his words. His eyes were unfocused, seeing another time and place – a place that now existed only in his dreams. 'He was a minor nobleman, powerful enough, and rich, but he was also violent and cruel. He treated Anya abominably, as if she were some *possession*. I saw things . . .' His words tailed off as he blinked away the awful memories. 'But it didn't matter what I saw. I was only a servant. I watched her shrivel under his brutality until I couldn't stand it any longer. I forced her to run away with me, to escape his tyranny, but I gave no thought to what would happen afterwards.'

Nomar's strange question to Pieri – when the storyteller had described how he and Yllen had come to be journeying together – made sense now. He had seen the parallel with his own tale – and the differences too.

'I'd loved her for years,' Nomar went on. 'And I think she came to love me eventually. But what I brought her at the last wasn't freedom but death. She died giving birth to Taryn. He's all I have left of her.'

'Have you told him all that?' Terrel asked.

'No. I thought he would blame me. In law he is a bastard.'

'In law, perhaps,' the healer conceded. 'But he was conceived in love, and that's much more important. He's a sensible boy. How could he blame you? If you tell him the whole story he'll think you're a hero. Even more than he does already.'

Nomar turned to meet Terrel's gaze.

'You think so?'

'I'm sure of it.'

Their exchange was interrupted then by an explosion of noise from the game players. Pieri had won, and had immediately been challenged to a rematch.

'I hope you're right,' Nomar said, gazing up at the stars. 'Either way, one thing is certain. He deserves the truth.'

'Don't wake him now,' Terrel advised as Nomar got to his feet. 'He needs to rest.'

'So do I,' Nomar replied. 'I'll tell him in the morning. Goodnight, Terrel.'

'Alone at last!' Yllen grinned, and Terrel realized that she was slightly drunk.

The others had finally retired to their respective huts to sleep. When Faulk had asked who would take the first watch, Yllen had surprised everybody by volunteering. Terrel had offered to keep her company and Faulk had nodded, clearly relieved to have someone who was completely sober sharing the duty. The soldier was the only one who thought such precautions were really necessary, but no one was prepared to argue with him.

'Is Nomar all right now?' Yllen asked with what seemed like genuine concern.

'I think so.' Terrel knew that her query was not entirely about his patient's health. His verbal attack the previous night was evidently still bothering her. 'You shouldn't take everything he says to heart.'

'I accept people as they are,' she said. 'All I ask is that others do the same for me. I'm under no illusions about who and what I am, and I certainly don't conform to Nomar's ideal of womanhood!'

'Not everyone can be as tolerant as you,' Terrel said. 'He's had a troubled past.'

'But people eventually have to take responsibility for their own life, to move on to the future.'

'Some don't have that choice.'

'You think his anger stems from something that happened when he was young?' she asked.

'Yes. His illness too, probably. That's my feeling, anyway. And I think that whatever brought on the attack last night was already affecting him when he lost his temper with you.'

'So he doesn't really think I'm a whore?' she asked quietly.

'No one can ever be sure what another person truly believes,' Terrel replied. 'But I don't think what you saw last night was the real Nomar.'

'If his own childhood was bad, it would explain why he's so protective towards Taryn.' Yllen was thoughtful now.

'And it can't have been easy bringing up his son alone.'

'Do you know what happened to his wife?'

'That's a private matter,' Terrel said evasively.

Yllen glanced at him, then nodded and didn't press the point.

'I suppose I disappointed him too,' she said.

'What do you mean?'

'When we joined you, maybe Nomar hoped I'd be the maternal type, help him with his boy. But I'm not like that. Taryn's better off with you.'

'Me? How can I be a mother to Taryn?'

'You're one of life's nurturers, Terrel. You'd make a better job of it than me, believe me.'

Terrel didn't know how to respond to that.

'I was watching the two of you earlier,' she added, by way of explanation. 'Growing up the way he has can't have been easy for Taryn, and I think you're bringing out a part of him that's been neglected until now. I mean, can you imagine Nomar making us laugh the way Taryn did with Jarek?'

Terrel found that he could not. Yllen's unexpected insight made him consider her other ideas more seriously – even as he smiled at the memory of the mule's antics – but she had moved on to more familiar territory now.

'As we're here,' she said, 'will you do some healing for me?'

'What is it this time?' Terrel asked wearily. Over the past few days Yllen had persuaded him to treat several minor ailments – some of which had seemed to Terrel to be entirely imaginary – and the suspicion was beginning to form that she somehow enjoyed the process for its own sake.

'There's no need to sound like that' she said, picking up on his tone. 'You don't have to do it if you don't want to.'

'What is it?' he repeated, more gently this time. In spite of his suspicions he had no wish to hurt her feelings.

'My elbow's very sore,' she said, holding it up in the firelight.

'Give me your hand.'

Terrel tried to remain objective when they touched, but there was an implied intimacy in the process that, for once, made him feel a little awkward. Nevertheless, he traced the patterns in her waking dream without difficulty and found an inflammation within the joint. The pain was easily dealt with, but it had been genuine enough and that fact made him feel ashamed of his earlier doubts. As he released her hand and opened his eyes, Yllen flexed her arm and smiled.

'Thank you.'

'The swelling should go down in a few hours,' he told her. 'You'll be fine in the morning.'

'A fine pair of lookouts we make, both with our eyes shut,' Yllen commented. 'It's a good job no one came to rob us.'

Terrel grinned, wondering what Faulk's reaction would have been if he'd witnessed their negligence.

'Do you think I'm attractive?' Yllen asked suddenly. She was not looking at the healer as she spoke but gazing into the dying fire, and in the soft light her charms were undeniable. However, the disconcerting question – coming so soon after their personal contact – left Terrel feeling distinctly uneasy.

'Yes, but I'm in love with someone else,' he blurted out.

Yllen laughed.

'Oh, I'm sorry,' she said. 'You're sweet, but you're not really my type.'

'Oh.' Terrel's embarrassment deepened as he wondered how he could have been so stupid. 'It's just that . . . sometimes other women have . . .'

Yllen saved him from having to complete his inarticulate explanation.

'And I'll bet they all had better hearts and less brains than I do,' she said, without rancour.

Terrel was silent for a while, thinking of the women he had met whom he'd come to love and who, in an equally chaste manner, had perhaps come to love him too. Ysatel had been more like a mother to him, but that had not been true of Esera or Ghadira. And his troubled relationship with Latira had been even less maternal in nature. There had even been a special bond between him and Tegan, though her heart was already given to another. They were all important to him – and they had each taught him something – yet they paled into insignificance when compared to Alyssa. But thinking of her now was too painful and so he turned his attention to his current companion.

'You must know you're very attractive,' he said. 'Why are you asking me?'

'I thought you might know why Faulk doesn't pay me any attention.'

Terrel realized he should have seen this coming.

'I don't think Faulk thinks about love a great deal,' he said.

'Never mind love,' Yllen replied. 'What's wrong with lust?'

CHAPTER ELEVEN

Terrel woke the next morning to find that the world had been painted a pale grey. His first bleary-eyed thought was that it must have snowed, but it was too warm for that. Then he wondered whether it might be some strange optical effect of early morning mist, even though the air seemed clear. Eventually he realized that the greyness came from a thin layer of fine dust that had been deposited overnight – an unwelcome reminder of the violent events they'd witnessed, and of the fires that were presumably still burning to the west. Later, Faulk confirmed that the sky had clouded over during his watch in the latter part of the night, but that the resulting drizzle had not been water but ash. It had coated everything it touched.

The weather was still overcast when the slightly subdued group of travellers set off once more. Now that Nomar had recovered his health they had all known that Terrel would choose to move on – and the taint that had fallen from the sky ensured that no one argued the case for staying in the village. Although it was not mentioned openly, it had seemed like a sign. Pieri, Lawren and Roskin were all suffering from mild hangovers, but they knew better than to ask for Terrel's help with their self-inflicted ills. Although Yllen seemed to be fine physically, she was unusually quiet and didn't want to talk to anyone. Faulk, of course, was his normal implacable self.

The company fell naturally into their now customary formation. Faulk and Pieri set a steady pace at the front, walking mostly in silence. The soldier spent much of the time scanning both the way ahead and the surrounding terrain, and even though Pieri was a storyteller by profession, he knew when to hold his tongue. The two men generally only spoke when it was necessary, to consult each other about some aspect of their route or any likely developments in the weather. Behind them came Nomar and Taryn. The boy had been entrusted with the task of leading Jarek – an arrangement that evidently suited both him and the mule – but on this occasion he was engaged in a serious discussion with his father for much of the morning. Watching them, Terrel guessed that Nomar was making good on his promise to tell his son about Anya. Taryn's reaction was reassuringly calm, his young face set in an unusually solemn expression. Next came Terrel himself, Roskin and Yllen, either singly or together as the mood took them. As usual, Lawren brought up the rear.

Shortly before noon they were trudging through coarse grass and wet bracken, crossing an area of open ground as they made their way to a sloping ridge between two hills. Terrel was walking on his own, behind Yllen and Roskin who were talking companionably now. From what he could hear, the healer surmised that they were discussing their respective marriages. Although neither had fared particularly well, they seemed to be finding some humour in their misfortunes, and Terrel was glad to see that for these two at least the sombre mood of the day appeared to be lifting. He was about to move forward to join them when a familiar but unwelcome trembling began deep within his body.

'Brace yourselves!' he yelled. 'There's an earthquake coming!'

Yllen let out a cry of alarm and up ahead, Pieri turned

round, looking puzzled. The others all took the announce-ment in their stride, having already benefited from Terrel's peculiar ability to predict tremors. Taryn touched Jarek's neck to reassure the creature, while Faulk looked around, assessing the area for any specific dangers.

'What do you mean?' Yllen asked Terrel, her voice shrill.

'He means just what he says,' Lawren told her, coming up beside her. 'You should sit down. There won't be as far to fall.'

Yllen looked at him uncomprehendingly.

'How—' she began, but got no further.

The tremor struck. The ground beneath them vibrated, emitting a deep, sonorous note. Fronds of bracken shook, rustling softly and shedding drops of water. Jarek brayed indignantly and staggered briefly, but seemed to take com-fort from Taryn's presence. Most of the adults found themselves sitting on the damp grass, either by design or because they had no choice. Yllen screamed briefly as she stumbled, but her fall was broken when she landed on top of Lawren.

Even in a previously stable land like Kenda, earthquakes were becoming a regular occurrence, and the travellers had all grown accustomed to them to some degree. While each tremor was still disorientating, and provoked a strange feeling of betrayal – if you couldn't trust the ground beneath your feet, what *could* you trust? – they had learnt to cope with the effects easily enough. In an open area there was little danger unless the quake was very severe – and this one subsided after only a few moments.

'You didn't need an excuse to jump on top of me,' Lawren said somewhat breathlessly. 'I'd've been quite happy any time.' The hunter had his arms round Yllen now, and seemed in no hurry to let her go.

'Well, at least we've found a use for you,' she replied, struggling to free herself from the one-sided embrace. 'You make quite a good cushion.'

She stood up, looked down at Lawren – who was still flat on his back – then grinned and offered him her hand. He took it and she pulled him to his feet.

'Glad to be of service,' he said, but Yllen had already turned her attention to Terrel.

'How did you know it was coming?' she asked as the healer righted himself.

'I just do. I can't explain it.'

'Everyone all right?' Faulk asked as the company gathered together.

They all nodded.

'Was it another fire-scythe?' Roskin asked. 'The Red Moon will be full tonight, won't it?'

'No, this was just an ordinary earthquake,' Terrel replied. He'd received no internal warning before the impact of the fire-scythe.

'A full Red Moon, eh?' Lawren said. 'No wonder you were so amorous, Yllen.'

'Shut up, you idiot,' she shot back, but she was smiling too, and even Nomar seemed amused by the exchange.

'Jarek's still shaking,' Taryn said anxiously. 'I tried to tell him it was coming but I'm not sure he understood.'

'You did very well, lad,' Pieri told him. 'Normally I'd have had to chase him halfway up that hill before I got him under control again.'

Taryn looked pleased.

'I think we're all a bit shaky right now,' Terrel said. 'Let's stop for a bit and have something to eat.'

Although no one ate much during the unscheduled stop, they all seemed glad of the chance to rest. Terrel noticed that after the excitement of the earthquake Taryn seemed to have retreated into a world of his own. He kept taking out the ring that hung around his neck and looking at it. His expression was impossible to read, but it was obvious what he was thinking about. Nomar sat close to his son, not speaking, but there if he was needed. Telling Taryn about his mother may have been something of a relief, but Terrel knew that the man had other secrets. Although one weight might have been lifted from Nomar's shoulders, he still carried a heavy burden.

Yllen was quiet too, leaving what conversation there was to the men. This revolved mainly around the route they were taking.

'If I'm right,' Pieri said, 'there should be a tavern about ten miles west of here.'

'Not enough beer for you last night?' Roskin queried.

'I'm not averse to the tail of the mule that kicked me,' the storyteller replied, 'but I wasn't thinking of that. I know the landlord of the place, and between us we ought to be able to earn our keep for a night.'

'You're going soft,' Lawren declared. 'Two nights in a dry cabin and you're already looking for another roof over your head.'

'And a soft bed if possible,' Pieri agreed unapologetically. 'Not to mention a decent meal. If memory serves, the man does wonders with roast pig.'

'Sounds good, if we can earn it,' Roskin said.

'We will,' Pieri said confidently, then amended his opinion. 'Well, *I* will anyway. A good storyteller's always welcome at a place like that. The rest of you can slave in the kitchens or something.'

'Thanks a lot,' Lawren muttered.

'Will it take us out of our way?' Terrel asked.

'It shouldn't do.'

'You don't sound sure,' Faulk said.

'That's because I've never approached it from this direction before. I'll have a better idea when we get to the top of the ridge.' Pieri pointed to the saddleback above them. 'But I'm almost sure we'll get there before nightfall.'

'Then let's go,' Terrel decided.

'What's the landlord called?' Faulk asked as they all began hefting their packs.

'Conal Bringer. Why? Do you know him?'

Faulk shook his head, but Terrel couldn't help wondering what had prompted the question. It wasn't like Faulk to be so inquisitive.

'What does he bring?' Lawren asked.

'Anything you can pay for,' Pieri replied. 'Conal's a businessman. He's not fussy about how he takes your money. But he'll pay a fair price if you give him something he wants.'

'Does the tavern have a name?' Roskin asked.

'It does. The Haven Inn.'

'What did you say?' Terrel said sharply, thinking he might have misheard.

'The Haven,' Pieri repeated. 'Why? Is that important?'

All that afternoon, as the storyteller led them into yet another valley, Terrel tried to convince himself that it was *not* an omen. 'Haven' was just an ordinary word, and a reasonable choice for a wayside inn that gave refuge to travellers. But as hard as he tried, there was a small, illogical part of him that could not set the coincidence aside. Fate had already played many tricks on him, and the fact that he was heading for an inn that bore the same name as the place where his long-lost love still lay – and on the night of the full Red Moon too – held a significance he could not dismiss.

He had not explained his reaction to his companions, and when it became clear that he wasn't going to enlighten them, they had not pressed the point, leaving the healer to his own musings.

To Terrel's relief, the tavern looked nothing like the grand but rather run-down mansion that had been his home for the first fourteen years of his life. This Haven was a sprawling, two-storey building that had probably begun its life as a simple, conventional rectangle, but which had obviously been extended several times on all sides – in a variety of styles and materials – so that the overall effect was of a jumble of connected dwellings.

The inn stood next to crossroads where several trails intersected and, judging by the size of its stables and other outbuildings, it was a popular place. Certainly the village that lay behind it was too small to support such a large establishment on its own account. A sign that swung from a pole at the front of the main house bore the single letter 'H', presumably as much of the word 'Haven' as the sign-painter's literacy had allowed.

Against all reason, Terrel found himself growing tense as Pieri led them through the sturdy gates at the front of the building. The large cobbled courtyard within stood between the tavern and the stables, and there were several fine horses tethered to a rail on one side.

'Got some gentry in, by the look of it,' Pieri commented, looking at the mounts.

'Will there still be room for a rough lot like us?' Lawren asked.

'Conal's used to all sorts,' the storyteller replied, glancing round the yard. 'Travelling players use this space sometimes.'

'We're not *that* rough,' Lawren said.

'And we're not going to put on much of a show,' Roskin added. 'You're the only actor we've got.'

Terrel chose not to contradict him.

'I'll go and see if Conal has a use for the talents we *do* have,' Pieri concluded. He disappeared into one of the outer rooms while the others waited, not sure what to do next.

'You'd think someone would be keeping an eye on those horses,' Lawren said. 'They're valuable beasts.' As he spoke one of horses turned its head and whinnied, and the rest started to fidget. 'I think Kephra's making them nervous,' he added. 'We'll go and do a little hunting while it's still light.' At a signal from his master, the tercel left his perch on Lawren's shoulder and rose into the air. The hunter set his pack down and strode off.

'I think it's Jarek that's making them nervous,' Taryn said quietly.

'A few rabbits will be useful for trade, though,' Roskin said. 'In case Conal doesn't want our services.'

When Pieri returned a few moments later he was smiling.

'We're in luck. Half the people who used to work here have run off and left Conal in the lurch, so he could use all the willing hands he can get. The place is almost full.'

'So much for a soft bed,' Roskin moaned.

'There's one room left,' Pieri added, 'which he's willing to give to Yllen. We'll all get a meal at the end of the night, and the rest of us can sleep in the hayloft over the stables. What do you think?'

'It sounds like a good deal to me,' Terrel replied. 'What does he want us to do?'

CHAPTER TWELVE

Conal Bringer – a huge bear of a man whose bulk dwarfed even Faulk – came out to inspect his new recruits and, with a shrewdness that belied his hulking appearance, assigned them to various duties. Nomar and Taryn were put to work under the watchful eye of the one remaining stable lad. They had to clear out the various stalls and refurbish them with fresh straw, settle the guests' mounts into their designated places, then groom and feed them. Jarek was given his own space, as far from the other animals as possible, and seemed perfectly happy with his latest accommodations.

Both Roskin and Faulk were first set to splitting logs for the Haven's fires, carrying several loads from the woodshed, before going on to draw water from the courtyard well, then refilling and lighting the inn's many oil lamps. Later in the evening, Faulk's intimidating presence proved useful in the tap room, persuading those clients who had had too much to drink that it was in their best interests to remain sociable. Diffusing any possible aggression was a role the soldier handled easily and with some aplomb, and he rarely needed to use more than a few words to achieve his purpose.

Yllen proved to be one of the most popular waitresses the Haven Inn had ever known. At first she complained about the menial nature of her assignment, but as the hours went by she began to enjoy herself in spite of the heavy workload. During the course of the evening she received two proposals of marriage and several offers of a less permanent nature, all of which she declined with a mixture of wit and good humour.

When Lawren returned with Kephra's latest kills – both rabbit stew and roast pheasant were swiftly added to the tavern's menu – he was told to join the remaining cooks in the sweltering, steam-filled kitchens. He quickly proved adept with a knife, skinning game, carving joints and chopping vegetables.

Terrel, whose prowess as a healer had already been advertised by Pieri, was excused such physical labour after Conal himself put him to the test. The landlord had a stiffness in one of his knees – the result of an old injury – which grew worse when the weather was damp. Terrel admitted he would never be able to rectify the damage, but he was able to relieve the pain in the joint and extend its range of movement considerably. His services were then offered to several patrons, all of whom were willing to pay for results. The healer was kept busy, dealing with a variety of aches and pains, a mild fever or two, and a man whose legs were covered with open sores. As always, Terrel did not claim to be able to effect an instant cure, but he did reduce the suffering of each of his patients, and increased the chances of their eventual recovery. They were all suitably grateful and – as agreed beforehand – Terrel passed on part of his earnings to Conal.

Naturally enough, as Pieri's skills were already known to the innkeeper, the storyteller was employed to entertain the customers – and to encourage them to eat and drink as much as possible. He told jokes and stories, played tunes on his whistles and, later in the evening, was persuaded to sing a few songs. Terrel only managed to catch part of his performance, but that was enough for him to realize that beneath his bawdy showmanship Pieri was indeed a talented musician. The coins that were tossed into his collecting bowl showed that others agreed with the healer's assessment.

During the course of the evening, the travellers overheard a great deal of gossip, and asked questions of their own whenever they got the chance. When their duties were finally over and they had finished their meal, they gathered together and compared notes.

'Everyone's talking about Vergos,' Roskin said. 'Whatever's going on there has got the whole country excited.'

'Yes, but what *is* going on there?' Terrel responded. 'I got a different answer from everyone I talked to.' Even though he had escaped manual toil, his extended healing session had left him weary and drained in spirit, and he was finding it difficult to think straight.

'I know what you mean,' Lawren said. 'One of the cooks told me Gozian has pronounced himself immortal and ordered his people to worship him. In return for their devotion he's been handing out lavish gifts to anyone who prays hard enough. But Conal's wife says that's rubbish, that it's Kaeryss who thinks she's a goddess, and who's promising to transform people's lives and make them all rich.'

'I heard something like that too,' Yllen put in. 'But it was all tied up with the Raven Cypher. Apparently, the part that's just been translated gives the location of a great treasure trove.'

'It all sounds like fairy tales to me,' Roskin commented, sceptical for once.

'I suppose at least we know now why those people abandoned their village,' Pieri said.

'You really think they'd have left a place as good as that, just for a wild-goose chase?' Lawren queried.

'Rumours are powerful things,' the storyteller replied. 'Who wouldn't want to follow the chance of easy riches?'

'But it's crazy.'

'I heard some unpleasant rumours too,' Nomar said. He was sitting with Taryn curled up at his side. Exhausted from his work in the stables, and not used to staying up so late, the boy was already asleep. His father glanced at him now, as if to check that he was beyond harm, before continuing. 'I heard that Vergos is in chaos, that there's looting and rioting in the streets, and Gozian's palace has been besieged by a mob.'

'What this all boils down to,' Faulk stated, entering the discussion for the first time, 'is that no one knows the truth of what's happening there.'

'You pays your money and you takes your choice,' Pieri agreed. 'No one I spoke to had actually seen it for themselves. It's all second- or fifth-hand tales.'

'What we have to do is decide whether to take any of it seriously,' Terrel said. 'And whether or not we still want to go there.'

'Please tell me you're not talking about Vergos,' Conal said, entering the room with a fresh pitcher of beer.

'What else?' Pieri replied. 'It's all anyone was talking about tonight.'

'Don't I know it,' the innkeeper said wearily, settling his considerable weight on to a bench. 'I'm sick of hearing about Vergos and its oracles, imaginary treasure, and people having visions of the moons falling out of the sky.'

'That's one I hadn't heard,' Terrel said, alarmed by this echo of his dream.

'It's all nonsense,' Conal muttered dismissively. 'But for some reason a lot of otherwise sensible people seem to want to believe it. Have another drink, and let's talk about something else.'

Most of the travellers accepted his first suggestion – though Terrel and Nomar declined – but Pieri did not want to change the subject.

'That's where your missing staff have gone, I'll wager,' he said once the landlord had poured the ale.

'Yes, damn their eyes,' Conal growled. 'The only good thing about all this gossip is that there's more people on the road. I'm glad of their custom, right enough, but what's the point if you don't have the staff to serve them properly? The last few days have been a nightmare.' He took a long draught from his own tankard. 'You lot turning up was manna from the moons. So drink up! You've earnt it.'

'Are you trying to get me drunk?' Yllen asked, all wide-eyed innocence.

'Well, lass, that's an appealing thought,' Conal replied with a grin, 'but I'd be a fool to try. My wife would not approve – and she's bigger than me. You wouldn't want to cross her.'

'I can vouch for that,' Lawren said. 'She's pretty handy with a cleaver too.'

'It's been a long time since I was called a lass,' Yllen said, laughing.

'How far is it to Vergos?' Terrel asked.

Conal scowled at the healer for bringing the light-hearted exchange to an end.

'On foot?' he said. 'Twenty, maybe twenty-five days. But you're surely not still thinking of going there?'

'We're hoping to find a passage on one of the river boats,' Terrel explained. 'Down to the coast.'

'Well, I don't want to tell you your business,' the landlord replied, 'but there's no way of knowing what's going on on the river right now. I wouldn't have thought it was worth the risk.'

'You just want us to stay here and work for you,' Pieri said.

'Of course I do!' Conal exclaimed. 'And so would you, if you had any sense. From the look of you, your lodgings haven't exactly been too cosy of late, and you'll get better food here than anywhere in Kenda. You've all got a few coins in your pockets for your trouble too, and there's more where that came from. It's a better prospect than chasing shadows in Vergos.'

No one said anything for a while, as the travellers exchanged glances and the innkeeper calmed down after his outburst. Having quickly summed up who was in charge of the group, Conal spoke directly to Terrel when he chose to break the silence.

'Promise me you'll stay for a few days at least. That way it's possible we can get you some reliable news about what's going on. All we've had so far is hearsay.'

'I can't promise that,' the healer replied.

'Then at least say you'll think about it, all of you. I'll make it worth your while.'

Terrel nodded, and Conal stood up.

'We'll talk again in the morning,' he concluded.

'Give my regards to your wife!' Lawren called as the landlord went out.

'Give them to her yourself!' he called back. 'When you come to work tomorrow.'

Terrel found his companions all looking at him expectantly, but he didn't know what to say.

'Well, what do you think?' Pieri asked eventually.

'I'm too tired to think.' He was indeed bone weary. And none of the group was used to being awake so late at night.

'We're going to have to pay for passage on a ship some-how,' Lawren pointed out. 'Some wages would come in handy.'

'But surely we could earn them in Vergos just as well as we could here,' Roskin countered.

'We don't know that,' Pieri said. 'Conal's right. There's no telling what's going on there.'

'I'm not sure I can afford any more delays,' Terrel said. He had the feeling now that he was *supposed* to go to Vergos.

'Well, let me know when you've decided,' Yllen said. 'I'm off to bed.' She stood up and looked directly at Faulk. 'You want to join me, soldier?'

The big man's face turned to stone. Whatever was going on inside his head, none of his thoughts showed in his eyes.

'I'm not going to ask twice,' Yllen told him. When there was still no response, the colour in her cheeks darkened slightly and there was a touch of anger as well as disap-pointment in her parting words. 'Suit yourself.'

It was only when she was out of earshot that Lawren broke the hush that had fallen over the group.

'Are you mad?' he gasped incredulously.

'What I choose to do, or not to do, is for me to decide,' Faulk replied flatly. 'And me alone.'

'But still—' the hunter began.

'Shut up,' Roskin said amiably. 'Not everyone thinks the same way you do.'

Lawren still looked mystified – and was obviously jeal-ous of Faulk – but he accepted Roskin's advice.

'It's time we all got some sleep,' Terrel said, ending the conversation.

Taking a couple of oil lamps with them, they filed out into the courtyard and crossed over to the stables. Above them the Red Moon glowed like an enormous jewel. Climbing the ladder to the hayloft – where they had already stored their packs – took a while because Taryn, who was being carried in his father's arms, did not wake up and had to be handed carefully from one person to the next. Faulk was the last in line and, as the others spread out their bedrolls on mattresses of straw, he climbed up and down the ladder several times for no apparent reason.

'Having second thoughts, are you?' Lawren said, unable to resist the temptation.

'No,' Faulk replied shortly, and did not elaborate.

It was only later, once the soldier had finally joined them and the lamps had been doused, that Terrel understood what Faulk had been doing. Remembering Pieri's earlier remarks, he realized the soldier had been memorizing the creaks made by the wooden rungs of the ladder so that he'd wake if they had any unexpected visitors in the night. As earlier events had demonstrated, when it came to protecting his companions, it seemed that Faulk took his duties very seriously.

Terrel lay in the darkness, listening to the shuffle of the horses below and the rustle of small nocturnal animals in the straw. In the distance an owl hooted. Sleep beckoned.

Terrel?

The healer sat bolt upright, suddenly wide awake. For a moment he thought he must have imagined the voice that sounded only inside his head, but then he saw the outline next to the top of the ladder. This visitor had been able to climb up to the loft without alerting Faulk.

Alyssa? His heart was pounding with a joy he could hardly contain.

The owl blinked and seemed to shrink in on itself.

I can't do this. Although her voice was hoarse and full of pain, it *was* Alyssa.

I've missed you so much, Terrel whispered.

Stay here. I'll try to come back tomorrow night when ...
The bird ruffled its feathers as if preparing for flight. *I can't ...*

Don't go! Terrel cried in alarm.

Tomorrow, Alyssa gasped – and then she was gone. The owl, which was just an owl once more, hooted in alarm and flew out into the yard, leaving Terrel with his emotions in shreds. Even though the visit had been agonizingly brief, and it was clear that she was still sick, one fact echoed thunderously in Terrel's brain. Alyssa was alive!

He sensed movement behind him and turned to see a shape moving in the shadows.

'What was that?' Taryn asked in a small, sleepy voice.

'Just an owl,' Terrel replied, but the words came out garbled, half choked, as he lost the last vestiges of control, and felt hot tears coursing down his cheeks.

Alyssa was alive.

CHAPTER THIRTEEN

What little sleep Terrel got that night was plagued by meaningless but vaguely ominous dreams, each fragmentary image apparently having no connection to any of the others. When morning came he felt as though his limbs were filled with wet sand and his head full of fog.

He surprised everybody by announcing that they would stay at the Haven Inn for one more night. Both Faulk and Roskin looked concerned by this development, but neither saw fit to argue with Terrel's decision, and the others seemed delighted by the idea. Conal's satisfaction at this turn of events was tempered when he discovered that his new employees were planning to move on the following day. He was heard to mutter, 'Better than nothing, I suppose,' before organizing his work force for the morning shift.

For Terrel, the day passed in a blur. Feeling the way he did, he knew that he would not be able to give any patients the attention they deserved, and so he decided not to offer any healing, telling people that he needed to rest. He suggested that Nomar take his place, and told Conal he would help his apprentice if it proved necessary – but also assuring him that Nomar was more than capable of treating most ailments. At first the landlord was reluctant to accept this arrangement, but after he agreed to give the other healer a try, Terrel heard nothing more and assumed that all was going well. For himself, Nomar seemed grateful for the vote of confidence and was determined to prove himself worthy of Terrel's faith. In fact, his biggest worry was what Taryn would do while he was working. The boy didn't want to traipse around with his father, and seemed intent on resuming his duties in the stables – on his own if necessary. Nomar wasn't happy with that, but then Roskin volunteered to help out with the horses as well.

The others were all engaged in similar tasks to the night before, while Terrel retreated alone and remained in the hayloft for the greater part of the day. As some guests left and others arrived, horses were led in and out of the stables below him. A heavily-laden cart appeared in the yard and its cargo was unloaded and taken into the tavern. Villagers came and went. But none of this activity meant anything to Terrel. He was in limbo, willing time to disappear.

Towards the end of the morning, during a lull in the comings and goings at the inn, Terrel heard the tell-tale creak of the ladder. He didn't really want any visitors, but when he saw who it was he didn't have the heart to send him away.

'Are you all right?' Taryn asked as he came to sit next to the healer.

'Just tired,' Terrel replied, sticking to the pretence he had adopted earlier.

Taryn nodded, his young face set in a solemn expression.

'Why were you crying last night?'

The question was not entirely unexpected, but Terrel still did not know how to answer it. The very real note of concern in the boy's voice made it even harder to lie.

'I won't tell anyone,' Taryn added, mistaking the reason for the healer's hesitation. 'Not even my father. I promise.'

'I was just startled,' Terrel managed.

'Don't you like owls?'

'No, I like them, but—'

'They make a funny noise, don't they? It was amazing no one else woke up.'

'Yes,' Terrel said. 'It was.' At the time he wouldn't have noticed if the entire party had been awake, but it was a relief to know that the encounter had been witnessed by only one other person.

'I cry sometimes when I don't know why,' Taryn confessed softly.

Terrel didn't know what to say to this. It occurred to him that if Yllen's theory was correct and he really did have some nurturing instincts, then he should have known how to respond. But he had no idea.

'What was your mother like?' Taryn asked, as if his thoughts had been following a similar pattern to Terrel's.

'I never knew her.'

The boy turned bright eyes on the healer.

'So you're like me,' he said.

'In a way,' Terrel conceded, but kept the truth to himself. At least Taryn still had his father.

'Did she die?' The question came out as no more than a whisper.

'No. I was sent away.'

'Why?' Taryn asked, with the tactless curiosity of a child.

'Because of the way I looked.' As far as Terrel knew, this was the truth – or at least a good part of it.

The boy thought about this for a while.

'That's stupid,' he said eventually. 'I wish I had eyes like yours.' His own were a warm golden brown, the colour of treacle.

'You wouldn't want these though, would you?' Terrel said, tapping his right hand on his leg.

'No,' Taryn admitted, looking slightly ashamed of himself.

'Then if I were you I'd be happy with the eyes you've got.'

'Yllen has nice eyes, don't you think?'

'I suppose so, yes,' Terrel agreed, wondering where this unexpected observation was leading. 'I've never really thought about it.'

'I like her. Do you?'

'Yes. I didn't think I would at first, but I do.'

'I'm not sure my father does, though. I don't know why.'

So that's it, Terrel thought. He wants to be friends with Yllen but doesn't want to offend Nomar.

'It can sometimes get complicated with grown-ups,' he said, wondering whether the boy was hoping that Terrel would take on the role of peacemaker between Yllen and his father. The healer had certainly had some practice as a go-between, but just at that moment he had no time for other people's problems.

'I know,' Taryn said, with a heavy sigh that would have been comical had it not been so full of genuine confusion.

'They'll sort it out between them,' Terrel assured him, just as Pieri's voice floated up from below.

'Taryn, are you up there?'

'Yes.'

'Well, come down then, if Terrel can spare you. There's something I want you to do.'

Taryn glanced quickly at the healer, who indicated the way out with a tilt of his head. It would be a relief to be on his own again.

Despite his self-imposed isolation, Terrel soon realized what Pieri had wanted Taryn for. At the storyteller's instigation, a sort of miniature fair had grown up in the courtyard, and he had found willing recruits among his fellow travellers. The recently emptied cart had been co-opted as a makeshift stage and Pieri was using his professional voice to pull in an audience for his songs. At the same time he was making outrageous claims about 'the smartest mule in the world', which provoked a good deal of heckling but also a certain curiosity among the spectators, who were mostly either tavern guests or villagers. When Taryn finally led Jarek out of the stables, he was greeted with laughter and derision. However, when Pieri asked the animal to do some simple sums, by tapping out the correct answers with one hoof, the interest level rose. By this time Terrel had moved round so that he could look out of the loft, and so he was able to watch as, at Pieri's prompting, Taryn got the mule to execute some peculiar steps and jumps — just as he had done in the abandoned village. The onlookers were both amazed and amused by these antics, and when Pieri offered to let anyone choose what Jarek should do next — on payment of a suitable fee, of course — there were several takers. Refusing only those suggestions that were physically impossible, Pieri directed proceedings like a master showman, while the mule walked backwards, turned his ears in opposite directions and put his head to one side, closed his eyes and pretended to sleep. He was also called upon to join in with one of Pieri's drinking songs, adding a suitably raucous note to the chorus, and to dance a kind of four-legged jig. This inspired some of the audience to dance themselves, and the atmosphere became even more festive. Throughout it all, both Taryn and Jarek seemed to be having the time of their lives, while Pieri was revelling in this original addition to his act. But they were not the only ones to enjoy themselves that afternoon.

Taking advantage of the carnival mood and the unexpectedly sunny weather, Conal began serving food and
drinks outside, and now that their morning duties were
over several of his employees were able to indulge themselves too. Roskin donned a splendid cape and transformed
himself into the Great Londolozi, offering to read palms.
His fortune-telling was generally light-hearted, with only a
few serious moments, but he did not lack for customers.
Lawren put on a show of his own, tossing pieces of raw
meat into the air for Kephra to catch in mid-flight,
taking – and winning – bets on the bird's performance.
And now that their taste for dancing had been whetted,
there was soon a queue of men waiting to join Yllen and
willing to pay the piper for a tune of their choice. Only
one of them tried to become too familiar as they danced –
and he suddenly found himself lying flat on his back on
the ground. No one else tried anything improper after
that.

Faulk stayed on the sidelines, remaining predictably
aloof from the various enterprises. He was his usual watchful self, keeping an eye on any potential trouble-makers
and also making sure that no one was tempted to disturb
Terrel. Of the healer's group, only Nomar was nowhere to
be seen, and Terrel assumed that he was being kept busy
inside the tavern.

The healer himself was reminded of the time he'd spent
with a troupe of travelling players on Vadanis, before fate
had forced him into exile. It had been an enjoyable time in
some ways, but he wasn't tempted to join in the revelry
now. No matter how many distractions were set before
him, he was consumed by the prospect of Alyssa's return.
I'll try to come back . . . The implied doubt in her words
was terrifying. The thought of what he'd do if she did *not*
come back was almost enough to drive him insane. It

would simply be too much to bear. The longing that had been blunted by her prolonged absence was now as sharp as a dagger again, making his heart ache and his stomach churn. But there was nothing he could do to hasten her return. He could only wait, wishing the day away, and wondering what was going on in that other Haven – the place that even now seemed so far away.

The fact that Alyssa was obviously still ill only added another layer of unease to Terrel's thoughts, but at least his worst fear – that she was already dead – had been set aside. Now at last he could allow himself to hope. Over a decade ago he had sworn to return to her, but during the last two years he had begun to wonder whether there would be any point in fulfilling his promise. Now he was more determined than ever to do just that. He *would* stand at her side again. For the time being he was not prepared to think of anything beyond that. Prophecies, the fate of empires, of the planet itself, all seemed irrelevant when set next to his need to see Alyssa again.

'And I'm a healer,' he reminded himself. 'What's the point in that if I can't heal *her* sickness?'

'Were you talking to me?' Faulk asked.

In his preoccupation Terrel had not even noticed the warning creaks of the ladder. He hadn't even realized that he'd been speaking aloud.

'No, no. Just thinking out loud.'

'Are you all right?' Only the soldier's head and shoulders were above the level of the loft floor, and he hesitated before coming any further.

'I'm fine,' Terrel lied.

'Do you mind if I come up?'

'Of course not.'

Faulk came to sit near Terrel, placing himself so that he could still see what was going on outside.

'I thought you ought to know that Conal's been trying to get some of us to stay even if you go on.'

'It's up to you. You've always known that.'

'I thought we were a team,' Faulk said, sounding uncertain for once.

'It has come to seem like that, hasn't it?' Terrel replied with a smile. 'But none of you owe me anything. I wouldn't blame anyone who wanted to stay on for a bit. Life here makes travelling seem rather less attractive.'

'So you're not angry with Conal?'

'No. He's just a businessman, like Pieri said.'

'I think he may be more than that.'

'What do you mean?'

'There may be people trying to stop us from moving on.'

'Stop us?'

'Yes.'

'But no one here knows what we're trying to do,' Terrel pointed out. 'Conal didn't even meet us until yesterday.'

'Unless Pieri led us here deliberately.'

The healer took a few moments to digest the implications of this remark.

'You think they're plotting against us?' he asked eventually. 'What for? That's crazy.'

Faulk did not respond.

'It doesn't make any sense,' Terrel added. 'How could Pieri have even known he was going to meet up with us?'

'There are ways,' the soldier replied mysteriously.

'What are you talking about?' Until that moment Terrel had regarded Faulk as the most level-headed and reliable of his companions, even though initially he'd had some qualms about his motives. Now he was beginning to doubt the big man's sanity. 'Are you sure you're not imagining all this?'

'I'm just saying it could be,' Faulk muttered. 'You're not the only one whose destiny's at stake here.'

'What?'

'I've already said too much. Just be on your guard, that's all.' He rose and crossed over to the ladder. Before he climbed down, he glanced at the healer again. 'And be careful of that woman,' he said.

Faulk disappeared from view, leaving Terrel even more anxious and confused than before.

By the time his next visitor arrived, dusk was no more than an hour away and Terrel was already on tenterhooks. Every time he heard a bird calling his pulse raced and he looked around expectantly. For some reason he couldn't explain, he thought it most likely that Alyssa would take the form of an owl again, but it was still too early for the nocturnal birds to be out and about, and in the meantime he wasn't going to ignore any other possibilities. It had occurred to him that his current situation mirrored the first time Alyssa had ever visited him in the shape of an animal. Then as now he had been sleeping in a hayloft, in a barn on Ferrand's farm, and Alyssa had borrowed the body of a barn owl in order to visit him, guided then – as she had been guided on each subsequent visit – by the ring he had made her. His astonishment on that occasion had been compounded by the fact that the ghosts had come with her, unseen by anyone but him. He had spoken aloud to the owl then – not yet knowing how to use psinoma – and that had got him into trouble. Had it not been for Sarafia, the first and youngest of his female friends outside the asylum, he might not have escaped with his life. He was older and more experienced now, but he was still startled when his latest female acquaintance made her appearance.

'Are you all right?' Yllen asked as she climbed up into the loft.

'Everyone keeps asking me that,' Terrel replied, trying to push aside the suspicions aroused by Faulk's warning. 'I'll be fine soon. I just need some rest.'

'So these are the gentlemen's quarters,' she observed, looking around. 'I like my room better.'

'So why are you here?'

'With all the dancing I've been doing, I've twisted my ankle. I thought you could . . .' She broke off when she saw the look Terrel was giving her, and smiled sheepishly. 'All right, so it doesn't hurt all that much. I just like the way your healing makes me feel.'

'I'm supposed to help people with *real* problems.'

'I haven't noticed you helping anyone today,' she countered. 'Besides, what harm can it do? Conal's going to want me to go back inside soon, and I'll be on my feet all evening. It'll be your fault if I end up limping tomorrow.'

This brazen attempt to manipulate him made Terrel laugh.

'You win,' he said, 'but I'm not going to do this again unless something really is wrong.'

'Agreed,' Yllen said with a grin. 'And I've got some gossip for you once you've finished.'

That was the last thing Terrel wanted just at the moment, but he could see that she was burning to tell him what it was. And so, once he had soothed away the mild pain in her ankle, he waited expectantly. The process of falling into Yllen's waking dream had calmed him a little, and it occurred to him that if she – together with Pieri and Conal – was up to no good, then he would surely have sensed some indication of it in her inner world.

'That's better,' Yllen said. 'Thank you.'

'So, what's this gossip you promised me?' he prompted.

'Oh, yes. Someone told me that Prince Karn – that's Gozian's son and heir – has been asleep for over a year. The amazing thing is, he's had nothing to eat or drink in all that time but he's still alive! Isn't that incredible?' In her enthusiasm for the tale, Yllen hadn't seen the series of expressions that had passed over Terrel's face. 'And he's not the only one, apparently. They call them sleepers and, according to Kaeryss, what's happening to them is all tied up with some part of the Raven Cypher.'

'That *is* amazing,' Terrel said quietly. If there had ever been any doubt that he should go to Vergos, it was gone now. The connection to his own quest had just become a lot clearer.

'So, are we still going?' Yllen asked. 'I mean, it sounds interesting, but I wouldn't want to fall asleep like that. It would be really boring.'

Terrel was saved from having to answer when Yllen suddenly burst out laughing.

'And whatever else is true, you certainly can't call my present life boring,' she exclaimed. 'You know, Pieri actually did me a favour when he got me into trouble with my husband. This is much more fun. Just don't tell him I said so.'

With that she got up and stepped carefully onto the ladder.

'Meeting a certain healer has been part of that fun,' she added with a smile.

'I could say the same about a certain woman!' Terrel called back as she vanished from sight. 'But I'm not her type, apparently.'

I'm glad to hear it, said a silent voice from the rafters.

CHAPTER FOURTEEN

The sheer relief of knowing that Alyssa had come made Terrel want to leap up and shout for joy. But he knew Yllen was still within earshot, and didn't want to get embroiled in any explanations. All that mattered was that — at last — Alyssa was with him again. And not only was she there — even sooner than he'd hoped — but, if his first impressions were correct, her voice sounded more robust, not quite as dragged down by pain.

I'm so glad you were able to come back.

It wasn't easy. There aren't as many open doors in the palace now.

This time Terrel heard the strain beneath her words, and realized she was pretending to be healthier than she was for his benefit.

Are you well? he asked anxiously, not really expecting a truthful answer.

Well enough, she replied.

Terrel could see the owl now, sitting very still in the shadows. The lighter-coloured plumage on her breast and heart-shaped face seemed to glow faintly in the dark. Terrel moved a little closer, hoping to see something in her eyes.

Don't lie to me, Alyssa. I love you, and I'm a healer. I want to help you.

This is not the sort of illness you can deal with, she told him wearily. *Sleepers are vulnerable in different ways.*

But I thought you were protected.

I am. It's the protection that's making me ill.

Her words confirmed what Terrel had suspected for some time. The elementals – and in particular the one on Myvatan, the only Ancient he'd been unable to heal – were responsible for Alyssa's plight.

Are all the sleepers affected like you? he asked, thinking specifically of Ysatel and her baby.

Some are better than others. It's probably concentrating on my room in the palace because of my connection to you.

Another layer of guilt settled over Terrel. He was responsible for the severity of Alyssa's illness, and the fact that she had made the effort to reach him now, in spite of the near certainty that it would expose her to even greater risks, made him feel even worse.

There must be something we can do, he said.

Keep believing, she replied. *We'll be together again, once this is all over.*

Will that be soon?

Sooner than any of us thought. One way or another.

Terrel's heart lurched with a mixture of hope and dread.

This will be the last swing of the pendulum, Alyssa added.

Although the healer was used to her sometimes oblique way of talking, he couldn't make any sense of this.

What do you mean?

You'd better ask the others.

Are they— he began, but had no need to complete the question.

Three transparent, softly luminous figures materialized in the loft. Although at first glance the ghosts looked exactly as Terrel remembered them, on closer inspection he saw subtle changes in each of them. Elam still had the sharp-featured face and gangling figure of the fifteen-year-old boy Terrel had known at Havenmoon, and was still wearing the tunic stained by the knife wound that had killed him. Shahan, the former imperial seer, was as imposing a presence as ever, his grey hair and long beard framing a lined, angular face with its great hooked beak of a nose. And Muzeni, the heretical astronomer who had died long before the other two, and in more peaceful circumstances, was slightly blurred as always, his features indistinct. His red cape was draped over other equally eccentric clothes. But in each of them — whether it was in the expression on Elam's face, the worry deep within Shahan's pale grey eyes, or the way Muzeni held himself so stiffly — there were intimations that something was wrong. Just as he had been delighted by Alyssa's arrival, Terrel was relieved and glad to see his spectral allies again, but he couldn't help wondering if they too were suffering for his sake. However, he had no chance to voice his concerns because as soon as the ghosts became aware of him they all began talking at once.

Terrel! At last! Shahan exclaimed.

How long have we got? Muzeni asked. *These calculations . . .*

Back to living in a barn, I see, Elam observed dryly.

One at a time! Terrel pleaded. *I can't hear myself think.*

It's been a long time, Elam said with a grin that was as welcome as it was familiar. *How are you doing?*

Not too bad. We—

Sorry, Terrel, Shahan cut in. *We've got so much to tell you, and there may not be enough time*. The seer glanced at the owl, which was still sitting hunched and unmoving. *Right now there are some things you need to know.*

This was not the way Terrel's meetings with the ghosts usually worked. Normally they would want to know where he had been and what he'd discovered before they passed on their own news and opinions. The fact that on this occasion their own messages were obviously so urgent deepened the healer's sense of disquiet.

How soon can you get back to Vadanis? Muzeni asked.

I'm not sure. Why?

Because the latest estimate for the next four-moon conjunction is that it will take place this winter, Shahan replied.

This winter? But that's—

I know, I know, the seer said. *Things are changing faster than any of us anticipated.*

I'm still not sure the calculations are correct, Muzeni muttered, consulting a phantom parchment held in his hand.

You're not sure? Terrel was aghast. This long-awaited confluence was the culmination of his epic journey, the time when, as Mentor, he was supposed to help the Guardian fulfil his heroic destiny – and they couldn't get their calculations right?

It's very complicated, the heretic responded defensively. *There are some unpredictable variables.*

Astronomy, unlike augury, was supposed to be an exact science. But the anomalies surrounding the Dark Moon had put paid to that.

It's what the seers in Makhaya are predicting, Shahan added, with a glance at his colleague, *and we can't do any better at the moment.*

So when is it supposed to be, exactly?

Fourteen days after midwinter, Muzeni replied. *That's eighty-three days from now.*

Two long months, Terrel thought. That's all the time I have. He felt a wave of despair wash over him.

And I've got to get back to the Floating Islands by then?

More precisely, you have to get to Tindaya, Shahan said.

Why there? Surely if I'm to help the Guardian I ought to go to Betancuria. That's where the Ancient is.

As far as we know the creature's still there, Muzeni agreed, *but we're basing our assessment on the latest interpretations of the Tindaya Code.*

You remember the new inscriptions, in the buried room Jax discovered? Shahan said. *Well, they refer to a sacred temple 'at the tip of the pendulum', and we think that has to be Tindaya itself. According to the passage we've been studying, both the Guardian and the Mentor are supposed to return there for the confluence.*

Return? But the elemental's never been there, Terrel objected. Neither have I, he thought privately, except as a bodiless spirit.

We don't know that for sure, Shahan said. *The Ancient's been around a lot longer than we have.*

You really think it would leave the mines and go up there? Terrel queried. *And what about the other three? They're part of the Guardian too.*

I didn't say it was all crystal clear, the seer replied. *The important thing is, can* you *get there in time?*

I can try, but I don't know how far it is to the coast. And it's not going to be easy to find a ship willing to take me to the Floating Islands.

Since when have you worried about anything being easy? Elam asked. *Unless you get there in time, everything else you've done will be pointless. You've* got *to do it.* There was an uncharacteristic earnestness in the ghost's words that lent them a chilling force.

I'll do it, Terrel vowed.

Good man, Shahan said.

What else can you tell me? Anything that might help me on the way? In the past he'd received hints – sometimes very enigmatic hints – from other parts of the ancient prophecy.

The two seers exchanged glances.

Because we haven't known where you were until now,

Muzeni said, *we've had to guess which sections might apply to this part of your journey. But the most likely section talks about 'avoiding walls of fire'.*

Always a good idea, Elam remarked.

We may already have done that, Terrel said, and told them briefly about the devastation caused by the fire-scythe.

There've been fireballs falling out of the sky in and around Vadanis too, Elam said, *but nothing as big as the one you saw.*

Then there's a reference to a 'city of sleepers', Muzeni said.

We're heading for a place called Vergos, Terrel said eagerly. *There are sleepers there, including the son of the king.*

That sounds promising, Shahan said. *There was mention of a meeting with a 'worldly king' in this city. It seems you're supposed to do something there.*

What?

That part's not clear, Muzeni replied. *It refers to setting some ravens free.*

Ravens? Terrel was excited now. He had the confirmation he'd wanted – that he was indeed meant to go to Vergos. He told his allies what little he knew about the Raven Cypher.

We're hoping to get a ship to take us from Vergos down the Syriel River to the coast, the healer went on. *That ought to be the quickest route.*

Shahan nodded approvingly.

You keep talking about 'we', Elam said. *Who are 'we'?*

And so Terrel explained about his companions. The ghosts listened in silence for the most part, asking only an occasional question, and having begun, Terrel decided it was time to tell them what he'd been doing since they'd last met. As succinctly as he could, he described his fateful encounter with the insane elemental on Myvatan. He explained that he'd done all he could to prevent it from wreaking havoc on the entire planet, but that he had been unable to heal it as he had the others. Although the ghosts knew his failure had not been for the want of trying, it was clear from their grave expressions that the Ancient's continuing illness was causing problems. Terrel then went on to give an abbreviated account of his journeys since then, and brought them up to the present.

You'll never guess what this place is called, he added, glancing at Elam.

What?

The Haven Inn.

Elam laughed, and looked at the owl.

It might have helped, Alyssa said quietly. *Names are important, even in a palace.*

Which reminds me, Elam said, turning back to Terrel. *Jax has been very quiet recently, and I'm starting to get worried. Have you seen anything of him?*

No. Not since I left Myvatan. The healer had been very careful not to get drunk or to use the glamour – either state could give his twin access to his mind – and nor had the prince invaded his dreams. Terrel wondered whether this was simply because of good fortune, or whether Jax had reasons of his own for not coming.

You should count yourself lucky, Shahan commented. *The prince has been antagonizing people recently.*

Doesn't he always? Elam queried. *I just hope our coming here doesn't lead him to Terrel.*

You think it could? the healer asked in alarm.

I'm not sure. We spy on each other, but not all the time.

There's nothing we can do about that now, Muzeni pointed out.

Has he killed anyone since Remi? Terrel asked.

Not that we know of, Shahan answered. *At least, not by using his skill as a fire-starter.*

Terrel shuddered, remembering the appalling sight of a fire-starter's victim burning up from within.

But his influence is growing all the time, Elam said. *Even the seers are being forced to admit that Dheran's becoming senile, and Adina's so tied up in her own schemes that most people think she's mad too. So as the supposed Guardian and the future Emperor, Jax already wields a lot of power.*

As always, mention of his parents filled Terrel with an unpleasant mixture of emotions.

There are some people arguing – privately, of course – that the lineage has been discredited, Shahan said, *and that the title should pass to one of Dheran's sons from a previous wife, but there's been no really effective opposition yet.*

And if the prophecy's right, court politics are irrelevant now, Muzeni declared. *There's no time to achieve anything that way. Especially if there's something to this pendulum theory.*

What is that, exactly? Terrel asked.

If what we've seen is correct, Shahan replied, *the islands are slowing down, like a pendulum coming to rest. No one can work out why it's happening, but the idea that they might stop altogether is causing panic.*

Terrel nodded. As far as the people of his homeland were concerned, land *ought* to move, and the empire's coming to a standstill would be seen as a disaster.

The last time it was Myvatan, Alyssa said, making one of her rare contributions to the debate. *This time it's Vadanis.*

It's happened before? Terrel exclaimed.

That's the theory, Muzeni confirmed. *But no one is sure exactly how it works.*

It makes prophecy a lot simpler if history just keeps repeating itself, Elam commented. *And on a positive note, if the islands* are *slowing down, then at least that should make your getting home a bit easier.*

And the sooner the better, Shahan added.

I'll leave for Vergos first thing in the morning, Terrel promised. *Regardless of who wants to come with me.*

The owl let out a low, mournful hoot, and the healer saw her pain reflected in the faces of the ghosts. It appeared that they too were being affected by Alyssa's illness.

We should go, Shahan said.

One last question, Terrel said hurriedly. *Faulk has the idea that someone might be trying to stop us. Do I need to worry about that?*

You should always choose your friends carefully, Muzeni replied.

And your enemies, Elam added.

That doesn't really help, Terrel began, but he was talking to thin air. The ghosts had all vanished in an instant.

I have to go, Alyssa rasped.

You'll come again though, won't you?

I still have your ring. Her voice was almost crushed beyond recognition – by a torment the healer could not even recognize, let alone relieve.

And then she was gone. The barn owl, freed from the usurper's control, flapped away into the evening, leaving Terrel staring morosely into space.

At the end of that evening, Terrel told the others of his decision to move on. To his surprise, no one raised any objections. Conal was clearly disappointed, and tried to talk him out of it, but when it became obvious that he was not going to change the healer's mind, the innkeeper accepted defeat graciously, thanking them for all the work they had done.

The travellers retired to get as much sleep as they could before resuming their trek.

Faulk roused Terrel before he felt really ready to wake.

'I think you'd better come and look at this,' he said.

The soldier led the healer out into the thin, grey light of dawn, and pointed beyond the inn to the western horizon. As Terrel stared, his foreboding turned to horror.

Every few moments a new red star blossomed in the sky. *Underneath* the clouds.

CHAPTER FIFTEEN

An hour later the whole of the western sky was suffused with a rosy glow, which made it look as though sunrise and sunset were happening simultaneously. By then the distant shower of fire-scythes had ended, but the ground still shook occasionally as various tremors ran across Kenda. Terrel's internal senses were in disarray, and he gave up trying to predict when the next earthquake would take place. He could only assume that the assault of the falling rocks had made the land unstable, causing the mild vibrations they were now experiencing. It was also apparent – from the ominous reflections in the cloud-filled sky – that fires were raging in the west.

'I still have to go on,' Terrel said when the others had gathered round him.

'Are you mad?' Conal exclaimed. The innkeeper had come to join them in gazing at the sky. 'You'd be walking into a forest fire!'

'There aren't any great forests in that direction,' Pieri said, obviously puzzled.

'Well, *something*'s burning,' the landlord commented.

None of them, least of all Terrel, could argue with that, but it did not alter his determination to set out as planned. In an odd way it even strengthened his resolve. It was obvious now that he really was going to have to avoid the 'walls of fire'. He was therefore pleasantly surprised when all the members of the original group announced their intention of going with him. The only one who seemed to be having any doubts was Yllen. She and Pieri discussed reverting to their earlier plan and heading east, but the advantages of travelling with a healer in such dangerous times were self-evident, and Terrel had the feeling that in some strange way Yllen was actually enjoying her adventures. In any case, the mismatched pair eventually decided to remain with the company.

An hour later – when most of the guests at the Haven Inn had decided to stay put, or were reversing the direction of their travel – the healer and his friends set off towards Vergos and the distant conflagration.

For the next few days they walked deeper into a realm of ever-increasing chaos. They were the only people travelling westward, and everyone they met looked at them as if they were insane. Many of these people were refugees who had been driven from their homes by the sky-born fire, and they told distressing tales of the catastrophes that had befallen them. There were also a number of wild rumours about the exact cause and extent of the disaster. Sifting through this piecemeal flow of information and hearsay, an appalling picture eventually emerged. Even stripped of its more fantastical elements, it was clear that it would be impossible to reach Vergos any time soon.

The entire sequence of events had, of course, begun with the fire-scythes. Over the course of a few hours, at least a hundred – some reports said *thousands* – had fallen on an upland region to the southeast of Vergos. Although each of them had evidently been much smaller than the one Terrel and his companions had seen from the mountain cave, the cumulative effect of the multiple impacts over a relatively compact area had been devastating.

Whole towns and villages had been obliterated in moments, livestock and crops had been destroyed by explosions or the fires that followed, and the air had become unbreatheable as poisonous clouds of smoke rolled over the surrounding hills. But it was what had happened subsequently that turned a local nightmare into a cataclysm whose tentacles were now reaching over a huge section of the country.

At a point near the centre of the airborne attack, the earth had split open in an explosive convulsion that seemed to originate from beneath the ground rather than above. A viscous red liquid poured out and flowed across the tortured landscape, following the contours of the terrain. It was so hot that everything it touched burst into flame as it was swallowed up by the remorseless advance. Only Terrel was in a position to understand what was happening. He had witnessed similar scenes in Myvatan, but had never thought anything like it could happen in what had seemed to be a relatively stable region. No one else knew that the red liquid was molten rock, and that the fast-growing mountain producing it was Kenda's first volcano.

Some time after the original eruption, the lava was still spewing forth, and there was no sign that the torrent was about to stop or even slow down. The blood flowing from that first gash in the planet's skin spread across the province in rivers of flame, forcing everyone in its path to abandon their homes and land and flee for their lives. What was worse, the split in the ground began to expand, slowly at first and then with murderous rapidity. In a series of earthquakes, a massive trench opened up along the centre of a hitherto peaceful valley that ran northeast from the site of the volcano, and all along its course fresh supplies of lava bubbled to the surface, forming an impassable barrier between one side and the other. And between the travellers and Vergos. The Tindaya Code's wall of fire had become a reality.

Time and time again Terrel and his companions tried to make their way westward, only to be forced back. Because altering course to the south would have meant heading towards the original source of the upheaval, they went north, hoping to find a place the ravine had not yet reached, or where the molten rock had cooled enough to solidify and allow them a perilous crossing. But each time they approached the valley it became clear that new outpourings of lava, intense heat, and air filled with ash and noxious gases, would make such an endeavour impossible.

Despite all this Terrel clung to the belief that they would still reach Vergos eventually, even though they were currently travelling further from the city with every step. Having begun the trek north and then been forced to go to the east as well, they had no choice but to continue that way, waiting for an opportunity to double back on themselves. But as the days passed and the healer was no closer to achieving even this goal, he became increasingly desperate, all too conscious of the deadline the ghosts had imposed upon him. At this rate he'd be lucky to reach Vergos by midwinter, let alone Vadanis. In his more pessimistic moments he began to wonder whether Faulk's suspicions might be correct, and there *was* someone – or something – trying to halt their progress. He knew that no human foe could have produced the wall of fire, but he'd seen the elemental on Myvatan do something similar, and even though none of the Ancients was anywhere near his present location, the possibility of one – or all – of them being responsible for the ravine could not be ruled out. The fact that it blocked their path so effectively made it seem almost like a deliberate act of sabotage rather than just a dreadful coincidence. To make matters worse, there had been no contact from Alyssa and the ghosts – the only allies who could have given him any advice about what he should do next. All he could do now was persevere in a task that was beginning to seem hopeless.

Matters came to a head on a day more than a median month after they had left the Haven Inn. The weather had been wildly unpredictable, veering from hailstorms and gales to unseasonably warm periods with virtually no wind, but on this occasion a soft, persistent drizzle had been falling all morning. The travellers were soaked and, at first, as they made their way towards the fissure for what seemed like the hundredth time, the increasing heat was welcome. However, as they got closer to the bottom of the valley – which was wreathed in what looked like fog but was probably steam – their nostrils were assailed by a sulphurous stench and the familiar, acrid smell of burning. They could see very little ahead of them, but most of the group had already decided that this latest attempt, like all those before it, was doomed to end in failure. Terrel had other ideas. As his companions faltered, he strode forward with an almost demented urgency. The healer's mind had been stretched tighter than a bowstring for too long and something had finally snapped. A small, logical part of his brain knew that he was being foolish, but he couldn't help himself.

It was Yllen who first recognized Terrel's intent.

'There's no way through!' she called after him. 'Come back before you get hurt.'

'It's all right,' he replied. 'The rain will have cooled it down. We're going to get across today, I'm sure of it.'

Even as he spoke he knew he was spouting nonsense. The earth beneath his feet was scorched black, and the humid air was getting hotter with every step. Ahead of him he could just make out a red glow within the mist, and yet the irrational belief persisted that a way through existed – and so he went on.

'Terrel, you can't—' Yllen shouted. 'Don't just stand there, you great lump. *Do* something!' This last was addressed to Faulk, who had come to a halt shortly after the healer had passed him and who was now staring into the fog, looking indecisive for once.

'Come on,' Lawren said. 'Yllen's right. If we don't stop him he'll get himself killed.'

The two men began to sprint over the rough ground and soon caught up with Terrel. Even then they hesitated, not wanting to use force unless they had to. The healer glanced at each of them in turn, his eyes glittering, but did not slow his pace.

'You—' Faulk began, half choking on the foul air.

'We have to get across,' Terrel declared. 'Today.'

'It's impossible,' Lawren gasped, putting a hand on the healer's arm.

Terrel shook him off angrily.

'No it isn't!' he shouted, then began to cough. Tendrils of smoke were curling up from his boots as they began to burn, adding a new taint to the fetid atmosphere.

Faulk and Lawren looked at each other, then acted in unison, grasping Terrel's arms and pulling him back. Although he struggled – displaying greater resistance than they had expected – he was no match for their combined strength and at length, still angry but resigned now, he was brought back to the rest of the company. Yllen and Nomar were instantly solicitous, but Terrel brushed them off and stomped away. For the rest of the day, as they continued their forlorn journey to the northeast, he spoke to no one.

By evening the rain had finally stopped but clouds still

massed above them, and when they reached a village the travellers all hoped that they could obtain shelter for the night. Even so, they approached the settlement cautiously. With so many displaced people on the move, desperation making many of them potentially dangerous, strangers tended to be treated with suspicion – and Terrel's group knew from experience that the manner of their reception was uncertain. The healer himself had calmed down by now, but as his earlier, almost manic energy had drained away he had sunk ever deeper into a black gloom. The thought that he had only one and a half median months to reach Vadanis made him feel ill. And his frustration at being no closer to his goal than when he'd first learnt about the date of the lunar confluence was threatening to unhinge him altogether. He had realized that – above the clouds – the White Moon was new, so that logic was at its lowest ebb, but even if that was influencing his irrational behaviour, it still didn't alter the fact that he had failed yet again. Vergos – and the Floating Islands – were further away than ever, and it seemed that there was nothing he could do about it.

'What do you think?' Faulk asked.

Terrel was so caught up in his own preoccupations that at first he did not realize the question had been addressed to him. When he looked up, and saw not only the expectant faces of his companions but also the village ahead of them, he had to make a conscious effort to bring his thoughts back to their present situation.

'It looks peaceful enough,' he decided. They had come across other settlements guarded by armed sentries, some of whom had seemed intent on attacking any strangers, whether they posed a threat or not. Terrel had seen one group – consisting mainly of ragged women and children – driven off by spears and arrows when they had approached the outskirts of a town. Such callous treatment of homeless wanderers inevitably reminded him of the 'unclean' in Misrah, and the way they had been abused or ignored by many of that country's more fortunate inhabitants.

'Do you want me to go first?' Yllen asked. A woman on her own was unlikely to be seen as much of a threat.

'All right.' It was a method they had used before, and even though Terrel knew some of the others didn't like Yllen taking such a risk, she seemed more than willing to try again.

'Just yell if you need any help,' Lawren told her.

'I can look after myself,' she informed him as she strode ahead.

'She's a different woman,' Pieri said quietly, once she was out of earshot. 'She'd never have done anything like this before.'

'Our redeeming influence, no doubt,' Lawren said with a grin, then tensed as a man came out of one of the huts and walked over to meet Yllen. A few words passed between them and then she turned and waved urgently, yelling at the same time.

'Terrel! They need a healer. Quickly!'

Terrel's skill was often a major factor in the group's obtaining a welcome, but just at that moment it was the last thing he wanted to hear. He groaned inwardly even as he began to hurry forward, driven more by habit and his responsibilities to his companions than by any real desire to help a stranger. The others followed in his wake, still wary but hopeful now.

'This is Haron,' Yllen said as they approached. 'It's his daughter who's sick.'

'She's in there,' the man said, indicating the nearest hut. His face was pale and drawn, sheened with an unhealthy patina of worry, and although he – like most people – was taken aback by the healer's strange appearance, he was clearly desperate enough to entrust his child to the new-comer.

'What's wrong with her?' Terrel asked.

'A fever,' Yllen said.

'We can't tell what it is,' Haron added. 'No one here's ever seen anything like it.' He was wringing his hands as he spoke. 'But it's getting worse. If we lose her too . . .' He faltered and swallowed hard.

'Ethilie's sister was killed in an accident a few days ago,' Yllen explained quietly.

'That's when the fever started,' Haron said. 'Please, I don't have much, but I'll give you whatever I can if you save her.'

'I don't need payment,' Terrel told him. 'I'll see what I can do.' Pity was beginning to override his earlier reluctance.

'Thank you, thank you.'

Haron ushered them inside, and Terrel saw a woman – presumably the girl's mother – sitting at Ethilie's bedside. There were several other villagers in the room, which made it seem very crowded, but he paid them no attention.

'This is Terrel, Khadia. He's a healer.'

The woman glanced up, her red-rimmed eyes widening in surprise, but she said nothing. She looked utterly drained and Terrel couldn't help thinking that the parents were almost in as much need of his help as their daughter. Khadia released the girl's hand and stood up. As Terrel took her place, he heard her whisper something to her husband, but he wasn't concerned with her obvious doubts. He had to concentrate on his patient.

Ethilie lay on her back on a narrow pallet. She was per-haps four years old, her round face framed by soft blonde curls, but Terrel remained indifferent to her beauty. What concerned him was the way her body was shaking convulsively, and the utter blankness in her staring eyes. He expected her hand to be hot when he picked it up, but her skin was surprisingly cool, almost cold – and that chilled him too. This was no ordinary fever.

He fell into the waking dream easily enough, but it was immediately clear that this too was like none he had encountered previously. It felt incomplete, stretched and unnaturally thin in places, full of unexplained patches of darkness. Gingerly, Terrel explored some of these voids, sensing connections he could not understand. It was almost as though there were links to another dream, another person, but he dismissed that idea as ridiculous and continued to learn what he could. For a long time he could find nothing wrong with the child – nothing that might explain her peculiar malady – but then, as he traced the patterns that related to her neck, he found them full of anomalies, impossible configurations. It was as if perfectly healthy bones were displaying the symptoms of a phantom injury – something that simply wasn't there. It made no sense. Nothing about this dream made any sense – until a memory from his own life made him look at it in a different light.

Terrel released Ethilie's hand and looked around.

'Can you help her?' Haron asked quickly.

'I think so, but there's something I need to know first. Was Ethilie's sister her twin?'

Haron nodded mutely, holding his wife in his arms. Khadia was weeping now.

'How did she die?' Terrel asked, hating to add to their pain but knowing it was necessary.

'She fell from a tree,' Haron said quietly. 'There was nothing we could have done. Her neck was broken.'

Terrel knew now what he had to do. Ethilie was not

going to like it, and it wasn't going to be easy, but there was no other option.

'What was her name?'

'Elise,' Khadia whispered between sobs. 'Her name was Elise.'

Terrel turned back to his patient. He was certain now that Ethilie would never be well until the links to her sister had been severed. It would be a cruel punishment, and one she did not deserve, but it was the only way to save her life. All he had to do was summon up the heartless resolve to complete the task. Only when Ethilie was convinced, both in body and mind, that her sister was truly gone, would she herself become whole again. But *all* the links had to be broken – and to achieve that Terrel not only needed to cauterize the wounds in his patient's waking dream, but also allow her to accept the separation from the person who had been the other half of her own self. And for that he had to find Elise.

Terrel placed his fingers around the cold, shivering hand and steeled himself for the ordeal ahead. But before he could close his eyes and begin the fall, the spectral figure of a man walked through the wall of the hut and stood near the bed. At his side, holding his hand with every sign of trust, was the ghost of a four-year-old girl with curly golden hair.

Is this who you're looking for? Jax asked.

CHAPTER SIXTEEN

What are you doing here? Terrel gasped.

You called me, Jax replied, feigning surprise. Then he smiled.

Terrel knew he couldn't take anything the prince said at face value, but wondered about his claim nonetheless. Was it possible that just thinking about his brother had been enough to make the unwanted connection? Or had it been because he was trying to heal one half of another set of twins?

I came to help, Jax said, all innocence. *This is Elise.*

He doesn't look like you, the girl remarked.

Some twins don't, the prince told her.

What *do* you look like? Terrel wondered. The last time he'd seen Jax, his brother had come in Elam's form – albeit altered to suit the prince's taste – and while he was bodiless he could change his appearance at will. It was possible that this ghostly figure looked like the real person. The healer had only glimpsed the true, flesh-and-blood prince once, and that had been from some distance, more than a decade ago. In fact, the only reason he knew who it was now was the infinitely familiar sound of Jax's voice. He would have known that anywhere.

Terrel turned his attention to the little girl.

Elise, I need you to help your sister. He couldn't fathom Jax's motives for being there and so decided to try to ignore the prince for the time being. There was no telling what his purpose was, or what it might mean for Terrel. His claim to have come simply to help was obviously a laughable pretence, but in the past the healer had occasionally been able to take advantage of his twin's abilities by playing on his vanity and self-interest. Right now Terrel had some healing to do, and the arrival of Ethilie's sister – however this had come about – was a blessing.

What are you doing to her? Elise asked.

I'm trying to make her well.

The little girl looked uncertain and glanced up at Jax, as if seeking his advice. The prince simply shrugged and looked mildly amused.

Why is she sick? the child asked warily.

I think it's because of what happened to you.

Why should I help her then? She sounded petulant now. *It was her fault.*

Terrel became aware of some unrest in the room behind him as the onlookers shuffled their feet and began to whisper. It was obvious that they could see neither Jax or Elise. As far as they were concerned, the healer was just staring at a blank wall, in silence, doing nothing. He couldn't allow them to think that for too long, but if he closed his eyes he risked losing Elise's attention.

All I'm asking is that you hold her hand, he said. *Like I'm doing. I'll do the rest.* He disliked lying to the child but couldn't see any alternative. *Nothing will happen to you.*

Elise looked uncertain again, glancing back and forth between her sister and the healer. The resemblance between the two girls was striking – except, Terrel reminded himself, that one was dead and the other still had a life to lead, if he could get it back for her. He could see through Elise's image to the wall beyond, but in every other aspect she appeared just as she must have done in life.

'What's going on?' Haron asked.

Terrel did not answer immediately. Alyssa had told him a long time ago that ghosts 'walked differently', and that in order to be aware of them he had to see 'round the corner' that separated their world from his. The fact that he was able to do so – at least in most circumstances – was still a mystery to him, although he was more or less convinced that it had something to do with his unique link to Alyssa. However, on several other occasions when he'd been in contact with both living and spectral people, he had found himself in a similarly awkward position. He had to balance how much attention he gave to each of the two worlds. Of course, Jax's presence complicated the issue. He was not a ghost in the traditional sense but the disembodied spirit of someone who was very much alive – although in practice the two things looked the same.

'I need some time,' Terrel said aloud.

Elise seemed to notice her parents for the first time then, and a look of such poignant longing passed over her angelic face that Terrel almost weakened in his resolve. He heard someone – probably Nomar – telling the girls' parents to have patience, but he kept his own focus on the ghostly child, and decided to try telling her the whole truth after all.

You have to do this, Elise. Not just for Ethilie's sake, but for your own. You're not meant to be here. You're supposed to move on.

But I want to stay here, Elise whispered.

You can't, Terrel told her sadly. *Your time in this life is over.*

Like Barker?

I don't know who he was.

Our dog. He died.

So did you, little one, Terrel said gently. *It's time to move on, but you can't do that until the bond between you and Ethilie is broken.*

But I don't want that.

The only alternative is to take her with you. And to do that she'd have to die too. Is that what you really want?

No, she said quietly. *It was just a game.*

What game? Terrel queried.

In the tree. We were pushing each other, seeing who could stay on the branch the longest. I won.

But you were the one who fell.

Yes, but that was afterwards. I caught her and stopped her from falling. Only then I pulled too hard when she was nearly back up. That's when I fell off. Ethi tried to catch me, but she's not as quick as me.

Terrel saw a mental picture of first one twin and then the other overbalancing, and realized that Ethilie's guilt at not being able to save her sister, as Elise had saved her, was part of the problem. Even though Elise was dead, her twin was unwilling to let her go, even to the extent of trying to join her in the next world.

Ethilie feels bad about that, he said.

It wasn't really her fault, Elise whispered.

Will you help me make her better?

Go ahead, Jax said unexpectedly. The prince had remained silent throughout the exchange, but now he let go of Elise's hand and waved her forward. Once again Terrel was suspicious, but he was unable to see what his brother's motive might be.

Elise reached forward slowly, her phantom hand hovering over her sister's.

Will it hurt? she asked timidly.

No, Terrel answered. *You just have to say goodbye, that's all.* I'm doing the right thing, he told himself. For both of them. I'm doing the right thing. He knew it was true, but he also knew it was going to cost them both a great deal of pain.

Elise made her mind up then, and a look of earnest determination settled upon her face. Watching her made

Terrel want to weep, and he was glad to close his eyes as the two matching hands came together.

The effect upon Ethilie was astonishing. Her waking dream emerged from the darkness, complete again. Even as he fought to remain objective, Terrel was subconsciously aware of the reactions of the other people in the hut when the child on the bed suddenly stopped shaking and her face relaxed into a smile. He alone knew that this was a false recovery, and that he would soon have to dash the onlookers' hopes.

He sensed the communion between the two girls, traced all its links and patterns, forcing himself to work out the best ways of severing those ties. He began slowly, aware that he would meet opposition from his patient, but also knowing that if Elise's resolve held firm he would be able to complete his bitter task. As the process went on, he came to admire her bravery. He sensed rather than heard the twins' last anguished goodbyes, and as they faded into silence he felt Ethilie's body twitch and struggle. He continued to hold her hand gently but firmly, hating the necessity of what he was doing.

And then it was done. When Terrel opened his eyes Elise was gone, though Jax was still there. Ethilie was alive and physically well, but convulsed by a tearing grief she was only just beginning to accept as real. As she howled in sorrow, Khadia swept her daughter up into her arms.

'What have you done to her?' she shrieked, her eyes blazing with maternal fury.

Terrel could not answer. He couldn't do anything.

Nomar leant down to whisper in his ear.

'The job's not over, Terrel. She still needs your help.'

The healer shook his head, feeling numb. He couldn't see the point any more. He was filled with a sudden loathing, not for the child but for the whole world, humanity in general.

He had done all he could. All he *wanted* to do. If that wasn't enough then it was no concern of his. The idea of even trying to enter Ethilie's waking dream again filled him with dread.

Nomar must have recognized Terrel's difficulties because he turned and spoke to the girl's distraught parents.

'My colleague is exhausted. I'm a healer too. May I try to help her?'

Terrel was only vaguely aware of subsequent events. He understood Khadia's reluctance to submit her daughter to another ordeal, but when Nomar was finally allowed to touch her, Ethilie's wails diminished and then fell away altogether.

'She is well,' Nomar assured them gently. 'The fever is gone. What you saw was her grief for her sister. The illness had been blocking her sorrow.'

'She is well?' Khadia whispered, grasping at the only piece of information she had been able to take in properly.

'Yes. She'll sleep now, probably for a long time. But when she wakes her heart will begin to mend.'

The atmosphere of relief in the cabin penetrated even Terrel's miserable cocoon, but it meant little to him. *His* heart felt as though it had been shattered. Unable to move, he remained kneeling where he was until Faulk put a hand under his good arm and pulled him to his feet. They began to walk slowly towards the door.

Now that was interesting.

Terrel had forgotten his brother was there, and his sudden tension made Faulk hesitate.

Now I'll know how to survive when you *die*, Jax added, laughing.

You'd be killing part of yourself, Terrel told him, remembering the vision on Tindaya when he'd seen into the future to the moment of his own death. He had to return to the mountain, but it didn't seem likely that he'd ever be able to get there now. It was just one more nonsensical aspect of his pointless existence.

Who said I was going to kill you? Jax asked, obviously intrigued. *I always thought you'd find a way to kill yourself sooner or later.*

Terrel did not respond, and the prince evidently lost interest in the idea.

This place isn't much fun, is it? he said. *It's no wonder your little friend doesn't visit you as often.*

Terrel hated it when Jax referred to Alyssa that way.

'Are you all right, Terrel?' Faulk asked.

'Just let me rest here a few moments,' he muttered.

Quite right, the prince said brightly. *I hadn't finished anyway.*

What do you want? Terrel asked wearily.

I don't know yet. It doesn't begin to compare to Myvatan, does it? I enjoyed the company of the wizards there. Still, things have been getting a little more interesting lately, but you've been hiding from me, haven't you? I didn't think you could do that.

Terrel was mystified. He had no idea what Jax was talking about, but he knew better than to reveal his ignorance. In the past the prince had only been able to torment him through dreams or – under certain conditions – by usurping the healer's own body. Even now, when he was able to travel independently, it seemed that he still needed the connection to Terrel to allow his spirit to wander. And now that connection had been renewed.

I actually lost track of you completely for a while, Jax added casually, as if he were having a conversation with an old friend. *And of course I've had other things to do with my time, now that I'm emperor in all but name. But still, you couldn't hide for ever, and now that I'm here I think I'll take a look around. Farewell, brother. For now, at least.*

CHAPTER SEVENTEEN

The travellers stayed that night in a large hut which, judging from the musty smell and the dust on the bare floorboards, had been used to store grain. The fact that it was empty now, with the worst of the winter still to come, spoke of hard times ahead for the villagers, but once they knew that Ethilie was on the road to recovery they were generous hosts. The food they provided was plain fare but welcome nonetheless, and the granary, while hardly luxurious, was soundly constructed and a dry and reasonably warm place.

However, before the travellers could settle down to sleep they were visited by a group of villagers intent on hearing whatever news and gossip the strangers might have brought with them. Terrel sat in a corner of the room, as far from the gathering as he could get, and took no part in the conversation. For the most part he was left undisturbed, with both their hosts and his own companions accepting Nomar's explanation about his exhaustion. This left him free to brood about everything that was making him feel so troubled.

His reaction to what had happened with Ethilie and Elise had been a devastating blow. He could tell himself until he was blue in the face that he'd done the right thing, but that didn't alter the fact that *what* he had done had caused a reat deal of suffering. The counter-arguments – that the alternative had been even worse and

that, in the long run, Ethilie would benefit from his treatment – meant nothing in the face of the agony he'd seen in
the girl's eyes that afternoon. But it had been his overwhelming feelings of disgust and resentment towards all
human beings, and not just those immediately involved,
that made him feel even more uneasy. Part of him hated
the cynicism to which he'd suddenly become prey, but part
of him recognized the truth of his reaction. He remembered something he'd said to Elam when they were boys at
the asylum – words that had haunted Terrel from time to
time ever since. 'Sometimes I hate the world so much I
wish I could destroy it all.' The reason for his discontent
on that occasion had been trivial compared to so much that
had happened since, but that didn't mean the sentiment
had not been genuine. And at this moment, Terrel remembered just how he'd felt.

His ability to heal had been the only constant reminder
that he was doing something worthwhile during his travels,
and if he was to lose his faith in that the future looked
bleak. Terrel had been grateful to Nomar for taking over
when he had, recognizing the needs of both Ethilie and
himself, and he couldn't help wondering now if it was time
for his fellow healer to go his own way. Nomar's skills had
developed considerably over the months they'd been
together, and Terrel suspected there was little more he
could teach him. He did not want the other man to be
tainted by the doubts and rancour that were now afflicting
his own mind.

Terrel's misery was made even worse by Jax's return.
The prince had been absent from the healer's life for so
long that he'd been able to put him from his mind. His
return was the last thing Terrel needed, and he simply did
not know how to cope with this added complication. The
mystery of how their contact had been re-established was

only one of the things plaguing Terrel now. Had it been something he'd done himself, as Jax had implied, or had Ethilie's connection with her dead twin been the significant factor? Had the ghosts' visit a month earlier opened the door through which the prince had stepped? And what was Terrel to make of Jax's assertion that he himself had been 'hiding'? He hadn't been aware of doing any such thing, but if that *had* been the case, what had changed to bring him out into the open again? However, the only important thing was that Jax was back. The thought of his being let loose in Kenda was unbearable. The prince's destructive talents as an enchanter and a weather-mage would give him ample scope to amuse himself. Because of the volcano and the earthquakes the situation was already volatile, and it would take very little meddling on his part to produce catastrophic results.

Terrel's thoughts made him feel so wretched that when the villagers produced some flagons of mead, he even considered getting hopelessly drunk. Although the impulse lasted only for a brief moment, the prospect of abdicating all responsibility was seductive. The healer knew that if he went ahead, the likelihood was that Jax would take over his body – and there was no telling what would happen then. If intoxication could offer him mere insensibility – a deadening of his feelings – he would probably have gone ahead. But Jax had robbed him of even that escape.

'It's Kaeryss who's calling the stones down from the sky.'

'No, no, it's Gozian. Peet told me the king's distraught because of his son and so he wants to punish everyone.'

The mead had loosened tongues and the villagers were repeating the various rumours that had reached them. Still sitting apart from the rest, Terrel wished they'd keep their fanciful theories to themselves and just go away. He wanted to be left in peace, even though sleep – and the dreams that might come with it – did not seem a very attractive prospect either. However, the next speaker captured his attention.

'I was told it was the king's wife,' one of the village men said. 'I heard she's supposed to be a sorceress, and she's used part of the Raven Cypher to conjure up a shadow-demon who can split rock and make the earth breathe fire.'

That sounded uncannily like the description of an elemental, and it set Terrel thinking. Was it possible that one of the creatures was actually there, in Kenda? The healer's first reaction was to reject the idea. He'd been convinced that he'd already found them all, and in the past none of the Ancients had ever seemed inclined to move any distance from their lairs. On the other hand he had no proof that either of these statements still held true. There *could* be more of them. One of them *could* have moved. And if one of the elementals *was* involved in the creation of the lava-filled ravine, it cast an unpleasant light on the way it had prevented Terrel from continuing his journey.

He was about to ask for more details about this so-called shadow-demon when he realized the conversation had moved on and the gathering was now engrossed in a discussion about music. Quite how this abrupt change of topic had taken place was a mystery to Terrel, but Yllen had evidently made some outrageous claim on Pieri's behalf which the storyteller was doing his best to play down – and several of the villagers were good-naturedly demanding proof of his prowess.

'I used to play well enough a while back,' Pieri conceded, 'but I'm out of practice now, except for these.' He held up a pair of his crude whistles.

'Anyone can wring a tune out of something like that,' one of his inquisitors said.

'What about a lute?' another asked. 'Could you play that?'

'I told you,' Pieri replied with a shrug. 'I used to be able to.'

The man got up and left the hut.

'His grandfather used to play, but since he died no one here's had the skill of it,' one of the others explained.

'That was years ago,' someone else added. 'It's probably useless now.'

'It'll be a challenge, then. If our friend here can bring it back to life then maybe he really is as good as Yllen says.'

Pieri shot his companion an aggrieved look, but she just smiled sweetly. The musician's grandson returned with his treasured possession and handed it over. Terrel expected Pieri to reject it immediately, but he did not. For a while he studied the instrument in an almost reverent fashion.

'This is fine craftsmanship,' he said eventually, looking up. 'The neck's warped a little and it would be murder to tune. And it really needs new strings.' He made no attempt to play so much as a note.

'So you *can't* play it?' the most sceptical of the on-lookers said.

'I didn't say that.'

'Well, go on then!' Yllen burst out, sounding half exas-perated, half amused.

When Pieri hesitated, Terrel realized that this was a sig-nificant moment for the storyteller. If he succeeded, then simply re-entering the world he had lost – or rejected – might be like tearing open an old wound. And if he failed . . .

Others were not so sensitive to the situation and urged Pieri on until finally he succumbed. Setting the lute in his lap, he plucked one of the strings. It took him a long time to tune the instrument, and the sounds it produced during the process were hardly auspicious. The lute groaned and whined, emitted a few pure notes but more that buzzed or sounded dull. This in turn provoked a series of humorous comments from the audience, which Pieri studiously ignored. Eventually he looked up, apparently noticing for the first time that everyone was waiting for him.

'I can't . . . It needs new strings,' he repeated.

'Play something anyway,' one of the villagers said.

'Most of us are tone deaf so it won't matter,' another commented, prompting some laughter.

Terrel knew that it *would* matter to Pieri and at first he thought the storyteller was going to refuse, but then Pieri ducked his head and set his fingers in place. A hush fell over the room. And when he began to play, all the other sounds in the world ceased to exist.

The tune he had chosen was gentle and lilting, under-pinned by a subtle rhythmic pattern on the bass strings, and highlighted by gossamer light phrases on the higher notes which were sometimes butterfly fast and sometimes achingly slow. Terrel felt his mood being transformed from moment to moment at the whim of the music, and he knew that on this occasion Pieri had not needed to use the glamour to enhance his performance. Even Yllen, who had presumably heard him play many times before, seemed both astonished and entranced by the delicate tracery of sound he had conjured up – and most of the villagers were open-mouthed in awe. While he was playing time seemed to stop, but when he finished – abruptly, in the middle of a passage – it seemed that the music had lasted for no more than a heartbeat.

In the stunned silence that followed, Pieri carefully set the lute aside, then jumped to his feet. Protests at his departure and expressions of delight and applause mixed with vehement requests for more, but the storyteller ignored them all. As he strode towards the door, he was shaking his head and muttering to himself. In the dim lamplight Terrel could not be sure, but he thought he saw tears in Pieri's eyes as he vanished into the night.

Nomar got to his feet and seemed to be about to follow him, but Yllen held up a hand.

'Leave him,' she said quietly. 'This is something he'll have to deal with by himself.'

Soon after that the villagers returned to their own homes, leaving the travellers to make their preparations for the night. The music had allowed Terrel to forget his problems for a while, and Nomar had obviously sensed the slight shift in the healer's mood because he came over to join him.

'That was quite something, wasn't it?'

Terrel nodded.

'There were a few false notes towards the end,' Nomar added. 'The lute was probably going out of tune again.'

'It all sounded beautiful to me.'

'But not to Pieri. I suppose that's why he stopped when he did.'

Terrel didn't think it was as simple as that, but he let the comment stand.

'Are you feeling better now?' Nomar asked.

'Not much.'

'We need people like you, you know. You give us all hope. For the future.'

Terrel was unable to respond. Nothing in the future looked hopeful to him.

'There's so much hatred, so much cruelty in the world,' Nomar went on. 'So many people who do only harm.

That's why healers . . .' He shrugged. 'You've taught me so much, but I've still got such a lot to learn. I won't fail you, Terrel, I swear. I just wish there were more like you. Perhaps Taryn's world would be different then.'

Terrel was almost overwhelmed by shame at that point, but he simply could not believe that he deserved such trust, such faith – especially when his own thoughts had suddenly become so cynical and bitter.

'I don't know exactly what you did today,' Nomar went on, 'but I know it was hard. For you as well as for the girl. But she—'

'She'd still be ill if you hadn't taken over,' Terrel cut in, finding his voice at last.

'No, not ill,' Nomar replied. 'I just gave her the will and the calmness of spirit to help her deal with her sorrow. Her fever, whatever it was, had already gone – and that was your doing. Keep believing, Terrel. You'll achieve everything you set your mind to, if you just believe you can.'

The echoes of the words he had shared with Alyssa left Terrel tongue-tied once more, and he wished he could share his friend's guileless optimism. But time, his greatest enemy, was marching forward while he was forced to stand still, and as night closed in and the ephemeral joy induced by Pieri's magic faded, Terrel sank back into the lonely darkness that was all his own.

'I may have some good news,' Roskin announced as he came back into the hut.

After the revels of the previous evening, the company had roused themselves a little later than usual. Indeed, Pieri – who had returned, unnoticed, during the night – was still asleep. The rest all looked expectantly at Roskin.

'There's been a huge avalanche a few miles north of here,' he told them.

'And this is *good* news?' Yllen queried.

'It is,' Roskin confirmed, 'because it fell across the ravine. So much rock came down that it's formed a bridge all the way across.'

'How did you find out?' Faulk asked.

'One of Haron's cousins lives out that way, and he arrived early this morning. He saw it for himself.'

'Has he actually crossed the bridge?' Lawren asked.

'No, but he's talked to people who have.'

'So it is possible then,' Yllen concluded.

'If this cousin can be believed,' Lawren said more cautiously.

'Why should he lie?' Roskin asked. 'He had no reason to cross it, but we do.'

'If we can get there fast enough,' Faulk said.

'What do you mean?' Yllen enquired.

'The bridge is built on foundations of molten rock,' the soldier pointed out. 'There's no telling when it might collapse.'

'Then we'd better hurry,' Terrel said, entering the conversation for the first time. 'I'm not going to miss this chance.'

'Are you sure?' Faulk asked. 'It could be dangerous.'

'We won't know till we get there,' the healer replied. 'But I'm going to try. You're all welcome to come with me or stay, as you please. The same as always.' He had already made up his mind to attempt the crossing, come what may. This time not even Faulk would be able to stand in his way.

Two days later, the travellers stood looking down on the tumbled mass of earth and boulders that made up the new bridge. 'A few miles' had turned out to be a considerable understatement, and to reach their present vantage point they had had to cross some difficult terrain. Despite his own melancholy fatigue Terrel had driven them on, aware that this might be his only chance to complete his journey on time. In his heart he knew it was probably already too late. Even if he managed to make the crossing now, it would still take them close to a month to reach Vergos, leaving him only a few days to get from there to the Floating Islands. That was surely an impossible task – but his new hope made him determined to keep trying.

'You still want to do this?' Lawren asked.

The ravine was wreathed in swirls of smoke and steam, and even from a distance they could feel the heat of the lava to either side, but the bridge itself appeared to be stable enough.

'Yes,' Terrel replied.

'It'll be rough going. There are no paths here. We'll be scrambling over rocks on our hands and knees just to get to the bridge – and there's no telling how hot it'll be underfoot.'

'I know all that. But I've got no choice.'

'We might make it,' the hunter added, 'but I don't see how Jarek can.'

'You'd be surprised,' Pieri said. 'He can be nimble enough when he needs to be.'

Lawren shook his head, his doubts obvious, but said nothing more.

'I'm not going to leave him behind,' Pieri went on. 'I'll turn back if necessary.'

'That's a choice everyone has,' Terrel said. 'I can't force—'

'Oh, shut up,' Yllen exclaimed. 'We're all coming – and if we break our necks it'll be our own fault, not yours.'

There were nods of agreement all round and even a few

smiles. Terrel wondered yet again what he had done to deserve such loyalty.

'The fumes down there are going to be bad,' Faulk commented.

'Tie a damp cloth over your mouth and nose,' Lawren advised. 'That might help a bit.'

'And we'll look like bandits,' Pieri added, 'so if we meet anyone else they'll keep out of our way.'

In the event, the crossing took the rest of that day, but they met no one. By nightfall they were all exhausted, bruised and blistered, but they were on the other side of the fissure – and the company was still intact. Even Jarek had made it across.

Now, at last, they could turn to the southwest and head towards Vergos and, beyond that, to the shores of the Movaghassi Ocean.

Even though Terrel drove himself and his companions as hard as possible, the journey to Vergos took almost exactly the median month that he had predicted. Their progress was slowed by the lack of good roads – or even tracks – in what was a largely barren and sparsely populated region, and by their own unavoidable need to replenish their supplies and to find shelter at night.

During their trek the travellers gathered what news they could from the few people they met. Conflicting rumours about what was happening in the city made it impossible to glean the whole truth of the situation, but it was clear that many people had abandoned their homes to go to Vergos – and on several occasions the group took advantage of the empty houses – mostly hovels – that had been left behind. The other main topic of conversation with any strangers was the weather. Even though there had been no sign of

Jax since he'd appeared with Elise's ghost, Terrel could not help but think of him when he heard reports of strange whirlwinds, sudden storms and unexplained fires.

However, it was not the possible results of his brother's malevolence that worried Terrel as much as the continued absence of Alyssa and the ghosts. Despite his own lack of progress, his allies had not come to him since their departure from the Haven Inn. Either they were still relying on him to reach Vadanis by the fast-approaching deadline – and were assuming that he'd be able to do this without any help from them – or something was stopping them from visiting Kenda. Neither possibility made Terrel feel any happier. All he could do was push himself forward and try to maintain some semblance of belief – a task that was becoming increasingly difficult.

When Vergos finally came into view, Terrel felt a small measure of relief – not because he really thought he would now be able to reach his ultimate goal, but because at least he'd soon be able to take the next active step. He had already decided that he could not afford to linger in the city – no matter how important the Raven Cypher might be – and that he would start to look for a passage on one of the river boats immediately. As always, his companions could make their own decision as to whether to stay with him or not.

As the travellers drew closer to Vergos, it became clear that the city sprawled out well beyond the original defensive walls, but when they reached the outskirts there was no one to be seen.

'The place is deserted,' Lawren said quietly in the unnatural silence.

'It can't be,' Roskin muttered. 'This is where everyone was supposed to be going.'

'Perhaps they've all gone inside the city walls,' Yllen suggested.

'Why?' Faulk wondered aloud. 'They're not under attack.'

'Well, *we* should go in,' Pieri reasoned. 'That's where we'll find any answers.'

And so they went on, passing through a huge stone archway under the city's battlements. The gates themselves stood wide open and were unguarded. In fact, there was no sign of anyone at all. But in the distance the travellers could now hear a sound, a vast murmuring, as if a gigantic swarm of bees had taken up residence in the heart of the city.

When they finally reached the source of the noise, the reason for the city's outer sections being empty suddenly became clear. The entire population seemed to be packed into the centre of Vergos, and every street was clogged with a heaving throng of people – who were all trying to get to the area in and around a vast square outside the royal palace. Everyone seemed to be in the grip of some form of mass hysteria, and the noise they made as they barged their way through was tremendous.

There was no way the travellers could hope to move in the crowd as a group, so they lingered at its edges and tried to find out what was going on by talking to others. They finally learnt that people were gathering to hear 'the Ravens' Voice', a prophet who apparently held the entire city in thrall. But they were unable to discover exactly why his words should be so important, or how long his oration was likely to last.

In the ensuing discussion, the more practical members of the group wanted to retreat and seek out possible lodgings for the night, while the others – Terrel among them – insisted that they should at least find out what the Ravens' Voice had to say. In the end they compromised, agreeing to split up and meet again later at an agreed point. Terrel, Roskin and Nomar – who, much to the boy's disgust, entrusted Taryn's care to Yllen – went on, forcing their way through the pulsating mass. Their progress was erratic and the crush was such that at times Terrel felt he was going to suffocate, but eventually they reached the edge of the great square.

Not only was the floor of the arena desperately crowded, but people were hanging from every window of the buildings that surrounded the square, clinging to balconies and roofs and any other available vantage point. Waves of sound swept through the crowd for no apparent reason. The trio were at last able to find their own spot from which to watch the proceedings, slipping into a gap on some steps when several women fainted and were carried away. The most extraordinary aspect of the entire gathering was that, as far as Terrel and his companions could tell, the prophet had not even made an appearance yet. The air of anticipation bordered on insanity, and it was clear that it would take very little to turn the scene into one of appalling violence.

Terrel looked around him with a sense of disbelief, and with a growing intimation of fear that was becoming more ominous by the moment. Both Roskin and Nomar seemed to be caught up in the same emotions, and none of them spoke. Like the rest of the throng, they waited.

Terrel had expected the prophet's eventual appearance to be greeted by a roar from the crowd, but when a black-robed figure emerged as if by magic, and stood surveying his audience from the parapet of one of the palace walls, the arena instead became eerily still and quiet. The Ravens' Voice raised his arms, like black wings, and spoke in a commanding tone that carried easily over the multitude.

'In twelve days from now,' he cried, naming the date of the lunar confluence, 'this world will end!'

The crowd murmured and shifted, waiting for what would come next, but Terrel was distracted by a gasp from his left. Glancing round, he saw that Nomar's face had turned chalk white, his eyes were wide and he was desperately trying to catch his breath.

'What's the matter?' Terrel whispered as the prophet began to speak again. 'Do you know him?'

'I'd know him anywhere,' Nomar replied in a voice shot through with absolute horror. 'I had thought – hoped – he was dead. His name is Araguz.'

CHAPTER EIGHTEEN

'Then he pointed to the sky, to the Amber Moon, and said "When it comes to the full, when they all do, the world will begin its last dream."'

The company were back together, in the cramped lodgings that had finally been acquired by a combination of coercion and bargaining with the owner of a large house. The negotiations had been aided by the proprietor's wife, who assumed that the travellers were pilgrims – like several others she'd already allowed into her home – drawn to Vergos by the charismatic teachings of the Ravens' Voice. She would have reached a very different conclusion had she been party to the conversation now taking place. The lady of the house was clearly already under the prophet's spell, but none of the three who had witnessed his latest performance were likely to become followers. Nomar's silent antagonism was obvious, Terrel seemed equally disapproving and even Roskin, who had been doing most of the talking so far, seemed to find the man's popularity inexplicable.

'He never did explain what that meant,' the would-be seer added.

'What phase is the Amber Moon in now?' Lawren asked.

'It's a new crescent, just one day old,' Terrel replied, remembering how all the faces in the crowd had turned to look up at the pale sliver of gold.

'And the others?'

'The White is four days past new, the Red half full and waxing.'

There was a pause while some of the group worked out what this would mean.

'So he could be right,' Pieri said eventually. 'They could all be full in twelve days' time.'

Terrel nodded.

'What about the Dark Moon?' Faulk queried.

'It's still waning, but it'll turn soon and it could be full then too.' The Dark Moon had always been the one the healer felt the closest affinity with, but since its orbit had begun to change, Terrel – like everyone else – had found it even more difficult to keep track of its movements. The fact that it was invisible during all its phases, and all observations depended on its blocking the light from the more distant moons – or the sun or the stars – meant that it was always going to be the hardest to judge accurately.

'So this could be a full confluence,' Lawren concluded.

'Yes,' Terrel replied, hoping the dread he felt in making this admission did not show on his face.

'I thought that was only supposed to happen every seventy-five years,' Yllen said.

'That was before the Dark Moon went mad,' Pieri told her.

'The Ravens' Voice was making a lot of the fact that it was happening less than twenty-five years after the last one,' Roskin added. 'He said the moons were punishing us.'

'For what?' Lawren demanded incredulously. 'How?'

'That was a little vague,' Roskin admitted. 'But he did say we all had to be ready for the next world.'

'He sounds like a madman to me,' the hunter growled.

'But a persuasive one,' Pieri pointed out. 'He's got an awful lot of people believing him.'

'The world's going to end in twelve days?' Lawren said scornfully. 'You don't believe that, do you?'

'*Something* is happening with the moons,' Roskin replied. 'You can't deny that. It's got to have some relevance, surely.'

'Why? They're up there and we're down here. What difference can it make? Are they going to fall on us like giant fire-scythes? The whole thing's insane.'

'He *is* insane,' Nomar stated quietly. 'But if Araguz gets his way the world won't *need* to end.'

They all turned to look at him. Nomar had not spoken a word since his earlier revelation about knowing the prophet's name. Despite his companions' prompting he had remained silent, his face a stern, rigid mask with only his eyes betraying the terror within. Terrel believed that his friend was in shock, and was glad Taryn had already been asleep when they met up again. He would not have wanted the boy to see his father in this state. While Roskin had described what they had seen and heard that afternoon, Nomar had stayed still and mute, and the healer had given up trying to coax him into talking, assuming that this would happen of its own accord once he was ready. It seemed that time had come now.

'If you're going to start talking in riddles too, then I'd rather you kept quiet,' Lawren remarked, but even he looked intrigued.

'What do you mean?' Faulk asked Nomar.

'I've seen this – *him* – before.'

'Seen what before?'

'I should be dead because of him,' Nomar said, staring blindly into space. 'I was four years old. And I drank poison.'

And so Nomar told his story, the story he'd kept locked up inside himself for so many years because it was too terrible to reveal to the world at large, and because he believed it could be safely consigned to the past – never to be forgotten but never to be repeated. All that had changed now. His nightmare had become real again.

The horror that suffused his memories transmitted itself to the others, who listened to his softly spoken words in a silence that grew deeper and more appalled as his tale unfolded. Terrel found the fact that Nomar was talking about events that had taken place on the night of the healer's own birth – the night when his destiny had been shaped by forces he could not control – even more chilling, and by the end he was not the only one blinking back tears.

'The entire Family died,' Nomar concluded. 'Over a hundred people, including my mother. I was the only one to survive. At least I thought so until today. And it's happening again here, only on a much bigger scale.'

For a long time no one spoke. They understood now why Nomar had refused to go anywhere near Senden.

'Do you really think Araguz could get everyone to commit suicide?' Lawren asked eventually. 'There's a huge difference between a cult following and a city full of thousands of people.' Under normal circumstances the hunter's question would have been rhetorical – imbued with the inherent scepticism with which he viewed all unnatural events – but on this occasion he was pleading his case seriously, obviously hoping someone would agree with him.

'He can do anything he wants to,' Nomar replied. 'He's an enchanter.'

'There's no such thing,' Lawren claimed, but his words lacked their usual conviction.

'You didn't see the way the crowd reacted to everything he said,' Roskin countered. 'They were drinking it all in.'

'Then why weren't the three of you affected?'

'I don't know,' Nomar said.

'You believed him when you were a child, didn't you?' Lawren went on. 'So why not now? And why are we all sitting here discussing this? If Araguz really is an enchanter who's got the whole city under his spell, we should be agreeing with whatever he says.'

'Perhaps we haven't been here long enough,' Pieri suggested.

'All I know is that it's happening again,' Nomar repeated. 'And we have to stop it. Perhaps we're the only ones who can.' He glanced round in appeal. 'Will you help me?'

'We should kill him,' Yllen stated venomously.

Most of the others were obviously startled by the ruthless nature of her proposal, but Nomar just shook his head.

'No. Even if we could, that's not the right solution. It may not even prevent the massacre. And I'm a healer, not an assassin.'

'But he's a murderer,' she objected. 'He deserves to die.'

'Are you absolutely sure it's the same person?' Faulk asked.

'Absolutely,' Nomar replied. 'He's a lot older, of course, but even if I hadn't recognized his face I could never forget that voice.'

'It was amazing how it carried so well,' Roskin murmured.

Terrel and Pieri exchanged glances.

'He even used some of the same words,' Nomar went on. ' "The moons move within the tides of my blood." I can still hear him saying that on the night Paradise came to the Family.'

'That's what you dream about,' Terrel realized. 'When the headaches come.'

'It's what I've been running away from all my life,' his friend agreed. 'But no more. You've given me the strength to face him now. You're the opposite of Araguz,' he told Terrel. 'He's the negation of all life. Healers enhance lives, even save them. I will not let him succeed again.'

'So let's kill him!' Yllen exclaimed.

'You haven't been listening to what I've been saying,' Nomar told her wearily.

'I'll do it myself if none of you have the stomach for it,' she declared.

Nomar laughed at that, surprising everybody – including himself.

'I'm glad I'm not your enemy,' he said. 'And I thank you for your support. But there has to be another way. If I become like him I lose everything.'

'But—'

'We don't have to decide now,' Pieri cut in. 'We've got twelve days to go – and in this city that's going to seem like a very long time.'

'What do you mean?' Faulk asked.

'Look at it this way. If people think the world's going to end, they'll react in one of two ways. Either they're going to be plunged into despair or they're going to make damn sure they enjoy themselves while they still can. No matter what happens there should be plenty of opportunities for us to get a feel for what's happening, and to work out a way of stopping Araguz. There must be others here with some power. Gozian, for one.'

'And Kaeryss,' Roskin put in.

'And if we can't get to them,' the storyteller went on, 'we ought to be able to find *someone* to listen to us. Like I said, we've got twelve days.'

'No, we haven't,' Terrel said. 'At least, *I* haven't.'

They all turned to look at him, unspoken questions in their eyes.

'I can't stay,' the healer explained. 'I have to find a ship and move on.'

'Would any be sailing now?' Faulk queried.

'I don't know,' Terrel admitted, 'but I have to find out. And if they're not, I'll have to look for another way.'

'Can't you stay for a little while at least?' Nomar asked, and his friend's obvious dismay made Terrel hate his predicament even more.

'No. I have to go.'

'You were the one I hoped would . . .' Nomar fell silent, waving away his own words.

'I thought you wanted to find out about the Raven Cypher,' Roskin said, his own disappointment plain.

'I have more important things to do.'

'Then this is where we part ways,' Nomar said sadly.

'Surely a few days won't matter,' Roskin persisted.

'I have to be back in the Floating Islands by the time of the confluence.'

'Why?'

'It would take too long to explain.' Terrel knew that even though this was true, his answer was unsatisfactory and less than his companions deserved.

'You'll never make it,' Lawren said.

'Even if you got a ship tomorrow, it would take that long just to reach the coast,' Pieri concurred.

'I've got to try,' Terrel insisted. 'I'm sorry, Nomar. I wish things were different, but . . .' He shrugged helplessly.

'We all have to do what we must,' Nomar said gravely. 'I shall stay and fight the evil that Araguz brings.'

'The rest of you should stay as well,' Terrel added.

'Nomar's cause is worthy of your talents. My course is my own.'

'I'll be coming with you,' Faulk said quickly. 'My destiny is tied to yours.'

Terrel glanced at the soldier, surprised by this overt declaration of intent – and wondering at the reason for it. None of the others looked quite so certain of their decisions.

'You choose your own paths, as always,' the healer said. 'Sleep on it. Then decide.'

Terrel and Faulk set off from their lodgings at first light, and the scene at the docks was reassuringly busy. The healer had told the others he would return to tell them his plans unless he was offered passage on a ship leaving immediately, in which case he was bound to take it. Their farewells had been brief and awkward, as though no one could quite believe that this really was the parting of the ways, but once they were outside, Terrel's heavy heart had begun to lift a little at the thought of making a start on the next stage of his journey. With only Faulk at his side, the weight of responsibility on his shoulders had lessened, and he tried not to think too much about the situation in which he was leaving his other friends. As he had told himself a hundred times, he had no choice.

The riverside was bustling with activity, with cargoes being unloaded and passengers disembarking from newly-moored ships, but it didn't take the two companions long to realize that their first impressions had been misleading. Everywhere they asked, the answer was the same. Boats were arriving, but very few were leaving – and certainly none intending to travel as far as the coast. Almost every available berth had already been taken, and with more vessels arriving hourly, the city's waterways would soon be clogged and impassable.

'It doesn't look good,' Faulk commented as they walked past a shipbuilder's yard, where the finishing touches were being put to a new craft within a dry dock. 'Perhaps we should consider other options. With so many people arriving and so few leaving, there must be horses in the city that the owners no longer want. We could get a pair for next to nothing and be on our way in no time.'

Bowing to the inevitable, Terrel nodded and was about to suggest that they do just that when he noticed a ginger cat hobbling down the gangplank of the nearest ship. Something about its crooked, painful gait gave him pause for thought, and when the wretched, moth-eaten creature began to limp directly towards him he stopped and waited.

'What is it?' Faulk asked, puzzled by Terrel's sudden preoccupation.

The cat stopped a few paces away from the healer, slumped onto its haunches and looked up at him with rheumy eyes. It was only then that Terrel saw the makeshift ring looped around one of the animal's tattered ears, confirming what his heart had already told him.

Alyssa? he whispered, torn between joy at her return and fear for her health.

We need to talk, she rasped, pain evident in every word.

In the next moment, three ghosts appeared in the midst of all the sailors and stevedores.

CHAPTER NINETEEN

'Are they here?' Faulk asked as he quickly scanned the area.

Can he see us? Elam was astonished.

I don't think so, Terrel replied. Aloud he said, 'Who are you talking about?'

'The invisible guardians,' Faulk said. He was still glancing around, his eyes wild. His usual calm seemed to have deserted him and he looked quite agitated. 'The ones who guide you.'

Guardians? Terrel thought, momentarily nonplussed.

If he can't see us, how does he know we're here? Shahan asked.

He's reacting to you, Alyssa told Terrel. *To the changes in you.*

The healer had done his best not to look at the mangy cat or the ghosts since Faulk's question, but his behaviour had clearly alerted the soldier to the fact that something unusual was happening.

We're wasting time, Muzeni grumbled. *What does it matter if—*

'It's not the warlock, is it?' Faulk asked, his hand going to the hilt of his sword.

'I don't know what you're talking about,' Terrel replied. He was thoroughly confused now, and at some point in the future he was going to have to discuss this peculiar development with Faulk, but this was not the time. The ghosts were getting impatient.

'It's in the prophecy,' Faulk said. 'He's your enemy.'

What prophecy? Terrel wondered, even as he saw a possible way out of his present dilemma.

'There are no enemies here,' he assured his companion.

Faulk relaxed a little.

Time to tell him something, Shahan urged. *We* do *need to talk.*

'My guides are here,' Terrel said, taking the plunge. 'I need to speak to them. Will you stand guard while I do?'

'Of course.' Now that his sense of purpose had been renewed, Faulk calmed down, though he remained watchful. He began to draw his blade but Terrel put out a hand to stop him.

'Don't draw attention to us,' he said quietly.

Faulk nodded, looking round as if, in spite of the healer's assertion, he expected to see enemies everywhere.

'Go and sit over there,' the soldier said, pointing to where some coils of rope were stored next to a warehouse. 'With the wall at your back I can guard you more effectively.'

Terrel did as he was told, settling himself on one of the coils. The cat came and curled up at his feet. Faulk frowned at this but evidently decided that the animal posed no threat, and took up his post as a sentry. The ghosts gathered round.

He's very protective, Elam remarked, with a glance at the soldier. *What did—*

I've been thinking, Terrel began, without preamble. *Can you transport me to Tindaya, in spirit at least? Like you did before?* The ghosts seemed taken aback by this and he went on quickly to explain his request. *It's just that there doesn't seem to be any other way for me to get there in time. I've still got—*

Even if we could, Shahan cut in, *there's no need for that now.*

But the confluence is in eleven days!

No, it isn't, Muzeni responded. *That's one of the reasons for us coming to see you.*

Terrel was dumbfounded.

But I thought—

It's not the first time the court seers have got their calculations wrong, Muzeni said with his habitual scorn for the denizens of Makhaya.

You got it wrong too on this occasion, Elam pointed out.

Yes, well. For once, the ancient heretic looked flustered. *I didn't have enough—*

Wait a moment, Terrel interrupted. *Are you really telling me there* won't *be a confluence in eleven days' time?*

The three visible moons will all be full that night, Shahan replied, *but the Dark Moon won't.*

Its orbit is changing faster than anyone expected, Muzeni added.

So it won't line up with the others? Terrel could still hardly believe what he was being told.

No, Muzeni confirmed. *As I said, they got the timing wrong. We all did*, he added with a glance at Elam.

And so did Araguz, Terrel murmured.

Who?

He's a prophet who seems to have got this entire city under his control. He's been predicting a great disaster for the night of the confluence. He did the same last time, twenty-five years ago.

Shahan and Muzeni exchanged a glance at this, but Terrel hardly noticed. He was still trying to come to terms with the repercussions of this new intelligence.

Nomar thinks he's going to try to get everyone here to commit suicide, he went on, *as some sort of sacrifice to the*

*moons, so that instead of being destroyed here they can go on
to the . . . next . . . world.* He faltered as he realized he was
talking to people who were actually *in* the next world.

That's not how it works, Shahan stated grimly.

*I know. He's obviously insane, but I think it's possible he
might be an enchanter, and there's no doubt about the power
he has over the people here.* Terrel realized that both the
seers were looking grave and Elam looked concerned too.
What is it? Do you know something about him?

Possibly, Muzeni replied, *but it's all tied up with other
matters.* He glanced at the cat, who appeared to have gone
to sleep. *Do we have time to explain properly, my dear?*

I think so, Alyssa grated.

Good. In that case—

Wait! Terrel commanded. Now that he seemed to have
obtained a reprieve, and it was no longer a matter of such
urgency for him to return to Vadanis, he realized he had
other priorities – and the sound of Alyssa's tortured voice
was very distressing. *Are you all right?* he asked her. *Is
being here harming you?*

Not really.

Her answer was not nearly enough to satisfy Terrel.

What do you mean? he asked.

This cat is making it worse, she explained irritably. *He's
hardly a perfect physical specimen, is he? And he's a* cat.
Alyssa disliked inhabiting felines, finding their self-centred
independence hard to tolerate. Ordinarily she would have
sought out another type of creature, but on this occasion
she'd obviously had no choice.

But within yourself, you are well? Terrel persisted.

Well enough, she replied impatiently. *You don't need to
worry about me.*

Yes I do, Terrel thought. And you know why. But he
was forced to accept her inadequate assurances.

Can we get on now? Muzeni asked. For once the usually acerbic heretic sounded concerned, almost gentle, as if he'd been aware of the unspoken part of the exchange.

Let me sleep, Alyssa said. *It's easier then.* She closed her eyes and Terrel turned back to Muzeni.

Go ahead.

Since our last visit, when we found out where you were, we've been able to concentrate our research on the relevant section of the Code. You remember we told you about a 'city of sleepers', where there was something you were supposed to do?

'Setting the ravens free', Terrel quoted, nodding. *We thought that must be a reference to the Raven Cypher.*

What you've just told us confirms that Vergos is that city. We found a passage which mentions a battle against 'the doomsayer'.

He's also called 'the bringer of the death-sleep', Shahan added.

Araguz, Terrel concluded.

A great deal depends on the outcome of that battle, Muzeni went on. *Apparently the Mentor needs the help of the whole city in order to achieve his final purpose.*

But that doesn't make any sense. Terrel was imagining the entire population of Vergos marching, like a crusading army, to the coast. *My final purpose is on Vadanis. How could they help me there?*

We're not sure, Shahan admitted, *but if Araguz gets his way and they're all dead, there's no way they can help you at all.*

Even as ghosts there are limits to what the dead can do, Elam said. He sounded almost apologetic.

Does the Code say anything about how the doomsayer is defeated? Terrel asked.

It doesn't even say he is defeated, Muzeni replied. *Just that there's a battle.*

The healer took a moment to absorb this unwelcome information.

But there must be something *that might help me*, he said hopefully. *Isn't that what the Code is for?*

There are some clues, Shahan conceded. *But I'm not sure how they help you at the moment.*

What he means is, they don't understand them, Elam said.

There are certain anomalies in the text, Muzeni explained. *From our standpoint they don't make much sense, but once you've explored the possibilities here in the city, and especially in the cypher, they may become clearer.*

The references to the Guardian are the most confusing, Shahan said. *At one point the Code seems to indicate that he's fighting against himself.*

Or itself, Muzeni added.

Or themselves, Elam completed.

Terrel was beginning to understand the ghosts' confusion.

Do you think the elementals are opposing each other? he suggested. *Have the other three decided that because the one in Myvatan is so deranged they have to turn against it?*

That seems the most likely explanation, Shahan said, *but we don't see how such a development would affect what happens here. And in any case, there are further complications.*

Oh, wonderful, Terrel thought. That's just what I need.

There are mentions of several alliances, which are very difficult to interpret, the seer went on. *Both sides in the battle evidently have some outside help, and there's an indication that one of the Guardian's allies – which we would normally translate as the Mentor – needs to make a sacrifice in order for them to defeat their enemies.*

What sort of sacrifice?

It's hard to tell, Muzeni replied, *but it seems to have something to do with a painted shield, and with the maker of that shield.*

Actually, the literal translation is 'father of the shield', Shahan put in with a mystified shrug.

And the shield is supposed to come from Tindaya and is 'imbued with sorcery', Muzeni went on.

We told you it was complicated, Elam said.

Terrel had encountered several different forms of magical shields before – the sharaken's dome that had sealed the fate of the Talazorian palace, the sandstorm that had protected him and Zahir's team at Makranash, and the wizards' pyramids on Myvatan – but he didn't see how anything like that might apply to his present situation. And certainly none of them could have been said to be 'painted', or to have a father. And none of them had come from Tindaya. It seemed unlikely that *anything* from Tindaya could be in Vergos.

One last thing, Shahan said. *When the battle is over, the winner is told to beware of 'a wall of water'.*

I thought it was a wall of fire? Terrel said, referring to the earlier warning.

That was before you came to the city, Shahan told him. *The water comes afterwards.*

This at least made a certain amount of sense to Terrel. He had managed to cross the lava–filled ravine.

Try to make sense of it all as you learn more here, Muzeni advised.

Or you could just forget all that and figure out a way to win anyway, Elam countered. *As I see it, you've got one huge advantage over this Araguz bloke. He still thinks the confluence is going to happen, and you know it won't.*

Can I afford to wait that long? Terrel queried doubtfully.

If you can defeat him sooner, so much the better, Shahan answered. *But Elam's right. It is a big advantage.*

And right now it's the only one I've got, Terrel thought. He glanced up at Faulk, who was still being as patient and vigilant as ever, and wondered which of his own allies might be destined to play a part in the events that were to follow. At least it seemed that now he would not have to abandon them. Nomar's determination to thwart Araguz had become the healer's own mission too. But although this thought provided him with a small measure of comfort amid all the confusion, Terrel had the feeling that the ghosts still had more to tell him.

Has anything else changed since we last talked? he prompted. *Are the islands still slowing down?*

Yes, they are, Muzeni confirmed. *And people in Makhaya are starting to panic.*

We're trying to work out where the islands might finally come to a halt, Shahan added, *but at the moment the changes are too erratic. The probability is that it'll be somewhere reasonably close to the coast of Kenda, which is good news.*

So the pendulum really is *coming to a stop*, Terrel marvelled. *Do you know when it'll happen?*

The seers exchanged another significant glance. Here it comes, Terrel thought, as fresh dread welled up inside him.

We have a fairly good idea, Muzeni replied, then hesitated, glancing at his colleague.

Just tell him, Elam exclaimed. *He's not a child any more.*

The bad news is that even though Araguz may have got the timing wrong, Shahan said, *he could well be right about the rest. The confluence won't be as soon as he thinks, but it* is *coming, and when it does it's possible the associated upheaval will be so great that all Nydus will be destroyed.*

The world *is* going to end, Terrel thought. That's when the pendulum will stop, when the moons line up and the Ancients decide our fate.

The time of change is coming to an end, Muzeni said, *and when it does there may be nothing of any worth left. The alteration in the orbit of the Dark Moon signalled the start, and the confluence will mark its final moments. The slowing of the pendulum – and the shorter than usual time between four-moon alignments – are both described, and provide confirmation of what we expected from the rest. This is what the apocalyptic vision in the Code describes.*

There are cycles within cycles, Shahan said, taking up the story. *Days, the various months, the seasons and the years – all fitting into neat patterns, one within the other. But some cycles are too big to be seen, because a human life span is just too short for us to notice them. It's one of these that is coming to an end.*

How do you know all this? Terrel asked bleakly.

It's in one of the new sections of the Code, Muzeni replied. *From the fountain room. Once we began translating it, it became clear enough. Whoever wrote the Tindaya Code, this is what they were afraid of – and what they were trying to warn us about. They failed to prevent a catastrophe. We can't afford to.*

Memories rose unbidden to the surface of Terrel's mind: the remains of an ancient fish embedded in rock halfway up a mountain; the crystal hill that had been split in two; the broken bridge – and all those remnants of vanished civilizations that he'd seen during his travels on Nydus, all the physical evidence of an unimaginable cataclysm that had happened before and was about to happen again. Which led him to the most obvious question of all, the one he was afraid to ask.

Do you know when it's going to be?

One hundred and thirty-seven days from now, Muzeni replied.

Terrel was taken aback by the precise nature of the answer. And by the fact that it was so soon. He'd been hoping it would still be years away.

You're sure of this?

As sure as we can be. The calculations have been done meticulously this time, and . . . there's another reason for us to be sure it's correct.

It predicts a date that's exactly twenty-five years after the night of your birth, Shahan explained. *That can't be a coincidence.*

Twenty-five, not seventy-five, Terrel mused, feeling numb.

You have to get back to Vadanis by then, Muzeni said. *To Tindaya, to be exact. That aspect of the prophecy hasn't changed.*

Four and a half median months, Terrel told himself. It was a lot better than eleven days, but it still didn't seem very long.

In the meantime, you've got work to do here first, Elam noted. *Are you up to it?*

I'll have to be, Terrel said, feeling the weight of responsibility threaten to crush him altogether. The fact that he now had the time to help Nomar – which is what he had instinctively wanted to do all along – was only a small consolation.

You'd better be, Elam said. *There are a lot of people depending on you.*

I think Terrel's aware of that, Shahan said quickly. *We don't need to burden him with any more problems.*

No! the healer declared vehemently. *Don't hide things from me, not ever again. Do you understand?*

Elam looked at his elders in mute enquiry. Neither of them spoke. Terrel was about to demand an answer when it came from an unexpected source.

There are too many links, Alyssa said. *Palace to palace. Whatever happens over the next few months is going to affect their world as well as ours.*

Is that true? Terrel was horrified. The one thing that softened the blow of any human death was the knowledge that there was another kind of life beyond it. If that certainty was taken away, then everything changed. *How will it affect you?*

We don't know for sure, Elam replied, *but it won't be pleasant.*

Unless I can do something about it, the healer whispered.

I'm sorry, Terrel, Shahan said. *I didn't want ... We're all relying on you.*

And we have every faith in you, Muzeni stated robustly. *You've done everything that's been asked of you so far.*

Except heal the Ancient in Myvatan, Terrel thought to himself, but he said nothing.

We've no doubt that you'll succeed, the heretic continued. *This is your destiny, Terrel – and we'll help you as best we can.*

As he spoke, the image of the old man seemed to blur even more than usual, and both Shahan and Elam frowned, wincing as if they were both in pain. The ghosts all glanced at Alyssa. The cat had risen slowly to its feet and was now stretching gingerly, as if wary of extending its muscles and joints too far.

Have to go now, Alyssa croaked.

The ghosts vanished before they had a chance to say another word and, even as Terrel watched, the ring around the cat's ear dissolved into nothing.

Alyssa! he cried, though he was almost sure she could no longer hear him. *Alyssa, I love you. I'll be back with you soon.*

The cat hobbled away, paying him no attention.

CHAPTER TWENTY

Terrel was still fighting the feelings of helpless disappointment and fear provoked by the abrupt departure of his allies when he heard the shiver of sound that meant Faulk had drawn his sword. He turned to see the soldier watching a group of young men who had been approaching – but who'd come to a halt on noticing the unsheathed blade and the menace in Faulk's stare.

'Take it easy, chief,' their leader said, holding out open hands. 'We're not going to harm you.'

'I'd like to see you try,' Faulk growled.

'Put your sword away,' Terrel advised, and as the big man reluctantly obeyed, the newcomers' attention switched to the healer. As always his appearance produced a series of reactions: pity mixed with contempt for his deformities, curiosity and alarm when they noticed his eyes. But this time there was something more, something he could not quantify.

'You should be careful,' the spokesman remarked. 'The guards don't like anyone but them carrying weapons in public places.'

Faulk did not respond, and the young man – who was clearly the most confident of the group and whose face was set in an insolent half-smile – returned his gaze to Terrel.

'We heard you were looking for a way to leave the city.'

'Not any more,' Terrel replied.

Faulk shot him a surprised glance.

'What's made you change your mind?' the newcomer asked.

'I don't see that's any of your business,' Terrel answered.

'It's just that . . . we wanted to come with you if you found a way.'

For a moment the four youths behind the leader looked taken aback, then they nodded their agreement. Once again Terrel knew he couldn't take their reactions at face value. There seemed to be some kind of suppressed excitement in their ranks.

'There's nothing to stop you going by yourselves,' he told them.

'Yes there is. We've tried everything we know,' the young man said, warming to his theme. 'We thought—'

'I'm sorry. I can't help you.' Terrel turned to his companion. 'Let's go.'

'No, wait.'

'Why?'

'We want to talk . . .' the spokesman began awkwardly. His comrades were turning round to look along the quay.

'I think I might be needing my sword after all,' Faulk said quietly.

A moment later a sixth young man appeared around the corner of a storehouse some distance away – closely followed by four uniformed guards. One of the original group beckoned to them, and amid a good deal of pointing and shouting the soldiers began to run towards them.

'I don't like these odds,' Faulk muttered.

'What's going on?' Terrel exclaimed. 'We haven't done anything wrong.' He was completely bewildered now.

'I don't think they care much about that,' Faulk replied.

His blade hissed from its scabbard once more and, beckoning for the healer to follow, Faulk strode towards the group who had waylaid them. Unnoticed by Terrel, they had shifted to block the alleyway that offered the only immediate escape from the dockyard. It took the young men only a few moments to realize that even at five to one the odds did not favour them – and although their leader and two of his cohorts had drawn knives, they scattered rapidly when Faulk threatened them. Ushering Terrel ahead of him and urging the healer to run, the soldier followed, glancing back at their pursuers. He was clearly not worried by the youths, but professional soldiers were another matter – and they were the ones giving chase.

The alleyway opened out into a small square, and by the time Terrel reached it he was already out of breath. They were now presented with several choices. Other than turning left or right, on to a comparatively wide street that ran parallel to the river bank, there were three small alleys on the opposite side of the square, all leading uphill. Faulk pointed to the narrowest.

'We'd be quicker if—' Terrel gasped.

'I want a confined space in case I have to hold them off,' Faulk told him calmly. 'And I'll have the advantage of height too. Go!'

Terrel went. After a few paces the alley turned into a stone stairway with high walls on either side and he pounded up the steps, feeling as if his lungs were about to burst. Behind them the sounds of pursuit were getting closer.

'You go on,' Faulk said when they reached the top of the flight. 'I'll see you back at the house.'

'But—'

'Don't argue. I can take care of them from here. And try to keep your eyes hidden if you can.'

Terrel was about to ask why, but Faulk just pushed him on his way then turned back, sword in hand.

*

An hour or so later, Terrel was crouching among bushes in a tiny, overgrown garden. He had no idea where he was, having lost his bearings some time ago as he'd followed a twisting route through the maze of streets and alleyways that made up much of the city. That was only a temporary problem however. He was more concerned about what might have happened to Faulk. He had heard sounds of combat as he ran, but because he'd known he would be no use in a fight he had obeyed Faulk's edict and got as far away as he could. Eventually, once he was reasonably sure he'd outrun any pursuit, he had slowed his pace, feeling the effects of the unaccustomed exercise. Long years on the road had developed his strength and stamina – he could walk at a steady pace for hours on end – but sprinting was always going to be difficult. His twisted leg was stabbing with pain and he thought the ankle might be swollen inside his specially adapted boot. He dared not take it off to find out in case he couldn't get it back on again. His chest ached too. But all this was a minor concern compared to what felt like his desertion of his friend and protector. For all Terrel knew, Faulk might be lying injured in the alleyway or trapped in a prison cell. He might even be dead. Although the healer fervently hoped none of those things was true, he couldn't help imagining the worst.

As he rested, hoping the garden's owner really was as negligent as its overgrown state made him appear, Terrel tried to work out exactly what had happened. The youths had obviously tried to keep them talking while one of their number fetched the guards, but why should they have wanted to do that? No crime had been committed, so why had the soldiers been interested? And if for some reason he had unknown enemies in Vergos, how could they have known where he was? Faulk's parting instruction implied that someone was indeed looking for the healer in particular, but hiding his eyes from view left him in something of a quandary. He had to be able to see where he was going so covering them wasn't practical, and squinting would only be partially effective – and might draw attention to him in any case. His only alternative was to use the glamour – and the last thing he wanted was to give Jax the opportunity to visit Vergos. Of course he could wait for dark, when remaining unnoticed would be easier, but that was assuming he could find somewhere safe to hide for the rest of the day. Dusk was still a long way off. Why *were* his eyes so important? They were his most distinctive feature, but that only led him back to the question of why his presence should have been of any interest to the guards, and he had no answer to that.

In the end, Terrel stayed where he was for as long as he dared, only moving on when he heard voices coming from the nearby house. Although it was still daylight he didn't want to get caught trespassing, and was beginning to feel the need of taking some kind of positive action. He told himself he'd be careful until he found his bearings again, and that he'd only use the glamour in the direst emergency.

Some time later, when he was beginning to feel a little more confident, he encountered his first problem. Up to that point none of the people he'd come across had paid him any attention, and although he'd kept his eyes downcast there had been times when he'd wondered whether this was really necessary. No one seemed to be regarding him with any suspicion. However, when he turned into yet another narrow alleyway and saw two guards walking towards him from the other end, he knew he was about to come under closer scrutiny. It was already too late to turn and flee. That would be suspicious in itself, and he doubted whether he could outrun another hunting party. That left only the options of disguising himself or finding another way to hide. Even though the soldiers were still some distance away, it would not be long before they reached him. Terrel could see only one chance of escape, and that was a low wooden door a few paces ahead of him on the right-hand side of the passage. Doing his best to look as if he belonged there, Terrel increased his pace and ducked into the opening. He tried the handle, praying it would not be locked and that whoever was on the other side would not raise the alarm.

To his great relief the door opened and he slipped inside, closing it behind him. He found himself in a dark room, cluttered with the sort of unwanted objects that had evidently outlived their usefulness in the house above. Flattening himself against the back of the door, Terrel kept very still, listening for any sound that might indicate he was not alone. But the room remained quiet, and he turned his attention to the guards' approaching footsteps. The two men did not seem to have altered their steady pace and he took this as a good sign. They were talking, and Terrel caught a snatch of the conversation as they passed by – but he was too concerned with the fact that they *were* going by to take much notice of what they were saying. It was only afterwards, when it seemed he was safe once more, that the words replayed themselves inside his head.

'. . . settling old scores.'

'The captain's been told to bring him in, dead or alive.'

'Yes, but who did the order come from? That's what I want to know.'

'No telling these days, is there? I reckon . . .'

The recollection of the phrase 'dead or alive' sent a chill through Terrel. Had the soldiers been talking about him? And if so, who had given the order for his arrest?

Repeating his earlier tactic, Terrel stayed where he was

until his own restlessness forced him to set off again. Although the room did not look as if it were used very often, the fact that the outside door had been left unlocked made him nervous. Finally he made up his mind to open it and peered out. There was no one in sight.

The far end of the alley led out on to a street he recognized and he realized, thankfully, that he was not far from the house where the company was lodging. However, the only reliable way of getting back there was to retrace their steps of the morning, when he and Faulk had seen no reason to conceal their presence in the city and had used the main thoroughfares. Now that Terrel knew roughly where he wanted to go, he could try to find an alternative route – but he knew from experience that once he re-entered the labyrinth of back streets it would be all too easy to get lost again. In the end the desire to rejoin his friends – and hopefully find that Faulk was alive and well – won out over the need for caution and he moved boldly into the flow of human traffic. All went well until he turned the last corner and entered the street that was his goal only to find himself almost face to face with an army patrol. Flight was clearly impractical, there was nowhere to hide – and he was maddeningly close to reaching safety. Instinct took over.

I have blue eyes, Terrel recited silently. Perfectly ordinary blue eyes.

For good measure he made them believe that his right arm was normal and that his legs were perfectly matched. And then he walked past the guards without looking their way at all. Several of the soldiers glanced at him curiously but then looked away again, apparently finding him of no interest.

Terrel had been confident that would be the case. He was more worried about the opening he might have given

Jax. However, there was no sign of the prince – either in the healer's mind or anywhere else – and Terrel began to hope he'd got away with it. The risk seemed to have been worth taking, and once he was safely past the patrol he was able to relax into his own appearance again. And the sanctuary of his lodgings was only a short distance away.

The first thing Terrel thought when he walked into the room and saw that Faulk was there – unharmed – was that he should have known better than to worry on his behalf. The soldier did not appear to have so much as a scratch on him, and was obviously delighted that the healer had also made it back safely. All the others – the entire group was there – seemed glad to see him too.

'We were just about to send out a search party,' Lawren told Terrel, 'but we thought that might just draw attention to you.'

'And Yllen persuaded us you'd get back on your own,' Roskin added.

'I have faith in you,' Yllen stated loyally, 'even if these idiots don't.'

'And now you've saved us the bother anyway,' Lawren concluded.

'And proved me right,' Yllen said smugly.

'We've even saved you some food,' Pieri told him, indicating the remaining portion of what had clearly been a substantial meal. 'Are you hungry?'

Terrel discovered that he was ravenous. He sat down and began to eat, talking between mouthfuls.

'You managed to take care of the guards, then.'

'There were only four of them,' Faulk said simply. There was no false modesty in his words.

'Four?' Lawren queried as the others glanced at Faulk in surprise.

Terrel realized the soldier had not told them the whole story.

'Do you know why they were after me?' he asked.

'It may not have been you they were after,' Faulk replied. 'I've had dealings with Gozian in the past.'

'I thought you'd never been to Vergos before,' Roskin said.

'I haven't. This was a long time ago, during one of his campaigns in the north. He didn't honour the agreement between us, so I took my men and went to fight for the other side.'

'And you didn't think to mention this before we got here?' Pieri exclaimed.

Faulk shrugged.

'It was a long time ago,' he repeated.

'Your men?' Yllen queried. 'Were you a general or something?'

'My rank wasn't important. They followed me because I was their paymaster.'

'And where are they now?' Pieri asked.

'The money ran out, so they went their separate ways.'

'Mercenaries are like that,' Lawren commented dryly.

'It's a more honourable profession than many I could name.' There was heat in Faulk's words for once – the equivalent of blazing fury in anyone else – and no one felt like arguing with him.

'It *could* have been Terrel they were after, though,' Roskin said, returning to the original topic. 'There's a rumour going round that the guards are looking for a stranger with silver eyes. Apparently there's a price on his head.'

Dead or alive? Terrel wondered.

'I overheard one of the boys on the dock telling the guards about your eyes,' Faulk said. 'I thought it was because it would be the easiest way of recognizing you again, but perhaps that's why they tried to corner us in the first place.'

'But how could anyone have known I was even in Vergos?'

'Maybe they didn't at first,' Pieri said. 'But people do tend to notice you. Word could have got around.'

'Either way, you'd better lie low for a while,' Lawren advised.

'But why would Gozian want me arrested?' Terrel persisted. 'I haven't done anything to him.'

'Maybe it's not Gozian,' Nomar suggested. 'Maybe it's Araguz. He seems to wield most of the power round here.'

'But he doesn't know anything about me either!' Terrel objected. 'I mean, I want to see him defeated, but how's he to know that?'

'You want to defeat him too?' Nomar said eagerly.

'Yes.'

'Then you'll be staying?'

'For as long as it takes, yes. I still want to leave as soon as possible, but this is something we have to do first.'

'What made you change your mind?' Lawren asked curiously.

Terrel glanced at Faulk but the big man remained silent, and the healer presumed he'd said nothing about any invisible guides.

'I've discovered something important,' he said, deciding not to answer the question directly. 'Something that changes everything, including my own plans.'

'What?' Nomar asked.

As Terrel hesitated, wondering how best to tell them the news about the confluence, the youngest member of the party answered the question for him.

'The Dark Moon's going to help us, isn't it?' Taryn said.

CHAPTER TWENTY-ONE

Taryn blushed when he realized that everyone was looking at him and he glanced at his father, obviously wondering if his comment had been a mistake.

'Don't be silly,' Nomar reprimanded him mildly. 'The moons don't help people.'

'Actually, he's right,' Terrel said. 'In a way.' And he went on to tell the group that the confluence Araguz was predicting was not going to take place.

'Because the Dark Moon won't be in the right position!' Taryn responded triumphantly.

'That's right,' Terrel agreed, wondering how the boy had reached the same conclusion as the seers.

'How do you know this?' Nomar asked, clearly torn between doubt and hope.

Terrel glanced at Faulk, but once again the soldier's face remained impassive. He would obviously go along with whatever Terrel chose to tell them.

'I studied astronomy with the seers in my homeland. I can read the skies. And I've always had an affinity with the Dark Moon in particular.'

'So you're absolutely sure of this?' Nomar queried.

'Yes, I'm sure.'

'Then that's good enough for me,' Lawren said. 'The question is, how do we use it against Araguz?'

'It's obvious,' Yllen said. 'All you have to do is wait for

the night in question and then challenge him. When people realize he's wrong about the moons, they won't listen to anything else he says.'

'That may be leaving it too late,' Nomar stated grimly. 'If he does what I think he will, the poison will already have been distributed and he may try to force people to drink it anyway. We can't run that risk.'

'And in any case, there's no guarantee we'd get the chance to challenge him,' Roskin put in. 'Why should anyone listen to us when *he's* speaking? That voice of his would drown us out.'

'I may be able to do something about that,' Pieri said, 'but Roskin's right. We'd have to be able to match him in getting the audience's attention. Gozian's not going to give *us* a spot on the castle wall.'

There was a pause while everyone considered this problem. It was Taryn who broke the silence.

'Why does he want to poison everyone?' He sounded puzzled rather than frightened by the idea, and Terrel realized the boy was the only one there who wasn't aware of his father's childhood ordeal.

'I know about him,' Nomar said. 'He's done the same thing in the past.'

'Killed people?' Taryn asked, wide-eyed.

'Yes.'

'Then why wasn't he punished?'

'That's what I've been saying,' Yllen said quietly.

'There was no one left to punish him,' Nomar explained. 'But we're not going to let him get away with it this time. That's what we've been talking about.'

For the moment the boy seemed satisfied, and the discussion resumed.

'A three-moon alignment still makes it a significant night,' Roskin said.

'There could be some tremors,' Lawren added, nodding.

'But not the apocalypse Araguz is predicting,' Terrel said.

'That was never going to happen,' the hunter said.

Terrel chose not to argue with him.

'In a way that's irrelevant,' Nomar said. 'What's important is whether Araguz can persuade enough people to *believe* it's going to happen.'

'And he seems to be doing a pretty good job of it so far,' Roskin said. 'Judging by what we've seen.'

'You mean at the rally yesterday?' Terrel asked.

'That, and from what we've learned today. While you were gazing at the moons and running away from guards, we've all been doing some investigating of our own.'

'Collecting gossip, you mean,' Lawren amended.

'Even gossip has to start somewhere,' Roskin said. 'We should be able to sift the truth from the exaggerations.'

'Even undiluted rumours can be useful,' Pieri added. 'They indicate what people want to believe and, like Nomar says, that could be important.'

'But it's not exactly a reliable source for us to base our decisions on,' Lawren argued.

'Well, for the moment it's all we've got,' Roskin said.

'We have some time,' Pieri said. 'We can try to learn more before we make any move.'

'Tell me what you've heard,' Terrel requested.

'This whole place is crazy,' Lawren muttered.

'Actually, given the circumstances, I'm amazed Vergos *hasn't* gone completely crazy,' Pieri responded.

'What?' the hunter exclaimed in disbelief. 'How can you say that?'

'I'll admit the atmosphere in the city is feverish,' the storyteller said. 'Fearful one moment, almost festive the next – but that's hardly surprising. Given what Araguz has been doing, I'm surprised law and order haven't broken down altogether.'

'The guards are seeing to that,' Roskin commented.

'Yes, but why are they bothering if the world's going to end in a few days? Why is anyone bothering to do anything? Because they *are*. In fact, trade seems to be booming. You must have seen that at the docks.' Pieri glanced at Terrel for confirmation. 'With so many extra people here, the opportunities for making money are endless.'

'Are you saying people don't believe what Araguz is telling them?' Nomar queried.

'I don't think most of them know *what* to believe.'

'There didn't seem to be much doubt in the square yesterday,' Roskin countered. 'You weren't there.'

'As far as I can tell, that seems to be the way of it,' Pieri conceded. 'When the prophet's there in person there aren't any doubts. But it's different when he's not. I've heard all sorts of arguments, and people's memories seem to be distorted, or full of contradictions. They can't even agree on what's been happening during the last few days.'

'But some of them are convinced, aren't they?' Roskin said, sounding defensive.

'Certainly,' Pieri admitted.

'Brioni, for instance,' Yllen said, naming the lady of the house. 'That's why she's filled her home with strangers – including us – and not asked for any rent. She even fed Taryn and me today. *She*'s not bothered about money.'

'That sort of generosity seems to be a common reaction among those who do believe,' Pieri said. 'They think they're going to die so they're trying to prepare themselves by helping others, giving away their possessions and so on.'

'Buying favours with the moons,' Lawren remarked contemptuously. 'For the next world.'

'Is that so ridiculous?' Roskin asked. 'It's certainly better than going to the other extreme. I agree with Pieri. It's amazing there hasn't been a massive outbreak of violence.'

'There's been some,' Pieri said, 'but there always would be in a city this size, especially when it's so overcrowded. And some of Araguz's converts are going mad with despair.'

'Which seems a much more logical reaction to me,' Lawren remarked.

'On the other hand,' the storyteller went on, 'there are some people who clearly don't believe the prophet, and a lot more who are carrying on as normal just in case he's wrong.'

Perhaps Araguz isn't strong enough to exert his influence over all the people all the time, Terrel thought. Perhaps he picks his moments for the greatest impact, and the rest of the time it's only those who are most susceptible to his skills as an enchanter − if that's what he is − who are convinced by him. It was reassuring to think that his enemy's powers might be limited.

'To me the most curious thing is that no one is reacting in the most obvious way of all,' Pieri added.

'Which is?'

'To run away.'

'No one's leaving the city,' Terrel confirmed.

'What would be the point of that?' Yllen queried. 'If the whole world's going to end, you might as well be here as anywhere else.'

'Especially if you think Araguz is going to lead you to Paradise,' Nomar added sombrely.

'And if it's not going to end,' Yllen concluded, 'there are plenty of opportunities here. That's obvious.'

'There might not be for much longer,' Lawren warned. 'Pieri and I did well today − ' he indicated the remains of their meal, ' − but I think food will be in short supply soon and people won't be so generous then. Vergos can't support this many people indefinitely.'

'It won't have to,' Terrel reasoned. 'All the visitors will be leaving in eleven days, one way or another.'

'I'm not sure it can last even that long,' the hunter said.

'Every room in the city is full,' Roskin added, 'and a lot of people are sleeping rough. We were lucky to find this place.' He waved a hand around the room, which had obviously not seen much use for some time before their arrival. The eight of them meant that it was crowded, but at least it was warm and dry – which was better than many of their recent sleeping places.

'And there are more people arriving all the time,' Terrel said.

'The riots we heard about may not be too long in coming,' Lawren predicted, referring back to the gossip at the Haven Inn.

'People are seeing omens everywhere,' Roskin added. 'It's no wonder there are so many rumours flying about.'

'Even if most of them are rubbish,' the hunter commented sourly. 'Almost everything we were told back at Conal's tavern has turned out to be wrong. Gozian hasn't declared himself immortal and there's nothing in the Raven Cypher about buried treasure.'

'What about Kaeryss?' Terrel asked. 'Is she calling herself a goddess?'

'Hardly,' Pieri replied. 'She's in prison.'

'That's what I heard too,' Roskin said.

'Do you know why?'

'I got a different answer from everyone I talked to,' the storyteller replied. 'Some said she was responsible for Gozian's son falling ill, others that she'd angered the king with one of her translations of the cypher.'

'I was told she was at odds with Araguz,' Roskin said. 'That there was a struggle for power in the court and he won.'

'Brioni said she was wicked and wouldn't accept the verdict of the moons – whatever that means.' Yllen shrugged.

'There's another theory going round,' Lawren put in. 'Some people think Kaeryss is the real power behind the scenes here. They reckon she's set Araguz up so that when something goes wrong he'll take the blame and she can take over.'

'But she's in prison!' Roskin objected.

'We don't know that for sure. For all we know she could have started that rumour herself, for reasons of her own.'

'She could even be one of the sleepers, like Karn,' Nomar said. 'That's what some people are saying.'

'Are there many sleepers here?' Terrel asked.

'No one really knows. They're all inside the royal palace.'

'Do you mean that only people inside the court have been affected?' Terrel asked. During his travels elsewhere, the strange affliction seemed to have struck at random.

'Either that or those from the outside were taken in when they fell ill,' Nomar replied.

'Why would the palace do that?' Lawren asked.

'I've no idea. Araguz may have had something to do with it, though. His rise to prominence coincided with when it started, apparently.'

'I don't think that can be right,' Terrel said.

'Why not?' Yllen asked.

'I've come across sleepers in other lands. Places where Araguz has never been.'

Yllen regarded him curiously, a slight smile on her face.

'You keep a lot of secrets inside that head of yours, don't you?' she commented.

'Doesn't everybody?' he responded.

'What we have to decide now is where we go from here,' Nomar stated with dour determination. 'How are we going to stop Araguz?'

'It would help if we could make sense of all these conflicting stories,' Lawren offered. 'There must be some way
to get at the truth.'

'We should make contact with as many people who *don't*
believe Araguz as possible,' Yllen suggested. 'I think we're
going to need all the help we can get.'

Terrel nodded, remembering the ghosts' advice. He was
going to need the aid of the whole city later on, so making
a few allies now could only help. 'Do you think there are
any more like the three of us?' he asked, indicating Nomar
and Roskin as well as himself. 'We weren't taken in by
Araguz when we were at the rally, even though everyone
else seemed to be under his spell.'

'We can't be the only sane people in the entire city,'
Lawren muttered.

'The only way to find out is to wait for his next appearance,' Nomar said.

'Or get inside the palace,' Yllen said.

'How would we do that?' Roskin asked.

'Brioni helped Taryn and I do some exploring of our
own today, and she told us something interesting too.
Taryn, why don't you tell everyone what she said.'

'Brioni has a brother who works as a secretary in the
palace,' Taryn said, obviously pleased to have been
included in the discussion. 'But he's been ill for a long
time. We thought Terrel could volunteer to heal him.'

'If we could get inside the castle, there are all sorts of
things we could learn,' Roskin said eagerly. 'That's where
the Raven Cypher is kept, for a start.'

'And where Kaeryss is being held,' Pieri added. 'It sounds
as if she might be an ally in any fight against Araguz.'

'There's just one problem with that,' Faulk said, speaking for the first time in a long while. 'If what happened
today is anything to go by, Terrel would be arrested as

soon as he shows his face anywhere near the palace. That wouldn't get us very far.'

'Then I'll have to do it,' Nomar responded. 'I can't match Terrel's skill, but I am a healer too.'

Terrel thought about suggesting he go to the palace in disguise. His earlier use of the glamour – and the fact that there had been no subsequent intervention from Jax – had given him a little more confidence. In the end, however, he decided to keep quiet for the moment. He was not ready to take that risk just yet.

'There may be other ways of infiltrating the court,' Pieri said thoughtfully. 'I've played for a few noblemen in my time. Perhaps I should offer my services for the end-of-the-world party.'

'This isn't a joking matter,' Nomar told him sharply.

'I know that, but if people think they're going to die, some of them are going to want to make the most of what time they have left.'

'Exactly how *is* the world supposed to end?' Lawren enquired.

'In an all-consuming fire,' Nomar intoned. 'In the smothering darkness of smoke and dust.'

'Now there's a cheerful thought,' the hunter murmured, looking disgusted.

'It sounds as though Araguz thinks Vergos is going to be hit by a fire-scythe,' Roskin commented.

'Funny you should say that,' Yllen said. 'According to Brioni, this city is built at the centre of a crater formed long ago by a great rock that fell from the sky. The crater's so big that the outer edges are a dozen miles away. One of the local legends says that eventually it's going to happen again.'

CHAPTER TWENTY-TWO

'How did you know about the Dark Moon?' Terrel asked Taryn as the travellers prepared for the night.

'I saw it,' the boy replied, though he sounded uncertain.

'In pictures?' Terrel guessed.

'I think so,' Taryn replied, looking confused. 'When you were talking . . . I just knew what you were going to say.'

'So did the pictures come from my mind?' The healer already knew that Nomar's son could show other people – and animals – his thoughts, and share his father's dreams on occasion. But if he could read the mental images of others without them even being aware of it, he had a rare talent, akin to psinoma.

'I suppose they must have done,' Taryn answered. 'No one else knew about the Dark Moon, did they?'

On impulse, Terrel formed a thought and directed it towards the boy, just as he would have done with Alyssa or the ghosts.

Can you hear me when I talk like this?

Taryn frowned but did not respond, and Terrel changed his approach. Instead of words he conjured up a picture from memory.

'Where's that?' Taryn asked immediately.

'It's the house where I used to live.'

'It's huge! Were your family rich?' The boy had obviously forgotten the conversation when Terrel had told him about having been rejected by his family.

'It wasn't *my* house. That's where I was sent. Lots of people lived there.'

'Is that where you're going back to?'

'Yes,' Terrel replied, thinking of Alyssa lying in a dungeon cell at Havenmoon. 'Yes, it is.'

Some time later, Terrel noticed Faulk and Yllen deep in what appeared to be a serious discussion. Ever since the soldier had refused her offer at Conal's tavern the relationship between the two of them had been rather frosty, with each tending to keep their distance from the other, so their conversation now came as something of a surprise. The fact that they were speaking in hushed tones, so that no one else could hear them, only added to the mystery.

As he watched, they both nodded at the same time and then Faulk looked up and beckoned to Terrel.

'What's going on?' he asked as he joined them.

'You and Faulk need to move,' Yllen said quietly. 'If they're serious about arresting you they'll find this place soon enough. Too many people have seen you here. Brioni, for one. She was asking about you earlier, and if anyone tells her the guards are looking for you I think she'll decide it's her civic duty to hand you over.'

Terrel was dismayed. The house was not the sanctuary he had thought it was, and the fact that Brioni and others had already seen him meant that it would not be safe to stay there even if he chose to use the glamour.

'She's right,' Faulk said. 'I know this complicates matters, but it's just too risky to stay here.'

'You mean we have to go tonight?' Just the thought of it made Terrel feel weary and dejected.

'That would be best,' Yllen confirmed.

'It'll be easier for us to go while it's dark,' Faulk pointed out.

'The rest of us can stay here,' Yllen added, 'and if anyone asks us about you, we'll just say you moved on and we don't know where you are.'

'But where will we go?' Terrel asked. 'Everywhere else is full.'

'I've got an idea about that,' Yllen replied, showing him a pair of large, ornate keys on a solid metal ring. 'You're not afraid of ghosts, are you?'

'It shouldn't be much further,' Yllen said, peering into the gloom at the far end of yet another street.

For some time now the three travellers had been making their way through lanes, many of which had still been bustling even though night had fallen an hour ago. Various lamps and torches had augmented the rusty glow of the Red Moon, which was an almost perfect semicircle in the sky above. For the most part they had kept to the shadows, and as yet no one had paid them any undue attention. In fact most of the glances directed towards them had focused on Yllen, but Faulk's intimidating presence had discouraged anything other than appreciative looks.

Terrel hated having to sneak out on the rest of his friends, but Yllen had pointed out that if any guards came calling, it might be better for them if they really *didn't* know where the fugitives had gone. She had volunteered to act as go-between, letting the two parties know what the other was doing. Terrel had not been able to argue with her logic, but it still felt as if he was abandoning the others, and not telling them where he was going could be taken to imply a lack of trust. When he had said as much, Yllen had promised to explain the situation to them if necessary –

adding that he could rejoin the company at any time when and if they judged the danger to be over.

They had left the house by a back entrance, passing by the stables where Jarek had been installed in the company of several other animals, and on the way out Terrel had thought he'd seen Kephra perched on the eaves. Yllen had led them on a circuitous route that avoided both the docks and the centre of the city. Moving from the residential area to a business district, they had passed various drinking dens, merchants' stores and several houses of ill repute – all of which seemed to be doing a roaring trade. As Pieri had observed, the atmosphere was peculiar, a mixture of frenzied excitement and desperation, and Terrel had been glad when they'd eventually passed into a quieter part of the town. Along the way they had seen several patrols, varying from two to eight guards, but the soldiers had had more than enough to keep them occupied without worrying about three apparently law-abiding citizens.

'There it is,' Yllen said as they reached the latest corner of their route.

She led them into a street even darker than the last, which appeared to be completely deserted. To their left a high wall hid whatever was beyond from the residents of the houses on the other side. Halfway along its length there was a gap in the wall, and it was towards this that Yllen was heading. When they reached the opening, Terrel saw that it was filled with sturdy but finely-wrought iron gates. Yllen tried first one of the keys and then the other in the ancient-looking lock. The second turned easily enough, and she opened the gate and ushered them into the moonlit darkness beyond.

'Welcome to the necropolis,' she said.

*

The cemetery was like a miniature city within a city – except that here all the inhabitants were dead. It was immediately obvious that the resting places within had been reserved for the well-to-do. Even the smallest tombs were built of fine stone and intricately carved, and some of the mausoleums were the size of a small mansion. It was equally obvious that the graveyard covered an enormous area.

'This place is massive,' Terrel said, finding himself whispering even though they were no longer in any danger of being overheard. 'How are we going to find the right one?'

'It should be over to the west,' Yllen replied, glancing up at the sky to check her bearings. 'It has two marble pillars either side of the entrance, and a statue of a white horse on top of the cornice.'

They began to thread their way through the narrow alleyways formed by the sides of the various tombs. It was an eerie netherworld, with touches of both the bizarre and the ominous. Gargoyles leered down from several of the rooftops, walls were decorated with florid inscriptions and carvings depicting scenes from the lives of those interred within, and images of the moons were everywhere, painted in all their various phases upon the stone or plaster. Apart from the interlopers' footsteps the silence was absolute, and the radiance of the Red Moon added a suitably macabre touch to the scene.

At last, as they came out into one of the wider thoroughfares, Yllen came to a halt and pointed.

'There it is,' she said. 'Your new home.' Unlike Terrel, she was obviously finding the entire escapade highly amusing.

'You wouldn't think it was so funny if you had to sleep in there,' the healer grumbled.

'I almost wish I was,' Yllen replied. 'It's not something you get a chance to do every day.' She led the way up the steps and between the pillars to the shadowed entrance. 'Besides,' she added, 'you have a big, brave soldier to protect you in case any phantoms put in an appearance.' She grinned at Faulk, who for once could not help smiling back.

'I'm not sure my skills would be much use against enemies of that sort,' he said.

'I wouldn't worry about it,' Yllen said, feeling for the lock with her fingers and then fumbling with the keys. 'They're probably all perfectly friendly.'

The key turned, making a harsh grating noise that seemed to echo very loudly in the confined space. However, even though it was no longer secured, Yllen was unable to move either side of the solid wooden door. She gave way to Faulk who managed to push them back without apparent effort.

'Big, brave and *so* strong,' Yllen murmured.

Inside, the air was cold and a little musty, but certainly not as unpleasant as Terrel had imagined it might be. It was so dark that they had to shuffle forward, tracing each step by sliding their feet over the smooth stone. Four small windows, high up under the edges of the sloping roof, allowed a tiny amount of moonlight to filter in, and as their eyes adjusted they were eventually able to make out a little more of their surroundings. A set of steps to one side led down into a crypt that was utterly dark, and the upper room was on two levels, with stone coffins lining the platforms on both sides. The centre of the cavernous hall was open, a plain stone floor divided into rectangular sections by ridges of dark metal studs, in readiness for the next members of the family.

'A spacious and elegant residence with guaranteed

privacy,' Yllen announced, her voice made hollow by the enclosing walls.

'It will do,' Faulk said.

'I'll try to bring your bedrolls tomorrow,' she added, serious again. 'You'll just have to make the best of it tonight.'

'We've slept in worse places,' Terrel said. 'We'll survive.'

'I'd better get back,' Yllen said, handing the keys to Faulk. 'You'll have to come and let me out.' She had taken the precaution of locking the cemetery gates behind them. 'Ideally, tomorrow you ought to see if you can find somewhere to keep watch. I'm not sure when I'll be able to come back, but I'll try to make it around dusk.'

Faulk nodded.

'We'll need food,' he said.

'Of course. I'll bring what I can. But if you get desperate you can always come and find us.'

The three of them walked back to the doorway.

'You might need to keep quiet during the day,' Yllen advised them, 'in case there's anyone about.'

'Can we lock ourselves in?' Terrel asked.

Yllen laughed.

'Think about it,' she said. 'Why would you need to lock a tomb from the *inside*?'

'Sorry,' Terrel mumbled, grinning at his own stupidity.

'The doors are so stiff I don't suppose anyone's likely to burst in on you anyway.'

'Won't Brioni miss the keys?' Terrel asked. He presumed that Yllen had stolen them.

'Not unless someone dies,' she replied.

For reasons he could not fully explain, Terrel wanted to delay the moment of her departure, but he couldn't think of anything else to ask her.

'I'll walk you back to the gates,' Faulk said.

'Why, thank you, kind sir.'

'Will you be all right going back on your own?' Terrel queried.

'Oh, yes. I might even see if the whorehouses are hiring any new staff. I'm joking!' she added when she saw the expressions on their faces. 'I do have *some* standards. See you tomorrow, Terrel.'

'I don't like this,' the healer said when Faulk returned.

'You'd like it even less if you got thrown in gaol.'

Terrel could not deny the truth of that. He had been imprisoned in various ways during his travels, and it was never a pleasant experience.

'You really think this is necessary?' he asked.

'Yes,' Faulk replied, and did not elaborate.

'I suppose this means you've decided we can trust Yllen now?' Terrel said a little later.

'I think we can. Right now we don't have much choice.'

'You still believe someone is trying to stop us?'

'Perhaps.'

'Maybe it's Araguz,' Terrel suggested. 'Or Gozian. Do you think it was a mistake to come to Vergos?'

Faulk shrugged.

Terrel had been trying to get the soldier to talk, but it was becoming obvious that an oblique approach would not work.

'This morning, at the docks, you talked about a prophecy. Will you tell me about that?'

In the darkness Terrel could barely see his companion, but he sensed that Faulk had become very still. When he didn't respond, the healer tried again.

'I know you believe your destiny is linked with mine. Is that because of this prophecy?'

'Yes.'

Terrel waited for the soldier to go on, and when he didn't he felt the first stirrings of anger.

'Come on! You can't just— What *is* this prophecy? Where does it come from? And why do you believe it?'

When Faulk finally spoke, his words were so chilling that Terrel wished he had not insisted on an answer.

'I went to an oracle,' the soldier said, 'to learn what I had to do to earn forgiveness for the murder of my brother. My twin brother.'

CHAPTER TWENTY-THREE

'You have a twin?' Terrel gasped. Even as the words passed his lips he knew it was an absurd reaction, but he couldn't help himself. He felt the intangible presence of his own brother hovering in the darkness.

'Had,' the soldier corrected him.

Terrel didn't know what to say. He knew Faulk was capable of violence, and had assumed that he had killed in his time – what veteran soldier hadn't? – but this was different. He would never have imagined that latent violence being turned against a friend, still less a brother.

'I'd never have taken you for a murderer,' he said eventually.

'It wasn't done in cold blood,' Faulk replied, 'and the laws of my homeland did not call it murder, but I know the truth of what I did.'

'Will you tell me about it?' Terrel asked.

'You haven't told me all of your story,' his companion responded. 'Why should I tell you mine?'

It was a reasonable point. There were a great many things Terrel had not told Faulk – or anyone else, for that matter.

'You don't have to tell me if you don't want to, but your story's linked to mine now. Will you at least tell me about the oracle that led you here?'

Faulk considered the request in silence for a considerable time, his body remaining perfectly still so that he became one more shadow among many. Terrel waited as patiently as he could, knowing better than to try to hurry him along.

'The oracle was in the hills above our village,' Faulk said at last, 'but when I went there I knew I'd never go home again.' He paused before continuing. 'There's a pool inside a cave. The level of the water never varies, whether there's been downpour or drought, and for most of the time it's dark in there. It's only on the nights when the White Moon is full that the oracle reflects the future.'

Terrel was immediately reminded of the oracle that had guided his own path when he'd been in Misrah. Then a white hawk had relayed messages with the help of symbols drawn in the sand. The consultation there had also taken place at the full of the White Moon, the moon of logic and precision – and of destiny.

'There are fish within its depths,' Faulk went on. 'They have no eyes and are pure white, like ghosts in a pool of life.'

That last phrase was also familiar to Terrel. He glanced at the circles tattooed on his left hand, even though he could barely see them in the gloom. Hamriya had likened them to ripples spreading out in a pool of water – which to the people of the desert was life itself.

'Ordinarily the pool is still, like a mirror,' Faulk explained, 'but it's when the fish come to the surface and indicate signs carved into the rock next to the pool that the reflections can be read. I was shown the eagle wind, which meant I was fated to travel long and far. In itself it wasn't much of a prophecy, but it was what came after that that led me here.'

The soldier was silent again then, and although Terrel knew it was still not time for him to speak his thoughts were racing. One of the symbols he'd seen at the oracle had been a bird the Toma called 'the eyes of the wind', and in the healer's mind it was forever linked to Zorn, another soldier who had suffered torments. Terrel had been able to help him, and hoped he could do the same for Faulk. But first he had to hear the rest of the story.

'I was told to seek out the man who carried the star beneath the water. It's the sign you wear on the cord around your neck.'

Terrel had not even been aware that Faulk had noticed the clay tablet he wore as a pendant. The nomads of Misrah called the symbol 'the river in the sky', which in that desert land had had special meaning.

'I was to follow that man,' Faulk concluded. 'He would lead me to a place where I could atone for what I had done, and be reconciled with my brother – in spirit, at least.'

If you come with me to Tindaya you may witness the reunion of another set of twins, Terrel thought. Faulk's tale had too many parallels with his own for them all to be coincidences, and he wondered just how much he should tell his companion.

'So now you know,' Faulk said.

'Not everything. You mentioned "invisible guardians" earlier, and something about a warlock.'

'They're creatures from another realm,' the soldier replied uneasily. 'Your friends and your enemies. I know nothing more of them. My skills are of this world.'

Terrel already knew who his friends were, and it seemed likely that Jax was the warlock – but there were other possibilities.

'Do you still think I have enemies in this world?'

'Why else are we in here?' Faulk replied.

Terrel began to laugh. He couldn't help himself.

'What's so funny?' Faulk sounded bewildered now – which only made the healer laugh all the harder.

'We're living in a *tomb*,' Terrel gasped when he was finally able to speak. 'Have you ever done anything like this before?' The absurdity of their situation had hit home with full force. 'Can you imagine the reaction of anyone outside who heard me laughing just now?' The thought of this threatened to start him off again and he knew he was teetering on the brink of hysteria.

'We'd better hope they didn't,' Faulk said. 'They might come to investigate.'

'They'd be more likely to run for their lives.' The bubble of hilarity that had filled Terrel's chest slowly deflated and his mood became as sombre as their abode.

'It's going to be a long night,' Faulk observed. 'We should try to get some sleep.'

As Terrel lay on the unforgiving surface of the stone, his thoughts churned, giving him no chance of any genuine rest. The fact that he was sharing his sleeping quarters with a murderer – or at least someone who thought of himself as such – and an unknown number of skeletons did not really bother him, but several other things did. So much had happened that day, and most of it had been unpleasant.

It was true that the ghosts' news about the timing of the confluence had been welcome, but the fact that it was now due to arrive on his twenty-fifth name-day meant that the seers in Makhaya would know it was twenty-five years after *Jax*'s birth. Because they still thought he was the Guardian, the prince would be expected to play his part in whatever events took place then. He too would be at Tindaya, and the vision Terrel had had of his own death there was now one step closer to being realized. It was not an encouraging thought.

Thinking back over the ghosts' visit, and about what

they had said, Terrel realized he had not told them about Jax's appearance in Kenda. Nor had he had the time to ask about what was happening on Vadanis and what the prince was doing there. His allies had at least helped clarify his plans for the next few days – although opposing Araguz was already imposing extra difficulties – but their abrupt departure had left him feeling sick with apprehension. It was obvious that they had somehow been forced to go, rather than leaving of their own accord, and the implications of that were unnerving.

Then there had been the discovery that he was being hunted by the guards, and the subsequent game of hide-and-seek that had eventually led him back to his fellow travellers. Their discussions had yielded some comfort, and a slightly better idea of what they were to do next, but running out on them later now made that alliance less than certain. All Terrel could do was hope that the others would understand his motives, and that Yllen could persuade them that they still needed to work as a team.

The idea of infiltrating Gozian's court somehow still seemed their best option, and Terrel had another reason – one he had not mentioned to the others – to think so. He remembered being told about the mention in the Tindaya Code of a meeting with a 'worldly king'. But how was this meeting supposed to take place if he was stuck here in a cemetery, leaving others to do all the work? It was even possible that he was *meant* to be captured and taken to the castle, and that his hiding here was only delaying his progress. Instinct told him this wasn't true, but logically he could not explain why. All he knew was that Gozian's palace might house people who were meant to be his allies as well as others who were his enemies. However, he had no way of telling which were which. He needed to defeat

Araguz; that much was plain. But who were the healer's allies and who were the prophet's?

It proved to be a very long night. And a cold one. When Terrel woke from a fitful sleep he was stiff and sore, and his hands felt like ice. The pale light of dawn was filtering down from the windows and he was able to see that Faulk was already awake, silently pacing up and down and flexing his arms. Terrel got to his feet and followed the soldier's example, groaning as he tried to warm frigid limbs. As he moved he was able to study his surroundings in a little more detail, picking out some of the carvings on the tombs. He couldn't make out any of the inscriptions, but a few of the relief sculptures were self-explanatory. One depicted a warrior on horseback, another a chariot race, while a third showed a woman surrounded by a stylized frieze of ponies. Horses had obviously played a major role in Brioni's family's history.

Once he had restored his circulation as best he could, Terrel began to wonder about what he was supposed to do now. Faulk had stopped pacing and was standing by the door, listening. Neither man had spoken so far, and the healer did not want to be the first to break the silence, so he took his place beside the soldier and tried to read the intentions on his shadowed face – with a predictable lack of success. Eventually he couldn't wait any longer.

'What are we going to do?' he whispered.

'I can't hear anything outside,' Faulk replied. 'I'm going to take a look around.'

'I'll come with you.' Terrel wanted to escape from the confines of the vault.

'It would be better if you stayed here,' the big man replied. 'For now, at least.'

He did not bother to explain his reasoning and Terrel

didn't need him to. Faulk was much more likely to be able to escape detection or capture if anyone else was about.

'I won't be long,' the soldier told him, then turned his attention to the door. Opening it gradually to minimize any noise, he slipped out and closed it again, shutting out what seemed like a very bright morning.

Terrel was left with only the dead for company.

Faulk was as good as his word, returning in less than half an hour, but that time had passed very slowly for Terrel. Each moment seemed to make the stillness and gloom more oppressive, and although he listened hard he couldn't hear anything from the outside world.

When the door grated open again, the healer jumped violently. Try as he might, he had not detected Faulk's approach. Quite how the soldier's boots could move over the stone steps without making a sound was a mystery to Terrel, but once he had recovered from the shock he was very glad that his companion was back. He was also pleased when Faulk did not immediately close the door again.

'We might as well have a bit of light and fresh air,' Faulk said. 'There's no one about.'

'Obviously no one rich enough has died recently,' Terrel said, hearing an unpleasant edge of hysteria in his voice.

'They're probably all waiting to see out the next ten days,' Faulk said. 'To decide whether it's worth being buried properly.'

It was such an uncharacteristically flippant remark that Terrel found himself at a loss for words.

'Either way it's good for us,' the soldier added. 'And I've found another hiding place, overlooking the gates, so we can watch for Yllen. We won't go thirsty either. There's a small fountain two rows over.'

'No food, I suppose?' Terrel asked. He was being facetious, but Faulk took the question seriously.

'Not that I've seen so far. I'll keep looking, but I think we'll have to rely on Yllen for our next meal.'

Dusk began to seem a long way off.

As the day wore on Terrel became increasingly frustrated and restless. He had ventured outside and done a little exploring, but that had not satisfied his need to be doing something positive. After his years of travelling, merely waiting, without purpose, was alien to him.

'This is ridiculous,' he complained to Faulk. 'I might as well be in prison for all the good I'm doing skulking about here.'

'Except that this is a prison you can walk out of whenever you want to,' his companion said, tapping the keys at his belt. 'When the time is right.'

'Do you always have to be so logical?'

'Would you rather I was illogical?' Faulk queried mildly. Terrel stared at him, then shook his head.

'Soldiers do a lot of waiting around,' Faulk added. 'You learn to make the most of it. Besides, Yllen should be here soon.'

'I hope so.' Terrel's stomach rumbled, emphasizing the point. Doing nothing was making him very hungry.

'I'm going to keep watch.' Faulk had already shown the healer the spot he had chosen for lookout duty. It was on the top of one of the larger mausoleums, reached by a narrow staircase. It was a place where they could remain in hiding, or make their escape back to their own tomb if anyone other than Yllen appeared at the gate. 'Will you wait here?'

'I'm going to get a drink,' Terrel replied, needing action of some kind. He was not really thirsty, and the first time he'd drunk from the stone fountain he had felt a little odd. It was not just that the water was so cold it burnt his lips; the fact that it sprang from a graveyard had been enough to make him queasy. However, it had tasted clean and fresh, and he had even forced himself to splash a little over his face and hands. 'Then I'll come back here.'

Faulk nodded, and the two men set off in different directions.

When Terrel reached the bubbling fountain he did not stop there but wandered on aimlessly, half-heartedly studying the various monuments. As dusk approached he returned to their hiding place, knowing that Faulk would worry if he stayed away too long. They had left the door ajar because the healer found it difficult to shift on his own, and Terrel slipped inside. As soon as he did so he froze, realizing that something had changed. Although there was no sound, no sign of any movement, he knew he was not alone. Faulk would have had no reason to hide, and for a brief moment Terrel wondered if Alyssa and the ghosts had come to meet him. An instant later that hope vanished in a sudden flare of light. The taper burned brightly in the gloom, then settled down as it was applied to the wick of a candle. In its glow Terrel saw an old man sitting on the floor, leaning back against one of the coffins. He seemed quite at ease, and his straggly beard and disreputable clothes made it obvious that he was not a representative of the authorities. He didn't appear to be armed, and when he looked up Terrel sensed the laughter hidden in his eyes.

'I think I preferred your previous lodgings.' The voice was frail and querulous, but beneath that Terrel recognized the humour behind the comment. It was so much like something Elam would have said that he wondered if the old man was a ghost – but he seemed much too solid for that.

'How did you get in here?'

'Oh, there's always more than one way into a place like this,' the stranger replied casually. 'And you left the door open. Careless, that.'

'Who are you? What do you want?'

'I'm a friend,' the old man replied. 'And I rather think this meeting is to help you get what *you* want, not me.'

The newcomer smiled, displaying uneven, discoloured teeth, and beckoned Terrel forward into the candlelight.

CHAPTER TWENTY-FOUR

Terrel stood where he was and glanced back through the open doorway. There was no sign of Faulk's return.

'Your companion won't be back for a while yet,' the old man said. 'Besides, it would be better if we kept this between the two of us – for now, at least.'

Terrel was utterly confused by this latest development. He sensed no threat in the stranger, and yet he didn't like the suggestion that his visit should be kept secret from Faulk.

'Why should I do that? He's my friend, after all – and I've no idea who you are.'

The newcomer smiled at that, but his next question was unnerving.

'You have quite a few people travelling with you. Are they all your friends?'

'Yes.'

'Just how sure of that are you?'

'I have no reason to doubt any of them,' Terrel stated loyally, even as a traitorous memory reminded him of his earlier misgivings over the travellers' motives.

'I hope you're right,' the old man said blithely. 'But in your situation it would pay to be on your guard.'

'What do you know about my situation?'

'People who have nothing to hide don't usually choose to sleep in a tomb.'

The logic of that statement was unanswerable, and Terrel was still at a loss. Part of him wanted to leave and go in search of Faulk, but he was sure that if he did so the stranger would be gone when he returned – and he had the feeling he could learn something from the old man. Common sense warred with curiosity.

'In any case, the big fellow may not have your perceptive nature,' his visitor added, apparently reading the healer's thoughts. 'He might not trust me.'

'Why should *I* trust you?'

'Because you want to. And because I'll prove my worth.'

'How?'

'Come and sit down. I'm getting a crick in my neck from looking up at you all the time.'

Curiosity prevailed. Terrel moved forward into the glow of the candlelight and sat down opposite the old man, who began talking without any further prompting.

'Gozian isn't the only one who's been looking out for your arrival, and I've—'

'What does Gozian want with me?' Terrel cut in.

'He thinks you may be able to heal his son. Though I doubt anyone can do that.'

'But how did he even know about me? I've never been here before.'

'Do you not know about the Raven Cypher?'

'I've heard of it.'

'Well, one passage refers to a "silver-eyed foreigner" who will arrive at a time of crisis and enable "the kingdom's heir" to join his parents. And you are a healer, aren't you?'

'Yes,' Terrel conceded, 'but if the prince is a sleeper, there's nothing I can do for him.'

'I told Kalmira that, but she wouldn't listen.'

'Who's Kalmira?' Terrel was sure he'd heard the name

before but at that moment he couldn't place it.

The old man looked surprised, then saw that Terrel's puzzlement was genuine.

'Gozian's wife,' he said. 'The Queen.'

It was the healer's turn to be taken aback, but before he could respond the visitor chuckled and explained.

'I don't look much like your idea of a courtier, do I? But you'd be surprised where a man of my talents finds himself on occasion.'

'What exactly *are* your talents?' Terrel asked, not sure whether to believe him or not. His words had the ring of truth, but he certainly didn't look like the confidant of a queen.

'I'm not in the habit of revealing trade secrets,' the old man replied. 'Let's just say there are ways into the royal palace that are open to me – which might be of use to you, don't you think?'

Terrel was still bewildered by the fact that a complete stranger knew so much about him.

'How did you find me if Gozian couldn't?' he asked.

'I have my spies everywhere,' his visitor replied with a gap-toothed grin. 'And they're a lot less clumsy than the royal guards.'

Terrel couldn't tell if he was joking or not.

'You know they tried to arrest me?' he queried.

'Yes. Some of them may have been a little overzealous in their efforts, but that's hardly surprising given what's going on at the moment. The balance of power within the palace keeps shifting.'

'Because of Araguz?'

For the first time the old man looked puzzled.

'Araguz?' he queried.

'That's the prophet's real name.'

'Really?' The laughing eyes sparked with interest – and

something more. 'I didn't know that. So the Ravens' Voice is human after all.'

From the way he spoke his enmity towards the prophet was obvious, and Terrel debated whether to tell him more, deciding against it for the moment.

'I knew you'd be worth meeting,' the old man said, thoughtful now. 'I wasn't sure until you changed your appearance and hid your eyes from the patrol. Then I knew I hadn't been wasting my time.'

'You saw that?' Terrel asked. The stranger seemed to have been everywhere.

'Let's just say I felt it. And I wanted to see you for myself before . . .' His voice died away.

'Before what?'

'Your friends are coming back. Be careful what you tell them.'

Terrel glanced towards the door and caught the sounds of a murmured conversation, still distant but coming closer.

'Watch for the fire between the horns,' the old man added.

'What?'

His visitor got to his feet without replying and blew out the candle. Terrel was blinded by the sudden darkness, but he heard the shuffle of feet as the old man moved away. As far as the healer could tell he was walking not towards the door but further into the tomb.

'Aren't you going to tell me your name?' Terrel called softly.

'You already know it,' came the fading reply. And then there was only silence.

A short while later Terrel was sitting on the steps outside the mausoleum in the company of Faulk and Yllen. He was still wondering whether to tell them about his peculiar visitor. Was the old man an ally – as Terrel wanted to believe? Or was he an enemy intent on tricking him? Perhaps he was simply a madman whose meanderings meant nothing. The healer suddenly wasn't sure of anything any more. He wasn't even sure he trusted his fellow travellers now.

He also couldn't help wondering where the stranger had gone. It was possible he was still hiding somewhere in the tomb behind them – though Terrel didn't believe that. There had to be another way in, and he was determined to find it later.

However, for the time being he was too busy devouring the food Yllen had brought. And in any case, she was doing enough talking for all three of them, having assumed that she was the only one with any news to relate. She had already described how the others had reacted to Terrel's departure. Nomar had apparently been quietly aggrieved and obviously disappointed, while Taryn had been upset. Roskin had been furious for a while, demanding in vain to be told where the healer was, but both Lawren and Pieri seemed to have accepted the new situation readily enough, though they too were clearly unhappy at their exclusion. However, the necessity of Terrel's flight had been brought home to them earlier that day.

'The guards came soon after daybreak,' Yllen reported. 'There were only two of them, and at first they didn't seem to be taking their duties very seriously. But as soon as Brioni told them about you their attitude changed. We were all questioned, and we stuck to the story we'd agreed earlier – that you'd left in the night, probably to get a ship, and none of us knew where you were.'

'Did they believe you?' Faulk asked.

'They seemed to. Even Taryn was convincing. Of course

I was the only one who actually *did* know where you were – and lying is one of my many talents! In any case they didn't seem to think it was worth arresting anyone. The strange thing is, the guards didn't give the impression they were looking for a criminal, but rather for someone their commander wanted to meet. They even said it would be to your benefit if you were found.'

'That's not the impression I got yesterday,' Faulk snorted.

'In the end they just gave up and went away,' Yllen continued. 'They posted sentries to watch the house, though – in case you came back, I suppose.'

'Are you sure no one followed you here?' Faulk asked anxiously.

'Absolutely. They didn't even see me leave. Well, they did, but they didn't know it was me.' She was wearing servant's clothes, presumably borrowed from someone in Brioni's household. 'I was just going about my business and taking Jarek along to carry the load.' The mule was tethered nearby, standing perfectly still with the stoic patience of its kind. 'No one took any notice of me, and with the route I took I'd certainly have noticed if anyone was following me.'

With the mule's assistance she had been able to bring not only food and drink but also the fugitives' packs and bedrolls. The night ahead promised to be a lot more comfortable than the last.

'But that's not all that happened today,' Yllen went on, eager to impart the rest of her news. 'We've all been out and about, seeing what we could learn. For a start we found that the guards are looking for someone with silver eyes because he's mentioned in the Raven Cypher. Can you believe that?'

I *can* believe it, Terrel thought. This confirmation of

part of the old man's tale made him more inclined to believe the rest.

'You don't seem very surprised,' Yllen remarked. 'You're in the prophecy!'

'If it is him,' Faulk said.

'Who else could it be?' she exclaimed.

'Does the cypher say anything about what I'm supposed to be doing here?' Terrel asked.

'I don't know,' Yllen replied. She seemed disappointed by their reaction. 'It must say something, but the people I talked to didn't give me any more details.'

'Any news of when Araguz is likely to make his next public appearance?' Faulk asked.

'No. But apparently they've been getting more frequent recently, so it'll probably be soon. A lot of people seem very confused about how they feel about him, and the ones who don't believe in him, who don't like what he's doing, are reluctant to talk to strangers.'

'Fear is a powerful weapon,' Faulk commented.

'Of course those who *are* convinced by Araguz react quite differently,' Yllen went on. 'They believe that they're doomed and that he's the only one who can save them. Brioni would do anything he told her to.'

'Including killing herself with poison?'

'I'm sure of it. All he'd have to do was assure her it was the only way to survive the disaster and move on to the next world.'

'But the disaster isn't even going to happen,' Faulk objected.

'*We* know that,' she replied, 'but they don't. Brioni refused to listen when I suggested that the confluence might not take place as predicted.'

'There must be sky-watchers in the city,' Terrel argued. 'People who could calculate the orbits accurately.'

'Vergos has always relied on the king's star-gazers to tell them about the moons,' Yllen answered, nodding. 'But no one's heard from them for some time. Apparently Kaeryss took over that role for a while, but since Araguz came no one's listening to her either.'

'So we're back where we started,' Faulk concluded. 'Until we can talk to someone inside the court we're not going to get any reliable information.'

'I've got some news about that too,' Yllen said. 'Nomar's talked to Brioni about trying to heal her brother. Even though she thinks he's going to die along with everyone else, she seems to believe it will benefit his spirit in the next life if he can be healed first. They're going to try to get into the castle tomorrow. It may not be easy, though, even for her. Security's pretty tight. Pieri found that out when he offered his services to the court. The guards sent him packing without even consulting their superiors. However . . .' She paused, her expression unreadable for once.

'What?' Terrel prompted.

'I'm not sure whether this is good news or bad, but Roskin did find a way to get inside the palace.'

'How did he manage that?' Faulk asked.

'Simple, really,' she replied. 'He got himself arrested.'

CHAPTER TWENTY-FIVE

'You mean he got himself arrested deliberately?' Terrel asked in amazement.

'That's exactly what I mean,' Yllen replied. 'At least, I think so. I don't know how else to explain it.'

'Why would he do that?'

'Somehow he got the idea into his head that they'd put him in prison near Kaeryss. He's obsessed with meeting her.'

'The man's an idiot,' Faulk muttered, sounding utterly disgusted.

'How did it happen?' Terrel asked.

'I'm not sure,' Yllen said. 'I only saw it from a distance. To give him his due, Roskin made sure none of the rest of us were implicated. He approached a group of guards, said something that made them angry, and they just marched him away. Pieri and I followed them to the palace gates. That was the last we saw of him.'

'You realize this may put you in danger,' Faulk told her. 'He doesn't know where we are, but he knows *you* do.'

'They may not connect him with us,' Terrel said.

'You want to take that chance?' the soldier replied, then turned back to Yllen. 'You must be careful. Watch your step.'

'Do you think Roskin would betray me?' she asked, sounding genuinely hurt by the idea.

'He may not have any choice,' Faulk answered grimly, his meaning obvious. 'He doesn't seem the type to withstand too much interrogation.'

'Well, I won't tell them anything even if they do catch me,' Yllen declared.

Faulk paid her the compliment of not contradicting her, though for once Terrel could read the thoughts in the big man's eyes.

'Whether you do or not doesn't really matter,' the soldier said. 'You're the only one who knows where we are, so if you couldn't come – either because you're in prison or being watched – we'd have to come out sooner or later, to find food if nothing else. We may have to consider—'

'Actually, Yllen isn't the only one who knows we're here,' Terrel said abruptly. During the conversation he had been considering his own dilemma – which finally boiled down to a single question. Do I trust these people? And he realized that he did. Despite the old man's warnings, he'd succeed or fail with the allies he already had.

'What do you mean? Who have you told?' Yllen asked. She and Faulk were both staring at the healer.

'No one,' he replied, then went on to tell them about his strange visitor.

Faulk immediately went to search the mausoleum. He went down into the crypt too, exploring every crevice and compartment. At one point Terrel and Yllen even heard the grating of stone as Faulk tried – without success – to prise open one of the coffin lids. Terrel did not expect him to find anything and eventually that proved to be the case.

'Well, he's not here now,' the soldier reported, brushing cobwebs from his hair and sleeves, 'however he got in or out. There's no other entrance that I can see.'

'Are you sure you didn't dream it?' Yllen asked.

'I know the difference between a dream and reality,'

Terrel replied. Most of the time at least, he added to himself as he remembered some unnerving experiences from his past.

'He was real enough,' Faulk confirmed. He too had taken Yllen's facetious question at face value. 'I could still smell smoke from the wick, and there were a few spots of candle wax on the floor.'

'So who *is* he?' she asked. 'And more to the point, is he really a friend?'

'If he was an enemy, he could have led the guards here by now,' Terrel pointed out.

'That counts in his favour,' Yllen conceded, 'but it might just be a matter of time. He could be waiting for night, when you won't be so alert.'

'It's not always easy to get the ear of anyone in authority quickly,' Faulk said. 'Especially when the army's involved.' He sounded as if he was speaking from personal experience.

'But he came alone in the first place,' Terrel argued. 'He could have brought the guards with him then.'

'Perhaps he was just testing you,' Faulk suggested. 'We don't know anything about this man.'

'So what it comes down to,' Yllen concluded, 'is whether you should move or not.'

'What would be the point?' Terrel asked. 'He found us here and we've no idea how. What's to stop him doing it again?'

'It sounds to me as if you *want* to trust him,' she commented.

'I do,' the healer agreed. 'I'm just not sure I should.'

'Well, if you do move to another tomb, you can still keep a look out for me. Otherwise we'll lose contact altogether. I ought to go.' She sounded reluctant, obviously wanting to stay and discuss the situation further, but Faulk nodded and stood up.

'I'll take you back to the gates,' he said.

'I hope you're right about him,' Yllen told Terrel as she got to her feet. 'I've got the feeling we're going to need all the help we can get.'

Terrel was left alone with his thoughts as darkness closed in. The sky above was clear, promising a cold night and a frosty morning, and he was glad that he now had his bedroll and some spare clothes to keep himself warm. A shooting star streaked across the heavens as he looked up. Once a sign of wonder and beauty, it now seemed an omen of ill fortune, and Terrel lowered his gaze.

Faulk was away longer than expected, and when he reappeared, a ghostly figure in the light of the newly-risen White Moon, Terrel had already moved their belongings inside the tomb.

'So we're staying put?' the soldier deduced.

'For tonight at least.'

Faulk accepted the decision without argument, but then spent some time spreading sand and grit on the steps outside the mausoleum, and also on the floor in several places inside, treading on each spot with his boots to test the sound of his alarm signals. Terrel knew that if the old man – or anyone else – came to their resting place that night, Faulk would be ready for them.

Terrel found himself standing in a large and richly furnished hall lit by more than a dozen oil lamps hanging from brackets on the walls. Such profligate use of light spoke of great wealth, and this impression was reinforced by the great blaze in a fireplace big enough to roast a whole ox. The opulence of the setting was enhanced by a variety of tapestries on the walls, the elegance of the timbered roof, and not least by the huge table of inlaid wood that dominated the centre of the room. The table was flanked by several finely crafted chairs, but only one – the largest – was occupied. The man who sat there was perhaps a decade older than Terrel. He wore a tunic of fine leather, and several of his fingers were adorned with gold rings. His face was set in a stern but thoughtful expression, his small dark eyes staring into space. A thin mouth was surrounded by a thick but neatly trimmed beard, and his black hair was cut short. To the healer he looked like a man who would be quick to anger and slow to forgiveness.

Standing behind his chair was a woman who was as elegant as the setting. Although her eyes were downcast in an attitude of subservience, Terrel could see that her face was beautiful and that the gown she wore, while simple in design, matched her grace and refinement. There were several other people in the room – all richly dressed – standing on the opposite side of the table from Terrel, but no one seemed to be paying him any attention and he did not recognize any of them. All eyes were fixed upon the seated man, who was clearly master of all around him. No one spoke to interrupt his deliberations. Finally he stirred and looked up at one of his courtiers.

'You risk much in questioning the decrees of our prophet.' Although the words were softly spoken, their menace was all too obvious.

'I do not do so lightly, sire,' the man replied. 'Our calculations . . .' He hesitated, glancing round at his robed colleagues – obviously hoping for some support – but none of them would meet his gaze. Before he could continue, a new voice from just behind Terrel's left shoulder captured the attention of the room.

'Calculations? How can mere computation stand against augury? Against fate?'

Terrel glanced round in sudden terror. The powerful,

arrogant voice was instantly recognizable. The presence of its owner had been unnerving even when Terrel had been some distance away, but now, as Araguz stepped forward, he was within touching distance.

From close to, his silver-grey eyes shone with an almost feral intensity, and the dark tattoos on his cheeks writhed like snakes. Terrel wanted to move away but found that he was rooted to the spot. Like everyone else, Araguz seemed unaware of the healer's presence.

I know the difference between a dream and reality. That claim now had a somewhat hollow ring to it. What's happening? he wondered. Is this a dream? He felt a sense of unaccountable amusement enfold him, making the experience even more bizarre.

Then the robed man spoke again.

'No one . . . least of all my colleagues and . . .' he stuttered, 'seek to question the cypher, but surely in such matters there is room for interpretation . . .'

'Interpretation?' Araguz roared, making his adversary start violently. 'You seek to quibble with *destiny*?'

'It is a matter of timing, not—'

'The time is set,' the prophet declared. 'It was set in stone centuries ago and the moons will confirm its accuracy, just as *I* have foretold.'

'With all due respect—'

'You know nothing of—'

'Silence!' The comparatively quiet voice of the seated man cut short the confrontation in an instant, slicing through their bluster like a sword.

Terrel had long since come to the conclusion that the man, whose air of authority dominated the room, could only be Gozian. He had a king's belief in his own infallibility but, unless Terrel was very much mistaken, there was a shrewd brain at work behind those fierce eyes. Now, as he pushed back his chair and got to his feet, everyone present – even Araguz – remained silent and still.

'These are important matters,' Gozian said. 'The Raven Cypher has guided the fortunes of this land for countless generations, and—'

The king's words were halted by a knock at the door, and a brief flicker of anger passed over his features.

'What now?' he muttered, then raised his voice. 'Enter!'

Terrel turned with the rest to look as the double doors were pulled back by servants, and his heart skipped a beat when he saw the face of one of the two new arrivals. The smaller of the men was a stranger, but the other was Nomar.

'What do you want, Coretzin?' Gozian snapped. 'Can't you see I'm busy?'

The elderly man looked flustered but was saved from having to answer by Gozian's queen.

'I asked him to come, my lord,' Kalmira said quietly, 'if Nomar here proved to be an effective healer.'

'I see.'

Terrel saw interest and hope spark in the king's eyes.

'I take it all went well, Coretzin?' Kalmira said.

'Yes, ma'am.' The physician had recovered his composure now. 'Secretary Bohem made an immediate and complete recovery. One might even say miraculous.'

'So, healer,' Gozian said. 'Do you think you can cure my son of the sleeping sickness?'

'Some maladies are beyond my skill, sire,' Nomar replied, 'but I will do everything in my power to help your son. However, my efforts have fatigued me and I do not have the strength to make the attempt at this late hour. I ask leave to wait until tomorrow.'

'As you wish,' the king responded, sounding less than pleased but apparently resigned to another delay.

'Thank you, Nomar,' Kalmira said. 'You give us new hope.'

Nomar bowed his head slightly. Throughout the exchange he had stood stiffly erect, holding himself with dignity and a weary pride that made Terrel glad to have helped him nurture his talent. Brioni's brother had obviously benefited from that skill and now, against all expectation, the other healer had gained access to the inner circle of the royal court. Terrel kept waiting for his friend to notice him, hoping he wouldn't give him away, but although Nomar's gaze had passed his way he gave no sign of recognition or even of being aware that someone was standing next to Araguz – for it was the prophet who caught his attention. And in that moment Terrel saw so much pain, so much pent-up rage, that he wondered how the Ravens' Voice did not shrivel up and die on the spot. Conversely, Araguz did not seem to realize he had a deadly enemy in the hall. All his energies were focused on returning to the debate with Gozian and the star-gazers.

'You may go,' the king said to Coretzin and Nomar, and the two men turned to leave. 'Now, where were we?' Gozian's gaze fixed first upon Araguz, then on his robed adversary. 'I think I should at least take a look at these calculations, don't you?'

'Sire, this is . . . unnecessary,' the prophet responded. 'These men are puppets of the sorceress whose misguided auguries have been responsible for so much that is wrong in Vergos. They are charlatans and I will prove it.'

'I must protest, sire—'

'Silence!' Gozian shouted. 'Give me the ledger.'

Something shifted inside Terrel then, and for the first time he wondered how he had come to be where he was. If this was a dream it was unusually vivid and self-contained. Yet what else could this vision be? He was not even sure he was really there at all. And what happened next made him wonder not just whether he was asleep but whether he was also insane.

The shift inside him wrenched him forward and he found himself pointing at Gozian. He had no will of his own now, no control over what was happening. He felt the link being established and grow in strength. The heat came next, pure power filtered and directed along the lines, concentrated with more precision than he had thought possible. He had done the same thing once before, but then it had been a reflexive bludgeoning; this was like the thrust of a rapier.

The healer's sensibilities were revolted by the results of his efforts – and yet he could only watch in horror as they unfolded before him. Gozian's face contorted in sudden agony, one hand clutching at his chest while the other dropped the star-gazer's ledger. He gasped, half choking, then coughed – and smoke issued from his mouth. As he collapsed, Terrel knew that the king's heart had burnt to ashes within his body. The fire-starter's technique that Terrel had once turned back upon Jauron in self-defence had been refined into an appallingly accurate weapon – and at last the healer knew who was responsible for his dream. It was not even *his* dream.

As her husband fell, Kalmira screamed and shouted for Coretzin to return. Then she knelt at the king's side as the other courtiers clustered round. Only Araguz did not move. Instead he turned his head and looked directly at Terrel. The fury in the prophet's glare was incandescent, and there was no mistaking at whom it was directed.

Unlike everyone else in the room, Araguz *could* see Terrel. And knew him to be a murderer.

CHAPTER TWENTY-SIX

Terrel woke to the darkness inside the tomb. It was still night but he knew that sleep was no longer possible. He had to get out into the open air, to see the real world beyond the suffocating confines of his shelter.

Disentangling himself from his bedclothes, he felt for his boots and pulled them on, then edged along the side of one of the stone coffins, moving by sense of touch towards the as yet invisible door. Before he had gone more than a pace or two there was a rustling in the shadows.

'Terrel?' Faulk asked, instantly alert. 'Where are you going?'

'I just need to take a piss,' Terrel replied awkwardly.

'Use the crypt,' Faulk suggested.

'I can't do that.' The healer found the idea unpleasant and even irreverent.

'No one down there's going to mind,' the soldier said in a rare moment of humour.

'I'd rather go outside.'

The door had become a little easier to open through use but it still cost Terrel some effort, and the grating noise sounded very loud in the stillness of the night. Once outside he went no further than the lower steps, where he sat down and let his eyes become accustomed to the starlight. Curiously the air seemed warmer outside than in, even though the sky was still clear, but just at that moment he was not interested in the unseasonable warmth. Even though the dream had released him, it still dominated his thoughts.

It had ended in confusion, with people shouting and running in various directions. Once it had become clear to Kalmira and the courtiers that Gozian was beyond all help, their panic had subsided and been replaced by a deep sense of shock and bewildered grief. Watching helplessly, Terrel had really only paid attention to the words of one man – words that had not even been spoken aloud.

You imbecile! Araguz had snarled. *What have you done?*

He won't be reading the ledger now, will he? Jax had replied smugly. Terrel heard his brother's answer as if it had originated in his own mind.

No, and he won't lead his people into the light of the Dark Star either, the prophet retorted. *If you weren't—*

If I wasn't what? Jax cut in, then began to laugh.

Araguz had said nothing further to his ghostly companion and Terrel had been left as a passive witness to the chaos in the hall. The mood was turning from sorrow and disbelief to anger when the prince had chosen to leave, returning his twin to his own body at the same time.

Thinking about it now, the healer still wasn't exactly sure what had happened, and his mind reeled with questions. Jax had shared Terrel's dreams before, but the healer had never followed the prince on his disembodied excursions. So why had it happened this time? Had it simply been a chance occurrence, or had Jax involved him deliberately? And if so, why? More to the point, could Terrel really believe what he had seen? Had those events actually taken place? It had certainly felt real enough, but with Jax involved it was possible that it had been an elaborate hoax, the sort of trick his brother would have taken great delight in playing. The final possibility was, of course, that it *had* all been a dream, his own dream – and that everything he'd witnessed was just a collection of phantoms from his own demented imagination. It was hard to believe that his mind could have come up with such a convoluted and yet realistic scenario, but Terrel could not rule the possibility out completely.

If, for the sake of argument, what he had seen had actually taken place, the consequences would be both far-reaching and unpredictable. There was no telling what effect the king's sudden death would have upon his people. With the city already in turmoil, it might easily precipitate the breakdown of law and order that Pieri had predicted. On the other hand, the power vacuum it left behind might be filled in several different ways. With Gozian's son and heir a sleeper – but still alive – the succession might well be disputed, and Terrel sensed that Kalmira and Araguz were not the best of friends. The prophet might well take this opportunity to strengthen his own hold on Vergos. However, it was also clear that Araguz had wanted Gozian to lead his subjects in the ritual drinking of poison at the supposed confluence, and so the king's death represented a possible disruption of his plans. But there was no reason to think that the Ravens' Voice could be stopped from going ahead, regardless of any changes in the royal household.

More disturbing still was the role Jax had played in all this. What was the link between him and Araguz? They both evidently delighted in death and destruction, and they were both enchanters. But there were differences too. The prophet was deadly serious about what he was doing, whereas for Jax Vergos was merely his latest playground. Was it possible that these two mismatched personalities had really forged an unholy alliance? The argument Terrel had overheard indicated that there was at least some friction in their relationship.

The only truly encouraging discovery – assuming that it *was* all true – had been that Araguz's scope as an enchanter was more limited than they had imagined. Even when he was physically present he was clearly not invincible. If he had been, the star-gazers would not have been able to oppose him. And it was obvious that Gozian had not been prepared to bow to the prophet's whim. It made the scenes Terrel had witnessed in the square even more mystifying, but it gave him a little hope for the battle to come. If the people in the court could defy Araguz, then so could others.

As this thought crossed his mind there was a small crunching sound behind him, and Terrel turned round to see Faulk emerging from the tomb. The soldier was frowning, and looked relieved when he saw the healer.

'What are you still doing out here?' he asked, sitting down beside him.

'I couldn't sleep.'

'Bad dreams?'

'You could say that.'

The bells began shortly after dawn, their tolling spreading out one to another until it seemed the whole city was vibrating with their ringing.

'Something's happened,' Faulk said.

Terrel could have told him what it was but he wasn't ready to share his vision yet, just in case it was a delusion. But he no longer believed that to be the case. The dream had taken another step closer to reality.

Throughout the morning the temperature continued to rise steadily until it was unusually warm for the time of year. Unpredictable gusts of wind raised small swirls of dust and dead leaves in the alleyways of the necropolis, and even though the sky remained a cloudless blue the sun seemed tinged with brown, as if its light were being filtered through dark gauze. Even when the sound of the bells gradually died away around noon, the atmosphere was so peculiar that – even from their isolated standpoint – it was obvious Vergos was in the grip of some strange malady.

Terrel and Faulk spent the day restlessly, unable to relax or take advantage of the weather. They saw no one. Nothing moved within the cemetery except the wind and a few passing birds. To Terrel's relief there was no sign of the old man, but as dusk finally approached there was no sign of Yllen either. With the darkness the cold of winter returned with an almost unnatural swiftness, and he and Faulk were soon shivering as they waited at their lookout station, peering through the gloom at the gates. Terrel had been relying on the fact that Yllen would arrive with news to either confirm or contradict his vision; as evening slipped into night, his frustration began to mount.

'I don't suppose she'll come now,' Faulk said eventually. 'Still, we've enough supplies for tonight.'

'I'm not worried about food,' Terrel muttered. 'Do you think something's happened to her?'

'We've no way of knowing.'

They were both wondering if Roskin had betrayed their go-between.

'We're more in need of news than provisions,' Terrel pointed out.

'Shall I go and see what I can find out?' Faulk offered.

Terrel shook his head. 'Not yet. She may still come.'

They waited for another two hours, then gave up and returned to their beds. By then Terrel didn't want Faulk to go; he had no wish to be left alone with his dreams.

In the event no more dreams came that night. The two men woke the next morning to the sound of drums and trumpets and, peering out through the crack in the door, they saw movement everywhere. It seemed as if the entire necropolis was now inhabited by the living, as an endless funeral cortege flowed in through the gates and spread out along the various avenues. There were a lot of guards, marching slowly, their expressions grave, or standing stiffly to attention at specific sentry points. Musicians added their dirges to the sound of the mourners' wailing.

'Someone important wasn't able to see out the last few days after all,' Faulk remarked. 'Someone *really* important.'

I should have seen this coming, Terrel berated himself. Where else would the king be buried? He knew now that the dream had been real and when, from the glimpses Faulk allowed himself, the astonished soldier concluded that it had been Gozian himself who had died, it was merely confirmation of that fact.

'Do you think Araguz murdered him?' Faulk whispered. 'To get him out of the way?'

Terrel did not respond to his companion's speculation. For reasons he could not explain he was not yet ready to describe what he had seen.

'There are guards everywhere,' Faulk added. 'I thought we might be able to mix in with the crowds, but it's too risky. We'll just have to lie low until this is over.'

The funeral went on far longer than they could possibly have imagined. Naturally enough, the royal mausoleum was the largest and most ornate in the necropolis. It was situated right at the centre of the graveyard, and most of the continuing ceremonies took place in and around that – but there were so many people involved and so many rituals to be carried out that events spilled into the surrounding area. Terrel and Faulk were effectively prisoners in their own refuge. The processions continued into the night, torchlight transforming the cemetery into a land of flame and shadows, while the thunder of drums and the murmur of voices drove back the usual silence. Terrel sensed anger among the mourners as well as sorrow, and he knew that Gozian's death would not go unavenged – even though the guilty party was actually far beyond the reach of justice. Whatever the extended lamentation said about the way in which the king had been regarded, it was clear that the situation in Vergos was now even more unstable than before.

It was only on the evening of the third day that the ceremonies finally came to an end and Gozian was left in peace. The prisoners' food had run out long before that, and they were ravenous as well as desperate for news by the time the last mourners left. Even then Faulk insisted on caution, making them watch and wait to make sure no sentries had been left behind. In the end, Yllen arrived before they were able to make a move.

'The city's full of rumours about Gozian's death,' she reported. 'As far as I can tell, the only thing everyone agrees on is that he didn't die of natural causes.'

'Murder?' Faulk queried between mouthfuls. Yllen had brought as much food as she could carry.

She nodded.

'There are all sorts of tales – everything from his being stabbed or poisoned to one claim that a sorcerer ate his heart to take the king's power.'

'Does anyone know who killed him?'

'There's a lot of speculation,' Yllen replied, frowning. 'But they say one man's been accused. And I've got a horrible feeling I know who it is.'

'Who?' Faulk asked.

'Nomar,' Terrel answered for her, hearing again some of

the unheeded shouts that had rung out in the hall while he'd been preoccupied with Araguz.

'How did you know that?' Yllen gasped.

'I saw it happen.'

'But—'

'In a dream,' he explained.

Faulk snorted in disbelief, his scepticism plain. Yllen was more willing to accept such insubstantial evidence.

'You mean Nomar really did kill Gozian?' she asked.

'No, but he was there,' Terrel replied. 'And he makes a convenient scapegoat.' In retrospect it was obvious that he would have been the most likely candidate to take the blame.

Faulk could contain himself no longer.

'You know all this from a *dream*?' he exclaimed.

Dreams are sometimes meant to show us things, Terrel thought. Alyssa had first said that to him when they were still at Havenmoon together – a lifetime ago.

'Call it a vision if you like.'

'Even so, can you trust such things?'

'Yes. On this occasion I think I can.'

'What difference does it make?' Yllen put in. 'Gozian's certainly dead, and what Terrel saw fits in with everything we've heard.'

Faulk looked baffled, but did not argue the point any more.

'So who *did* kill Gozian?' Yllen asked.

'I don't know,' Terrel lied, 'but it involved sorcery. His heart burned up within his chest.'

'That was one of the rumours!' she exclaimed. 'I didn't repeat it because it sounded so ridiculous.' She broke off and looked up, startled by a slight thrumming noise in the air. A pair of birds were flying overhead, shadows flitting across a darkening sky.

'What's happened to Nomar?' Terrel asked. 'Do you know?'

Yllen shook her head.

'He went to the palace with Brioni three days ago,' she told them. 'No one's seen either of them since.'

'Where's Taryn?'

'At the house. He's frantic, poor kid. Pieri's with him now.'

'Have you found out anything that might help us?' Faulk asked. 'We need to decide what to do next.'

'Not really. There's still no sign of Roskin. Pieri's tried several approaches but with no luck. Lawren's been off on his own most of the time, doing something with Kephra, but I'm not sure what. He told me she's behaving very oddly, even allowing for the fact that she's not used to the city.'

'It's probably this strange weather we've been having,' Faulk said. The last few days had seen bouts of unusual warmth interspersed with cold spells, a few short-lived thunderstorms and fitful winds.

'Probably,' Yllen agreed. 'I've even heard people talking about whirlwinds, but I've not seen any myself.'

Terrel couldn't help wondering whether Jax was responsible for these meteorological anomalies, but he decided it didn't really matter at that moment.

'What about you?' Yllen asked. 'Have you learnt anything?'

'We've been stuck here,' Faulk told her. 'There were guards everywhere during the funeral rites.'

'So the old man didn't come back?'

'No,' Terrel said. 'The funeral probably kept him away too.'

'I don't think that would have stopped him if he'd wanted to see you.' Yllen was clearly intrigued by the mystery of the old man.

They sat in silence for a while.

'I do have one other piece of news,' she said eventually.

'What?'

'Word is that the Ravens' Voice is supposed to be appearing before his adoring public again tonight.'

'Why didn't you tell us that before?' Terrel cried, jumping to his feet.

'And spoil your digestion?' she replied. 'Relax. It's not until later. Around midnight.'

'Do you want to go?' Faulk sounded pleased by the thought of some action.

'I think we have to, don't you?' Terrel answered.

CHAPTER TWENTY-SEVEN

'By this evil deed Gozian was denied his rightful place in the time to come.' The prophet's voice rolled out over the multitude in resonant waves. 'But before he died, the king entrusted me with the guiding of his people.'

Terrel knew this to be a lie but he was in no position to discredit any of Araguz's claims. Everyone around him was mesmerized by the Ravens' Voice, and even if the healer could have made himself heard, he knew no one would have listened to him.

The scene in the great square was both eerie and frightening. Terrel would not have thought it possible, but the crush of people was even greater than the last time. A thousand torches and lamps, both within the crowd and around the perimeter, painted the night in ever-shifting colours, while in the sky the White and Red Moons – both of which were about three-quarters full – cast their more serene radiance over the sea of upturned faces. The knowledge that they were waxing towards their full, which – together with the Amber's – was only five days away now, lent an urgency to Terrel's thoughts. He still had no idea how to prevent Araguz from carrying out his murderous plans, and felt a lump of dread in the pit of his stomach.

Overruling Faulk's objections, Terrel had decided that the three of them should split up before approaching the square, reasoning that they were less likely to be recognized individually than as a group. They had tried to keep within sight of each other and, although this proved difficult, the healer had managed to catch a glimpse of the others every so often. However, when the black-garbed prophet had finally made his appearance, stepping out onto the same parapet as before, all eyes had turned to him. By then Terrel had manoeuvred himself into a position only a few paces from the castle wall, and he had been watching Araguz in profile. Little of what he had said had made much sense, but his hold over his audience was undeniable. Only the healer and his two companions seemed to be immune to the prophet's influence – and Terrel had no idea why that should be.

'But our time is coming!' Araguz cried now, pointing to the moons. 'When the sky is consumed by fire, the only salvation will be in the true light of the Dark Star.'

At this a second figure stepped out onto the balcony, and the massed crowds murmured their surprise. Terrel recognized Kalmira at once and wondered whether her appearance was voluntary. He was too far away to make out the expression on her face but, unless he was being deluded by wishful thinking, her movements spoke of reluctant participation. Araguz handed something to her, which she appeared to hang around her neck.

'This is the key that unlocks the door to Paradise,' the Ravens' Voice declared, but before he could go on a third figure appeared on the balcony – and this time Terrel would have known who it was even if he'd had his eyes shut. Jax had not stepped forward as the queen had done but had simply materialized in mid-air, deepening Terrel's sense of dismay. The only other person to react to the prince's arrival was Araguz, who turned away from the crowd and fell silent. Even Kalmira, who stood only a few paces from the ghostly figure, was clearly unaware of his presence, and Terrel realized that no one else could see his twin.

Even as the healer watched, certain now that Jax must be an ally of the prophet, the prince turned to look directly at him, pointing with an imperious, spectral finger. Araguz soon mimicked his actions, shouting for the guards. Too stunned to react immediately, Terrel realized his danger too late. His neighbours were drawing back a little, staring at him as if he were a criminal, but even so, in such an overcrowded arena flight seemed almost impossible. For a few moments he stood petrified, vaguely aware that both Faulk and several guards were pushing their way towards him. The animosity that surrounded him now was palpable and he knew he could expect no help from the onlookers. His only hope lay in the one talent he had hoped he'd never have to use again.

Panic made summoning up the glamour difficult to control, and he knew that to the bystanders his appearance probably seemed blurred and indistinct, but he was able to manipulate it sufficiently to disguise his most distinctive features – the colour of his eyes and the crooked nature of the limbs on his right side. He did not stop there, however, and changed their perception of his hair and the shape of his face. At the same time he belatedly began to move, pushing his way into the crowd which was now milling about in confusion.

Ignoring the shouts all around him, Terrel pressed on blindly, not really knowing where he was going but desperate to move, to put some distance between Araguz and himself. At one point he almost blundered straight into a patrol, but they ignored him and this made him feel a little more confident. The guards were all looking past him, searching the crowd for a face that was no longer there, and one of them actually shoved Terrel aside as they moved forward.

One of the disadvantages of using the glamour was that it also hid him from his friends. There was no sign of either Faulk or Yllen, and they would have no way of following him now. Terrel felt bad about abandoning them, but that was a problem he would have to deal with later.

Hello, brother.

The one person who could see through Terrel's disguise had caught up with him, crushing his new-found hope.

This is entertaining, Jax remarked cheerfully. *Where are you going?*

Terrel did not reply.

You can't hide from me, the prince added. *I know what you look like* inside.

What are you doing here, Jax? Terrel muttered as he made his way through the crowds, working towards the corner of the square.

Don't you know? The prince's mocking tone made it clear that he was enjoying himself.

Terrel turned to glance back at the distant parapet. Araguz and Kalmira were gone but Jax was still standing there. A moment later he vanished, leaving behind only the sound of laughter that echoed within the healer's mind before fading into silence. Terrel looked round, not sure whether his twin was really gone or whether he'd chosen to follow him, but he noticed nothing out of the ordinary. Although the crowds were thinning slightly now and he was able to move more easily, he could see that there were still a lot of guards in the area and so, somewhat reluctantly, he kept up the internal litany that changed his appearance. When he was finally able to make his way out of the square, moving as part of the human tide now flowing back out into the rest of the city, he began to wonder where he should go. Back to the necropolis? Or to Brioni's house? In the event he was not given any time to consider this decision. Another patrol came into view and their leader immediately pointed to Terrel.

'There he is!'

After a moment's stunned disbelief, Terrel fled. As it became clear that he really was the guards' prey, and the glamour was no longer effective, he abandoned the disguise and resumed his natural appearance. Dodging in and out of the stream of people, he plunged into an alleyway, hoping to lose his pursuers in the city's maze. As he ran he saw the patrol leader's face again in his mind's eye. There had been something wrong with his eyes, a strange lifelessness. And then Terrel understood. Jax was an enchanter after all and, as others had found to their cost in the past, some people were more susceptible to his manipulations than others. It had not taken the prince long to find a guard who suited his purpose – and as he'd pointed out earlier, Terrel could not hide from *him*.

The sounds of pursuit were getting closer all the time and Terrel's twisted leg was hurting him more and more, but he ran on, gasping for breath. Turning another corner he came to a halt as he discovered that a group of guards had circled round so that he was now surrounded. They were closing in fast. Just as he realized that he was trapped, Terrel glanced down a side alley – one he'd ignored moments ago because it was a dead end – and saw a torch burning above a small plain door. But what caught his attention was not the flames but the incongruous carvings to either side. Two stone horns sprouted from the lintel like a bizarre hunting trophy, prompting a memory to stir in the healer's tired brain. Watch for the fire between the horns. That was what the old man had told him – and if he was ever going to decide to trust his mysterious visitor, now was the time to do it. The guards were getting closer by the moment.

Terrel heard them shouting and glimpsed black shapes whirling around the soldiers' heads, causing them to strike out as if they were under attack. He had no idea what was going on but took advantage of their unexpected distraction to duck into the alley, forcing his aching limbs into one last effort. Before he reached the door it opened, and he stumbled inside and fell in a heap upon the floor. The door closed behind him and he found himself in utter darkness.

For a while the only sound was that of his own tortured breathing, but then he heard movement and voices in the alley. The guards were evidently searching for him, sounding confused as they shouted back and forth. Terrel found it hard to believe that they hadn't seen him go through the door and expected them to smash it down at any moment. He thought about crawling away into the darkness but stayed where he was and lay perfectly still, afraid that any noise might betray him. But nothing happened and, after what seemed like an age, the footsteps outside moved away.

'For them the doorway wasn't even there.'

The familiar voice drifted out of the darkness, startling Terrel. Although the old man was clearly close by, he was completely invisible.

'What do you mean?' Terrel whispered.

His unseen companion ignored the question. Instead there was a scratching sound and a sudden flare of light as a candle was lit.

'Why are you helping me?' Terrel asked.

'Aren't you worthy of my help?' the old man replied.

'I'd like to think so, but . . . Who are you?'

'You still haven't worked that out?'

Terrel shook his head, conscious of the fact that he had disappointed his saviour.

'You can call me Cobo.'

Terrel had heard that name before but for the time being he couldn't place it. He was about to ask more but a fluttering overhead distracted him. A bird appeared on the sill of a skylight above them.

'The coast is clear,' the old man said. 'We can go now.'

'Go where?'

'To the palace. There's someone there I want you to meet.'

Vergos was quiet in the aftermath of the prophet's gathering. The crowds had dispersed with remarkable speed and most of the streets were deserted as the two men made their way back towards the centre of the city. Despite several attempts on Terrel's part, Cobo would not tell him anything more about what had happened or who they were going to see, leaving the healer to his own speculations. A dozen questions were buzzing in his brain, but on one issue he was now decided. He was committed to the old man. All Terrel's instincts told him that Cobo was trustworthy – and the fact that he'd saved the fugitive from the guards counted in his favour. Although a small, cynical part of the healer's mind wondered whether his new ally's actions might simply have been designed so that he'd be the one to gain credit for the capture when they reached the palace, he dismissed that notion as unworthy. One way or another, Terrel's fate was in the old man's hands.

As they drew closer to the castle, Terrel began to wonder whether he was about to see Nomar or Roskin again – and then he wondered whether any of his other companions had been captured.

'Do you know what happened to my friends?'

'The big fellow got away,' Cobo replied, 'though I don't think he's going to be very pleased with you when you see him again. I'm not sure what happened to Yllen, but that young lady can take care of herself.'

'You know her?' Terrel asked, surprised by the old man's use of her name.

'By reputation,' Cobo replied with a smile. 'I've followed Pieri's career with interest for some time. Such a waste of talent, don't you think?'

The vague memory that had eluded Terrel until then snapped into focus.

'You're the king!' he exclaimed. 'The King of the Marketplace.'

'At your service.' The old man nodded, obviously pleased to have been recognized at last.

The 'worldly king', Terrel added to himself. Ever since he'd learned of Gozian's death he had been wondering about the reference in the Tindaya Code. But it was clear now, and his confidence in his decision to trust Cobo went up another notch.

'You're the one who taught Pieri how to use the glamour.'

'If that's what you want to call it. He was one of my better pupils, but I doubt he could match you.' Cobo came to a halt. They were now in sight of one of the small side entrances to the castle. 'Can you pass through unnoticed?'

It took Terrel a moment to work out what the old man meant. He had used the glamour to make himself invisible once before, but only when he had been keeping perfectly still. Walking past sentries was another matter.

'I doubt it,' he replied. 'In any case, I'd rather not use what skill I have at the moment.'

'Why not?'

'It's complicated,' Terrel said, not really wanting to explain about Jax.

'Suit yourself,' Cobo said with a shrug. 'I'll do it, then. Take my hand and don't speak until I do.'

Terrel did as he was told and allowed himself to be led out into the open and towards the gateway. There were several guards there, but as Cobo marched inside no one paid the new arrivals any attention. Overhead a raven croaked loudly, and Terrel realized for the first time how the old man knew so much about what went on in the city. Little could be hidden from spies who could take to the air. His respect for his guide rose once more.

A short while later the two men were climbing a staircase into a section of the palace that appeared to be deserted. Everywhere else had seemed to be in turmoil, with guards, servants and courtiers hurrying in all directions in spite of the lateness of the hour, but in these quarters all was still and silent. Terrel had half expected to be taken down to the dungeons, where prisoners were likely to be kept, but Cobo clearly had another destination in mind.

Pausing at a door, the old man listened for a moment, knocked lightly three times, then twice more. There was no response from within but he opened the door anyway and ushered Terrel inside. At first Terrel thought the room was empty, but then the soft candlelight revealed a slight movement beside a table on the far side of the room.

Queen Kalmira turned to look at the healer with an unreadable expression on her beautiful face.

CHAPTER TWENTY-EIGHT

'It's good to see you again, Meddler,' Kalmira said. Her voice was soft and her use of what was obviously a pet name for Cobo spoke of fondness as well as familiarity.

'And you, ma'am,' he replied gravely. 'I'm sorry for your loss.'

Kalmira did not respond and her expression did not change, but Terrel could see her sadness and grief. Queen or no, her marriage to Gozian had clearly been more than a matter of political convenience. She was obviously controlling her emotions with some difficulty, and Terrel wanted to say something to comfort her – but there were no words that could do that.

'This is Terrel,' Cobo said, more businesslike now. 'I have no doubt he's the one we've been waiting for.'

Kalmira studied the healer for a long moment, and he felt as though he was being measured in some way.

'Can you read thoughts, Terrel?' she asked eventually.

The question was so unexpected that it took the healer by surprise, and he hesitated before answering.

'Sometimes,' he admitted awkwardly. 'When I was a boy I was taught the secret of psinoma by a man who follows much the same path as Cobo here. There are certain people with whom I can converse without the need to speak aloud, and with others I can have some contact on occasion. But most thoughts are private,' he added hurriedly, 'and I would not . . . I could not intrude.'

'So you don't know what I'm thinking now?'

'No, ma'am.'

'That's probably just as well,' Kalmira said, and the first ghost of a smile crossed her face. She waved her visitors to chairs and Terrel had the feeling that they were settling in for a long conversation. Kalmira appeared close to exhaustion and her face was pale and drawn, but she held herself erect and he could sense her inner determination. The healer's own tiredness was forgotten now as he wondered why he'd been brought to the queen's apartments.

'Some would say you have the eyes of an enchanter,' she remarked. 'Do you have that power?'

'No, ma'am.'

'But you are a healer?'

'Yes.'

'Do you think you can cure my son of the sleeping sickness?'

'If what I've heard is true, I fear not. I have encountered sleepers before, and their malady is beyond ordinary healing. But I will try, nonetheless, if you give me the chance.'

'That's what Nomar said,' Kalmira murmured.

'Where is Nomar now?' Terrel enquired, hoping he'd earned the right to ask some questions of his own.

'He's been imprisoned,' the queen said, pain showing in her eyes once again.

'He's innocent, ma'am,' Terrel claimed. 'Nomar could no more kill a man in that manner than he could fly to the moons.'

'In what manner?' Cobo asked curiously.

'I heard . . .' Terrel began, then faltered. He was not yet willing to admit that he'd witnessed Gozian's death, but he did not want to lie. 'Nomar is a healer,' he said. 'Such abuse of his talent is unthinkable.'

'All men may kill if they think they have reason enough,' Kalmira said mildly, 'but I do not think Nomar is guilty either.'

Terrel felt a measure of relief, but knew he was still on dangerous ground.

'Such vile sorcery is rare in this world,' the queen went on. 'If it had suited his purpose I would have suspected the prophet of murdering my husband, but given his plans that would make no sense at all. Yet who else could it have been?'

'What plans?' Terrel asked.

'Gozian was to have led our people in the ceremonies on the night of the confluence. For most the prophet's influence would be enough, but the royal seal of approval was supposed to win over any waverers.' She paused, fingering a small leather pouch that hung on a cord around her neck. 'Now it seems that duty falls to me.'

'Let me see that,' Cobo said, holding out his hand.

Kalmira slipped the cord over her head and passed it to him. The old man loosened the bag and let its contents fall out onto his palm. The three of them stared at a single white tablet. It looked as innocent as a piece of chalk but Terrel knew it was not. Cobo raised it to his nose and sniffed delicately.

'Shadowbane,' he concluded. 'The same as all the others I've seen. The apothecaries in the city have been kept busy for some time now, seeking out the plants and distilling the essence.'

'It's poison?' Terrel asked.

'Deadly, even in tiny quantities,' the old man confirmed. 'There's enough in this pill to end the lives of three men.'

'Or one woman,' Kalmira said quietly.

'Some of them are being sweetened with honey,' Cobo added. 'For the children.'

Terrel felt his gorge rise. He realized now that he had seen a lot of people wearing pendants like the queen's. He had assumed they were some sort of talisman, but having learned their real purpose, the fact that so many of the city's inhabitants had accepted them made him feel sick.

'But surely you would never think of swallowing it!' he exclaimed.

'I may not have any choice,' Kalmira replied calmly. 'There are times when it seems your only option is to do what the prophet says.'

'But you *know* he's evil!' Terrel burst out. 'And he's a fraud.'

'Is he? What if he's right? What if the fire that carved out this land returns to fill the sky? No one could survive that, and his way could be the path to salvation.'

'No! You can't believe that. You mustn't! Suicide can never be a solution. Araguz is mad. All he wants is to prove his own warped power by destroying everyone here. He did it once before.'

Kalmira looked taken aback by his impassioned outburst, and Terrel continued before she could respond.

'Even if the great fire he's predicting does eventually come, it won't be when he says. The three visible moons will line up in five days' time but the Dark Moon won't be full until two days later. You would all be dying for nothing!'

In the stunned silence that followed his feverish words, Terrel had to force himself to remain calm. He sat back in his chair and took a deep breath.

'I'm sorry,' he said quietly. 'I didn't mean to shout.'

'We should be safe enough here,' Kalmira said, 'but perhaps it would be better if you kept your voice down a little.' She glanced at Cobo, then returned her gaze to the healer. 'You seem to have a good deal to tell us. I assume Araguz is the name by which you know the prophet?'

Terrel nodded, then told them about Nomar's childhood and his unexpected survival after Araguz had left everyone else in Senden to die. Then, without revealing the exact source of his knowledge, he repeated his assertion about the moons.

'So the world is not going to end?' Kalmira said.

'No.' At least not yet, he added to himself.

'A few of the star-gazers thought as much, but it's difficult to argue with the Ravens' Voice.'

'Araguz has to be stopped,' Terrel went on fervently. 'We can't let him murder thousands of people.'

There was silence for a while.

'You see,' Cobo said eventually. 'He *is* the one.'

Terrel had evidently passed some kind of test.

'How much do you know of the Raven Cypher?' Kalmira asked.

'Not much.'

'It's ancient, and much of it was destroyed long ago. No one took what was left seriously until recently, but now it seems that many of the things it predicts are coming true – the fire-scythes, the sleeping plague, the changes in the cycles of the moons. Kaeryss was the first to realize what was happening but she found it hard to persuade the court that her findings were important. Even Gozian was sceptical, and when Araguz arrived he turned everyone against her – including my husband.' The queen sounded bitter now.

'Where is Kaeryss?'

'She's a prisoner in her own rooms. I managed to save her from the dungeons at least, but she's well guarded and no one's been able to speak to her for several months.'

'But she had already translated several new sections of the cypher before she was confined,' Cobo put in.

'Yes,' Kalmira agreed, making an effort to raise herself out of the gloom that had begun to enfold her. 'And that's why we're so interested in you,' she told Terrel. 'As is the way of oracles, many of the symbols are confusing, and even when they're decoded we're often left with riddles. But some things were clear enough, specifically a reference to a "silver-eyed stranger" and his allies. Most people assume that's Araguz. I did too until I heard about you, and now that I've seen you some of the other anomalies are beginning to make more sense.'

'What is the stranger supposed to do?' Terrel asked, hoping for some guidance.

'Save Vergos and all its people from disaster,' Kalmira replied.

'Which is exactly what Araguz claims to be doing,' Cobo added. 'It's just that I'd rather we were saved by a different method.'

'So you can understand why we wanted to meet you,' the queen went on. 'I was about to have proclamations posted all over the city but the prophet forbade it – calling it unnecessary, and meddling with fate. So it was left to my old friend here.'

'But Araguz was anxious to find you as well,' Cobo added, 'though for very different reasons.'

I *was* wanted dead or alive, Terrel thought. Dead by Araguz; alive by Kalmira.

'Exactly how am I supposed to save Vergos?'

'That's not clear,' the queen admitted. 'Especially as the stranger seems to be called by several different names, and is described differently in various passages. For instance, at one point it says that protection can only be provided by a "child of pain".' She gestured towards

Terrel's crooked limbs. 'At least that seems to make sense now. But in one section he's also referred to as a "man with two heads".'

The double-headed man? Terrel wondered, remembering the desert oracle and the time when his spirit had remained, ghost-like, at Makranash while the nomads had carried his body away from the sacred mountain. Was he supposed to divide himself in the same way again? And if so, to what purpose? Or could it perhaps refer to the time when he and Jax had occupied the same space? Or . . . The possibilities seemed endless.

'That doesn't help a lot,' he said.

'What does seem certain,' Kalmira went on, 'is that you need the help of your allies in order to succeed, and that the process involves "powers of the mind" – what most people would call magic.'

To some, Terrel knew, his healing was a form of magic. It did not feel like that to him, but when something was outside the normal realm of understanding it was easy to see how it came to be attributed to sorcery. But he didn't see how his skills could be used to thwart Araguz's plans.

'We were rather hoping you would know what to do,' Cobo said. His rueful tone indicated that he had seen Terrel's confusion.

'You'll need to be careful, whatever you do,' Kalmira added. 'Kaeryss believed that another part of the cypher indicated your betrayal by one of your allies, although that translation was disputed by some.'

So I need their help, Terrel thought, but I can't trust them. Wonderful.

'Our main advantage,' he said, repeating an earlier argument, 'is that we know the confluence is not going to happen. For a start we could go to the star-gazers and—'

'It's too late for that,' the queen cut in. 'Araguz has had

them "removed". No one knows where they are. He didn't believe their claims. He just thought they were trying to discredit him, so he got rid of them.'

Just as Jax got rid of Gozian when he threatened to take those claims seriously, Terrel thought. Judging by Araguz's fury at the time, the prince had acted on his own initiative – an impulsive urge to destroy anything or anyone who opposed his purpose. Yet his actions, while not of the prophet's choosing, had given Araguz an even greater degree of power within the court.

'Things would be different if my son was still with us,' Kalmira said.

'Why?'

'A woman will never be accepted as ruler here. That's why I am a poor second choice for Araguz. The nobles are already divided over the succession, some saying that while Karn still lives he is the only rightful king, others that he is as good as dead if he cannot be woken. If the prince were awake, he would at least be a figure around whom we could rally in trying to oppose the prophet. Karn disliked him from the start – which is why he is ill now.'

'You think Araguz had something to do with his becoming a sleeper?' Terrel was certain this could not be true but he was interested in why Kalmira might think it was.

'I cannot prove it,' she replied, 'but the evidence speaks for itself. There were no sleepers until Araguz came to Vergos, but soon after he arrived those courtiers who seemed less than captivated by his charms fell ill. Anyone who was convinced by the prophet's arguments was spared. I tried to warn my son but he is headstrong and he spoke out in defiance of his father. That very night he fell into an endless sleep.'

Terrel was stunned. He had been convinced for a very

long time that there was some connection – albeit ill-defined – between the elementals and the sleepers. The idea that it was possible for anyone to interfere with the mysterious and apparently random process that created the comas had never occurred to him before. If Araguz was able to create sleepers at will then Terrel had to revise his thinking completely or – even more worryingly – he had to consider the possibility that the prophet had some sort of link with the Ancients. Then something else occurred to him. Could it be that Araguz was actually another Mentor, like Terrel himself? The healer did not want to believe this, but it did make a horrible kind of sense. Araguz could be the human equivalent of the mad elemental on Myvatan – somehow manipulating the power of that malevolent entity to further his own ends. But if that *was* the case, another Mentor – a sane one – could surely reverse the process. Terrel's thoughts fled not only to Karn but much further afield – to Alyssa.

'You have an idea?' Cobo queried.

Something of his speculation must have shown on Terrel's face, and yet now doubts were assailing him. He had never been able to contact any of the elementals at will. Very specific conditions were necessary, which were entirely beyond his control. And even when he had been able to converse with them, there had been no suggestion – not even a hint – that they might enable him to 'heal' the sleepers.

'No, not really,' he replied. Unless you can arrange an eclipse for me, he thought. He turned back to Kalmira. 'One of the rumours I heard before I reached the city was that you were a sorceress who was able to summon shadow-demons.'

'Me?' The queen looked utterly mystified. 'No, no. Kaeryss once told me she thought Araguz spoke to demons who did his bidding, and offered to protect me from them, but I didn't take her seriously.'

'Gossip has a way of distorting the truth,' Cobo observed.

'Do you believe in demons?' Kalmira asked.

'I'm not sure what I believe any more,' Terrel replied.

'We have all the faith we need,' the old man declared. 'None of this would matter if the world was going to end in a few days. But it isn't. That belief is enough for me to know that we have to stop Araguz.'

Terrel nodded, though his mind was still reeling from all he had learned.

'What do you want me to do?'

'Come and see my son,' Kalmira answered promptly. 'Much would change if you could rouse him.'

'Now?'

'Yes.'

They took advantage of Cobo's skills on more than one occasion on the way to the prince's quarters, but when they reached them all was quiet.

'I can't even trust my own guards any more,' Kalmira whispered ruefully as they slipped down a final corridor.

Inside his chamber, Karn lay unmoving on the bed. Terrel had seen many sleepers before and knew that his own skills would be useless to counter whatever held them captive. But he knew he had to try anyway, if only to satisfy Kalmira. As he moved across the room he heard the creak of another door and the queen's gasp of shock, and knew they had been discovered. The sight that greeted him when he turned around confirmed his worst fears.

'So, healer,' Araguz remarked. 'We meet at last.'

CHAPTER TWENTY-NINE

Terrel's earlier experience had not prepared him for the shock of Araguz's physical presence. The tattoos on his face and forearms emphasized his sinister appearance and his eyes had an eerie light in them. Naked evil flowed from him in cold waves – as if he were a creature of ice rather than flesh and blood. It reminded Terrel of the terrible sense of madness that had assailed him when he'd first set foot on Myvatan, the snow-bound home of the last of the elementals. He found himself shivering, wondering how he could ever hope to oppose such a foe.

'You *are* a healer, aren't you?' the prophet queried.

'Yes.' Terrel saw that there were several guards in the room now, though he had no idea how they had got there. Glancing round, he saw Kalmira trying to remain dignified yet looking smaller somehow, as if the prophet's mere presence diminished her. However, Cobo was nowhere to be seen. Terrel had not been aware of anyone leaving the room but it was possible the old man had used his special talents to escape.

'But you can only deal with your patients' bodies,' Araguz stated in a patronizing tone, 'and you are able to treat only one at a time. I, on the other hand, minister to men's souls and I will heal an entire city, an entire kingdom, at the same time.'

By killing them? Terrel thought. The idea of Araguz claiming to be a healer of any kind was utterly repugnant, but he said nothing, and the prophet seemed more than happy with the sound of his own voice.

'I'm told you've travelled widely,' he remarked. 'Tell me, have you ever been to an island called Myvatan?'

The question was so unexpected that Terrel had no need to reply. Araguz read the answer in his face.

'I see you've heard of it, at least. It's a remarkable place. The darkest star guided me to its frozen wastes and I carry its essence with me to this day.'

The hideous possibility that Araguz was somehow connected to the insane elemental seemed even more credible now. If he really *had* been to Myvatan, it was more than likely that at some point he would have drunk meltwater from the central glacier – the same glacier that had trapped the Ancient and driven it mad. And once the link had been formed . . . The chains don't stop at the coast of Myvatan, Alyssa had said – and Araguz might just be living proof of that fact.

'I can call upon its power when appropriate,' the prophet added, deepening the healer's unease.

Terrel felt a subtle, almost gentle, probing into his mind then, and recoiled instinctively. He found himself thinking about Havenmoon, without knowing how or why. Araguz smiled and withdrew.

'Not so innocent, then,' he remarked. 'You don't have much to say for yourself, do you?'

'I only speak when I have something worth saying,' Terrel replied.

The prophet's smile fell away as he switched his unnerving gaze to Kalmira, then back to the healer.

'Did you come here to revive Prince Karn?'

'I came to see if I could help him, yes.'

'An admirable ambition, and one that should not pass in secrecy. Our contest should be more public.'

'Contest?' Terrel queried.

'Bring them,' Araguz said tersely, beckoning to the guards.

Terrel found himself back in the lamp-lit hall of his dream, the hall where Gozian had died. Even though it was now very late – closer to dawn than midnight – there were a large number of people present, including several stern-looking men whom Terrel took to be the nobles Kalmira had mentioned. The queen herself was standing to one side, her head bowed either in deference or defeat. She had not spoken a word since they'd been surprised in the prince's quarters. Karn's body had been laid upon the long table, and Araguz stood next to the king's empty chair, the focus of everyone's attention.

'Some of you may have heard of this silver-eyed stranger,' he said now, pointing at Terrel, 'and wondered whether it was him, and not me, who is referred to in the Raven Cypher as Vergos's saviour of destiny. I think it's time we tested that theory. Terrel here claims to be a healer, as do I in a different manner. Let us see who has the greater power over Gozian's heir.'

At this a subdued murmuring rose in the hall, rapidly quelled when Araguz swept the gathering with his gaze. The general air seemed to be one of distrust and uncertainty, but Karn's fate was obviously important. Terrel already knew what the outcome of the 'contest' would be. He knew – and was certain the prophet also knew – that he would not be able to do anything for the prince. And yet he would have to try. This was Kalmira's last hope and if, in seeking to prove his own worth, Araguz really did revive her son, it might unwittingly prove the prophet's downfall.

In a way, the question of why Araguz needed to convince the watching courtiers of his power was more
interesting. As an enchanter, he should be able to force
them to accept his dominance. Terrel wondered whether
the Ravens' Voice needed to conserve his sorcery for a
time when it really mattered – the night of the false confluence. The prophet might be mad, but Terrel knew from
personal experience that lunatics could be cunning on
occasion. The healer had also realized that although his
adversary was clearly insane, Araguz truly believed in his
own obsessive vision of the world – and its end. What
Terrel saw as mass murder, Araguz knew to be genuine
salvation, the only hope of a doomed people. That sort of
fanaticism was going to be difficult to oppose.

When the prophet beckoned to Terrel, he moved forward even though his limbs felt numb. As he placed his
hand on Karn's he knew at once that – like all sleepers –
the prince was beyond his help. The waking dream was
still there, but so far away that he could never hope to
reach it. He tried for a while anyway, aware of Kalmira's
gaze upon him, but it was no use. Terrel stood back and
looked around.

'Well?' Araguz prompted.

'I can do nothing for him,' Terrel admitted.

The prophet waved him aside then, and approached the
table himself. Placing both hands on the prince's head, he
closed his eyes and stood perfectly still. The temperature
in the room dipped noticeably, and a kind of low thrumming filled the air. A sick dread threatened to overwhelm
Terrel as, against all reason, Karn's limbs began to twitch.
As the hall filled with gasps of amazement, the prince sat
up, swung his legs off the side of the table and stood
before them. All his movements were stiff and jerky, as
though he was a puppet manipulated by invisible strings,

and the expression on his face was one of blank incomprehension. His eyes were dark caverns, empty and limitless.

As Kalmira came forward, her arms outstretched in welcome and her face revealing both joy and disbelief, Karn's lips moved, but no sound emerged. He did not respond to his mother's greeting, nor did he seem capable of further movement. The queen stopped short of the embrace she had been longing for, and her doubts resurfaced. Hope was soon replaced by fear and revulsion.

'This is not my son,' she hissed.

Karn lurched forward then, reaching out with claw-like hands, but Kalmira drew back and he faltered.

'The moons have chosen his path,' Araguz announced. 'I will revive him again in time to greet the darkest star, but for now it is his fate to sleep.' At a gesture from the prophet the prince collapsed to the floor.

Kalmira fainted then, and Terrel stared at the scene in horror. He knew that there had been nothing of Karn in the zombie-like creature Araguz had conjured up, but he also knew that the prophet's performance – even though it had produced nothing more than a grotesque travesty of human life – had been enough to convince the courtiers where the greater power lay.

Araguz turned to face Terrel, then beckoned to some of the guards who had escorted them from the prince's chamber.

'Take this charlatan and throw him in the dungeons with the other unbelievers,' he commanded.

A skeletal fish was swimming through the air, weaving its way between the spires and towers of a beautiful mountaintop temple. Far below, in a darker, colder place, a frozen sea beckoned, turning red as the earth beneath it split open and Nydus bled fire. Terrel felt himself being dragged down into that smoke-churned abyss, but he clung to the light and the serenity of the mountain, turning his eyes away from the depths. He knew that if he were to fall that far he would never rise out of the darkness again. The ice would become his prison, locking him in an endless sleep.

The tug of war continued, and he knew he was not alone in fighting the malevolent forces that were trying to pull him down. He glanced up and saw Havenmoon, its many windows glowing with a welcoming light. Swimming like the fish before him, he moved towards the house and knew that he was free.

Terrel woke and realized that he was anything but free. However, it was not the icy cold of a hibernation without end that confined him, but a bare space between solid stone walls. His heart raced with fear as he wondered how much time had passed. Sunlight did not reach down into the dungeon cells, so he had no way of telling whether it was day or night. Sleep had been a long time coming, and he was hungry now, and stiff – but not as cold as he'd been before. For a while he couldn't work out why, but he soon found the source of the unlooked-for warmth. The red crystal in his pocket was hot to the touch, and when he took it out it was glowing softly, allowing him to see the meagre limits of his cell. Nothing like this had happened since he'd left Myvatan, and he wasn't sure what had triggered it now. Over the next hour the stone cooled and grew dull, and darkness reclaimed its domain, but by then Terrel had had time to consider what had happened and put a possible interpretation to his dream.

The connections to Myvatan were obvious, bringing with them renewed dread that the elemental there was indeed Araguz's ally. Terrel had the feeling that if he had slipped into the frozen sea he would not have returned; he would have become a sleeper. But something – the crystal, perhaps – had prompted other images, of the temple and Havenmoon, which he'd been able to cling to and thus avoid Karn's fate. If all that was true, he had no doubt that the prophet had been responsible for his peril and that Araguz would now be aware that the healer was protected in some way. What this meant in terms of his future treatment was something he could not begin to imagine.

Terrel looked up as he heard footsteps in the passage outside his cell. The torchlight that showed through the bars of the small grille in the door grew brighter, and then a face peered in. A key turned in the lock and bolts were drawn back before the gaoler pulled the door open.

'On your feet.'

'Where are we going?' Terrel asked nervously as he got up.

'Not far. We need the space, that's all. You're going to have to share.'

Terrel still had little idea how long he'd been confined, and the prospect of some company gave him a tiny moment of hope – until he realized he could be made to share with anyone. It was possible that the prison held ordinary criminals as well as Araguz's enemies, so he was doubly relieved as well as surprised when he was thrust into a cell with Nomar.

His delight turned almost instantly to concern. His friend was clearly in a bad way. From the hollow look in his eyes and the numerous cuts and bruises marking his face it was clear that he had been mistreated, perhaps even tortured, and the smile that greeted Terrel was undercut with pain. Wasting no time on words, Terrel went to kneel by the other man. His healing was a struggle at first, in part because he was out of practice, but he was eventually able to ease Nomar's pain. The process ended when his patient shook him off.

'Enough,' Nomar croaked. 'You've done enough. Save your strength.'

Terrel was nowhere near satisfied, but he respected the decision and withdrew his hand.

'What happened to you?'

'Some people got the idea that I'd killed Gozian,' Nomar replied hoarsely. 'It's ridiculous. I still don't know what happened to him, but I had nothing to do with it.'

'I know.'

'They tried to get me to admit I was guilty,' Nomar went on, his voice gaining a little strength, 'but when Araguz came to see me he seemed more interested in finding out who was protecting me. I didn't know what he meant at first, but then I realized that no matter how hard he tried he couldn't bend me to his will. There's some sort of shield around me that even an enchanter can't penetrate. I thought it must come from you. I didn't tell them anything.'

Terrel had already seen what keeping silent had cost his friend.

'It's not me,' he said, 'but I—'

He broke off as the door to the cell opened again and another prisoner was pushed inside. The newcomer fell in a heap on the floor and groaned, then looked up, his face breaking into an incredulous grin.

'Hello, Roskin,' Nomar said. 'This is getting to be quite a reunion.'

'What are you two doing here?' Roskin gasped, his initial pleasure fading quickly as the door slammed shut and the reality of their situation reasserted itself.

'We got on the wrong side of Araguz,' Terrel replied. 'What about you? Yllen seemed to think you got yourself arrested deliberately.'

Roskin didn't answer immediately but moved to lean against a wall, wincing as he did so.

'Are you hurt?' Terrel asked. 'Do you want me to help you with the pain?'

'No, no. I'm fine.' Roskin settled himself and took a deep breath. 'Yllen was right. I can't believe I did anything so stupid.'

'So it's true?'

The would-be seer looked shamefaced as he nodded.

'I got the idea into my head that if I could just get inside the palace I'd be able to meet Kaeryss.'

'And did you?'

'Yes, as it happens, but not until after I'd been down here a few days.'

'What happened?'

'They made some of us work in the kitchens, and I was sent to Kaeryss's quarters with her meal. I wasn't able to talk to her for long, but it was fascinating.' Roskin's eyes shone at the memory.

'I thought she was supposed to be in gaol,' Nomar said.

'She's a prisoner in her own rooms,' Roskin explained. 'I don't know why they're treating her like that. But we talked for a while, and she told me Araguz had tried to turn her into a sleeper! Can you believe that?'

I can believe it, Terrel thought, now more convinced than ever that the prophet had tried to do the same to him.

'But he failed,' Roskin went on, 'so he had to find other ways of discrediting her.'

'So she's protected too?' Nomar surmised.

'What do you mean?' Roskin was looking puzzled now.

'Doesn't it seem odd to you that none of us have fallen

under Araguz's influence?' Terrel replied. 'Nomar and I both think there's some sort of shield around us.'

'So what's protecting us?' Roskin asked.

'Not what,' Terrel said. 'Who.'

'You know?' Nomar queried.

'I can't be sure,' the healer replied, 'and it doesn't explain why Kaeryss is immune – but I think I do.' Everything had crystallized in that moment, vague suspicions turning to near certainty. A painted shield imbued with sorcery, a shield that had a 'father', and the dream images that had saved him the night before. A child of pain. Those pictures could only come from one source.

Terrel turned to look at Nomar.

'Your son is even more remarkable than we thought,' he said. 'It's Taryn who's protecting us.'

Nomar looked amazed, unable to believe what he was being told.

'Taryn?'

'I'm sure of it.'

'That's good enough for me,' Roskin said. He got to his feet, moving without any sign of pain now, and Terrel felt a tremor of disquiet.

Roskin rapped on the door in a pattern that sounded like a prearranged signal. Moments later a guard appeared and unbolted the door.

'This has been very interesting,' Roskin said, 'but I have to go now. I think Araguz will be fascinated to learn of your theory, don't you?'

Before either Terrel or Nomar could react, Roskin slipped out into the corridor and the door clanged shut behind him.

CHAPTER THIRTY

The cell Nomar was now sharing with Terrel was close enough to the open air for a little sunlight to filter down and allow them to recognize the passing of day to night and back again. A full day had gone by since Roskin had left, and they were still none the wiser about what was happening in the outside world. The frustration Terrel felt at this situation was terrible, but it was nothing compared to the agonies his companion was going through.

Nomar's rage when Roskin had revealed himself to be a traitor had been frightening to behold. He had screamed in an impotent frenzy, completely beyond the healer's control. When his fury had finally died down, Nomar had slumped into a period of utter despair which in turn brought on one of his debilitating headaches. Although he had been quite incapable of calming his friend down earlier, Terrel was able to help him through this stage of his reaction, bringing him at last to an exhausted sleep. At the same time, Terrel had had to deal with his own feelings of guilt. He felt wretched at the thought of having brought Taryn into danger by his unguarded words, and wished that he had heeded earlier warnings about treachery. But it was too late to do anything about that now.

The only hope left to the two men was that either their remaining allies would be able to protect Taryn and defeat Araguz without them – using the failure of his prediction to discredit him – or that either Cobo or Faulk, if they were still free, might come to their rescue before the fateful time arrived. But as the hours crawled by and nothing happened, neither possibility seemed very likely.

In the end it was not one of their friends but their deadliest enemy who came to visit them. Evening had already cast their gloomy cell into almost total darkness, so when they saw flickers of torchlight in the passageway and heard footsteps and the muffled sound of voices, they grew tense, waiting to find out what was going on.

The light came closer and after one of the gaolers had glanced in to check on the prisoners, Araguz's face appeared in the grille. Before their visitor could speak, Nomar uttered the howl of a wild animal and hurled himself at the door in a useless attempt to reach his nemesis. The prophet stepped back quickly, well out of reach, looking genuinely shocked that anyone should feel such enmity towards him. The gaps between the bars were too narrow to allow Nomar to get his arms through, and one of the guards banged his truncheon against the metal to discourage him from even trying. Terrel stepped forward and put a tentative hand on his companion's shoulder, feeling his muscles tensed to the rigidity of stone, and after a moment Nomar pulled back – although the hatred he could not control burned in his eyes as he glared through the window.

'Think,' Terrel whispered. 'He couldn't stop you trying to attack him.' The healer was hoping Nomar would realize – as he had done – that this meant the enchanter was not yet able to control them as he could other people. It meant that Taryn was still protecting them – and if Nomar's son was free then there was still hope. Terrel felt his friend relax a little as he reached the same conclusion.

'I come to offer you my help,' Araguz said, stepping forward again now that the prisoners had drawn back a little.

His claim was met with frank disbelief, but that did not seem to bother him.

'I am not a cruel man,' he added, 'even to those who oppose my holy purpose. Because those of you in the dungeons won't be able to attend the rituals tomorrow night . . .'

Tomorrow? Terrel thought helplessly. He could not believe it had come so soon.

'. . . other arrangements must be made,' Araguz went on. As he spoke he pushed two tiny pouches through the grille. They fell to the floor with barely a sound. 'I give you these in case you decide to accept salvation. It will be your choice, to be saved or not. You'll know when to take them. If not, you will be punished for your crimes, consumed in the great fire and denied the new life that the darkest star will grant to the rest of us. I hope you will choose the right course.'

He genuinely believes he's being merciful, Terrel thought incredulously. He believes swallowing poison is the right thing to do!

'You're a murderer and a madman,' Nomar said, and Terrel was astonished to hear that his friend's voice was now controlled and almost calm. 'But I am the one who can save you, not the other way around.'

Araguz was obviously taken aback. This was clearly not the reaction he had expected.

'Don't you recognize me, Araguz?' Nomar added. His use of the prophet's real name was another shock to their visitor. 'My bones should have been dust by now, like all the others you left at Senden.'

The prophet's face was a picture of horror, and Terrel felt an alien pressure building up inside his head – only for it to be relieved by the glimpsed memory of a mountain cave. Taryn was still protecting them.

'I was the only one of the Family to survive,' Nomar went on, his tone still measured but burning with the intensity of a lifetime's buried memories. 'And they died for no reason. You got it wrong then, and you've got it wrong now.'

'No!' Araguz screamed, finding his voice at last. 'You defy the moons!'

'The moons will defy you,' Nomar spat back. 'Take your pills away. We have no need of them. Better still, take a few yourself. And do it now, before you destroy us all.'

'Unholy fool!' the prophet shouted. 'I am the guide to all the rest. When the ceremony begins, then is the time to step out on the road to Paradise.' He grew calmer and a wolf-like smile spread over his ageing face. 'And when I do so, your son will be coming with me.'

Nomar's hard-won control deserted him then, but his screams went unheeded. Araguz had gone.

After that, the waiting became even more of a nightmare. While Terrel was certain that Taryn was not yet in the prophet's hands, Araguz's parting words had implied that he soon would be. Had his boast been based on knowledge, or on wishful thinking? There was no way of knowing, and the healer swung back and forth between undirected anger and despondency. Neither he nor Nomar slept much that night, but when daylight returned they felt even worse. There were only a few hours left now.

In the feeble, pallid light that reached their cell, Terrel eyed the pills – which lay untouched at the base of the door – and began to wonder about the future. If the worst came to the worst, and Araguz succeeded in getting everyone else to take the poison, it would leave the two men trapped inside the prison that would eventually become their grave. Swallowing the tablets would at least be a quicker end than starving to death.

Stop thinking like that, he told himself sternly. There's still time.

But, as if to emphasize the morbid nature of his ideas, no one brought them any food or water that day – and although that was the least of their concerns as dusk fell, it did nothing to improve their mood of increasing despair. They called out until they were hoarse, but provoked no response. It seemed that even their gaolers had forgotten their existence.

There was never any possibility of either of them sleeping that night, but as they stared blindly into the pitch black of their darkened cell Terrel suddenly found himself dreaming. At first the images were confused and fleeting, but as they gradually became more coherent he understood what he was seeing. What was more, he sensed that Nomar was seeing it too. Taryn was showing them both 'pictures' of what was happening outside in the city.

Taryn's attention, like most of those in the immense crowd around him, was divided between watching the heavens and the parapet where Queen Kalmira was standing next to the Ravens' Voice. It had been cloudy earlier in the day, but now the sky was clear and the three visible moons, all glowing at the height of their brilliance, were slowly moving towards each other. The boy tried to work out where the Dark Moon was by seeing whether it blocked the light of any stars, but he hadn't been able to locate it yet. Few people would even know it was there until it began to move in front of the other moons. On the castle balcony, Araguz had been talking for some time, extolling the glories of the moment to come. Everyone around

Taryn hung on the prophet's words and seemed to be accepting them wholeheartedly, their faces rapt with a curious mixture of excitement and fear. They all wore pouches around their necks, and many fingered them nervously. There was a cord round Taryn's neck too, but his bag was empty.

Taryn felt the enchanter's power, but it washed over him, leaving him unaffected. However, he knew that Araguz's talent was made more potent – not less – when the greatest number of people were involved. In a massed gathering like this, the blind faith he induced fed on itself, intensifying as it passed from one person to the next and back again. The boy glanced anxiously at his companion, who held onto his hand. Lawren seemed tense, but he too was unaffected by the Ravens' Voice.

'Will it be soon?' Taryn whispered.

'I hope so,' Lawren replied. 'Not much time now.' The hunter glanced up at the sky, his keen eyes searching out not only the bright moons but other smaller shapes in the darkness.

'Do you really think—' Taryn began, then broke off as the Ravens' Voice rang out louder than ever.

'Only after the black night of the darkest star will we all find peace!'

The spell the prophet had cast over the entire city was made plain in that moment as an impossible silence fell over the square. No one moved or spoke. They hardly seemed to breathe. It was at once the most incredible and the most terrifying thing Taryn had ever witnessed. He wanted to shout out, to call for his father, but he could not. His eyes, like those of everyone there, turned from the parapet to the sky above, where the three moons seemed to be almost touching. The confluence was only a short time away.

'The only true light comes,' Araguz intoned. 'Watch.'

A movement in the crowd nearby distracted Taryn and he looked around, wondering who would dare to defy the Ravens' Voice. He saw a figure pushing his way through the throng and was delighted to see that it was one of the travellers. Lawren had noticed him too.

'Nice timing,' the hunter remarked quietly. 'Now I can go with Faulk. Look after the boy, will you.'

'It'll be a pleasure,' Roskin replied.

Terrel and Nomar were screaming at the walls of their cell.

'No! No! Don't go with him,' Nomar cried.

But it was too late. Lawren had vanished from Taryn's field of vision, after exchanging a few more words with the newcomer, and the boy had trustingly put his hand into Roskin's.

'Pictures,' Terrel gasped. 'Not words, pictures. That's what we need to send him.' He tried to envision a scene with the boy escaping from the traitor's clutches, but the link did not seem to work in the other direction. Roskin was talking to Taryn now, his words unheard by the distant observers, and whatever was being said did not seem to upset Nomar's son at all.

'Do you want to go inside the palace?'

'Do you know where my father is?' Taryn responded eagerly.

'I know exactly where he is,' Roskin replied. 'Come on.'

'Shouldn't we wait for the others to start?'

'Start what? Where are the others?'

Taryn pointed, looking up at the battlements above and to the right of the parapet. Roskin followed his gaze but could not pick out what the boy had seen. It was only when the music began that he realized what was happening.

CHAPTER THIRTY-ONE

The music was beautiful. It was also impossibly loud – as though a thousand lutes had struck up the same tune all around the square, and even in the sky. Each one played in perfect harmony with the rest, each beat matched exactly, yet each had a singular voice, a subtle variation from its partners.

And the music was more than sound. It had a magic all of its own – enough to break the hold of Araguz's spell. The crowd shifted and murmured, confused now, their attention divided.

Roskin began to pull Taryn through the mass of people. Then, when the boy couldn't go fast enough for his liking, he picked him up and carried him towards the castle gates.

Terrel and Nomar could hear the music even in the underground cell. Despite being muffled by layers of stone its beauty was still recognizable, and if they did not know how such incredible volume was being produced, they both knew who was creating the wondrous sounds.

'It's Pieri, isn't it?' Nomar said. 'He's on the battlements.'

'Yes,' Terrel agreed. 'And Yllen's with him.' There had been a third figure there too, but he'd vanished almost as soon as Taryn had looked their way, and Terrel had not recognized him.

'What are they doing?' Nomar wondered.

'I've no idea, but it seems to be upsetting Araguz's plans.' A bubble of hope and excitement welled up inside the healer.

Then, abruptly, the pictures began to sway and lurch, and they could no longer see properly.

'What's happening?' Nomar cried in panic. 'What's he doing to Taryn?'

Terrel was as disorientated as his companion, but at that moment the relayed images were superseded by real light, coming from the corridor outside their cell. He stood up but Nomar stayed where he was, frantically trying to hold on to his son's visual messages.

Cobo's face appeared in the grille and, as his heart leapt, Terrel heard the longed-for sound of the bolts being drawn back.

'Come on,' the old man rasped, breathing hard. 'If you want to challenge Araguz there's not much time left.'

'But Taryn!' Nomar exclaimed.

'This is the only way we're going to save him,' Terrel said as the door swung open. 'By beating the prophet at his own game. Let's go.'

Blinking in the harsh new light, Nomar stumbled after the healer.

As Cobo led them through the various levels of the palace, it soon became obvious that they had no need of stealth. In contrast to Terrel's earlier journey within these walls, there was no one to slow their progress or even question their right to be there. It seemed that everyone was in or around the square.

At first the music was the only sound they could hear. But as they neared their destination Terrel became aware of the low rumbling of the crowd and Araguz's voice raised above the noise, shouting orders that the healer couldn't yet make out. As they began to climb another set of stairs, with Cobo's laboured breathing making the supreme nature of his effort obvious, Nomar turned to Terrel.

'If anything happens to me,' he gasped, 'look after Taryn.'

'Nothing's going—'

'Promise me!' Nomar demanded, almost bringing them to a halt as he grabbed Terrel's arm.

'Come on!' Cobo wheezed, noting their hesitation with alarm.

'I promise,' Terrel said.

They ran on.

A few moments later their goal was in sight. On the far side of the room they'd just entered was an open doorway that led out on to the balcony overlooking the square. There were several courtiers and guards in the room, but they all seemed to be in some sort of a trance and none of them made any attempt to stop the trio from making their way across the chamber.

As they emerged into the moonlight – and into the full force of the music – Terrel instinctively took note of the moons. They were overlapping now, moving towards the moment when the Red and White would vanish behind the Amber, but – much to Terrel's relief – there was no sign of the Dark Moon in front of them. There was time yet.

As they had known from Taryn's pictures, there were only two people standing on the parapet. Kalmira did not even look at them as they arrived, but Araguz spun round and glared. Below them the crowd's murmuring rose in volume at the sight of the newcomers.

'Blasphemers,' the prophet hissed. 'This is your doing.' It was not immediately obvious what he was referring to, but his next words made his meaning clear. 'But my guards are on their way up to the battlements. This vile music that seeks to make a travesty of the sacred night will soon be silenced. And then all will be well again.'

Not so much time after all, Terrel thought. He knew as soon as the music stopped that the spell the Ravens' Voice had cast over the gathering would be renewed. If he was ever going to challenge Araguz it had to be now. But before he could act Nomar stepped forward, and Terrel knew that this was the moment his friend had been waiting for all his life, ever since he'd crawled away from his mother's corpse. This was Nomar's battle.

'The Ravens' Voice is false!' Nomar cried, and his words rolled out like thunder across the square.

This was Nomar's battle, but he was not fighting it alone. Like Pieri's music, Nomar's voice seemed to come from everywhere, louder than any human sound, and Terrel guessed that someone, probably Cobo, was using the glamour to make sure that everyone there heard what was being said. The fact that the crowd had become silent, waiting for the next utterance, was proof of his success.

'There will be no confluence this night!' Nomar roared. 'The Dark Moon will prove the prophet's augury is false.'

'He's lying!' Araguz cried, his own augmented voice booming over the music that was still ringing out. 'This world will end tonight in fire and smoke. Your only hope – your only certainty – of being saved is to take the elixir when the time comes.'

'Poison will not save you,' Nomar told the crowd, then turned to face his adversary. 'I challenge you. Give me some of this elixir. If the confluence takes place and the Dark Moon blots out the other three, I will swallow it. But if it does not, I will cast it aside – and so will everyone else here.' He turned back to the throng. 'Is this a fair challenge?'

The response was a rumbling avalanche of sound that slowly grew in volume until its meaning was unequivocal. Terrel expected Araguz to be apprehensive now but the prophet was smiling, apparently quite sure of his ground.

'I accept your challenge,' he replied with equal fervour, tossing over a small pouch as he spoke. There could be no doubt that Araguz believed his own prediction.

Terrel glanced up at the sky again. The furthest moons were more than half covered now, but the Amber Moon was no longer complete. A black shadow was advancing across its glowing surface, as if it were a golden cheese and someone had taken a neat bite out of its edge. For a moment the healer felt horribly nervous, wondering if the ghosts had got it wrong. If the confluence that night *was* complete, then they were all doomed.

'Will you take my hand to seal your oath?' Nomar asked.

The prophet looked surprised, then moved along beside the balustrade.

'This seals your oath too,' he said as their hands clasped together.

It was only a few moments later, when Nomar showed no sign of releasing his grip, that Terrel realized what his friend was trying to do. He was trying to *heal* Araguz, to rid him of his madness and murderous intent. That he could even contemplate doing such a thing for his mother's killer was a mark of how far Nomar had come as a person, as well as a healer. You're a better man than I, Terrel thought, willing him to succeed.

'Your tricks won't work on me,' Araguz said contemptuously, his voice pitched so that only the people on the balcony could hear. 'I am protected too.'

Nomar stepped back, staggering slightly. Even in failure his efforts had drained his strength. Terrel thought he was going to fall, but Nomar righted himself and stood defiantly erect. He put a hand to his temple, and Terrel realized that facing the man responsible for his nightmares was likely to induce one of Nomar's crippling headaches. He could only hope it would not come too soon.

Everyone turned to watch the moons again. The Red and White were now no more than crescents, flanking the Amber, and the Dark Moon's bite was bigger than before, but it was not progressing as fast as the others. We were right, Terrel thought jubilantly. It's not going to happen! He glanced at Araguz, who was looking nervous, having presumably begun to have his own doubts about the oath he had sworn. A few paces away, Nomar was clearly in a lot of pain, his brow creased and his eyes half closed. But Terrel knew his friend would not accept any help now. The music continued to swirl over the city, and ripples of sound ran through the crowd as they too watched the sky-borne drama unfold. Most of them did not even notice the hundreds of small shadows that moved among the stars.

All at once a disturbance in the room behind them made all those on the balcony turn round. Roskin came towards them, carrying the struggling figure of a young boy.

'I've found him!' Roskin called breathlessly as he staggered on to the balcony and dumped the child beside Araguz. Taryn immediately jumped to his feet and was about to run to his father when one of the prophet's hands snaked out and grabbed the boy's collar. An instant later his other hand was holding a knife at Taryn's throat. It had all happened so fast that no one had had the chance to react. As Taryn froze, terrified, Nomar simply stared in horror. Neither Terrel nor Cobo dared move.

A slow smile spread over the prophet's face.

'Your son has remarkable talents,' he said, 'but they won't protect him from my blade. The tip is coated with shadowbane. Even the slightest graze will prove fatal.'

Nomar's face had turned white.

'Don't hurt him,' he breathed.

'On one condition,' Araguz replied.

'What?'

'I've had enough of you and your tiresome challenge. Swallow your elixir and I'll let the boy go.'

As Nomar hesitated, a ghostly figure materialized next to Terrel.

Hello, brother, Jax said cheerfully. *What have I missed?*

Terrel did not reply, having no idea how the prince's arrival might affect the course of events. Araguz – the only other person who could see the prince – was less reticent.

It's about time you showed up, he complained silently. *I've been—*

Sorry, I'm sure, Jax cut in, glancing up at the sky. *But you promised me something more exciting than this.*

Before Araguz could reply, Terrel found his own telepathic voice.

Don't help him, Jax. He's just using you for his own ends. At the same time, the healer was trying to keep an eye on the moons and on Nomar – who had taken the tablet from the pouch Araguz had given him, without ever taking his eyes off his son. The prophet seemed momentarily distracted by Terrel's intervention, but the knife was still almost touching Taryn's neck.

'Don't do anything stupid, Nomar,' Terrel said aloud, hoping his friend would give him some time to turn the new situation to their advantage. 'There's another way to settle this.'

Why are you listening to him? the prophet asked Jax. *Get on with it.*

What's that music? the prince asked, ignoring them both.

Evil, Araguz hissed. *Kill the one who's making it, Jax. Burn his heart.*

No! Terrel cried. *If you're going to kill anyone, kill the prophet. He's the evil one here.*

Are those my only choices? Jax enquired. He seemed to be enjoying himself immensely.

Fool! There is no choice. Araguz's silent voice was filled with disdain. *You risk the souls of this entire city. Unless—*

I don't like being called a fool, Jax stated quietly. In yet another of his mercurial changes of mood, the prince was becoming irritated and impatient.

Blasphemer, Araguz spat. *Imbecile!*

Terrel felt the first stirrings of sorcery, the lines snaking out. A fire-starter's talent was the most appalling misuse of power, but if ever a man deserved to be killed it was Araguz. The healer found that he was willing on Jax's murderous intent, feeling almost as if he was actually part of the process.

All that changed in the next instant when one of the small shadows in the sky grew larger, and a raven fluttered down awkwardly – landing on the ground at Terrel's feet in a muddle of black feathers.

You can't let Jax kill him, Alyssa said urgently. *You have to stop him.*

Why? Terrel was utterly bemused now.

Don't argue, she snapped. *Just do it!*

Stop! Terrel cried, aiming his thoughts at the prince.

Keep out of this, Jax growled, the heat rising within him and in Araguz.

You can't do this. Stop it now. Terrel reached out, finding that he really was part of the process, and did his best to disrupt the fire-starter's chains.

What are you doing? Jax was outraged. *You can't . . .*

I can, Terrel declared. *Stop this now, Jax.*

Their struggle ended in deadlock, with them both paralyzed and unable to pull back. The man with two heads had fought himself to a standstill. Araguz was safe for the moment – though Terrel did not know why he should want to keep him alive – but the healer was not able to do anything else. The raven seemed to recover itself and flew off, croaking indignantly. Alyssa's fleeting visit was over, and Terrel's last hope of understanding had gone with her.

He looked around and saw that the others on the balcony were still frozen where they stood, but he could do nothing to influence the outcome of the confrontation now. All his energies were needed to contain Jax's vicious rage.

'Time to make up your mind, Nomar,' Araguz said, regaining some of his earlier confidence. 'You were right when you said you should have died a long time ago. But this way you can at least save your son.'

Nomar's eyes were haunted, full of pain and helpless longing. He started to say something, then thought better of it. In one swift movement he put the tablet in his mouth and swallowed convulsively. Taryn screamed and began to struggle in spite of his own danger, even as Terrel's mind rang with repetitive, useless denials. A tremor ran through Nomar's body and his face contorted in agony.

At that moment the music stopped. The night was suddenly full of a thousand different snippets of birdsong, but that soon died away. Araguz smiled, tightening his grip on Taryn, as the crowd below grew hushed.

Nomar clutched his throat and collapsed to the ground.

CHAPTER THIRTY-TWO

'Behold!' Araguz cried, his voice enhanced again by his own version of the glamour. 'The darkest star comes!' He pointed with the knife in a dramatic gesture and everyone looked up at the sky.

The Red and White Moons were now reduced to the thinnest of slivers, crescents peering out from behind the Amber – which itself was almost half hidden by the seemingly inexorable progress of the sky-shadow. Held immobile by the continuing internal struggle with his twin, Terrel could only watch and hope. The night grew darker, the stars seemed to shine brighter in contrast, and silence fell over Vergos as the last of the birds returned to ground, their unnatural songs at an end.

At last the two more distant moons disappeared altogether, and the onlookers held their breath as the Dark Moon continued to edge across the Amber.

'Welcome to—' Araguz began, then faltered, sounding uncertain for the first time as the city and the land on which it stood trembled. The prophet had finally realized what Terrel had known for some time; the confluence was never going to come to completion. It was clear now that the Dark Moon was not moving across the centre of the Amber but sliding across a little to one side, and now – even before it reached the midpoint of its traverse – the Red and White Moons were beginning to emerge slowly from their hiding place. The crucial moment had passed – and Araguz had failed to meet the challenge of his fallen opponent.

The prophet tried desperately to reassert his authority.

'Eat!' the Ravens' Voice implored the whispering crowds. 'Take the elixir, or the fire will—'

'Don't listen to him!' A new voice entered the conflict and Terrel knew at once who it was. Her words were louder than was natural but he would have recognized Yllen's voice anywhere. 'The prophet is false,' she went on. 'He has failed the challenge. There is no confluence, no fire.'

The crowd seemed to hover in indecision, not sure who to believe. The enchanter's will warred with the evidence of their own eyes.

'Eat!' the Ravens' Voice repeated, his eyes wild. 'Or I will slit his throat.'

The knife was back at Taryn's neck, but the threat meant nothing to most of Araguz's audience. There was one person, however, to whom it meant everything.

Nomar rose up from the dead, mouth open in an incoherent roar as he charged towards his nemesis. The prophet gaped in disbelief, and Cobo took advantage of his distraction to lunge forward and grab Taryn. Araguz slashed out reflexively and blood spurted, but Terrel, still held fast by his battle with Jax, could not tell from whom it came. The knife clattered to the floor, and both Taryn and the old man landed in a heap under the balustrade just as Nomar reached his enemy. His assault was unstoppable, channelling the pent-up fury of a wild animal into a single goal. In threatening his son, Araguz had released Nomar from his beliefs as a healer and made him capable of the violence he so abhorred.

Terrel watched in horror as the two men collided, Nomar driving his forehead into Araguz's face as the force of his charge lifted the prophet from the ground. What happened next seemed inevitable to Terrel, and he was powerless to prevent it. The impact of Nomar's ferocious attack threw Araguz backwards, and both men toppled over the balustrade and fell to the unforgiving stone of the square below.

Seeing this, Jax gave up his own attempt to kill Araguz and Terrel found himself free to move. Leaning over the parapet, he saw the two men, still locked together as they smashed to the ground. Neither of them could possibly have survived such a fall – and Terrel was distraught. Not only had he lost a friend, but he hadn't been able to obey Alyssa's urgent instruction to ensure that Araguz was not killed. The 'father of the shield' had made his sacrifice – just as the Tindaya Code had predicted – and the inhabitants of Vergos had been saved, but the healer still knew he'd failed. He looked away, no longer able to bear the sight below him, and it was only then that he realized there were others in need of his help.

Thankfully, Jax was nowhere to be seen, but Kalmira had collapsed and Taryn was curled in a heap, sobbing desperately. But Cobo was in an even worse state, lying on the floor in a pool of blood. Terrel went to the old man first and knelt beside him. As he did so, another tremor shook the city and the healer suddenly felt very warm, but he took no notice of these things. As soon as he looked into Cobo's eyes he knew there was little hope. The old man had already lost a lot of blood and the poison from Araguz's blade had worked its way through his body. Even so, Terrel took his hand and tried to bring him back.

'Don't waste your strength,' Cobo breathed, then forced a weary smile. 'It's my time. He's the one you need to look after now.' The old man's eyes flickered towards Taryn.

Terrel drew back, knowing that Cobo was right but unwilling to just abandon him.

'Set the ravens free, Terrel,' the old man whispered. 'I won't be needing their services any more.'

The healer looked up and saw that all around, on the balustrade, on all the nearby ledges and sills, a great flock of night-black birds had gathered, their bead-bright eyes fixed on their fallen master. They were the ones who had carried Pieri's music far and wide, allowing the prophet's spell to be broken. The voices of the true ravens had muted the Ravens' Voice.

Your job is done, Terrel told them silently. *You can go now.*

When he looked down again, the smile was still on the old man's face but the King of the Marketplace was dead. Terrel wished him well on his journey to the next world, and went to try to comfort the living.

'Terrel? Terrel! Are you there?' Faulk's voice rang out in the silence, startling the healer.

Once Taryn's sobs had subsided the world had become an unnaturally quiet place – but Terrel hadn't really noticed that until now. All his attention had been concentrated on the boy who had just lost the only parent he'd ever known. Nomar's son was clinging to him, trembling like a newborn calf, as the sounds of movement came from the room behind the parapet. A moment later Faulk came out into the multi-coloured moonlight, his face flushed and sheened with sweat. His sword was in his hand, but Terrel saw at once that there was no blood staining the blade. On seeing the healer, the soldier's expression betrayed his relief, but there was sorrow and bewilderment in his eyes too.

'Are you all right?' Faulk asked as he came to a halt.

Terrel nodded, looking round. Roskin was nowhere to be seen. Kalmira still lay where she had fallen.

'And Taryn?' the big man asked, sheathing his sword.

'He's unharmed,' Terrel replied. In body at least, he added privately.

'That's something,' Faulk said heavily, as Lawren emerged from the doorway and took in the scene before him. For once the hunter seemed at a loss for words.

'Have you seen Araguz?' Terrel asked.

'Yes,' Faulk replied. 'He's dead, and so is . . .' He fell silent, all too aware of Taryn's grief.

Terrel nodded in acknowledgement. He had expected nothing else.

'But that's not all,' Faulk went on. 'Everyone else in the city has fallen asleep. We're the only ones left awake.'

At first the healer's brain refused to accept what he'd heard.

'Everyone?' he breathed.

'We can't rouse a single person,' Lawren confirmed. 'It's the same up here as in the square. They're all sleepers.'

A city of sleepers, Terrel thought. The unnatural silence made sense now, but he could not quite believe it until he had seen for himself. He glanced at Kalmira, who was still unconscious – as were all the courtiers in the nearby room. Awkwardly cradling Taryn in his mismatched arms, Terrel rose to his feet and looked out over the square. The entire arena was littered with thousands of unmoving bodies, and the healer finally understood what must have happened.

Having been thwarted in his original intentions, Araguz – even as he fell to his death – had exacted a terrible revenge on the population of Vergos. The second tremor Terrel had felt had been no ordinary earthquake, and the heat had come from his red crystal, confirming that the mad elemental had indeed been involved. Only those whom Taryn protected had escaped, which meant that all their efforts to save the city's inhabitants from a dreadful fate had been in vain – because they had now been condemned to another. And Terrel had failed in his own endeavour. There was no way now that the 'entire city' could help him in his ultimate task. Their lives, like those of all Nydus's sleepers, hung in the balance.

'Where are the others?' Lawren asked.

'I've no idea where Roskin is,' Terrel replied, hoping he'd never see their treacherous companion again, 'but the last time I saw Yllen and Pieri they were up on the battlements.'

'I'll go and find them,' the hunter said, running off at once.

'What's he doing here?' Faulk asked, looking down at Cobo.

'He was a friend,' Terrel replied. 'I'm not sure any of us could have survived this without his help.'

The soldier looked sceptical, but Terrel was too tired to explain fully.

'He's dead,' he added simply.

The healer was beginning to find Taryn an increasingly heavy burden, but realized that – incredibly – the boy had fallen asleep in his arms. Terrel knew that grief affected people in different ways, and there was no telling how the ordeals of the past few days had drained Taryn's strength. Even though he might not have known what he was doing, the effort involved in protecting the rest of the company had obviously exhausted him.

'Look after Taryn for a while, will you?'

Faulk took the sleeping child from Terrel and the healer turned his attention to Kalmira. It took only a brief examination to confirm that she was indeed a sleeper, and Terrel reflected grimly that the Raven Cypher had been right after all. The queen *had* rejoined her son – just not in the way she had hoped. Both their spirits were in limbo now.

A short time later Lawren returned in a breathless rush.

'They're still up there,' he told them, 'but Pieri's badly hurt. You need to get to him fast, Terrel.'

Terrel did his best to keep up with the hunter as he retraced his steps, and when they arrived at the battlements he was gasping for air and aching all over. However, the sight that greeted him was enough to make him forget his own fatigue. Several guards, now fast asleep, were sprawled nearby and the lute Pieri had been playing lay on the ground, smashed beyond repair. Yllen was sitting with Pieri's head cradled in her lap, tears running down her face. The musician's eyes were closed and his tunic was stained with blood.

'Terrel! Thank the moons,' Yllen cried when she saw him. 'Help him, please.'

The healer wasted no time in kneeling beside them and taking Pieri's hand. As Terrel fell into the waking dream his patient opened his eyes, smiled and tried to speak. What emerged was no more than a whisper that bubbled ominously in his throat, but his words were clear enough.

'That's a fine instrument. I should like to play it again sometime.' He was clearly unaware of the lute's fate.

'Quiet now,' Yllen said softly. 'Terrel's here.'

As he followed the paths and patterns of the storyteller's inner world, Terrel knew he had almost come too late. He could deal with the pain, but some of the damage that had been done was very serious, and it would only heal – if it ever did – after a long convalescence. It was not just the stab wounds themselves – though they were bad enough – but there were traces of poison too, a dark shadow within the dream. He did what he could to counter its malign influence and tried to set Pieri on the way to recovery, then withdrew.

'Will he be all right?' Yllen asked immediately, her anxiety plain.

'He'll live for now,' Terrel replied, 'but it's going to take him a long time to recover.' Pieri had fallen asleep where he lay.

'He was only hurt because he tried to protect me,' she said tearfully. 'He made my voice loud, so everyone could hear me, but then the guards came and . . .' She broke off, unable to finish.

'You both did a wonderful job,' Terrel told her, not knowing what else to say. He was feeling utterly drained and wasn't sure how much more he could take.

By the time dawn came, Pieri and Taryn had been installed in two of the palace's many bedchambers. Yllen stayed to watch over her friend, but Terrel knew he had to go and see for himself what had happened to Nomar. As he was about to set off, Taryn woke up and followed him out.

'I'm coming too.'

'No, I don't think—'

'I want to see him.' The boy's face was set in such a look of determination that Terrel did not have the strength to argue.

Faulk led them to where Nomar and Araguz lay on the stone flags of the square. The prophet's body was in a crumpled heap, but Nomar had been laid out on his back, his arms crossed over his chest. He looked quite peaceful, but as a healer Terrel sensed that his injuries had been devastating and death instantaneous. His friend had been broken beyond all hope of repair.

'Are you sure he's not just sleeping, like all the rest?' Taryn asked quietly. The boy was standing with Terrel, holding the healer's hand as they looked at his father.

'No, little one. He's dead. I'm sorry.'

'It was my fault, wasn't it.'

'What?' Terrel was aghast. 'No! Of course not!'

'But if I hadn't been there . . .'

'Your father loved you. He'd have done anything to protect you. But this was *not* your fault. I think he always knew his fate was linked with Araguz, and that's how it turned out.'

Taryn said nothing for a while and Terrel couldn't tell whether he had accepted this rather glib rationalization. All the healer knew for certain was that Taryn could not be allowed to accept the blame for his father's death.

'Was it the poison that made him angry?' the boy asked. 'He hates fighting.'

'I don't know,' Terrel replied, feeling helpless now. At first he'd assumed that Nomar had not really swallowed the tablet and had only pretended to collapse. But it was also possible that by surviving his poisoning as a child he'd built up a certain immunity to the venom in shadowbane. It was even possible that Nomar had known he would die from the poison eventually, and had used the last of his strength to make sure Araguz died with him.

'Are we going to leave him here?' the boy asked.

'No,' Terrel replied, marvelling at the child's courage. 'We'll find somewhere to bury him properly.'

They said their final farewells to Nomar and Cobo that afternoon. Lawren had retrieved Jarek and found a cart which the mule pulled through the streets to the necropolis. Faulk used the keys to let them in through the gates and led them to the tomb he and Terrel had shared earlier.

Once inside they found two empty coffin spaces and laid the bodies inside. No one knew quite what to say or do after that, although they all wanted the occasion to be marked somehow. Eventually, Pieri – who had insisted on coming with the others, in spite of still being in pain and very weak, and who'd had to be persuaded to ride on the cart – whispered something to Yllen and then took her hand in his.

Yllen looked nervous and embarrassed, but then she closed her eyes and began to sing. Her voice was lighter and less resonant than Pieri's, but everyone heard his influence in her delivery. The song was a lament in a language none of the others knew, but its heartfelt poignancy touched them all.

After that, Faulk and Lawren manoeuvred the waiting stone slab that formed the lid of Cobo's tomb into position. As they moved to do the same for Nomar, Taryn – who until then had been remarkably composed – began to take off the cord that held his mother's ring.

'What are you doing?' Terrel asked.

'I think he should have this, don't you?' Taryn said, his voice trembling.

'I think he'd want you to keep it,' the healer said. 'We'll leave him a different treasure.'

'No. I don't have anything else.' Taryn sounded determined now.

'Well, all right. If you're sure.'

The boy nodded, leant over the side of the coffin and placed the ring over Nomar's heart.

'Goodbye, Father,' he said quietly and turned away.

Terrel nodded to Faulk and the second lid was set in place. The mourners filed out into the wintry sunlight. Just before Faulk closed and locked the mausoleum for the last time, Taryn glanced back and raised one hand in a little wave, a gesture that made Terrel feel as if his heart would break. He thought he was the only one who'd seen it, but a moment later Yllen burst into floods of tears, which did not stop until Pieri had held her in his arms for some time.

As they walked slowly away from the tomb, Terrel looked back, half expecting to see some of the ravens paying their last respects. But there were no birds in sight. The ravens were free now.

Looking down at the child who walked beside him, Terrel's thoughts turned to the last wishes of the mausoleum's other new resident. If anything happens to me, look after Taryn. Whatever else happened, that was a promise the healer was determined to keep.

Faulk took it upon himself to dispose of Araguz's body, but he didn't tell the others what he had done with the prophet's remains, and nobody asked him about it.

'There's nothing more we can do here,' Terrel said later that day.

'So what happens now?' Faulk asked.

'We go on to the coast.'

The remaining members of the company had spent most of the day recovering from their various ordeals, but at dusk both Terrel and Faulk had become restless. They had gone up to the battlements and were now looking out over the city.

'We'll have plenty of horses to choose from,' Faulk observed.

'I'd rather go by boat if we can,' Terrel said.

'But there's no one to sail them,' the soldier objected.

Terrel was about to explain his reasoning when he was distracted by a peculiar sight in the distance. To the southwest, where the Syriel River snaked its way towards the ocean, the golden light of the setting sun was glittering on something moving very fast.

'What's that?' Terrel asked, pointing.

Faulk stared, squinting against the glare, then whistled in surprise.

'My guess is it's a tidal surge running up the river,' he said. 'A big one, by the look of it.'

Terrel studied the phenomenon, not sure how anything to do with tides could affect the river so far inland.

'It happens after two or more of the moons are full,' Faulk explained. 'This is more powerful than most, because three were full last night and the fourth was close too. Even so . . .'

A wall of water, Terrel thought, recalling Shahan's warning.

'Will it get as far as the city?' he asked.

'I'm not sure,' Faulk replied.

The answer to Terrel's question came only a short time later. As the surge drew closer, it became clear that it was growing more – not less – powerful as it sped inland, because as the river narrowed the water was compressed into a smaller and smaller space. By the time it reached the outskirts of Vergos it was a small mountain of churning foam that carried everything before it, overflowing the banks and flooding the surrounding areas. When it reached the city its impact was explosive, lifting ships into the air and dashing them down again, inundating buildings and sending miniature tidal waves down many of the streets and alleys. The devastation would normally have been accompanied by massive loss of life but for the fact that the docks and the nearby areas were deserted. Even from the safety of the castle, high above the river, watching the deluge left Terrel feeling shaken, and made him think that perhaps travelling by horseback might not be such a bad idea after all.

'All the shipping on the river's been smashed into firewood,' Faulk reported the next morning. 'The whole area's a mess.'

The company had spent the night in the comfort of the palace, and were now gathered together to discuss their plans. Even Pieri was there, looking pale but alert, having benefited from Terrel's continuing ministrations and a day's rest. Faulk had gone down to the docks at first light and had returned with dispiriting news.

'That's that, then,' Lawren said.

'Actually, there's a ship that *did* survive,' Faulk said. 'It was in dry dock – except that it's not dry any more. It might be the sort of craft we could handle.'

Everyone considered this idea for a few moments.

'Of course we can,' Yllen exclaimed, laughing suddenly. 'I mean, look at this crew. Two able-bodied men who've never sailed before, one man with only two sound limbs out of four, one invalid, a cabin boy and – worst of all – a woman! How can we fail?'

'And a mule,' Pieri added. 'Don't forget the mule.'

'Exactly,' Lawren said, picking up on their good humour. 'Look at it this way. We'll be on a river, so we can't possibly get lost or go the wrong way. And we'll be travelling downstream, with the current. How hard could it be?'

Despite their joking, the idea was clearly taking hold.

'All right,' Faulk said. 'I just hope none of you are too superstitious.'

'Why?' Lawren queried. 'What's the problem?'

'The name of the ship,' Faulk replied. 'She's called the *Dark Star*.'

PART TWO

THE DARK STAR

CHAPTER THIRTY-THREE

With their limited manpower it took the company several days to prepare the *Dark Star* for her maiden voyage, but Terrel counted the time well spent. Apart from familiarizing themselves with the layout of the ship and the ways of operating her sails and rigging, they were also able to load up enough provisions to see them through a month if necessary. For once, finding food was no problem at all; they simply took what was needed from the city, knowing that no one there would have any use for it. By doing this they gave themselves the option of sailing all the way to the coast without having to stop on the way. Lawren joked that this was a good thing, because once they set off they probably wouldn't be able to stop even if they wanted to.

The problem of navigation was taken seriously in spite of such light-hearted remarks. It turned out that although Faulk was not a sailor, he had been a passenger on ships many times and knew enough to get them started – and Terrel began to remember some useful information from his voyages to and from Myvatan. However, with such a small and inexperienced crew no one was under any illusions that it was going to be easy. Common sense combined with trial and error would get them so far, but luck would be a factor too. On several occasions Terrel wondered if they were doing the right thing – but each

time, seeing the enthusiasm of his companions, he decided
that they were.

They returned to the palace every night to rest in comfort and to check on Pieri's progress. The storyteller was
still in bed and he was not improving as fast as Terrel
would have liked. In fact it was Pieri's condition that made
travelling by ship their preferred choice. Faulk and Yllen
claimed to be good riders. Although Lawren and Taryn
had never ridden before, they could probably have coped
on suitable mounts, and Terrel would have done so under
protest, but there was no way Pieri could travel on horseback. Both he and their supplies could have been loaded
on to carts, of course, but they had no way of knowing
which roads to follow – or indeed what condition they'd be
in after the recent upheavals. The river did at least guarantee a continuous and unmistakable route to the sea. All
in all, the *Dark Star* seemed to be their best chance – and
even though Terrel faced the voyage with some trepida-
tion, he was still eager to be on his way.

At last, late one afternoon, all was as ready as it could
be, and the company trudged back up the hill to the palace
knowing that their journey would begin again the next
morning. As they threaded their way through the square,
trying not to think too much about the sleepers all around
them, Terrel felt a mixture of anticipation and sorrow. He
had several regrets about what had happened in Vergos,
and in many ways he would be glad to leave, but he sensed
that he still had some unfinished business there. That
night he found out what it was.

At first Terrel thought he was dreaming, but when he
opened his eyes properly the figure he'd imagined at the
foot of his bed was still there. She was holding an oil lamp
that was burning low, casting her features into dull shadows.

'Who are you? How did you get in here?'

'This palace has been my home for years,' the woman replied. 'Even your watchdog can't sniff out all the ways of moving around in here.'

Terrel guessed that she was referring to Faulk, who had checked the apartments thoroughly and who was now sleeping in the adjoining room. The fact that his visitor had been able to get past the soldier without disturbing him made it clear that she had remarkable talents – but Terrel already knew that. Any ordinary person would have been a sleeper.

'You're Kaeryss,' he said.

The prophetess nodded her head in acknowledgement, setting her lamp down upon a table. Terrel still couldn't see her eyes properly, and for some reason this made him even more nervous.

'What do you want?'

'I have a request. A very simple one. And in return I'd like to offer you what little help I can.' She held out a small roll of parchment.

Terrel leant forward and took it from her. Once unrolled it was clearly a letter, but he couldn't read much of the text. The signature at the bottom was plain enough, but while some of the words were familiar many were not, and the meaning of the whole was beyond him.

'What's this?'

'You're planning to travel by boat, I believe,' Kaeryss replied. 'I think that's a wise choice, but the Syriel River is not called Kenda's Sorrow for nothing, and tidal surges aren't the only peril you will face. This is a letter to some friends of mine. They live in a village called Blackwater, the first you'll come to beyond the crater rim. They're skilled in the navigation of these waters, especially closer to the ocean where the currents become more treacherous. I have asked them to give you whatever assistance you require.'

'You don't think they'll be asleep?' Terrel queried.

'It's possible,' she admitted, 'but I have a feeling this malignancy doesn't extend beyond the outer limits of the ancient crater. So if you can get that far, they should be able to help you reach the coast at least.'

'And beyond?'

'I can't promise that. The ocean is another matter entirely.'

Terrel glanced at the letter again, wondering whether it was genuine. He sensed no deception in her spoken words, but without being able to read the letter properly he couldn't be sure of its content or its true meaning.

'You had a request,' he said, wanting to know the cost of this bargain.

'I'd like you to remember us,' she replied. 'Everyone here in Vergos.'

'That's all?'

'That's all.'

'What good will that do you?'

'Vergos will live again one day,' she answered. 'I have to believe that. And unless I'm very much mistaken, our fate, along with many others, depends upon your mission. There's no doubt now that you are part of the Raven Cypher, and with all that's happened I'll probably learn a lot more before too long.'

'Does the cypher say what I should do next?' Terrel asked curiously.

'I think you know that already,' Kaeryss replied with a slight smile. 'All I know for sure is that you have to leave. I'm trying to ease your path.'

'Thank you,' the healer murmured, not knowing what else to say.

'I'm the one who should be thanking you,' she said. 'If it hadn't been for your intervention, my friends would be dead now rather than sleeping.'

'Why aren't *you* a sleeper?'

'I'm old enough to have learnt a few tricks. I couldn't compete with Araguz when it came to controlling other people, but I was damned if I was going to let him control me. He had to use other means to keep me out of the way.' Her distaste for the prophet was obvious. 'Not that it did him much good in the end,' she added with a certain degree of satisfaction.

'Do you intend to stay here?' Terrel asked. 'Alone?'

'I shan't be alone.'

For a moment the healer was nonplussed, but then he realized who would be keeping her company – and how, in spite of her earlier isolation, she knew the prophet's real name.

'Roskin,' he said quietly.

'I won't ask you to forgive him,' she said, 'but he knows now that what he did was wrong, and he's keen to make amends if he can. He'll stay here with me and help me continue my work.'

Terrel was glad Roskin had kept out of sight. He'd wondered if the traitor had become a sleeper, but thought it more likely that he'd fled – fearing the wrath of those he had betrayed. He had good reason to be afraid. When the healer had told the others what the would-be seer had done, Faulk and Lawren had become ominously quiet, while Yllen had been all for seeking him out and tearing him limb from limb.

'Can you trust him?' he asked now, unable to keep the bitterness from his voice.

'I think so. And if not . . .' She shrugged. 'I have little left to lose.'

So Roskin's got what he always wanted, Terrel thought – to work beside Kaeryss on decoding the Raven Cypher. The ironies of fate never ceased to amaze him. He glanced down at the letter once more.

'Remember us, Terrel,' Kaeryss repeated softly. 'All of us.'

When the healer looked up again, he was alone in the room.

The next morning Terrel told the company about his nocturnal visitor and showed them the letter. Neither Faulk, Lawren or Yllen could make head nor tail of it, but Pieri and Taryn spent some time going through it word by word and came to the conclusion that, as far as they could tell, it was exactly what Kaeryss claimed it to be – unless any hidden messages had been concealed within the text. In the meantime, Faulk was angry with himself for the failure of his security measures.

'No harm came of it,' Terrel pointed out.

'I know,' the big man responded. 'But it could have done.'

The others helped persuade Faulk that searching the castle now would be pointless, and Terrel was glad he'd decided not to mention Roskin. If Yllen and Lawren had known he was still there, their attitude might well have been different.

'So, should we trust her?' Lawren asked as they completed the last of their packing.

'I see no reason not to,' Terrel reasoned. 'If she'd meant me any harm she could have killed me in my sleep.'

'But if we get as far as Blackwater by ourselves, why would we need help from sailors?' Yllen asked.

'Because the further we go the harder the navigation gets. I'd rather not end up drowning in a shipwreck.'

'We can go to the village anyway,' Faulk said. 'And see what we think before we show anyone the letter. By then we'll have some idea how well we can manage on our own.'

This compromise seemed to satisfy everyone, and the travellers set off for the docks – with Pieri leaning on Lawren's arm, and Taryn leading Jarek. Riding on a cool but sluggish breeze, Kephra circled above the silent city as if on lookout duty.

Three torturous hours later, they finally managed to manoeuvre the *Dark Star* out of the flooded dock and into the main course of the river. The effort involved had been disheartening, and almost bad enough to make them want to give up, but through a combination of stubbornness, hard work and ingenuity they succeeded with only minimal damage to the vessel's starboard bow. Because all the scrapes and bumps had been above the water line, no one was unduly worried as they edged out through the shattered lock gates – but it was still an enormous relief when they reached relatively open water.

They proceeded cautiously, finding that steering was not so easy when the current was flowing in the same direction as they were. At times the rudder seemed to have a mind of its own. They had only set one small sail and the wind was not strong, so they were moving slowly enough to mean that any collision would hopefully not be too serious, but in the event they managed to make their exit from the city with no more than a few alarms. In fact their biggest problem was the uncertainty about the amount of debris in and under the water – remnants of all the less fortunate craft that had been destroyed by the tidal surge.

It was only when the river was finally out in open country, and the crew were feeling a little more confident in their own abilities, that they discovered they had one more passenger than they'd realized. A large ginger and white cat emerged from wherever it had been sleeping and began a leisurely circuit of the deck, as if inspecting its domain.

Terrel's heart leapt, but he realized very quickly that Alyssa was not present. For the most part the cat paid scant attention to the humans on board, although – much to the boy's delight – it graciously allowed Taryn to stroke its neck and rub the soft fur under its chin. However, it took an instant dislike to Jarek, hissing and spitting at him from a safe distance. The mule, who seemed to be taking his first nautical adventure in his stolid stride, simply ignored the smaller creature, treating its presence on the deck with lofty disdain. On the other hand, Kephra eyed the cat suspiciously from his perch atop the main mast and made no move to come any closer.

The cat, whom Taryn instantly named Paws, accepted some food as if it had expected nothing less and then retired to sleep once more. Terrel could not help smiling at the animal's proprietorial attitude, but when he thought about it, he realized Paws had as much right to be on board as any of the travellers. According to the laws of Kenda, they were all pirates now.

CHAPTER THIRTY-FOUR

The next three days provided ample evidence that the company did indeed need help in handling their stolen vessel. It took them that long to reach the unremarkable range of hills and rocky escarpments that marked the extent of the ancient crater. This was in part because the river meandered a great deal, but other factors – mainly their own incompetence – were of greater significance. Even though the water was calm for the most part, controlling the *Dark Star* proved more difficult than they had imagined, especially as the twists and turns of the river's course also meant that they had to cope with the constantly changing direction of the wind. Fortunately, the reed-encrusted banks were generally soft enough to make their occasional slow collisions more of a nuisance than a real danger, but there were other, more time-consuming mishaps. The level of the water seemed to rise and fall without discernible reason, and they ran aground twice – getting free only after several hours of fruitless toil and rising tempers, when the river itself relented and rose sufficiently to float them clear. Another factor was that almost imperceptible currents made it hard to keep the ship on course. At one point, when a tributary so small that it ought not to have made much difference joined the main flow, the travellers encountered a series of whirlpools which swung the *Dark Star* round so fiercely that for a while they were drifting sideways, completely out of control. However, their own cautious approach meant that they were never in any real danger of sinking, and at times they even managed to extract a certain amount of humour from the situation. But they were all aware that their progress was painfully slow.

Because none of them felt brave enough to sail on in darkness, they were forced to moor each night. They achieved this by dropping anchor from the stern and then allowing the craft to drift, securing her to a bank whenever possible. It was a haphazard method but they didn't have the skill to do anything more professional. The worst of it was that raising the anchor again the next morning was always very hard work, even with the ingenious system of wheels and ratchets that had been installed by the *Dark Star*'s builders. Faulk and Lawren bore the brunt of the manual labour, though the others all did what they could to help. Pieri, fretting at his own enforced idleness, even suggested a way of using Jarek to pull up the anchor, but that proved to be impractical.

While they were still within the boundaries of the massive crater they encountered no other shipping of any kind. Moreover, they saw no one on either bank. Any houses and settlements they did see appeared to be empty, but there was no way of knowing whether the occupants had abandoned their homes or become sleepers. They spotted quite a few animals wandering over the quiet fields, but all human life seemed to have vanished.

'No, no!' Lawren shouted. 'We need *more* sails, not less.'

'We're going too fast as it is!' Faulk yelled back. The soldier was at the tiller, his legs braced against the deck and the muscles in his arms straining as he fought to keep the *Dark Star* on course.

'Yes, but we can't just run with the current,' the hunter countered. 'We'd have no control at all.'

'All right, all right,' Faulk conceded. 'But hurry up. I'm going to need some help here soon.'

The ship was moving faster than it had ever done before, riding a current that was quickening all the time. They were heading towards the mouth of a ravine, where the Syriel had cut its way through the hills at the rim of the crater. Once they were inside, the banks would no longer be composed of forgiving mud and vegetation. The river here was flanked by cliffs of solid rock. At the same time the channel narrowed so that the flow increased its speed, making the possible consequences of any collision much more serious. By the time they'd realized what was ahead of them it had been too late to do anything about it. One way or another the *Dark Star* was going to go through the canyon. The only question was, would she come out of it in one piece?

Lawren was now directing Terrel, Yllen and Taryn as they scurried about, setting the extra sail. Terrel did what he was told, making the best use of his limited physical abilities, while trying to keep an eye on Taryn at the same time. The boy had become adept at climbing the rigging – almost like a spider tiptoeing across its web – but Terrel still found it hard not to worry about him. On this occasion all went smoothly for once, and as the new sail snapped into place and Taryn returned to the deck the healer felt the *Dark Star* steady herself and ride the waters more confidently. As Lawren dashed back to help Faulk, leaving Yllen to oversee the tying off of the last ropes, Terrel was able to look about for the first time. What he saw made his stomach clench and his pulse race even harder.

They were probably moving no faster than a man could

run, but after their ponderous progress during the earlier part of their journey this seemed very fast indeed. Although the river here was still wide enough to accommodate six or seven boats side by side, the enclosed nature of the defile and the solid walls of rock on either side made it seem much more narrow. Terrel was relieved to see that the surface of the water was placid – flowing smoothly rather than churning into rapids – but there was a lot of silt in this section of the river which made it impossible to tell how deep it was. He kept telling himself that many ships, some of them much larger than the *Dark Star*, had made the journey to and from Vergos on numerous occasions, proving that these waters were navigable. If Faulk was able to keep them in midstream they should be safe enough.

However, that was quite a big 'if'. The extra sail had given the helmsman a greater degree of control but, with the following wind, it had also increased their speed. Any mistake now would be disastrous, and even with Lawren's help Faulk was clearly having to strain every sinew to keep the bows pointed straight ahead. At the same time, Yllen and Taryn were continuously making small adjustments to the ropes, either on their own initiative or in response to instructions from the stern. Their course wavered every so often, and twice they came much too close to the cliffs for comfort. On both occasions they managed to sail on, but by then the only one on board who was still calm was Jarek, who actually seemed to be enjoying the fresh breeze in his face. Terrel wished he could have shared the mule's stoical acceptance of the world around him but he was too afraid – for himself and for his companions.

When at last the ravine began to widen out again, their hopes began to rise. They were soon able to see the wide plain that spread out beyond the hills, and knew they were through the worst. The current slackened and the river slowly returned to its benign self until it was just as gentle as it had been before, and its banks also became less hazardous. The crew were all smiles, congratulating each other, but their overwhelming feeling was one of relief. Nevertheless, with their new-found confidence they kept the extra sail aloft, allowing them to move more rapidly than they had done inside the crater.

An hour later, they saw a village up ahead.

'Is that Blackwater?' Taryn asked.

'It must be,' Terrel replied.

'So all we have to do now,' Lawren remarked, 'is see whether we can stop in time to moor there.'

'You've done well to get this far on your own,' Marlo commented, 'but why didn't you get a crew in Vergos? There are always men available.'

'What's going on there?' Tighe asked. 'Not so long back everyone seemed to want to go to the city, but no one's come back out again for months – until you.'

'Doesn't make much sense,' Kelli said.

The three men had been among those who'd helped the travellers come ashore. The manner of the newcomers' arrival had caused considerable amusement among the locals – until they recognized their true plight and came to their assistance. The ship's somewhat uncontrolled approach to Blackwater had been complicated by the fact that several small boats were already moored there. Because of this, the *Dark Star* had ended up tied to the far bank and the company had been ferried across from there. Their inexperience in handling the vessel had been painfully obvious to the villagers, but if anything this had only made their welcome all the warmer. The people of Blackwater were hungry for news.

'It's going to be hard to believe,' Terrel warned them. By tacit agreement the healer had been left to do most of the talking, and it would be up to him to decide what and how much to tell their hosts. So far he felt that their welcome had been genuine, though that might change once they knew more. But Terrel realized he had to tell them something.

'The entire population of Vergos, everyone inside the ring of hills, has fallen into a sleep from which they can't be woken,' he said, provoking gasps and looks of frank astonishment. As he went on to tell the villagers about Araguz and the sleepers, he couldn't help wondering if he was doing the right thing. The people here seemed honest enough, but it had not been lost on Terrel and his companions that the city was now ripe for plunder – if anyone dared go there and did not fall asleep themselves.

'All of them?' Tighe whispered.

'We *knew* something was wrong!' Kelli exclaimed.

'The last few ships that tried to go through the gorge had to turn back,' Marlo explained. 'They all told us the same story. Not only were the winds against them, as well as the current, but they began to feel ill, as if they were going to faint.'

'But they were fine once they'd turned round,' Tighe added.

'Now we know why,' Kelli said. 'The place must be cursed.'

'And yet you all managed to stay awake,' Rivas commented. He was the village's senior elder, and had formally greeted the newcomers and invited them into his home. Since then he had said little, leaving the talking to the younger men, and his intervention now introduced the first note of scepticism into the conversation.

'I'm a healer,' Terrel said. He had been ready to explain

how they had escaped from the sleeping sickness, having decided that a convenient lie would be much less complicated – and more believable – than the truth. In any case, it was always a good idea to advertise his talent, which he could offer to their host at some later point. 'I was able to protect us for long enough to get away. The rest of the people there weren't so lucky.'

'Well, no one's going to want to go there now,' Marlo remarked.

'It'll be bad for us if trade dries up entirely,' Tighe said. 'How long's it going to last?'

'I have no idea.'

'We'll manage,' Rivas declared.

'Is there any news of Kaeryss, the prophetess?' Kelli asked. 'Is she asleep too?'

'Do you know her?' Terrel asked, avoiding the question.

'She was born and raised here,' Rivas answered. 'She was a strange girl, but very bright, very talented. She wasn't meant to stay in a place like this.'

'But she's never forgotten us,' Marlo added. 'We've all benefited from her generosity at one time or another. It'd be a shame if she's been caught up in this mess.'

'Did you meet her?' Kelli asked.

'Yes, we did,' Terrel replied. 'And I have some good news, at least. She's still awake, though she's the only one left there.' It was another expedient lie, but this time designed to hide the truth from his own companions, not the villagers. By now the healer had made up his mind to trust both Kaeryss and her friends. 'In fact I was able to talk to her for a while, and she gave me this to show to you.' Taking the scroll from the pocket inside his jerkin, Terrel passed it to Rivas.

The old man gave him a measuring look, as if wondering why the letter had not been produced immediately, but then he nodded. The elder clearly understood and approved of Terrel's caution.

'Fetch Ganz for us, will you?' he said to Tighe. 'Ganz is the scholar amongst us,' he explained as the young man went out.

'Can I ask you something?' Terrel said.

'Of course.'

'Blackwater is so close to the river. How did you survive the recent tidal surge?'

The elder looked a little taken aback.

'It was a big one,' he admitted, 'but we know when such things are coming, and once the boats were up out of the water there was no real danger.'

'I'd have thought the whole village would have been swamped,' Terrel persisted. 'The wave was huge when it reached Vergos, and it did no end of damage.'

'Really?' Rivas was definitely surprised now. 'That is most unusual. It must have built up again further upriver for some reason.'

Terrel couldn't help wondering what had caused the anomaly. It seemed that a lot of strange forces were operating in and around Vergos – but he didn't get the chance to pursue the topic because Tighe returned then with another of the village elders. Rivas handed the letter to Ganz, who read it aloud to the gathering. It was exactly as Kaeryss had described.

'And that's her signature all right,' Ganz added.

'Then it seems we're honour-bound to do as she asks,' Rivas concluded. 'I have to say that that would have been my inclination anyway, even if you'd simply asked. But Kaeryss's words have done your cause no harm.'

'We'll go,' Marlo said immediately. He glanced at Tighe and Kelli who nodded their agreement eagerly. 'But we'll need one more.'

'Valko,' Kelli suggested promptly.

'Will four of you be enough?' Terrel queried.

Marlo grinned.

'You can give us a hand now and then if you like,' he said, 'but she looks like a nice craft and I reckon she'll handle well enough. It's actually quite easy when you know what you're doing.'

'Thank the moons!' Yllen breathed, unable to remain silent any longer. 'If we'd been stuck with our present captain for much longer I think mutiny would have been our only chance.'

Even Faulk had the good grace to join in with the laughter.

CHAPTER THIRTY-FIVE

Another two nights passed before the travellers set sail again. Having been reassured that it would take between twelve and fifteen days to reach Leganza, the port at the mouth of the Syriel River, Terrel had not been quite so desperate to move on. This would still leave him over three median months to reach Vadanis, and now that he knew he was so close to the shores of the Movaghassi Ocean it did not seem too daunting a task. The reason for the delay was because the sailors going with them needed some time to set their affairs in order. Although they were all single, and seemed excited about the voyage, they wanted to make sure that their families did not suffer during their absence – especially as they had no idea how long it would take them to find work on a ship to bring them home again.

Valko turned out to be Kelli's brother, and the two looked so alike that at first Terrel thought they must be twins. They both had hair the colour of old thatch, wispy beards and deep brown eyes, and were the same height and build. But Valko was the younger of the two by a little over a year, and was much quieter than his brother. Even so, it was sometimes hard to tell them apart, and the travellers often found this disconcerting. In particular, it was noticeable that Faulk became awkward when dealing with the brothers together. It wasn't hard to work out

why, and Terrel wondered if their presence would prompt
the soldier to talk about his twin and the events that had
separated them for ever. However, the healer had no
intention of raising the topic himself – in spite of his
curiosity.

During their time in Blackwater Terrel did some healing, combating fevers and a few cuts and sores, but he did
not find even these comparatively simple tasks as easy as
he had once done, and at times he began to doubt his own
talent. But although his ministrations did not seem as
effective as he would have liked, his efforts were appreci-
ated nonetheless.

One of his more successful treatments alleviated the
pains Ganz had been suffering in his back. Terrel spent
some time with the elder, who – apart from being the only
villager who could read and write fluently – was also the
settlement's moon-watcher. Together they confirmed that
no two full moons would coincide for the next months at
least, which meant they need not be too worried about
tidal surges on their journey to Leganza.

The sailors consulted Ganz too, on this matter and
others, before they left, but they also spent a fair amount
of time inspecting the ship – and converting the holds that
would ordinarily have been used to carry cargo into their
own sleeping quarters. They brought some fresh food
aboard to augment the travellers' supplies, as well as some
other goods with which they intended to trade once they
reached the seaport.

On their last night there, the travellers were invited to
join the entire village for a farewell meal. The plain fare
could hardly have been called a feast but the celebratory
atmosphere made up for that. Even though Terrel had told
the villagers only that he was trying to go home, everyone
seemed to feel they were playing a part – no matter how

small – in important events, and many of them seemed to envy the four sailors their forthcoming adventure.

When morning came, the whole village was out on the river bank to see the *Dark Star* cast off.

It didn't take the travellers long to feel that they'd placed their ship – and themselves – in good hands. With four experienced sailors on board it was immediately obvious that their progress would now be much smoother – and faster. Lawren and Taryn continued to help when they could, learning from the experts, but somewhat to Terrel's surprise Faulk was now content to be just a passenger. Yllen was also happy not to have to tackle the ropes, and spent most of her time with Pieri, who was still resting. For himself, the healer was happy to be on his way again, but was also weighed down with several concerns.

Foremost among his anxieties was his double failure at Vergos. Not only had he failed to keep Araguz alive, as Alyssa had demanded, but he had left the city's entire population in a state of comatose inactivity. From a selfish point of view, this meant they would not be in any position to help him later on. Together with his friends he had at least managed to save them from death, but that provided little consolation and, what was worse, Terrel still had no idea why Alyssa had insisted that Araguz should not be killed. If he knew that, a lot more might become clear – even if such clarity might not be very pleasant. However, the chances of Alyssa and her ghostly retinue being able to visit him and provide such an explanation remained slim while he was travelling on water. For that reason, whenever they moored at night – an operation completed with considerable proficiency now – Terrel always tried to spend some time ashore if possible, just in case Alyssa was able to open one of the palace windows.

In the meantime he had other people to worry about, two in particular. Pieri's health was improving, but only very slowly. Although he was occasionally well enough to leave his bed and join the others on deck, he tired easily and the illness would then take hold again. He remained determined nonetheless, often joking about his own infirmity even though everyone could see that he was suffering. Terrel was troubled by the fact that his own healing efforts seemed to be having little or no lasting effect. Either his gift was failing, or the influence of the poison seeping through Pieri's body was so malevolent that no cure was possible. Neither diagnosis was encouraging.

Terrel was also concerned about Taryn. He was a remarkable lad, who had already displayed a resilience the healer could only admire, but he was also something of a mystery. Periods of almost manic activity alternated with times when a dull lethargy crept over him and made him listless and uncommunicative. No matter how brave a face he put on it, the loss of his father had hit him hard and, knowing that, Terrel felt the responsibility of Nomar's last words to him even more acutely. It had been taken for granted – not least by Taryn himself – that the boy would stay with the travellers, but Terrel wasn't sure how long the company would remain intact. After they reached the coast, it was possible that they would all go their separate ways. The healer already knew that Faulk would travel with him to the Floating Islands, and Lawren had said that he probably would too, but Yllen was uncertain – and no one had even bothered Pieri with the problem. So where did that leave Taryn?

Instinctively Terrel wanted to honour his promise and keep the boy with him, but could he subject a child to the rigours and uncertainties of such a voyage? Would he be better off staying in his own country, with Yllen for

instance? In the end it might well come down to what
Taryn himself wanted to do, but Terrel had no intention
of forcing him to make any decisions just yet.

The matter was complicated by the part the child had
played in recent events. If he truly was the 'painted shield'
mentioned in the Tindaya Code – and Terrel was unable
to argue with that supposition – it meant that Taryn was
connected to his own fate. The question was, had the
boy's role begun and ended in Vergos, or was there more
to come? The fact that, according to the Code, the shield
was supposed to come *from* Tindaya and not go to it only
confused the issue further. Taryn had never been anywhere near the ruined temple. It was yet another reason
for Terrel to wish he could speak again with Alyssa and
the ghosts – a wish that didn't seem likely to be granted
any time soon.

'How's Pieri?' Taryn asked as Terrel came up on deck
after his latest visit to his patient.

'Much the same,' the healer replied gloomily. 'I don't
seem to be doing him much good. I wish ... I wish I
could find the root of his illness, but it always seems to
elude me.' He'd been about to say that he wished Nomar
was there to help but had caught himself just in time.

'I'm sure you will eventually.'

Terrel was grateful for the boy's confidence, but wasn't
sure he deserved it.

'How many days since we left Blackwater?' he asked,
wanting to change the subject.

'Six,' Taryn replied. 'Marlo says we should reach a
place called Alimi this afternoon. He knows people there,
so we should be able to get some news.'

The *Dark Star* had still not passed any ships of compar-
able size on their way downstream. They had seen several

small boats and ferries manned by the local people, but it seemed that all long-distance trade had come to a halt. No one could tell them why.

'We're almost halfway to Leganza now,' Taryn added knowledgeably.

Terrel saw his chance and forced himself to take it before he was tempted to put the discussion off again.

'Have you thought about what you're going to do when we get there?' he asked.

'Not really.'

'You know I have to go back to the Floating Islands.'

Taryn nodded.

'Well, I'm not sure how I'm going to do that, and—' Terrel tried to explain.

'Isn't Marlo going to take us?'

Terrel noted the eagerness in Taryn's voice, and also his assumption that he'd be included in the party.

'I'm not sure this ship is built for the ocean,' the healer said. 'And besides, Marlo may not want—'

'He'd love it,' Taryn cut in. 'He told me.'

'He knows about the Floating Islands?'

Taryn immediately looked shamefaced.

'I told him,' he admitted. 'I'm sorry. I didn't know it was a secret.'

'It's all right,' Terrel said quickly. 'I'd have told him myself soon anyway.' In fact the healer was quite glad the boy had done his work for him – and that the reaction had been enthusiastic rather than appalled.

With his broad muscular build and air of innate self-confidence, Marlo was the natural leader of the sailors and had, in effect, become the *Dark Star*'s captain. He still deferred to either Terrel or Faulk at times, asking if they were happy with what he planned to do, but as far as the day-to-day running of the ship was concerned his authority was unquestioned. If Marlo was prepared to sail out into the Movaghassi Ocean, Terrel had little doubt that the other sailors would be happy to go with him. Assuming they really could navigate the ship in the open sea, this was excellent news. Finding a crew to undertake the voyage to his homeland had always been one of Terrel's major worries. Whether the *Dark Star* was sturdy enough for the trip was another matter – and one he would have to discuss with the sailors.

At that moment, however, he was more concerned with Nomar's son.

'Can I ask you something, Taryn?'

'Of course.'

'I promised your father that I'd look after you – and I will. But that means deciding what's best for you.'

The boy's expression had clouded over at the mention of his father, but he said nothing.

'Going to Vadanis might be difficult and dangerous,' Terrel said, 'and when we get there you'd find a lot of things strange.'

'I don't care about that,' Taryn said in a small but defiant voice.

'Well, you need to think about it. For instance, you might feel better staying in Leganza with Yllen.'

'Isn't she coming too?' The boy's dismay was obvious.

'I'm not sure,' Terrel replied. 'An ocean voyage could be very hard for her, and with Pieri ill . . .' He shrugged.

They were silent for a while, leaning on the gunwale and watching the river bank slide by.

'You don't have to decide now,' Terrel said eventually.

'I think my father would have wanted me to stay with you,' Taryn said, then looked unsure of himself. 'If that's all right.'

'Of course it is. If that's what you really want.'

Taryn nodded, looking relieved, and Terrel began to wonder just what his promise would finally entail. Looking after a small boy had not figured in his thoughts and hopes concerning his own future. Having children of his own had always seemed such a remote possibility that he'd given it little thought. Simply being able to return to Alyssa and be with her had been his goal for so long he hadn't dared look beyond that – and his imagination balked at it now. He did know that the situation might well be rather more complicated if he arrived with a six-year-old boy in tow.

'Can I ask *you* something?' Taryn enquired timidly, interrupting the healer's reverie.

'Go ahead.'

'What's her name?'

'Who?'

'The lady who's asleep in the house where you used to live.'

'How do you—' Terrel began, then stopped, remembering an earlier conversation with Nomar's son when they'd discussed the 'pictures' Taryn could produce and see in other people's minds. Terrel had shown him Havenmoon – and immediately after that he'd thought of his love, lying in her dungeon cell.

'Her name's Alyssa.'

'She's very pretty.'

Terrel smiled.

'I think so,' he said, then frowned. Whenever he tried to conjure up an image of Alyssa in her own form, his memory betrayed him. He could describe her huge, child-like eyes, their rich brown hue contrasting with her uneven crop of hair which was the colour of sunlit straw. There were so many details he could recall – but he couldn't *see* them. All he had were ideas and words, and Taryn couldn't interpret them. And yet he knew Alyssa was pretty. He had seen a picture in Terrel's mind that Terrel couldn't see for himself.

'What's the matter?' Taryn was anxious again now.

'Nothing. It's all right,' the healer said, hastening to reassure him. 'I just haven't seen Alyssa in a very long time.'

'And that makes you sad.' It was a statement rather than a question.

'Yes,' Terrel said quietly, hardly trusting his voice to say anything more.

'But you'll be able to see her soon,' Taryn said, reassuring the healer in his turn. 'When we get to Vadanis.'

I hope so, Terrel thought. With all my heart, I hope so.

CHAPTER THIRTY-SIX

Terrel first recognized that something strange was happening when Jarek bellowed and began turning round in circles as if he were chasing his own tail. The healer had seen dogs exhibit similar absurd behaviour but it was quite out of character for the mule. Until that moment he had been grazing contentedly in his usual steadfast manner, but now he seemed positively demented, braying almost continuously and snapping his jaws at nothing as he went round and round. Although Terrel couldn't help laughing at first, he soon realized that there was something seriously wrong with the beast. Looking about, he saw that no one else was in sight and he muttered under his breath, cursing the circumstances that had led to his being left alone to deal with this unexpected situation.

The *Dark Star* was moored at a stone quay on the outskirts of Alimi. Marlo had left the ship in the hands of the other sailors while he and Faulk went into the town in search of news, and the rest of the travellers had taken the chance to stretch their legs on firm ground. The mooring had also offered a rare chance for Jarek to go ashore, and so he'd come with them when they headed towards the nearby common land. Since then Yllen and Pieri had returned to the ship, Lawren had gone off somewhere with Kephra to hunt, and Taryn had disappeared without Terrel noticing. The healer had been lost in thought, walking aimlessly amidst the bracken and coarse grass – until Jarek went mad.

Approaching cautiously, Terrel tried to pitch his voice to soothe and reassure the animal.

'Whoa, boy. Easy now. What's got into you?'

Jarek continued to spin round, and Terrel had to step back to avoid a collision, but the animal did eventually begin to slow down. When the mule finally came to a standstill, he was trembling from head to hoof and seemed on the point of collapse. Flecks of foam had collected round his mouth and his tongue hung down, dripping saliva from his exertions. Terror showed in his eyes – and something more. It was only then, with a sudden surge of excitement, that Terrel saw the ring entwined in the hairs atop one of the creature's ears.

Alyssa? What's going on?

I can't do this. Her voice sounded faint and racked with pain. Terrel wasn't even sure she was talking to him.

You have to. Elam's voice appeared in Terrel's head even though he couldn't see him anywhere. *Just for a little while.*

The palace isn't safe any more, Alyssa whispered. *Windows dark.*

What's going on? Terrel repeated. *Elam? Where are you?*

I'm here. Hang on, Alyssa. I'll be as quick as I can.

Terrel could see the ghost now, but he was just a hazy outline standing next to the mule.

Is she all right? Terrel asked, knowing it was a stupid question. It was abundantly clear that Alyssa was not all right.

I still love you, Terrel, she said. *None of this changes the way I feel.*

He knows that, Elam told her gently. *Let me talk. We can be done quicker then.*

What's the matter with her?

No one's really sure. Being here's not doing her any good, but there are things you need to know, and I had to come because the others are too busy.

Elam's hoarse voice betrayed his own discomfort and Terrel wondered what news could possibly be worth such suffering. Alyssa's obvious agony made him feel as if his own heart was being encased in a crushing layer of ice.

Tell me, he ordered.

I'm just passing on messages, Elam said. *I'm not even sure what some of them mean. The first is that the shield may not work much longer. There are gaps in it, and you need to be careful to avoid them. The next is that Vadanis isn't where it's supposed to be. The three-moon confluence turned the islands' course and you'll need to take that into account. Third—*

Where are they in relation to Leganza? Terrel cut in.

Where? Elam replied. *I've no idea. You're the one who has to work it out. The third thing is that Jax is turning Vadanis into a floating fortress. He's found something in the Code about invaders, and even though everyone thinks he's mad he's insisting on guarding the entire coastline. You may have some problems coming ashore.*

Is that it? Terrel asked as Jarek's legs almost gave way beneath him.

There's one more thing. Were you able to save the people of Vergos?

Yes and no. They're alive, but they're all sleepers.

All of them?

All except Kaeryss.

The ghost nodded.

We think now that it was supposed to happen like that, he said.

Really?

Is Araguz a sleeper too?

He's dead.

Oh. Elam's phantom expression turned from one of satisfaction to doubt. *That could explain a lot. Araguz wasn't supposed to die.*

Why?

He's with us now, Elam replied, then his image flickered and faded to nothing.

Close it. Close it! Alyssa screamed silently. *He's—*

Her voice, her presence and the ring vanished from Terrel's world, leaving him in a state of shock. The mule was himself again now but he was still shaking.

'What's the matter with Jarek?' Taryn asked as he ran past.

'I don't know,' Terrel replied truthfully. Ordinarily, when Alyssa left a host animal which had been affected by her illness the creature recovered immediately. This time the effects seemed to be lingering.

Taryn went up to the mule and patted his neck and nose, speaking softly all the time. The boy's attention had a calming influence, though there was still a wildness in Jarek's eyes.

'We should take him back,' Taryn said. 'Pieri will know what to do.' He began to lead Jarek away and Terrel followed mutely, his mind still struggling to cope with what had happened.

Elam's messages had been a mixture of good news and bad. The idea that Taryn's shield might be failing hardly seemed to matter now that they'd escaped Araguz's malign influence, and Vadanis' position in the ocean was never going to be predictable, so that wasn't vitally important either. The fact that they might have to fight their way ashore was discouraging – but surely it would be impossible for Jax to guard the entire coastline. In Terrel's opinion, none of these snippets of information were worth the risks Alyssa and Elam had run to bring them to him, and he still wasn't sure what to make of the last – that the population of Vergos were meant to have become sleepers but Araguz was not meant to die. Good news balanced with bad – but in the healer's mind they should have been the other way round. How could the fate of the city's inhabitants be anything but bad? And why was the prophet's death not a good thing? How else were they supposed to have defeated him? *He's with us now.* Recalling Elam's final words sent a chill through Terrel. It was a frightening thought that Araguz might be just as dangerous an enemy in the ghosts' world as he had been in Terrel's.

Yet the single most unnerving aspect of the whole encounter had been the state of the messengers themselves. Elam's image had been less substantial than ever before, and Alyssa's torment had been all too obvious – but the healer couldn't work out what had caused these anomalies. Apart from clearly being in pain, Alyssa had been frightened too – and close to panic at the end. Her comment about the palace not being safe made Terrel wonder if the Ancients had turned on her.

The healer came to an abrupt halt as another dreadful possibility occurred to him. Alyssa's wandering spirit shared certain similarities with the ghosts', and Araguz was in their world now. The prophet had some sort of connection with the sick elemental in Myvatan. Had he been instrumental in making Alyssa's illness so much worse? Elam's parting words took on a chilling new significance. *He's with us now.*

Ahead of him Jarek stumbled, and Taryn had to coax the mule into moving on. At the same time he saw that Terrel had fallen behind and called out.

'Are you all right?'

Terrel did not reply, but he began walking once more. He was not sure he'd ever be all right again.

That night Terrel slept only intermittently. Each time he woke to darkness, his mind started wandering again. At one point it occurred to him that Alyssa's choice of host might have affected her wellbeing. In some ways a mule was similar to a horse, and Jarek was old and hardly in the prime of life, so it was possible she'd found him less than ideal – just as the ancient cat in Vergos had made the process difficult for her. He wondered why she hadn't picked another animal. Terrel understood why she'd avoided Paws, but Kephra would have seemed the perfect host. Had it just been bad luck that she'd settled on Jarek? Or had she had no choice in the matter?

Questions also ran through his head about what Muzeni and Shahan were busy doing, the problem of locating the Floating Islands in a vast ocean, and the decisions he would have to make when they reached Leganza. Marlo and Faulk's trip into the town had garnered no new information about the lack of shipping on the river, and this also occupied his thoughts for a while.

At some indeterminate point in the night, when he'd finally been able to drift into an uneasy sleep, Terrel was woken by a loud thump from above. He listened for a while and heard some footsteps on deck, but there didn't seem to be any cause for alarm and he was content to leave the investigation of the noise to others.

He dreamt of a hill in the middle of pleasant countryside, a green and rolling landscape. All that changed when the ground shuddered and then began to move with a thunderous noise that shattered the fragile, false peace. The hill was torn in two, dragged apart by forces too immense to comprehend, exposing seams of glittering crystal.

But the devastation did not stop there. He saw the beds of oceans rise up to become mountains, their waters inundating the existing land all around and creating new seas. He saw volcanoes strung out like jewels on the tortured surface of the planet, reshaping its contours and filling the air with fire and smoke. Cities crumbled or were swept away. Whole empires vanished. The sky turned grey, then black. The sun and moons were hidden from view, leaving the few survivors cowering in the frigid gloom.

The great cycle was complete. History began again.

Terrel woke feeling chilled and yet covered in sweat. The sunlight angling through the porthole made him feel a little better, but he knew it would be a long time before he'd be able to shake the night's images from his mind.

Dressing quickly, he went up on deck to find everyone else gathered near the main mast. They were talking quietly, and it was only when Terrel drew closer that he saw Jarek lying stiffly on his side. It was obvious now what had caused the disturbance in the night.

'What happened?' Terrel asked as he joined the others.

'I don't really know,' Kelli replied. 'I was on watch when I heard him bray and I turned round to see what was bothering him. He just keeled over without warning. It all happened so fast – he was dead by the time I reached him.'

CHAPTER THIRTY-SEVEN

The company left Alimi in low spirits. The loss of his old friend made Pieri miserable, and his mood infected everyone else. Jarek's body had been left behind for the townspeople to dispose of, and Terrel had hoped that once they were on their way again Pieri's spirits might lift a little. In the event the opposite was true. His patient no longer seemed willing to make an effort to help himself, and spent the whole day in his bed. With Terrel's own efforts still having only a minor and temporary effect, Pieri seemed set into a decline – which did nothing to make the healer feel any better. He had come to the conclusion that the timing of Jarek's death was no coincidence. The mule might have been old but he had not seemed to be in ill health before, so Alyssa's hasty visit must have somehow hastened his demise. This in turn implied that there was something seriously wrong in Alyssa's realm, making it even less likely that she'd be able to return with the ghosts to give Terrel any advice. He'd expected to feel better the closer he got to Vadanis – with the end of his monumental journey now in sight – but events were conspiring against him, and he too was sunk in gloom.

He did not think his situation could get much worse, but three days later it did.

This time it was the ship's cat who raised the alarm.

Terrel had gone down to his cabin to fetch an extra layer of clothing because a cold wind had sprung up – and now that they were on a much wider stretch of the river there was nothing to protect them from the chill blast. He had found Paws asleep on his bed, but thought nothing of it. The cat treated the entire vessel as his personal preserve. It was only when Terrel had put on an outer shirt and was pulling his jerkin back over his head that the first yowl split the air. When the healer had managed to struggle into his clothes and could see again, Paws seemed to have been inflated to twice his normal size. His fur was sticking out straight, his back was arched, and he was clawing at the bedclothes as his tail lashed from side to side. He was hissing fiercely, spitting his fury at something at the far end of the cabin. When Terrel followed his gaze, his heart sank.

Hello, brother, Jax said casually. *That's not your little friend, is it?*

The prince's outline was slightly blurred, and fainter than normal, but – unlike Elam – Jax did not appear to be aware that anything was wrong. He was looking around the cabin with every sign of interest.

What do you want? Terrel asked. He had realized too late the significance of one of the ghosts' warnings. Taryn's shield had not just been protecting the company from the enchanter's power, but had also been hiding them from Jax. His twin had evidently found one of the gaps.

Let's go and see, shall we? the prince replied, and floated up through the ceiling of the cabin.

Terrel dashed up on to the deck, fearing the worst. Unseen by anyone else, Jax was gazing at the sails and rigging, then at the expanse of water all around them.

You're not really thinking of sailing this tub all the way to Vadanis, are you? he asked.

Why not? Would that worry you?

Jax laughed.

Of course not, he said. *Besides, you'd drown before you were halfway there.*

I crossed the ocean before, remember? On a craft a lot smaller than this.

It was Jax who had been responsible for his brother's exile on a makeshift raft.

That was just dumb luck, the prince said.

Terrel chose not to argue. His brother's statement was too close to the truth for comfort.

Let's do a little experiment, Jax went on.

'No!' Terrel cried, only realizing he'd spoken aloud when several of the others on board glanced round. He had feared that his twin was going to use his murderous skill as a fire-starter again, but now he saw that the prince had other ideas in mind.

You've no need to do this.

Jax ignored him and set to work. The wind veered abruptly to an entirely different direction, and as the sails flapped and banged the *Dark Star* heeled over to port. Marlo immediately began yelling orders and, quickly recovering from their surprise, the sailors ran to make the necessary adjustments. The ship was soon running smoothly again, on a different tack.

Very impressive, Jax mocked, *but that was nothing, really. How about this?*

'Is he here?' Faulk asked, coming up beside Terrel. 'Is the warlock here?'

'Yes,' Terrel replied, wondering how Faulk had known. 'Tell Marlo to be ready for anything.'

'Where is he?' the soldier asked. He drew his sword, his eyes flashing with anger.

'That's no use,' Terrel said. 'Go and tell Marlo we could be in for some rough weather.'

Faulk ran off, though he was still looking around and trying to locate his invisible foe. The *Dark Star* lurched again, and water slapped against the side of the hull. A new wind swept through the rigging.

For the next hour the ship was subjected to a series of impossible changes in the weather. The wind varied in both strength and direction, squalls of rain and hail fell from a clear sky to splatter across the deck, and the waters around them churned and swirled in inexplicable waves and currents. For a while Marlo and his crew – together with Faulk and Lawren – did what they could, making constant adjustments in a futile attempt to keep up with all the changes. But their efforts were in vain, and the dangers mounted until eventually they decided to give up and furl all the sails, for fear that the masts would be torn away if they did not. After that the *Dark Star* wallowed at the centre of its own private storm, pitching and yawing as it was buffeted by the ever-changing onslaught of the elements. By then only Marlo and Faulk were left on deck, clinging to the tiller in the hope of retaining the last vestiges of control over the craft's movement. Everyone else had been ordered below.

Finally Jax produced his masterpiece, a small whirlwind that began life over the distant shore, then turned into a waterspout as it headed towards the crippled vessel. It struck with the force of a small tornado, threatening to capsize the ship. Even below deck the noise as her entire framework shuddered and groaned was incredible, and Terrel didn't think the *Dark Star* could possibly survive. But in the next moment the storm was gone. The sudden silence was broken only by the ship herself as she righted with a series of creaks and sighs.

When they all ventured out on deck, they weren't sure Marlo and Faulk would still be there. They were, but both men were battered and bruised as well as soaked to the skin. The damage to the ship was also less than Terrel had feared. The foremast had split and was now leaning at a drunken angle, and some of the sails on the mainmast had been stripped away and lay in tatters across the deck and over the side. But everything else was salvageable and the hull appeared to be intact. The weather was relatively calm once more, and the group began the long and arduous task of clearing up. No one could quite believe what had happened, and only Terrel knew how it had come about. What was more, he was certain that – had Jax wanted to – he could have sunk the *Dark Star* or run her aground. The fact that he had done neither made Terrel uncomfortably aware of the most likely explanation. The prince had simply been toying with them.

Marlo had been worried about finding a berth for them to dock in Leganza, but when they finally reached the city port that proved to be the least of their problems. There were far fewer ships than was usual, and so they were able to moor at one of the quays without delay. The matter of the harbourmaster's fee had been discussed earlier, and Marlo had assured Terrel that he'd be able to negotiate a delay in payment so that they could do some trading first, and he went off to do that as soon as the ship had been secured.

Before then money was not something the healer had thought about a great deal, but he was forced to do so now. Apart from the fees, which ought not to be too onerous, there was the question of repairs to the *Dark Star*. That was going to be expensive and as yet Terrel had no idea how they were going to afford it. The alternative was to sell the ship. Even in its damaged state it would surely fetch more than enough to secure a passage to the Floating

Islands for himself and whoever else wanted to go.
However, that presupposed they'd be able to locate a buyer
and a captain willing to risk his own vessel on such a venture. Neither objective was by any means certain and, as
the sailors had already declared that once she was refitted
the *Dark Star* would be perfectly capable of an ocean
voyage, finding a way to pay for the repairs seemed to be
the better option.

The last part of their journey to the mouth of the Syriel
River had been slow and laborious. As they had neared the
sea, the increasing tidal effects had made navigation harder,
especially with the ship's reduced manoeuvrability. The
currents in the estuary seemed to run in all directions,
changing for reasons that were not apparent to Terrel. He
had marvelled at the way the sailors coped with the conditions as they limped on towards Leganza, and now that
they were there and another stage of his long trek was over
he was determined to go on to the last. Staring at the endless expanse of the Movaghassi Ocean, and thinking that
the Floating Islands might only be just beyond the horizon, he had silently renewed his oath to Alyssa. One way
or another he would return to Vadanis. Nothing would be
allowed to stand in his way.

To that end, he and Faulk went ashore soon after Marlo
to begin their enquiries. They soon learnt the reason for
the lack of activity in the dockyards. The entire nautical
community seemed convinced that the Syriel River was
cursed. The few vessels that had tried their luck since the
three-moon conjunction had all foundered or had been
driven back by a peculiar set of circumstances, and now no
one was willing to take the risk. As a result the trade
flowing through Leganza had been drastically reduced as
captains looked for better fortune in other ports.

There were many rumours concerning the source of the

curse – varying from fire-scythes and earthquakes to plague and sorcery – and Terrel quickly learnt not to reveal where he and the travellers had come from. The people they did talk to reacted with horror when they admitted to having come from Vergos, thinking that perhaps they carried the curse with them like some infectious disease. In fact the only thing the citizens of Leganza seemed to regard as more insane than sailing up river was trying to travel to the Floating Islands. No matter how tentatively Terrel raised the subject, the reaction was always the same; a declaration that such a journey was impossible, and incredulity that anyone would be mad enough even to try. The prejudices about his homeland that the healer had encountered in Macul were duplicated here – several people informed him either that the islands were unpopulated or that the deformed barbarians who did live there were no better than rabid animals. By the time they returned to the *Dark Star*, Terrel was feeling distinctly discouraged.

'He's asleep,' Yllen said, referring to Pieri, as she joined the others in the largest of the cabins. 'What have you decided?'

'Nothing yet,' Terrel replied. He had already told the gathering about the failure of his earlier investigations, and although he wasn't sure where they were supposed to go from here, he knew they had to come up with a plan of some sort. He turned to Marlo. 'How long can we stay here?'

'At the moment, as long as we like,' the sailor replied. 'But the fees are charged on a daily basis, so the longer we stay the more it's going to cost. I got us the best rate I could, and if we get the chance to do a little trading we should be able to cover it for a while.'

'So the question becomes, do we sell the ship or try to earn enough to get her repaired?' Terrel concluded.

'With trade here at such a low ebb, finding a buyer isn't going to be easy,' Tighe commented. 'Especially with her in this state.'

'On the other hand,' Kelli put in, 'the repair yards are probably looking for work, so we should be able to fix her for a good price.'

'I can ask around if you like,' Marlo offered.

'Do that,' Terrel said. 'But before we decide anything I need to be sure of one thing. If we do manage to get her repaired, are you going to be willing to take me out to the Floating Islands?'

'Yes,' Marlo replied, and it was immediately obvious that the four sailors had already discussed the matter. 'But we do have a problem. None of us has any idea where the islands are, and we can't just search at random. It would take for ever. So unless you can tell us where to aim for, or find somebody who can, we'd be crazy to try.'

'I'm no navigator,' Terrel admitted, seeing no point in lying. Even if he had been able to remember the charts he'd once seen that plotted the movements of the empire, its course had changed in recent times.

'There must be someone in this town who would know where to look,' Lawren said. 'Even if no one's ever actually been to the islands, surely they'd want to know where they were, if only to avoid running into them.'

'We need a pilot,' Kelli said, nodding. 'The best are usually captains with their own ships, but there are normally a few independents in a place like this.'

'So if we can find a pilot who's willing to come with us, and we can make good the damage from the storm, you'll do it?' Even as he spoke Terrel knew that both tasks were easier said than done.

Marlo grinned.

'Try and stop us,' he said. 'We haven't enjoyed ourselves so much in years.'

'The stories about the islands don't bother you?'

'Why would *you* want to go there if they were true?' Valko countered, making one of his rare contributions to the debate.

'My brother's right,' Kelli added. 'When are we likely to get a chance like this again? I'd love to go.'

'Are you sure?' Terrel persisted. 'It will mean being away from your families much longer than you'd expected.' He paused, noting that they still looked eager. He had been about to mention the possibility of Jax attacking them but decided against it. It would have been too demoralizing, and he would not have known how to explain it anyway. He could only hope that it would not happen again.

'They'll be fine,' Marlo said.

'Besides,' Tighe added, 'how could we go back and tell our tale and admit we turned down such an opportunity? We'd never be able to hold our heads up again.'

'All right,' Terrel said. 'But there's only one way I'm going to be able to pay you for your services.'

'Pay us?' Marlo queried, looking insulted. 'What are you talking about?'

'Once you've put me ashore on Vadanis, along with anyone who wants to go with me, the ship is yours,' Terrel replied. 'We won't have any more use for her.'

'You're joking,' the sailor breathed, his rugged face a picture of astonishment.

'How else are you going to get home?' the healer asked.

Marlo glanced at his fellow villagers, then grinned again.

'It's a deal,' he stated.

'Don't get your hopes up yet,' Terrel warned. 'We've

got a lot of obstacles to overcome before we get to that stage.'

'Perhaps I can help with one of them,' Lawren said. As he spoke he took a leather bag from an inside pocket and tossed it over to the healer. When Terrel loosened the drawstring and upended the pouch over the bed, a shower of gold coins fell out. Everyone stared in amazement.

'I've been saving up for my old age,' Lawren remarked, provoking several disbelieving glances.

Yllen burst out laughing.

'You lying toad!' she exclaimed.

'Oh, all right,' he said with a grin. 'I took them from the palace in Vergos. It seemed a shame to leave all of it just sitting there.'

'You stole it?' Terrel asked.

'I don't see that it's so different from us taking this ship,' the hunter replied. 'She didn't exactly belong to us either, did she?'

Terrel had to admit he had a point, and found himself at a loss for words.

Lawren turned to Marlo.

'If you do ever get to take this ship back up the river,' he said, 'you should think about changing her name. If her rightful owners in Vergos ever wake up, they might be a bit peeved.'

'They'll probably think she was destroyed with all the rest,' Yllen reasoned, 'but it's not a bad idea. I always connect the name with Araguz – and I think we'd all like to forget about him.'

'Will this be enough for a new mast and sails?' Terrel asked, fingering the pile of coins.

'More than enough, I reckon,' Kelli said.

'Are you sure this is what you want to spend your money on, Lawren?' the healer queried.

'Just take it,' the hunter replied impatiently.

'Thank you.' Terrel didn't know what else to say.

'So now all you need to do is organize a search for your pilot,' Yllen concluded. 'While you get started on that, I'm going to check on Pieri.'

'You think we'll find a navigator here?' Faulk asked as she went out. 'After what we heard today it doesn't seem very likely.'

'There might be other ways to go about it,' Marlo said. 'I could ask the harbourmaster for some help.'

'And we can always sail down the coast,' Tighe added. 'Try some of the other ports if we don't have any luck here.'

'In the meantime, we should get the repairs under way as soon as possible,' Kelli said.

'Are you happy for me to arrange that?' Marlo asked Terrel.

The healer never got the chance to answer, because at that moment Yllen burst back into the cabin.

'Come quickly!' she said, her voice sharp with fear. 'Pieri's got worse. He's coughing up blood.'

CHAPTER THIRTY-EIGHT

It was late that night when the crisis finally passed. Terrel was exhausted, even though he knew he'd done little to assist Pieri's partial recovery. The storyteller's mysterious ailment was hidden deep within the waking dream — deeper than anything Terrel had ever come across before. Whenever he managed to catch up with it, it would always slip from his grasp.

He had been able to ease Pieri's pain and stop the internal bleeding, but he was no closer to establishing the underlying cause, let alone curing it. Although the storyteller's illness was unusual, Terrel still wasn't sure whether it was that or his own failing gifts that were defeating him. Pieri was sleeping when the healer finally left him, and his life was no longer in any immediate danger, but beyond that Terrel could not say.

Leaving his patient in Yllen's care, he climbed up on deck to clear his head and to get some fresh air. The night was cool and salty, overlaid with the myriad odours generated by any port. Looking up at the cloudy sky, Terrel breathed deeply, listening to the distant swell of the mighty ocean and wondering how soon he would be out upon its waves.

A little while later, having obviously convinced herself that there was nothing more she could do for Pieri, Yllen came out to join the healer. She too looked weary as she smiled in greeting.

'Thank you for helping him,' she said quietly. 'I know it's costing you a great deal.'

'I don't seem to be achieving very much,' Terrel replied.

'Don't be too hard on yourself. He'd be dead now but for you.'

'I don't know. I can't connect with him, somehow. Perhaps I'm just not meant to be a healer any more.'

'Don't be an idiot,' she chided him. 'There are enough of us around without you starting.'

'Will you—' he began, then fell silent.

'What?'

'I was going to ask if you'd let me try to heal you. You usually seem to have an ache or pain somewhere or other.' He smiled ruefully. 'But it wouldn't be a fair test. I'm so tired I'm not sure I could do anything right now.'

'Try anyway,' she insisted. 'My shoulders are really stiff.'

Somewhat reluctantly, Terrel made the attempt. In theory the experience had not changed. He was able to seek out the problem and do his best to ease it in the usual way, before withdrawing gently. But he couldn't be sure that what he was doing was genuinely effective.

'Much better,' Yllen declared, flexing her shoulders, but her smile was too bright and her words lacked conviction.

Terrel knew he had disappointed her, but didn't have the heart to tell her that he'd seen through her pretence.

'We should get some rest,' he said.

'I've got an idea,' Yllen said suddenly. 'About connecting with Pieri, I mean. We need something to liven him up, to make him *want* to live.'

'It would certainly help,' Terrel conceded. A patient's attitude always influenced their rate of recovery or decline.

'Well, I know just the thing,' she exclaimed. 'A lute! If we could just get him playing again . . .'

It seemed a forlorn hope to Terrel, but Yllen looked so

optimistic that he didn't want to contradict her. But he did point out one obvious problem.

'A good lute would be expensive. All our money's committed to repairing the ship. Even if you could find one, how would you pay for it?'

Yllen did not respond, but there was something in her silence that Terrel could read easily enough.

'You stole something from the palace too,' he said. 'Didn't you?'

'I borrowed a few things from Kalmira,' she corrected him. 'Just some bits and pieces she wouldn't miss, but they should fetch enough for what we need.'

Terrel laughed.

'You and Lawren have more in common than I thought,' he commented. 'I'm surrounded by thieves.'

'I'm insulted,' Yllen claimed, but her smile told another story. 'I did know Kalmira, you know. She'd have been glad to let me have a few of her jewels.'

'I'll take your word for it,' Terrel replied, then grew serious again. 'But are you sure you want to spend it on a lute he may never play? You may need—'

'He *will* play it,' she interrupted. 'In any case, I can always get more money but I'll never find another friend like Pieri.'

The next three days saw a great deal of activity but produced few results. The *Dark Star* was moved to a new mooring within a shipwright's dockyard and the refitting was under way, but it wouldn't be completed for some time yet. Meanwhile, the travellers spent most of their time trawling through any of the city's haunts where a pilot might be found. They found several, but each refused point blank to have anything to do with such a foolhardy enterprise. The few who would even discuss the matter rationally claimed it was impossible anyway – that no charts existed to show the position of the notorious moving islands, and that even if they did they would be so far out of date that no one would be stupid enough to try to follow them.

As Terrel and Faulk returned to the ship to compare notes with the others, the healer was wondering whether they ought to move on to another port as soon as the *Dark Star* was seaworthy.

'We must have covered every likely spot in the city by now,' he muttered. 'We're not going to find anyone.'

'Maybe one of the others will have had better luck,' Faulk said as they crossed the gangplank, though he didn't sound very optimistic.

It was Valko who confounded their expectations.

'Well,' he began hesitantly. 'Kelli and I found someone who used to be a pilot, and who claims to know where the Floating Islands are.'

'Really?' Terrel exclaimed, his pulse quickening.

'Don't get your hopes up,' Kelli warned, then nodded to his brother to go on with the story.

Work on the *Dark Star* had stopped for the night, leaving the company in sole charge of the vessel again. They had gathered to eat and talk, but all thought of food was put to one side as soon as Valko made his announcement.

'His name's Daimon Zarro,' he said. 'Apparently he was quite a famous sea captain in his time.'

'In his time?' Terrel queried warily.

'Yes. He's old now. Must be sixty, at least, and from the looks of him he's been retired a long time.'

'He's also a hopeless drunk,' Kelli added.

Wonderful, Terrel thought. Just what we need. A decrepit drunken has-been.

'What makes you think he's telling the truth, then?' Lawren asked.

'Surprisingly enough, quite a few people confirmed his story,' Valko replied. 'At one time he owned three ships and used to pioneer new trading routes, but he fell on hard times and lost the lot.'

'All because of some woman, apparently,' Kelli added. 'Drove him crazy.'

'We always get the blame when you men mess things up,' Yllen complained.

'Anyway,' Valko went on, 'he's been drowning his sorrows ever since.'

'Where did you find this venerable old hero?' Tighe asked.

'At a tavern called The Caltrop. It's not far from here.'

'I know it,' Marlo said. 'It's one of the lowest dives in the city. The beer's like pisswater and anything else they serve there'd rot your guts in no time.'

'How would you know?' Tighe enquired, eyebrows raised.

'I was young and foolish once.'

'But the rotgut's cheap,' Kelli pointed out. 'That's why Zarro goes there.'

'He claims to have sailed past the Floating Islands many times,' Valko went on, 'and that he still has the charts to prove it.'

This sounded rather more promising. Even if the old man was too far gone to help, his charts could be priceless.

'Did he show you these charts?' Lawren asked, sceptical as always.

'No. He said they were in a chest at his lodgings.'

'And you believed him?'

'Personally, I wouldn't trust the old beggar at all,' Kelli stated. 'I'm not sure he's capable of walking two paces one after the other, let alone navigating a ship. His brain's addled.'

'I don't know,' Valko said doubtfully. 'There was something about him.'

'The smell on his breath,' his brother declared.

'No, I mean underneath all the drink and the shabby clothes . . . I think you should talk to him, at least.'

'He's our only possibility so far,' Faulk pointed out.

'Will he be there now?' Terrel asked.

'I expect so,' Valko replied.

'Then let's go.'

The Caltrop turned out to be just as disreputable as Marlo had described, and Terrel was glad to have Faulk – as well as Valko and his brother – at his side as they entered the taproom. Inside it was dark and rank, and the atmosphere turned even colder as the strangers arrived.

'Is he here?' Terrel asked quietly.

'Not that I can see,' Valko replied. 'He usually sits over there.' He pointed to an empty alcove.

'Let's ask the landlord,' Kelli said, and led the way to the bar.

The innkeeper soon confirmed that Daimon had left a while ago, though he couldn't tell them where the old man lived.

'But he'll be back here by noon tomorrow, without fail,' he added. 'You lads want a drink while you're here?'

'Maybe tomorrow,' Kelli replied. 'Thanks for your help.'

'You're welcome, I'm sure,' the landlord responded sourly.

The next morning a search of a different kind was brought to a rather more successful conclusion. About an hour before noon, Yllen returned with a lute that she'd bought for Pieri. Lawren had acted as her escort on the shopping trip and was full of admiration for her trading skills.

'I wouldn't like to haggle with her, I can tell you,' he remarked.

'It's a good one too,' Yllen said proudly. 'I may not be able to play but I can tell that much. Pieri's going to be so surprised.' Her own excitement was palpable and Terrel couldn't help smiling, even though he suspected she might be in for a disappointment.

The three of them went down to the invalid's cabin, where they found Taryn watching over him. The story-teller was barely awake, but when he saw the lute he roused himself and a little of the old light crept back into his eyes.

'What's that?' he croaked.

'It's for you,' Yllen told him, helping him to push him-self up into a sitting position and then handing him the instrument.

'It's beautiful,' he whispered.

'I knew you'd like it.'

Pieri ran his thumb gently over the strings.

'And it's in tune,' he said admiringly.

'Play something,' Yllen requested.

'I can't. Maybe later.'

'Of course you can. It'll be good for you, and we'd all like to hear you play again, wouldn't we?' She glanced round at the others, who nodded their agreement.

'I can't,' he repeated. 'I need to sleep.'

'Just one little tune,' she pleaded. 'For me.'

Pieri looked up at her, an odd expression on his lean face. Then he settled himself and turned his attention back to the lute. Yllen smiled in anticipation, but when he began to play she found it hard to keep her composure. He'd chosen the chorus of a drinking song, an infantile melody without variation or subtlety, set to a leaden rhythm. Even in such a simple task his once nimble fingers moved clumsily, and the magic that had imbued his craft when he'd played in Vergos was notable only by its absence. When he finished, after a mercifully short time, no one knew quite how to react. Pieri closed his eyes and his head fell back, his hands drooping limply at his sides as if he were completely exhausted.

'That was beautiful,' Yllen said softly as she stooped to take the lute from him.

'Thank you,' he whispered, but he could not have seen that her eyes were bright with unshed tears.

It was only when they were outside the cabin that Yllen broke down and wept. She fell into Lawren's arms, and the surprised hunter reacted instinctively and held her until her sobbing had subsided.

Terrel went to The Caltrop with the same three cohorts as before. They arrived well before midday in the hope of catching Daimon before he went in – and hopefully still sober – but the old man eluded them somehow. After a while Kelli went in to check and returned shaking his head in annoyance.

'He's inside,' he reported. 'And he's already three sheets to the wind.'

'Well, we might as well try now we're here,' Terrel decided.

The old man was in his favoured alcove, a half empty glass on the table before him. His matted thatch of hair and thick beard were streaked with silver, and his complexion was pockmarked and ruddy. Watery eyes regarded the newcomers with indifference.

'Go and get drinks for us and one of whatever he's having,' Terrel said quietly.

'You sure you want him to have some more?' Kelli queried. 'You may never get any sense out of him.'

'It's just a peace offering,' the healer explained.

As the two sailors crossed to the bar, Terrel went over to the former pilot, with Faulk close behind him.

'Captain Zarro, my name's Terrel. May we join you?'

'What for?' the old man replied, eyeing the curious pair suspiciously. Terrel's deliberate use of his formal title had obviously intrigued him.

'Just to talk,' the healer replied. He couldn't tell which the drunkard found more unnerving, his own eyes or Faulk's menacing bulk.

'Buy me a drink and we can talk,' the old man muttered after a moment's calculation.

'It's on its way.' Terrel sat down on the bench. 'They tell me you're a sea pilot.'

'Used to be,' Daimon mumbled.

'Could you be again?' Terrel asked as the sailors arrived with four tankards of beer and another glass filled with the clear liquid the old man was imbibing.

'You the fellow wants to go to them Floating Islands?' Daimon asked, perking up a little.

'Yes.'

'You don't *look* mad.' He cackled at his own witticism, his thin frame shaking under several layers of ragged brown clothing.

'I'm not,' Terrel said, keeping his expression serious. 'That's where I come from – and I want to go home.'

That got the old man's attention. He froze with his original glass poised halfway to his lips and stared at the healer.

'You're joshing me, boy, ain't you?'

'No.'

Daimon tossed back the contents of the glass with a shudder, then set it down and picked up the full one.

'Can't be done,' he stated shortly, before taking an almost genteel sip of his new drink.

'Why not?'

'Too dangerous. I've seen them things, you know, plenty of times. At the front there's a great bow wave, taller than a schooner's mast. Astern there's a wake that'll suck you under like a drowning rat, and at the sides the currents are way too strong. There's no way in.'

Paradoxically, this catalogue of perils reassured Terrel. It made it more likely that the old man really had observed the empire.

'My people travel between the islands,' the healer pointed out, 'so it can't be that bad.'

'Not the same thing.'

'Are you saying their skills are greater than yours?'

Daimon took another pull of his drink, watching Terrel over the rim. Fumes from the spirit filled the air between them.

'You're not drinking,' he observed.

'It's a bit early for me.' Terrel had no intention of touching a drop, and he noticed that none of his companions was drinking either. Marlo's warning about the quality of the inn's beer had clearly been heeded.

'Early. Late. What's it matter?' Daimon asked.

'If you don't think you're up to the job yourself,' Terrel said, 'will you at least show us your charts?'

'I never said I wasn't up to it. I said it can't be done.'

Terrel shrugged.

'Same thing,' he said.

The two men stared at each other, then they both grinned. Terrel's three companions didn't know how it had happened, but some sort of agreement had just been reached.

CHAPTER THIRTY-NINE

'Moons! These are ancient.' Kelli was handling the unrolled map carefully, as though afraid it might fall to pieces beneath his touch. The healer was looking over Kelli's shoulder, and when he saw the chart – which was faded and frayed in places but still clear enough – he felt a glimmer of recognition. The coastal outlines that marked the rim of this section of the Movaghassi Ocean were unfamiliar, but the convoluted patterns etched upon the expanse of the sea reminded him of similar diagrams he'd seen in the library at Havenmoon, before all the books had been burnt.

'Where did you get this?' Kelli asked.

'Drew 'em up meself,' Daimon replied with a touch of rather pathetic pride. The old man had led them to his lodgings – a dirty and cluttered attic in the roof of what appeared to be an abandoned warehouse. As soon as he'd reached the top of the stairs and unlocked the door with shaking hands, Daimon had gone straight to a flagon and poured himself a drink in a grimy tin cup. The colourless liquid – which certainly wasn't water – had seemed to refresh him and his laboured breathing had eased, but he'd still slumped into a chair before pointing to a rack on the wall that contained dozens of deep pigeonholes, most containing scrolls of one sort or another.

'Is this really the course the Floating Islands took back

then?' Valko asked. He was kneeling next to his brother as he smoothed the map out on the floor.

' 'Course it is,' Daimon replied, draining his cup. 'Still would be if the Dark Moon hadn't shifted in its tracks.'

The sailors looked up at Terrel.

'Looks right to me,' he confirmed.

'You a cartographer too, eh, boy?' the old man grumbled. 'What right've you got to question me?'

'But the islands won't be holding this course now?' Faulk asked.

'Not since the time of change began,' Daimon muttered, sounding aggrieved. 'Everything went crazy then, not just the moons. Tides, the whale runs, everything. I was glad I wasn't at sea any more.'

That was a transparent lie, Terrel thought, switching his attention back and forth between the map and the old man. You'd be out there now if you had the chance – and I might just give it to you.

'So how can we tell from this where the islands are now?' Faulk asked.

'Won't have changed that much,' Daimon declared blithely. 'Pass that flagon over here.'

'Don't you think—' Kelli began.

'Don't lecture me, boy!' Daimon shouted, his sudden vehemence coming as a shock. 'Pass it over.'

Faulk went to fetch the jug and took it to the old man, who helped himself.

'Anyone else want a jigger?' he asked.

No one took him up on his offer.

'So how do we work it out, then?' Terrel queried.

'Bring it over here,' Daimon demanded impatiently. 'And light the lamp. I don't see so well these days.'

Once the map was in place and they were gathered round the ex-captain, Daimon began explaining that the various loops and turns of the islands' course corresponded to different phases of all four moons, pointing out various examples of what he meant. Although Faulk and the sailors were soon out of their depth, Terrel was able to follow his reasoning. The old man seemed to recognize this and began to address himself directly to the healer.

'There are annual and seasonal influences as well, of course, but the lunar effects are the most significant.' Even his voice seemed to have become more authoritative now that he was talking about his own sphere of expertise. His cup was set aside, forgotten for the moment.

'So if everything had gone on as normal,' Terrel said, 'where would the islands be now?'

'In spring they'd be in this section,' Daimon replied, 'but to get an accurate position you need to pinpoint the next full or new moons.'

Terrel thought about this for a few moments.

'Three days' time,' he said. 'The Dark Moon will be full and the Amber Moon will be new on the same night.'

The old man began tracing lines with his finger, until he was satisfied he had found the right configuration.

'Here,' he said, tapping a spot at the end of one of the smaller loops. 'Just about the closest they ever get to Leganza.'

'But if they've been slowing down,' Terrel suggested, 'they might not have reached there yet?'

'Slowing down? How do you know that?'

'Messages from home,' the healer replied evasively, and the sailors glanced at him in surprise.

Daimon chuckled.

'There's more to you than meets the eye,' he remarked.

'How long will it take to sail there?' Terrel asked.

'Depends on what ship you've got.'

'A two-masted cutter,' Kelli replied. 'A good one.'

'Well, assuming you know what you're doing, and you get the usual mixture of good and bad fortune with the weather, I'd say about a long month.'

They were silent for a while.

'So, are you going to come with us?' Terrel asked eventually.

'I might,' Daimon replied. 'If you make it worth my while.'

'I'd have thought the adventure would've been enough for a man like you,' Terrel said, grinning.

The old man snorted derisively.

'Pilot gets a fee,' he informed them. 'One tenth of all profits, usually.'

'We're not going to trade. You're welcome to a tenth of nothing.'

'Then what's it worth to you, boy? What's this map worth to you?'

'I'd offer you gold enough for all the liquor you can drink,' Terrel said, 'but you can get that sitting here by the looks of things. Come with us and you'll get something money can't buy. You'll get to be a pilot again. And you'll be the first man in a thousand years to guide his ship to the Floating Islands.' He knew he had the measure of the old man now. 'Wouldn't you like to meet some barbarians?'

'If they were all like you, then it would almost be worth it,' Daimon replied thoughtfully. 'But just to make sure, I'll take what gold and drink there is on offer too.'

'Agreed.' Terrel held out his good hand to seal the deal. Looking slightly bemused, Daimon took it.

'Can we really trust him?' Kelli asked as they walked back to the ship. 'You saw what he's like.'

'I think he'll be a different man if we give him a purpose in life,' Terrel replied.

'I hope you're right,' Faulk said. 'The idea of being guided by a man who's dead drunk half the time is not particularly reassuring.'

'Especially when, by his own admission, his skills and his map are long out of date,' Valko added. The younger of the two brothers seemed to be having second thoughts now.

'Exactly,' Kelli went on. 'We all know things have changed with the moons, which means the islands might be nowhere near where he thinks they are.'

'But we're not going to find a better place to start looking, are we?' Terrel argued. 'Don't forget, Vadanis alone is over five hundred miles long, and there are smaller islands all around it. It ought to be easy enough to spot.'

'Five hundred miles is nothing in the Movaghassi,' Kelli said. 'You can sail for months and not see any land – and that's the sort that stays in one place.'

'Well, it's still the best chance we've got,' the healer maintained. 'In fact it's our *only* chance.'

'We could have just bought the map from him,' Faulk said. 'Why do we need to bring him along?'

'I'd rather have him with us to interpret the charts as we go,' Terrel explained. 'None of us has ever been out there before.'

'A drunk navigator is better than no navigator at all,' Valko said, nodding.

'That's debatable,' Kelli remarked, then turned to Terrel again. 'Are you likely to be getting any more messages from home?' He was obviously hoping the healer would explain a little more about what he'd meant, but Terrel had no intention of doing that.

'I doubt it.' He hadn't given up hope of seeing Alyssa and the ghosts again, but once they were at sea the chances of that happening would be remote.

'So we're really going to do this, then?' Valko said, caught between doubt and excitement.

'We are,' Terrel replied, trying to sound more confident than he felt. 'As soon as the ship's ready.'

Three days later, it was ready. During that time most of the company's efforts had been concentrated on restocking their provisions for what promised to be a long and uncertain voyage. At the same time, Faulk and Valko had appointed themselves as unofficial guardians of their pilot. Daimon had been down to the dockyards to inspect the *Dark Star*, and had pronounced that she 'would do'. Marlo had bristled at this, muttering about the old man's damned cheek, but he had been restrained by his colleagues when he'd been tempted to insult their visitor. As the captain of the ship in all but name – and as prospective part-owner – Marlo was proud of his charge, and became defensive if anyone dared to criticize her. Daimon didn't care two hoots about that, of course, and he also made it plain that there was no way he would stop living his life the way he wanted – and this meant that his daily sojourns to The Caltrop continued, and a considerable stock of his chosen liquor was added to the supplies on board.

That afternoon Terrel had sent a message to Daimon telling him that all was ready for them to sail the next morning. Faulk had returned saying that the old man had insisted on being left alone for the night – 'to set his affairs to rights' – and that he would be at the quayside at first light.

'What's the betting he won't show up?' Kelli asked.

'He'll be here,' his brother responded.

'Drunk or hungover?' Kelli queried.

'Does it matter?' Faulk wondered. 'As long as he's here. Once we're at sea we can throw all the gutrot overboard if necessary. There won't be anything he can do about it then.'

'Except refuse to help us steer a course,' Lawren pointed out.

'I'm not sure he'd be much use to us sober anyway,' Valko said. 'He's been drunk for so long the lack of drink would probably kill him.'

All the company, except Pieri, were gathered together again for one last meal before the *Dark Star* left port. There was a feeling of excitement in the air as the antici-pation built up, but there was sorrow too, because they had come to the parting of the ways. Yllen had decided, and Terrel had agreed, that Pieri was not well enough to brave the rigours of a long ocean voyage. She had therefore arranged to move him to a room in a nearby tavern later that evening. She would be staying in Leganza too, to nurse her friend and earn their keep once the last of her ill-gotten gains had been spent. The decision had not been reached lightly, and had saddened everyone. Taryn in par-ticular had been miserable for a while, but Yllen had no intention of changing her mind. In fact her greatest sorrow was not having to say goodbye to the rest of her friends, but knowing that Pieri would probably never play music again. He had not even picked up the lute since he'd first handled it, and now it stood forlornly in a corner of his cabin – a testament to lost hope.

Lawren had also been torn between continuing the adventure and staying in the city. One of his main con-cerns was the welfare of Kephra. The tercel was already suffering from the huge disruption to his normal life, and was certainly not equipped to hunt at sea. Lawren had always said that his objective in joining the company had been to reach the coast. Now, faced with a journey to a strange and possibly inhospitable land, no one could blame

him for deciding to stay in Kenda and return to his old
life.

That left only Taryn's fate to consider and everyone,
including the boy himself, had decided that he should stay
with Terrel. Even so, Nomar's son was unusually quiet
that evening, and the imminent separations made the meal
a sad occasion for Terrel too. The sailors, likeable company
though they were, could not replace the camaraderie of the
original group, and as of the following morning all that
would be left of that were Faulk, Taryn and the healer
himself.

When the meal was almost over and thoughts were
turning, reluctantly, to the need for farewells, it was
Faulk – the last person Terrel would have expected to
speak out – who best put their joint feelings into words.
Raising his cup – which contained nothing more potent
than water – first to Yllen and then to Lawren, he spoke
calmly but with evident feeling.

'It's been an honour and a privilege to travel with you,'
he began. 'And Pieri too. I shall miss all of you, just as I
miss Nomar.' He glanced at Taryn, who looked down at
his feet, hiding his face. 'I hope our paths cross again one
day.'

Terrel could see that Yllen wanted to make light of his
sentiments, but she could not. In the end she simply raised
her own cup in response.

'Me too,' she said quietly.

In the silence that settled over the cabin then, a faint
sound reached them from outside.

'Listen,' Yllen breathed, her face lighting up in one of
her glorious smiles. 'It's Pieri.'

The music grew a little louder and more confident, but
they still had to strain to catch its ethereal beauty. Without
a word, everyone rose and made their way as quietly as

they could to the storyteller's cabin. Yllen, Terrel and Taryn slipped inside, kneeling on the floor, while the rest crowded round the open door and then kept absolutely still in order to listen.

The magic was back. Pieri's fingers were moving with a fluent dexterity the onlookers could barely comprehend, but this performance had nothing to do with technique. The player and his instrument had ceased to exist as separate entities. There was only the music.

It flowed from him in waves that swelled and subsided on a tide of undiluted emotion, evoking in each listener a series of feelings and images that came partly from their own memories and partly from a realm beyond imagination, beyond the normal world. If the music in Vergos had been about power and purpose, designed to be heard by thousands, this was its artistic opposite, an intensely personal vision that needed no audience nor any reason to justify its existence. Pieri's eyes were closed as he played, his gaunt face enraptured, and he seemed quite unaware that anyone else was present.

As the music made a seamless transition from one entrancing melody to the next, Yllen turned to glance at Terrel, her face glowing with happiness.

'He's going to get better now,' she mouthed silently, then turned back before the healer could respond.

For some reason Terrel saw the Dark Moon then, outlined by a delicate halo of purple light. His moon was full that night, and Pieri's sorcery had made it visible for once. No dreams, Terrel thought. This is not a dream. The Amber Moon was new, hidden from the eyes and minds of men. The sky-shadow and its unknown forces held sway.

The moment passed and Terrel was able to observe his surroundings again, as the music leapt up to new heights of invention, glittering in the sunlight of its own making before beginning a long, slow spiral that would bring it back down to the earthbound silence. The sailors, who had never heard Pieri play before, were transfixed – but so was everyone else. Terrel knew that they were witnessing something very special, a culmination of all Pieri's skill, his art, his life. Something final.

When he reached the end, Pieri held himself perfectly still, his fingers poised over the strings until the last vibration had run its course, and for those few moments everyone in the room held their breath. Then Yllen gave a little sigh, and Pieri opened his eyes and smiled.

'Yllen?'

'That was beautiful,' she breathed.

Terrel realized then that Pieri was blind, unable to see even though his eyes were open now. The poison had taken his sight from him, but had left him one last outlet for his passion. It also meant that Pieri thought he was alone with Yllen.

'I always loved you,' the storyteller whispered, his voice pitched so low that only Yllen and Terrel, who was the next closest, could hear him. 'From the moment we met.'

Yllen was aware that something was wrong now, and her face grew pale as she looked into his unseeing eyes. Terrel felt horribly awkward, an unwilling eavesdropper on a very private moment – but if he were to move Pieri would know he was there. Yllen did not seem to know or care who was watching.

'You love me?' she murmured, sounding bewildered.

'Everything I've ever played has been for you,' he told her. 'Of course I love you.'

'Why didn't you say?' It was all she could do now to keep her voice from breaking.

'I did,' he replied. 'All you had to do was listen.'

'To the music,' she said, understanding at last.

Pieri reached out, and Yllen shifted so that he could touch her hair, then her cheek. It was a gesture of such tenderness – of joy mixed with regret – that Terrel knew for certain what was coming next. The healer had heard somewhere of a species of bird that were reputed to give vent to their haunting song only once, in the moments before they died. He knew now that he had just heard such a song.

Pieri smiled again and moved his hands back to the lute.

'Listen,' he said softly.

One last delicate phrase floated into the air, a fleeting melody, and then a beautiful, yearning chord that faded into silence as Pieri's life faded from the world.

Yllen turned her tear-stained face to the healer.

'Do something, Terrel,' she implored.

'I can't,' he replied simply.

Pieri's brief encore had taken the last of his strength, and by then everyone knew it. He had said everything he had wanted – or needed – to say.

'No,' Yllen said quietly. 'No, no, no. Not now. Not now.'

Seeing what was needed when nobody else could, Lawren came forward and lifted Yllen to her feet. She resisted at first, but allowed herself to be held eventually and then led away. Faulk scooped up Taryn and carried him out too, while the sailors hung back uncertainly, leaving Terrel alone with the musician.

Pieri's last smile was still frozen on his face when the healer gently closed the dead man's eyes. Somehow that made the task even harder.

CHAPTER FORTY

'Any debt you owed him for what he did for you is paid now,' Terrel said.

'You really think so?' Yllen whispered, dabbing at her eyes.

'You gave him the greatest gift he could have asked for,' the healer assured her. 'The chance to play once more before he died. You heard him. How could there have been a better end than that?'

They were walking slowly back from Pieri's funeral, following the rest of the company. The storyteller had been buried in an unmarked grave in a cemetery outside Leganza. No stone or memorial marked his resting place but, at Yllen's request, the lute had been buried with him. The others had all questioned her decision but she had been adamant, telling them simply, 'He'll need it.' Terrel hoped she was right. Even in the world of ghosts, such music would surely be highly valued.

'It was amazing, wasn't it?' Yllen conceded. 'I just wish—'

'He made his life, not you,' Terrel said, cutting her off gently. 'And we can't change it now.'

'How did you get to be so wise?'

'I've learnt from all my mistakes,' he replied. 'There have been so many I can't help *but* be wise.'

Yllen smiled ruefully.

'I hope I can do the same,' she said quietly.

'I was the one who let him down,' Terrel added. 'I should have been able to heal him.'

'No. I was angry with you at first, because you'd always been able to work your wonders for everyone else. But this was different. I know – and he knew – that you did all you could.'

'It still wasn't enough.'

'I take it back. You're not wise at all. How can you blame yourself for not doing more than was possible?'

'I've seen people do the impossible before,' he replied. 'Why can't I?'

'You will, Terrel,' she told him. 'When your time comes, you will.'

Pieri's death had not changed Yllen's mind about her own plans. She was weary and heartsick, and the prospect of a long sea voyage did not appeal to her. The *Dark Star*'s departure from Leganza had been delayed in order for her crew to pay their respects to the dead. Even Daimon, who *had* arrived at the docks on time, had attended the burial – but when the ship sailed the next day, Yllen would not be on board.

The following morning the goodbyes were brief, and the *Dark Star* moved smoothly out towards the open sea. As the four sailors set the ship on her way – and Daimon slept off the previous night's drink – Terrel stood with Faulk and Taryn in the stern and waved to Yllen and Lawren, who had come down to the quay to see them off. As they turned to go, Lawren put a tentative arm around Yllen's shoulders and she made no attempt to shrug him off. Terrel had wondered earlier whether the hunter's worries about Kephra had just been an excuse for him to stay with

Yllen, and as he looked at the two of them together now, he couldn't help thinking they would make a good match. He watched until they were no more than specks in the distance, and by then the rise and fall of the *Dark Star* was enough to tell him they were in open water. Terrel turned to look forward, out over the ocean that contained his home.

Daimon had decreed that rather than sail directly towards the projected position of the Floating Islands, they would travel northwest along the coast of Kenda, enabling them to call in at several lesser ports and then go on to Daghlet Isle – an offshore settlement – before heading out into the deep. The purpose of this was twofold; to replenish their supplies – especially fresh water – and to try to gather news and information. In the event they were successful in the first of these objectives but failed completely in the second, learning nothing that would aid their search. And so, after twelve days of hugging the shoreline, they set their course westward and committed themselves to the vast expanse of the Movaghassi Ocean.

Once they were out of sight of land, navigation became less a matter of observation and more an abstract science. There were still clues to be gleaned from the wind and clouds, the colour of the ocean and even the types of fish they saw, but getting an accurate fix on their position was a matter for careful calculation. Marlo and Daimon had evolved a wary but effective partnership – cross-checking each other's bearings whenever they measured the sunrise or sunset or studied the alignment of the moons and stars, before plotting their readings on to Daimon's charts. They usually consulted Terrel about any change of course, but that was just a polite formality. The healer never had any reason to challenge their findings or the decisions based upon them.

The old man drank every day, but never became so inebriated that he was unable to work when necessary. Although he slept at odd times and ate sparingly, there were occasions when he seemed to be growing younger as the voyage progressed. After only a few days at sea he began to stride the deck with confidence, when even those who were stone cold sober sometimes staggered and missed their footing. His eyes lost the dull patina bequeathed by city life, and although he could still be surly and impatient, he soon became an accepted member of the crew. He even formed a bond of friendship with Paws, finding in the cat's silent and self-centred company an ease that was harder to achieve with his human colleagues.

As the days passed and the only way of measuring their progress was by the minute changes in the markings upon the pilot's map, the company's most tireless enemy was boredom. The monotony of the unchanging vistas could easily have led them to think they were making no progress at all. The sailors were kept busy enough coping with the ever-changing demands of the weather, and both Faulk and Taryn were able to help out on occasion as their own knowledge grew, but Terrel did not trust himself with rope or canvas. The immensity of the ocean – which he had braved once before, in very different circumstances – intimidated him, and the constant movement underfoot made him doubly conscious of his own physical shortcomings. As a result he spent a great deal of time simply gazing ahead, wishing time away and waiting for the first sight of land.

On a clear day, exactly one median month after they had

left Daghlet Isle, Terrel was in his usual position in the bows of the ship when Taryn came running up.

'Marlo and Daimon want to see you,' the boy informed him, pointing back towards the stern.

Terrel went with the messenger and saw that the two men were arguing over a chart which was fixed to a wooden board.

'We're here,' Daimon stated without preamble.

'He's right,' Marlo added. 'I wasn't sure at first, but I am now. This is where the Floating Islands should be.'

Terrel looked around with a sinking heart. In every direction, all he could see was the ocean.

That night Terrel returned to Vadanis, but only in a dream. Instead of a ship's cabin, he was lying in the hayloft of a barn. He recognized it as the place where he'd slept at Ferrand's farm, the place where Alyssa had first re-entered his life in the shape of an animal – in this case an owl. But there was no sign of the bird now, and when his visitor arrived it was by more conventional means, climbing up the ladder from below. At first he didn't recognize her, but then the shape of her face and the colour of her eyes and hair became familiar, even though much else about her had changed. Sarafia had been eleven years old when he had known her, but now she was a grown woman.

'What am I doing here?' she asked, looking puzzled.

'Isn't this where you live?'

'No. I left the farm a long time ago. My dream came true.'

It took Terrel a moment to remember what that had been.

'The travelling players?' he guessed.

'Yes, I'm a member of the Great Laevo's Theatrical

Company,' she announced with a flourish, waving her arm
grandly and almost falling off the ladder.

'Laevo?' Terrel exclaimed. He too had been a member
of that troupe, first as a prompter, then as a stand-in
actor. 'I knew him.'

'I know,' Sarafia replied. 'You're quite a legend among
the actors.'

The dream began to shift.

'Will I ever see you again?' she asked quickly.

'I don't know.' It was the same answer he'd given her at
their parting more than a decade earlier.

Then Terrel found himself in a town square, where
bonfires were burning and crowds of people moved
between rows of merchants' stalls. There was a heady
scent of flowers in the night air, mixing with the smoke
and the aromas of food and drink. Then that too was
gone, as a great darkness swallowed everything.

Out of the void came a miniature star that grew swiftly
in brightness, illuminating the scene around it. Terrel just
had time to recognize the glorious temple from Taryn's
vision before that also disappeared.

He was back on the ship now, but sitting in the bows.
Directly ahead of him, the Red Moon was rising in its full
glory. But as it climbed above the horizon it became clear
that it was rising over land, not sea.

'But it doesn't make sense,' Marlo protested. 'We'd be
going back the way we've just come.'

'I know,' Terrel replied. 'Let's just say I've had another
message from home. The Red Moon was rising, which
means we were heading east, and it was full, as it will be
in three days' time. This is what we have to do.'

'It's possible the islands moved in behind us after we
sailed past,' Daimon conceded. 'But if we were that close

I'm surprised we didn't spot them. And it would mean we'd be outside the normal range of their course. They wouldn't be where they're supposed to be at all.'

'They aren't,' Terrel responded confidently, recalling Elam's advice. 'Turn the ship round. We've got to choose one way or another, and if I'm wrong we'll soon find out.'

'You're the boss,' Marlo said, though he was obviously sceptical, and then he turned and began yelling orders to his crew.

They spotted the islands even earlier than Terrel had expected, at dusk on the second day. Although they were still some distance away there was no mistaking the fact of their existence. The healer gazed at the smudge on the horizon with a number of emotions welling inside him. By this time tomorrow I'll be there, he thought, hardly daring to believe it had come at last.

And when he realized that they would indeed be arriving on a night when the Red Moon was full, he knew where he was meant to go ashore.

'The most direct route would be to go round the northern tip of Vaka,' Terrel said. 'That's the small island directly in front of us. It's connected to Vadanis by an underwater bridge. But if we do that, it'll be obvious that we're coming from the open sea. My people aren't used to foreigners, and I'm not sure what sort of reception we'd get.' He saw little point in repeating Elam's warning that Jax was in the process of turning Vadanis into a floating fortress. 'So I suggest we go to the south, then cross over the bridge. That way it'll look like we're pilgrims coming from Vaka or one of the more southerly isles.'

'Pilgrims?' Marlo queried.

'There are celebrations at the full of the Red Moon, in

a town called Tiscamanita,' the healer explained. 'The main festival's in the autumn, but I suspect they get quite a few visitors each long month.'

'But once the people there get a look at the ship, they'll probably realize we're not from around here,' Tighe said. 'So that story won't hold water for long.'

'It won't have to,' the healer replied. 'All you have to do is get me, Faulk and Taryn ashore, then you can set off again. It'll be getting dark, and if we're lucky you might not even need to dock. There may be ferries operating in the harbour.' Although it was in Tiscamanita that Terrel had seen the ocean for the very first time, that had been from the top of a tower near the centre of the town. He had never got as far as the docks, and so wasn't certain how things worked there.

'How shallow is the water over the bridge?' Daimon asked.

'I'm not sure, but I've seen ships using the channel so it must be navigable.'

'The currents are going to be tricky, though,' Marlo commented.

'Which way are the islands travelling at the moment?' Kelli asked.

'Almost due south,' Daimon replied. 'So the main flow will be parallel to the coast here. We'd be going with it along the strait.'

'But the islands are moving so slowly,' Marlo added, 'it shouldn't be much of a problem.'

'There'll be a fair bit of turbulence caused by the other outlying islands,' Daimon said, 'but again it shouldn't be too bad. What worries me are the transitions on to and off the underwater bridge. There's bound to be some trouble there. But I'm willing to give it a go if you are. Terrel knows this place better than any of us.'

The sailors exchanged glances, then nodded their agreement.

'It'd be a shame not to go ashore, though,' Kelli remarked, 'having come all this way. Aren't you curious to see what this place is like?'

'We'll see how it plays out,' Marlo replied cautiously, although it was clear that he too would be disappointed if they didn't get to see more of the Floating Islands. 'Let's just see if we can get there without sinking first, shall we?'

It proved a relatively simple task to guide the *Dark Star* into the deep-sea channel between Vaka and the group of smaller islands further to the south. Once there – as Daimon had said – the currents were unpredictable, but they weren't too violent and the ship rode the uneven swell with ease. Ahead of them lay the vast bulk of Vadanis itself, and looking at it now even Terrel found it almost impossible to believe that it was actually moving. The healer had been away for so long that the firmly held belief that land *ought* to move had been eroded to the point where it seemed unnatural, an optical illusion created by the passage of the ship.

Such philosophical notions were soon set aside, however, when two things happened almost simultaneously. Another ship appeared from a channel between two of the southern isles, heading north along the coast of the mainland towards Tiscamanita. Moments later Kelli, who was on lookout duty in the bows, spotted the leading edge of the underwater bridge that linked Vaka to Vadanis. Its position was marked by a curving line of white on the surface of the water, and by the brighter blue of the shallow sea beyond.

'Slow down,' Daimon ordered, taking charge quite naturally. 'Circle round if necessary. Let's see how they tackle the boundary before we try.'

The other vessel was travelling quite fast, steering close to the mainland now in order to avoid any contact with the slow, rolling 'bow wave' that was piling up in front of Vaka's south-facing shore. When they reached the edge of the shallow water they did not slow down at all. If anything they accelerated, turning their ship so that it cut across the line of rough water at a right angle. For a few moments she bucked, her bows and then her stern dipping violently, but then she was through and riding smoothly over the bright-coloured surface of the strait.

'Logical,' Daimon muttered. 'Let's see if we can do the same.'

The crew set about raising more sails, and Marlo brought them around, following the other vessel's path as closely as possible. Daimon kept up a stream of advice, which was accepted without question. The old man was no longer a drunk. For a short time at least he was a pilot again.

The churning line of white foam seemed to rush towards them at alarming speed, and it was difficult not to imagine the hull being ripped apart by the roiling mass. When the *Dark Star*'s bows dipped, everyone on board had their hearts in their mouths, but then she rose again, seeming almost to take wing, as the stern disappeared into a trough of blue-green water. It seemed impossible that any craft could survive such an unnatural angle, but a moment later she levelled out and sailed on in an almost comically serene manner. The sailors whooped and hollered their delight, hardly believing what they had just done.

Such was their relief that their ship was still in one piece that it took a while for anyone to notice that there were now several other craft in the strait. Most were smaller than the *Dark Star*, and they all appeared to be heading north.

'Looks like you were right, Terrel,' Marlo commented. 'We're not the only ones heading towards Tiscamanita. We might get mistaken for locals after all.'

They positioned themselves near the back of the small flotilla, and sailed on. Nobody on the other vessels seemed to be paying them any undue attention, and Terrel took this as a good sign.

Crossing over the trailing edge of the underwater bridge was no bother at all. Compared to their earlier experience, there was hardly a ripple to mark their passage into deep waters again. Soon after that, the harbour at Tiscamanita came into view. This proved to be a large inlet, guarded by two promontories. Terrel noted fortifications on both sides of the entrance, but once again no one seemed to be interested in the *Dark Star*.

Once inside the harbour it was obvious that they were in shallow water again, even though they hadn't noticed the transition this time, and the surface was perfectly calm. Several ships rode at anchor while others were moored at jetties, and a number of small boats made their way to and fro among the larger craft. At first glance everything appeared to be much like any other bustling but peaceful port, but then Terrel noticed several groups of soldiers patrolling the quayside, and he began to worry again about the safety of the ship and her crew. At his suggestion they anchored in open water, and almost before they had stopped moving a small skiff drew alongside.

'Anyone to go ashore?' one of the oarsmen called.

'Three of us!' Terrel yelled back. 'We'll be ready soon.'

Terrel, Faulk and Taryn collected their packs and said hasty farewells to the sailors, thanking them for all they had done.

'The *Dark Star* is yours now,' the healer told them.

'Enjoy your travels. And don't forget to give her a new name when you get home.'

'We will,' Marlo replied. 'We're going to call her the *Musician*.'

For a moment Terrel could not speak.

'Enjoy your travels too,' the sailor went on. 'Who knows, we may even come ashore ourselves later.'

'Watch yourselves if you do,' Terrel warned, pointing out the military presence.

'Are you coming or not?' the oarsman yelled.

'We'd better go,' Terrel said, saddened by yet another parting.

'I'll drink a toast to you tonight, lad,' Daimon promised.

'I bet you will,' the healer responded, smiling.

'Good luck,' Valko said.

'And welcome home,' Kelli added.

'I've got a little way to go before I'm truly home,' Terrel replied, 'but I couldn't have got this far without your help.'

With that he pulled his hood forward over his face, hoping to hide his eyes a little, and followed Faulk and Taryn down the rope ladder to the waiting boat.

'The fare's two phinars apiece,' one of the oarsmen said as they pulled away.

'Fine,' Terrel replied, knowing full well that they had very little money between them – and none that would be recognized here.

'Where do you want to go?'

'The nearest landing place.'

'That'll be Redshank Breakwater. For an extra phinar each I could take you to Seneschal Quay. It's a lot closer to the town and the markets.'

'The Breakwater will be fine.'

'Suit yourself.'

When they were halfway to the shore, the boatmen obviously grew suspicious, especially as Terrel had kept his face hidden.

'Let's see the colour of your money,' one of them demanded.

'When we land,' Terrel answered.

'No. Now.' The men stopped rowing. 'You'll pay me or we'll throw you over the side and let you swim for it. If you can.'

There was a swift shiver of sound as Faulk's blade was drawn from its sheath.

'That would be a mistake,' he said quietly.

The oarsmen stared, weighing up the situation.

'You have a choice,' Faulk told them. 'Take us to the shore and then row away. Or you can swim from here and I'll do the rowing. Which would you prefer?' When they did not respond, he added, 'Of course, there is a third alternative, but I don't think you'd like it much.' He tapped his sword against the side of the boat for emphasis.

A short while later, Terrel and his two companions were clambering up over the shingle and driftwood of a tiny bay at the outer edge of Tiscamanita's dockyards. Behind them the boatmen rowed away, arguing loudly.

Even though he knew they could not afford to remain where they were for too long, Terrel did not set off immediately they reached solid ground. He could hardly believe that it had happened at last. The unknown road had finally come full circle. For the first time in more than ten years, he was standing on the soil of his homeland.

PART THREE

TINDAYA

CHAPTER FORTY-ONE

The prospect of actually setting foot on Vadanis had seemed so remote for so long that Terrel had not been able to think beyond the point he'd reached now. But as the reality of their situation gradually sank in, he began to realize that there were many more obstacles to overcome before he reached Tindaya and tried to fulfil the demands of fate or prophecy. They had no usable money, no possessions of any value, and no obvious means of earning their keep now that his healing skills had become unreliable. There were soldiers everywhere, and even if Jax hadn't told the guards to be on the lookout for him specifically, they would certainly be watching for any foreign 'invaders'. Terrel was with two companions who knew nothing of this land, and whose accents would betray them as soon as they opened their mouths. Faulk's threats to the oarsmen, which had provoked bewilderment as well as fear, had already made that much clear. Although the spoken language of the empire was remarkably similar to that of Kenda, some vocabulary was different and pronunciations varied. In fact it was amazing that any similarities existed at all. Terrel could only think that in the distant past, before the islands' self-imposed isolation, there had been a connection between Vadanis and the Kendan mainland – certainly a much closer one than there had ever been with Macul, whose language was entirely different. However, that was of little concern now. Terrel had more immediate problems to deal with.

'Where should we go?' Faulk asked, assessing the surrounding area.

They were on rough ground, near the end of a deserted wharf, and some distance from most of the activity in the harbour. If the boatmen raised the alarm the travellers would be spotted easily in such an isolated spot, and they were conspicuous even to a casual observer.

'We won't be so noticeable in a crowd,' Terrel decided. 'We'll head for the centre of town.'

'Lead on,' Faulk said. He too was obviously keen to distance himself from the scene of his confrontation with the oarsmen.

'If anyone approaches us,' Terrel added, 'leave the talking to me.'

As they set off along the wharf, the healer added another disadvantage to his list. Even though he hoped Taryn's shield was still in place, he was already aware of gaps in its protection, and he dared not disguise himself using the glamour now that he was in Jax's territory. He would just have to keep his eyes hidden as best he could, and hope no one recognized him by his awkward gait. There were presumably a large number of strangers in the town for whatever events were to mark the full of the Red Moon, and he would just have to trust that he and his companions could lose themselves among the throng. The amount of activity in the harbour certainly indicated that Tiscamanita would be busy.

Having been inspired to go ashore there, it now seemed a good idea to leave the town as soon as possible. Their best chance of doing that in a way that was both practical and would give them a realistic opportunity of evading the soldiers was to fall in with some of the pedlars, travelling

merchants who had brought their wares to the market. To
that end Terrel decided to head for the town's main
square, a place which held several memories for him –
some good, some decidedly bad.

. After they had been walking for a short while, the bulk
of the town came into view. Daylight was fading and the
Red Moon had risen, adding its glow to that of the sunset.
Terrel picked out the silhouette of the tower he had
climbed on his previous visit – and felt a brief moment of
nostalgia for the boy he had been then, innocently unaware
of all that was to come.

They were still in the dockyard area, but now there were
other people on the quays as a few vessels moored for the
night. No one paid the three travellers any attention, and
Terrel began to feel a little more confident. He told himself he had no need to hurry. The one thing in his favour
was that he still had a whole long month in which to get
to Tindaya. Unless he did anything stupid, that ought to
be plenty of time for the journey. However, this thought
was followed by the realization that it was *only* one long
month until his destiny was played out. The next time the
Red was full, the other three moons would match its
power – and then the Dark Moon would blot them all
from the sky.

The healer's nervousness returned in full measure when
several soldiers ran past them, heading towards the place
where they'd come ashore. The guards seemed intent only
on speed, and weren't checking any of the people nearby,
but it could only be a matter of time now before the
search widened. Faulk touched Terrel's arm and pointed
out into the harbour. Several small boats, carrying men
wearing the uniform Terrel recognized as that of the
Imperial Guard, were converging on the *Dark Star*. The
healer was just hoping the sailors would have the sense to

make a run for it when he realized they were doing precisely that. The anchor was being raised and sails hoisted. From this distance it was impossible to tell exactly what was happening, but Terrel thought he heard the sound of hails floating over the water. When these were ignored, a few arrows were fired at the ship. However, the boats were no match for the *Dark Star* once she got under way and she soon outran her pursuers, who broke off long before the ship crossed over into the ocean proper.

The travellers were not the only ones who'd watched the encounter with interest, but they were the only ones to feel sorrow at the departure of the foreign vessel. The oarsmen had clearly raised the alarm – and Terrel and his companions were truly on their own now.

As they went on they became aware of increasing military activity, but none of it seemed very organized – and because the travellers tried to keep out of the way of the patrols as much as possible, they never felt under any direct threat. From various conversations he chanced to overhear, Terrel gained the impression that most of the local inhabitants either resented the presence of the Imperial Guard or found their antics amusing. It seemed to the healer that the soldiers themselves had probably viewed the assignment as a chance to enjoy themselves – especially at the full of the Red Moon – and that they had never really expected to be called into action. The report of newcomers with strange accents disembarking from an unknown ship had changed all that, but the military response had been haphazard and ill-directed. Having chased off the 'invading' vessel, it was even possible that they thought they'd done their duty now – for what danger could be posed by just two men and a boy? Nevertheless, the very fact that the soldiers had taken the alarm seriously confirmed Elam's report about Jax's fears. The healer took an almost vindictive pleasure in having thwarted his twin – for the time being at least. I'm here now, *brother*, he declared silently. And there's nothing you can do about it.

Once they reached the huge paved square that was the hub of Tiscamanita, Terrel realized why the town was so busy. Although the real Moon Festival took place only once each year – at the full of the Red Moon closest to the autumnal equinox – *this* full was the closest to the spring equinox, and thus the gathering was the second largest of the year. As they entered the arena he saw that the bon-fires near the corners of the square were not as big as those he remembered. The crowds were not as great and fewer stalls had been set up, but otherwise it was much the same as his previous time there under the lovers' moon. As if to emphasize that point, a replica of Kativa's Shrine – a bizarre wooden sculpture depicting a vast number of red roses – stood on its traditional site at the exact centre of the square. Terrel – or rather Jax using Terrel's body – had been responsible for burning down the original monu-ment, something that had caused him a great deal of trouble at the time, as well as shame and confusion. His subsequent escape from the authorities and the indignant citizens had taken place in the same arena a few days later.

'What are we doing here?' Faulk whispered in his ear.

'I'm not entirely sure,' Terrel replied. 'But many of these stall-holders are travellers, and we may be able to offer our services to one of them in exchange for a ride.' The healer had half expected to see Babak peddling his potions and elixirs, but there was no sign of his former tutor. In reality, Terrel knew that such a meeting had been too much to hope for.

Taryn began to laugh now, wide-eyed in astonishment at

everything going on around them – the sales patter of the merchants, the antics of the jugglers and fire-eaters, the musicians and food sellers – and Terrel recalled his own reactions as a fourteen-year-old boy. It had been almost overwhelming for him then, but in his short life Taryn had already seen and experienced so much more. And yet now – even though he knew they were in a potentially dangerous situation – he was just a child again, with a child's wonder and curiosity. Terrel smiled, but the weight of responsibility he'd taken on with his promise to Nomar settled a little more heavily on his shoulders.

A face the healer recognized emerged from the crowd then, and he turned away instinctively, trying to sink back into his hood. The newcomer paid no attention to the travellers as he walked rapidly past, deep in conversation with the younger man hurrying along at his side.

'And you will report to me, and only me. Not the soldiers, not Seneschal Cadrez. You understand?'

'Yes, Underseer,' the younger man replied.

'Good. There are times when . . .'

As they strode out of earshot, Terrel turned to look at their retreating backs. He'd remembered the older man's name now. It was Hacon. Ten years ago he had been a deputy to Uzellin, who was then Underseer of Tiscamanita and who had tried and failed to exorcise a 'demon' from Terrel – and had then inadvertently allowed his prisoner to make a very public escape. Uzellin's position in the town had probably not survived that debacle, and at some stage Hacon had obviously been promoted. What was more interesting was that there was clearly some friction between the military and spiritual leaders of the community. Terrel couldn't help wondering whether the divide had been caused by the possibility of his own presence.

A loud burst of laughter disturbed his train of thought.

It drew the three travellers towards a makeshift stage set up not far from the fire in the northern corner. By the time they were able to see what was going on, the play being performed there had evidently switched from comedy to romance; there were only two actors in view now and the man was down on one knee, proclaiming his love.

As soon as he saw them, Terrel was transfixed with amazement. The man was clearly too old to be playing the romantic lead, and his make-up made him look slightly grotesque – but his impassioned voice made the onlookers forget such shortcomings. All but the least sensitive of the men in the audience envied him his eloquence while the women were entranced, no doubt wishing they could be wooed in such a gallant manner. However, it was not the acting or the play that held Terrel's attention but the identity of the actors. The lover on his knees was Laevo, and the object of his theatrical devotion was Sarafia.

'You know them?' Faulk asked quietly, glancing round to make sure he could not be overheard.

'Yes.'

'Do you think they'll help us?'

'I hope so,' Terrel replied. 'It certainly can't hurt to ask. Travelling players don't usually have much time for the authorities, so I don't think they'll betray us.'

The trio had made their way round to an area at the side of the stage. They had to wait to make contact until the play and then the encores – which featured a medley of songs performed by the entire company – were over and the collection tins had been taken round. Even now Terrel was intent on a careful approach. The circumstances under which he'd left the troupe had not been ideal. The true nature of his eyes had been revealed in an on-stage incident following the first total eclipse Vadanis had ever experienced, and many of the actors had been both frightened and angry. After all this time Terrel didn't know how many of the original group would be left, but he didn't want to take any chances. Ideally he wanted to approach Sarafia first, to test out what his reception might be. The fact that his dream had correctly identified her as a member of Laevo's cast, and that she had not been antagonistic was encouraging, but hardly conclusive. However, as he knew only too well, dreams were sometimes meant to tell him things – and he had no intention of letting this opportunity slip away.

As the actors and their helpers took a breather before preparing for their next show, Terrel saw his chance. Sarafia had wandered over to a nearby stall selling woven rugs, and was idly looking at the wares as she sipped from a cup of water. Leaving Taryn in Faulk's charge, Terrel went to join her.

'How are you, Sara?'

She turned to look at him, peering into the shadows under his hood.

'Do I know you?' she began, then gasped. She had seen the healer's hands – one deformed, the other marked with four tattooed circles.

'Don't make too much fuss,' Terrel said quickly. 'And don't use my name.'

'But . . . Why, what's the matter?'

'I can't afford to be recognized by the guards. I was hoping you might help me.' He had turned to face her now, so that the firelight would show her enough of his face to know he was in earnest. As she stared into his eyes, he saw memories stir. After a moment she smiled.

'It was real,' she whispered.

'What was?'

'I dreamt about you,' she replied. 'Three nights ago. You were here, in Tiscamanita. That's why I persuaded Laevo to come. He doesn't usually like performing in big towns, especially when there's any sort of festival. Too much competition, he says. And now you're here! I can't believe it.'

'I had a similar dream,' Terrel said, wondering whether he had been calling for help in his sleep, directing the friends he thought he could rely upon to come to his aid.

'Really?' Sarafia was shaking her head in amazement now.

'You told me your dream came true. That you'd escaped from the farm.'

'I ran away,' she admitted, looking guilty. 'But I had to. I love what I'm doing now.' She paused. 'What have you been doing since then?'

'It would take too long to tell you,' Terrel replied apologetically. 'Do you think my friends and I could travel with the troupe for a while?'

'If it was up to me, yes, of course. But it'll be Laevo's decision. Shall I ask him?'

'Am I really a legend among the actors?'

'Oh, yes! You've no idea how many stories there are about your time with the company.'

'Good or bad?'

'A little of each. Wait here. I'll fetch Laevo.'

Terrel moved away from the stall, seeking the shadows, and after a little while Sarafia returned with Laevo in tow. The actor was fiddling with his costume and muttering to himself, but when he looked up his painted face almost exploded with astonishment.

'Moon's blood!' he breathed. 'It's the enchanter.'

'I'd rather not be called that,' Terrel replied, grinning in spite of his nervousness.

'Sara tells me you want to rejoin the troupe.'

'We do.'

'We?' Laevo queried. 'How many of you are there?'

'Me and those two over there.'

'Can they act?' The actor glanced over at Faulk and Taryn, who were watching the exchange closely.

'I've no idea. We just need to get out of Tiscamanita without attracting any attention.'

Laevo nodded, smiling.

'I know that feeling,' he said.

'Is there anyone in the company who would still remember me?' Terrel asked.

'No, just me. Though they all know you by reputation.'

'So I'm told.'

'You made quite an impression back then,' Laevo confirmed. 'Let's hope you do so again, *after* we leave town, of course.'

'So we can come with you?' Terrel said hopefully.

'Why not?' the actor replied with a shrug. 'It's time we had a bit of fresh blood in our act.'

Sarafia gave a little shriek of joy and flung her arms around the healer.

'That's quite enough of that,' Laevo mumbled. 'How do you two know each other, anyway?'

'Sara saved my life before I even met you,' Terrel replied.

'And he made me see I could do anything I wanted if I set my heart on it,' Sarafia added.

'Oh, so nothing important then,' Laevo responded, deadpan. 'Sara, we've got another show to do.' He turned back to Terrel. 'You and your friends stay backstage – and don't get in the way.'

'Thank you,' Terrel said, then turned and beckoned to Faulk.

As Taryn came forward at the soldier's side, he glanced up and fixed Sarafia with a solemn gaze.

'You were in the dream,' he said.

'Did T— Did he tell you?' she asked, squatting down to face the boy at his own level.

'No. I saw . . .' Taryn hesitated, looking up at the healer, uncertain now. 'I didn't . . .'

'Is this your son?' Sarafia asked.

'No,' Terrel replied. 'But we're all the family he's got now.'

'Not any more,' she said with a welcoming smile that was directed at the boy. 'Young man, you're now part of the Great Laevo's Theatrical Company.' She looked up at Terrel and Faulk. 'You all are.'

CHAPTER FORTY-TWO

After an initial period when Terrel was treated with equal amounts of awe and suspicion, the company accepted the newcomers readily enough. Faulk's strength proved to be a valuable asset, and Taryn displayed such dramatic talent that he was eventually able to take on various juvenile roles written especially for him by Laevo. And while Terrel refused to appear on stage, he occasionally took on his old role as prompter, and also helped Laevo mark up any changes to the scripts – even suggesting a few amendments of his own. The three friends never asked for a portion of the profits from the shows, accepting only food and a place to sleep each night, so the actors were given no cause to complain on that score. And they all enjoyed listening to Terrel tell stories of his adventures. These tales were carefully edited, omitting any mention of Ancients or prophecies and concentrating on the exotic nature of the lands he had travelled through. The simple fact that he had actually visited foreign realms – unlike any resident of Vadanis in countless generations – was enough for his tales to seem fantastical to his audience. Laevo was already planning to use many of Terrel's experiences in new plays, but the healer had made him promise not to do so until after he'd left the company. The veteran actor grumbled at this, complaining about the fact that their performances had to be so much more 'respectable' these days, and implying that he would like nothing better than to present some rather more sensational material. When Terrel asked about the reasons for his dissatisfaction, Laevo told him that since Prince Jax had come to power, both the local underseers and detachments of the army were being used to monitor performances. Satirical burlesques such as those they had performed during Terrel's earlier tenure were no longer considered acceptable. In the past Laevo would have ignored such injunctions with contempt, but now he could not afford to. Other actors had been put out of business or even imprisoned simply because of alleged insults directed against the imperial family.

Terrel found this news unsettling, especially as it meant the troupe came under rather more scrutiny than would have been the case in those earlier years. But there was nothing he could do about it. He simply made sure he remained in the background, leaving the showmanship to others.

Because Faulk and Taryn were the first foreigners any of the actors had ever met, they were also the subject of a great deal of curiosity, in part because they appeared so normal and not the barbarians that common belief proclaimed all people from static lands should be. They fitted in well, their accents becoming less conspicuous as time passed, until they were almost regarded as ordinary members of the company.

Their exit from Tiscamanita, the day after the moon gathering, had been largely uneventful. They had seen several detachments of guards half-heartedly checking the progress of the departing traders and visitors, but Laevo was clearly well known to most of them and so the company's wagons were simply waved through. Terrel had experienced an unnerving moment when he'd spotted Seneschal Cadrez sitting on his horse at the side of the road, but he too paid little attention to the caravan and the healer had been able to remain hidden.

Since then he had settled back into life on the road with something approaching contentment. Laevo had even asked Terrel which way he would prefer to go, claiming that all roads were equally valid to a travelling artist. The temptation for the healer to ask to go northeast – towards Havenmoon – had been tremendous, but he had resisted, saying instead that he wanted to go south, without specifying his final destination.

Another reason for the healer's pleasure in the continuing journey was his reunion with Sarafia. She was just a few years younger than Terrel, and in the time since he'd last seen her she had grown from a romantic girl to a romantic young woman. He was delighted that she had been able to fulfil her ambition to experience a wider world than the confines of the farm where she'd grown up – even though he sensed the pain she felt at the separation from her parents. In turn she was astounded by all he had done, and she never tired of hearing him speak about his travels. She also doted on Taryn, spending a lot of time with the boy, who recognized in her playful nature a kindred spirit. She even got him to talk about his parents, something Terrel had always failed to do. Taryn still had periods of misery or quiet melancholy that no one could alleviate, but at other times he was happy – and this was something that gladdened Terrel's heart.

Terrel joined in with the applause as the last actors came off the stage, congratulating each of them in turn. Then, as he was about to turn away – preparing to join the company for the late meal at the nearby tavern – he suddenly froze in place. Now that the stage lamps had been doused, he could see that it was no longer empty. Elam's spectral shape hovered over the boards, his face creased with an anxious uncertainty.

Elam?

At the sound of his voice the ghost turned, and relief flooded his face. When he didn't move, Terrel walked out on to the stage, pretending to be collecting some props.

Where's Alyssa? he asked. He had not heard or seen any animal nearby.

She's not here, Elam replied.

Why not? Panic clutched at Terrel's heart.

She's sick, but you know why. Once this is over she'll be fine.

How can you know that for sure? Terrel wondered hopelessly.

I don't think you'll see her again until then, Elam added. *But nothing's changed between you. She still loves you. Even I can see that.* He tried to grin, but only half succeeded. In the past, Elam had made fun of the growing bond between his two friends. Now he was serious. *She knows you're coming back for her.*

The news that Alyssa would not be able to come with him to Tindaya was dreadful, and it was a while before Terrel recovered enough of his wits to see that there was another mystery here.

So how did you find me without her? he asked.

The soldiers aren't the only ones looking for you, Elam replied. *And don't forget you're on home territory now, mine as well as yours. Even without the ring we have ways of following your progress.*

That was good news at least, but Terrel's hopes were dashed almost immediately.

Mind you, Elam added, *as soon as you get much closer to Betancuria, none of us will be able to come to you.*

The elemental's still there?

Yes, and its influence is far wider, probably because of the links with the others. We can't get within a hundred miles of the place. That's one of the reasons I had to come now.

A hundred miles, Terrel whispered, trying to recall the maps of Vadanis he had seen and translate the distance into practical terms. *But that means you won't be able to come with me to Tindaya!* The sacred mountain could be no more than eighty miles from the mining district.

No, Elam confirmed sombrely. *You'll be on your own, I'm afraid.*

The healer's heart sank still further.

Do you have any *good news for me?* he asked plaintively.

Not much, his friend admitted. *I just wanted you to know that we haven't forgotten you, that's all.*

Thanks. I appreciate that.

What are friends for? Elam said. *And I do have some things to tell you that might be useful.*

Are the others coming? Terrel asked, thinking that Shahan and Muzeni were usually the ones to pass on such information.

They can't. They have other things to take care of, and it's taking up almost all of their energy. Besides, if they came now they might bring others with them. I was able to slip away. To be honest I prefer it this way.

His explanation sounded alarming.

Who might come with them? Terrel asked, but realized he knew the answer even before his friend replied.

Araguz, Elam said, confirming his fears. *Not all our enemies are in your world.*

So that's why they didn't want him to die, Terrel thought dismally. We're not rid of him even now.

Anyway, you *don't have to worry about him,* Elam continued, *but, as I said, there are other things—*

Can you move? Terrel cut in. He had been standing in the middle of the stage for no apparent reason for some time now, and sooner or later someone was bound to ask what he was doing.

I'd rather not go too far, Elam said. *This isn't as easy as it used to be.* Simply remaining in Terrel's world was obviously costing him some effort.

All right. Hang on a moment. Terrel went back and collected his copy of the script, then returned and sat on the edge of the stage where there was just about enough light to pretend to read. Moving as slowly and as carefully as an old man, Elam came to sit beside him.

You're not the only one who misses Alyssa, he muttered as he settled himself, then looked aghast at his own tactlessness. *Moons, I'm sorry. That was a stupid thing to say.*

It's all right. You never were the soul of discretion. The two friends exchanged rueful smiles. *What is it you want to tell me?*

Well, the first thing is that Jax is getting nervous. It's finally sunk into his thick skull that, as the supposed Guardian, he'll be expected to do something at the confluence. He's putting a brave face on it, but it's obvious he's way out of his depth. The court seers keep coming up with suggestions from the latest interpretations of the Code, but none of them make any sense when you apply them to Jax. Which isn't surprising, really.

Can't the seers work out they've got it wrong?

Some of them are having doubts, Elam admitted, *but you're dealing with court politics here, as well as astrology, and that always muddies the waters. The point is that Jax seems to think you have a role to play too.*

What?

It's the first thing he's got right in years, Elam stated caustically, *but it means that the soldiers he has out looking for you aren't going to kill you. In fact, they may even take you where you want to go.*

To Tindaya? Terrel exclaimed in disbelief.

Jax may think he needs you to help him fulfil his role, Elam explained. *Or, knowing him, he may just want someone else there to take the blame if something goes wrong.*

The healer remembered his twin mocking him with the notion that they made a good team. At the time Terrel had wanted to deny any semblance of truth in that idea, but now it seemed Jax might be taking it rather more seriously. And there was an argument that said he ought to as well. On the other hand, if his own vision had been correct, the prince might want the guards to bring his banished brother to Tindaya so that he could kill him himself.

I'd rather not rely on any help from Jax or his soldiers, Terrel said. *I'll get there on my own.*

That's probably best, Elam agreed. *But at least it means there's still hope if you* are *captured.*

Terrel nodded.

What else? he asked.

The islands—

But before Elam could complete his reply they were interrupted by one of the actors, who called out to Terrel from the side of the stage.

'Are you coming, Legend?'

'In a while,' Terrel called back. 'I'm making some corrections to the cues in the second act. I'll join you later.'

'Don't wait too long,' the actor advised. 'The food'll be gone soon, the way this lot pack it away.' He waved and wandered off after the rest of the troupe.

Legend? Elam queried, spectral eyebrows raised.

That's what they call me, Terrel said with an embarrassed shrug. *I didn't want my real name to get too well known.*

Fair enough. Where were we? Oh, yes. The islands are still slowing down. And guess when the seers have calculated they'll come to a complete stop.

Terrel had no need to guess. He already knew. Everything was converging on a single night, now less than a median month away.

There's even a theory that the islands' course has been thrown off so badly that we're going to be trapped in a channel between two underwater ridges, Elam went on. *And we'll never be able to get out, even if we do pick up speed again. If that happens we may eventually get dragged up against the mainland – at a place called Kenda, apparently.*

Returning to where we came from? Terrel murmured, as a theory of his own began to form.

What?

The healer explained about the similarities between the languages of the empire and Kenda.

Perhaps our connections with the mainland were closer than anyone would like to admit, he went on. *Perhaps the Floating Islands were once* part *of the mainland – before they broke free and began moving.*

It's possible, Elam conceded doubtfully. *But it doesn't really matter now though, does it?*

Maybe not.

Oh, I nearly forgot. Shahan found a section of the Code indicating that when our time of change ends, another one begins. Something about moonlight and movement. He said you might be able to work out what it means.

Terrel laughed.

I probably will, he said. *When it's too late.*

'Is it the warlock?'

Taryn's voice floated up from the deeper shadows in front of the stage. The boy had approached unnoticed and was now looking at Terrel, his eyes full of fear.

'No,' the healer assured him. 'There's no warlock here.'

'Then who is it?'

Can he see me? Elam queried.

I don't think so, Terrel replied, *but he knows something's going on.*

I'm not surprised, the ghost remarked, sounding both curious and impressed.

Terrel wanted to ask what he meant, but Taryn was still waiting for an answer.

'This is a friend.'

The boy relaxed a little.

'A ghost?' he asked quietly.

'Yes, but you mustn't tell anyone about him. It'll be our secret, all right?'

'All right.' Taryn nodded solemnly. 'Laevo sent me to find you. The meal's almost over.'

'Tell him I'll be in soon,' the healer said, marvelling once again at the child's acceptance of extraordinary events. 'I need to talk to my friend for a bit longer.'

Taryn trotted off as Elam whistled in surprise.

Do you know what he's doing?

Protecting us, you mean? Yes, I—

It's much more than that. Who is *he?*

His name's Taryn Veress. He can create pictures in his mind, and they form the shield you told me about.

Elam didn't seem to be paying much attention to what Terrel was saying. The ghost was still staring at the boy's retreating figure.

There are connections, he said. *Hundreds of them.* His focus returned to Terrel as Taryn was lost from view. *Connections to my world.*

His father—

No. It's more than that, Elam declared. *Something strange happened with him. He was dreaming even before he was born. We all do that, of course, but his were different. And when his mother died she left him all the pictures from her memory – and all the pictures she'd inherited from her mother. I think some of them have been passed down from mother to daughter through a huge number of generations.*

Struggling to absorb this idea, Terrel picked up on the obvious inconsistency.

But Taryn's a boy.

So he's the end of the line, Elam said, nodding to himself. *The reason for all that sacrifice and effort.*

Sacrifice? Terrel queried.

I get the feeling they may all have died in childbirth.

But that's awful, the healer exclaimed. He was horrified by the idea, but he couldn't just set it aside. The phrase 'a child of pain' had taken on a whole new meaning.

Maybe that was the only way they could be sure of passing the pictures on, Elam guessed. *In any case, Taryn's here now.*

I'm lost, Terrel confessed. *What does that mean?*

According to the Code, the shield is supposed to come from Tindaya, isn't it?

But he's never been there.

No, but one of his ancient ancestors might have been, Elam said, *especially if Vadanis was once part of Kenda.*

The temple! Excitement was coursing through Terrel now. *One of Taryn's pictures is of a place he's never seen, a beautiful temple on a mountaintop. It looks nothing like the ruins we have now, but—*

It could be what it looked like in its heyday, centuries ago, Elam completed for him. *And Taryn is a descendant of someone who saw it and survived the catastrophe that destroyed it. One of the few.*

But how could an ancient memory protect us? Terrel wondered.

Who knows? Perhaps Taryn's ancestor was a wizard.

'Imbued with sorcery', Terrel quoted.

The point is, he's here now, Elam repeated. *And he's going to Tindaya with you.*

They did all this just to protect me?

Looks like it, but we may never know for sure. Perhaps they wanted us to rebuild the temple.

But it's too late for that.

Well, you have more allies than we could have hoped for, Elam said. *Perhaps they're relying on you too.*

Something about the way he said this sent a chill through Terrel. He remembered the conversation in Vergos when the ghosts had told him that their world was going to be affected by what happened in his.

You've found out something new, haven't you, he said.

Not new, exactly, Elam replied. He was obviously reluctant to explain further, and this deepened Terrel's sense of unease.

Tell me.

Our world doesn't work in the same way as yours, Terrel. But have you never wondered why there are no ghosts from the time before the last great upheaval? Someone who could explain all this to us?

I assumed they'd have moved on.

If they have, it's to a place none of us can find.

Then what happened to them? Terrel asked.

If the worst happens, none of us will survive either, Elam replied. *Our world will be devastated too.*

CHAPTER FORTY-THREE

After that there didn't seem to be much to say, and Elam was obviously ready to go. Before doing so, however, he held out his hand and Terrel met it with his own. He felt nothing more than the faintest whisper of a touch, but it meant a lot nonetheless.

You'll get through this, Terrel, Elam assured him. *We all will.*

Take care, the healer replied. *Look after Alyssa for me.* He knew he was asking for the impossible.

She'll only tell me she can look after herself, his friend said. *But I'll do what I can.*

Come back and see me again . . . if you're able to.

I'll try, Elam promised. *Good luck.*

And you.

The ghost's wavering outline vanished then, and Terrel went to the tavern to join the others.

The next evening was one of the rare occasions when the troupe camped on open ground rather than in or near a village. There would be no show that night, and most of the actors were glad of the time off – though work did not stop entirely. There were costumes to be mended, scenery to be repainted and maintenance on the wagons to be carried out, as well as tending to their horses and the usual domestic chores. But later on, as the company gravitated to the campfire, there was time for some idle chatter and a few jokes. As usual the actors eventually asked Terrel to tell them more about his travels, but on this occasion he declined, claiming he'd done enough talking for a lifetime.

'The same can't be said of you, can it, Faulk?' Laevo remarked. The soldier's taciturn nature and calm demeanour had made him something of a challenge for some of the troupe. 'What about you giving us a story?'

There was a chorus of agreement from around the fire.

'I have no skill with words,' Faulk stated warily.

'The quintessential man of action,' Laevo declared. 'But I can't believe you have no tales to tell. What about the legends of your country?'

'I leave them to people who can do them justice.'

'But won't you try?' Sarafia asked. 'Please?'

Her appeal seemed to carry greater weight with the soldier, and for a moment he hesitated. There were more expressions of encouragement from the rest of the actors, and finally Faulk relented.

'A legend, then,' he said quietly.

'Tragedy or comedy?' Laevo asked, as if he were preparing to take notes.

'Tragedy,' Faulk replied heavily, and Terrel felt a shiver of apprehension.

For a few moments the only sounds were the crackling of the fire and the distant soughing of the wind.

'In my country,' Faulk began, 'the men of the mountain villages have a reputation as fierce and cunning fighters. Traditionally, many of them make their way in the world as mercenaries, fighting for the local kings. In one such village, in the middle of a winter blizzard, twin boys were born to the wife of a renowned soldier.'

Terrel knew then that this was not just any story Faulk was telling. It was his own.

'They were small and sickly infants at first, but they were strong-willed, and they survived and grew into strong and healthy youths, destined to be soldiers like their father.'

'What were their names?' Laevo asked, leaning forward to push a stick back into the fire.

Faulk fell silent, his eyes blank, as if he did not understand the question.

'Don't interrupt,' Taryn hissed indignantly, and the others smiled. Laevo accepted the rebuke with good grace and sat back again.

'Their names were Galen and Zidan,' Faulk said, 'and as they grew to manhood they were each other's equal in every way. They looked alike, they spoke with the same voice, they even thought alike. And when it came to skills with bow or spear or sword there was never anything between them. They could both run the mountain trails for hours without becoming tired. They could lift great weights and endure the bitter cold of the snowfields. They even shared the same tastes in food. They were closer than any two brothers have ever been, before or since, and nothing could separate them. But then something did. Love.'

At this there was a kind of collective sigh around the fire and several nods, as if the audience had been expecting something like this. Faulk paid them no attention. He was staring into the flames but seeing another scene altogether. Terrel wondered what had prompted his friend to reveal the secrets of his past in such a way. Perhaps by presenting it as a fable he could distance himself from it, and thus try to exorcise the demons within. The healer was the only other person there who knew that this was no legend – and Faulk had been very careful not to look his way since he'd begun his story.

'Her name was Eden,' Faulk went on, and from the way he said it Terrel had the feeling that, unlike the earlier names, this one was real, but the soldier's expression remained as unreadable as ever.

'As if to prove they could do nothing separately,' he went on, 'the twins both fell in love with her at the same time, with the same relentless passion. At first Eden was flattered, but she soon saw that they were faced with an insoluble problem. She could only marry one of them – and how could she choose between identical men? To her credit she refused to do so, declaring she would have neither, but that wasn't good enough for Galen and Zidan.

'Despite her opposition, the brothers were determined to decide the issue with a series of contests. Whoever prevailed would win the right to ask for her hand. The tournament consisted of all the pursuits by which a mountain man is usually judged – trials of strength and stamina, of a clear eye and a steady hand. But, as before, there was nothing to choose between them. Each arrow hit the heart of the target, each spear throw matched the last. A race that lasted all day ended with them coming home side by side, each straining for the advantage in vain.

'As Galen and Zidan became more desperate to win, Eden grew angry and afraid. She was the only one who saw that all these trials were made to test the mettle of a hunter or a warrior, not the merits of a husband or lover. She begged them to stop, knowing it could only end in heartache for both loser and victor, but they were deaf to her pleas. The contests grew more brutal and exhausting, but still neither would give in, and at last – as Eden had foreseen – they lost all reason. They agreed to a final bout, a sword fight, man to man in the warriors' ring.'

Terrel knew what was coming next because of Faulk's earlier confession, but even he was not prepared for all the twists in the end of the tale.

'With the whole village watching, they traded blows for

an hour, each drawing blood, but neither would yield to the other by stepping out of the ring of stones. They were mad, their original purpose forgotten. Their whole world had shrunk into that small circle, and nothing outside it existed.

'Finally, Eden – who had remained silent until then – declared she would watch no more and ran off. In that moment, Galen proved his love for her was the greater because he was distracted, glancing round to follow her flight. In doing so he left himself open to one of Zidan's thrusts, which he was only able to partially deflect. The blade pierced his side, just below the ribs, a shallow wound but bad enough to bleed profusely. Yet Galen still had no thought of admitting defeat, and he knew he must act quickly before he lost the last of his strength. He launched an uncontrolled but furious attack, which Zidan only just managed to fend off. Both men were now almost spent, but Galen was near the point of collapse. Zidan began to back away, not wanting to cause any more damage and knowing he had only to wait in order to be victorious – but his brother would have none of that. He charged, taking them both to the very edge of the ring. But then he twisted his ankle on one of the stones and lost his footing even as he attacked. As he fell he was unable to avoid a thrust he would normally have been able to turn aside. Galen was impaled upon the blade and collapsed.

'It was only when his brother died in his arms that Zidan realized what he had done. He had murdered half of himself. As tears mingled with the blood and sweat on his face, he begged for forgiveness, but Galen was beyond words then and his eyes were fading stars.'

It was very quiet in the circle around the fire now.

'Zidan's grief was terrible, his guilt unbearable, but the worst thing was the knowledge that it had all been for

nothing. When Eden learnt what he had done, she refused
to have anything to do with him, would not even look at
him. A few days later she married someone else – a man
she did not love – to punish Zidan for his pride and stupidity. And so the half-man left his village home and lived
in exile. He became a wandering soldier, selling his skills
to the highest bidder, and in time he became a commander, a man renowned for his ruthless determination in
battle. He gained respect and even a little fame, but he
never found any peace of mind.'

And no love, Terrel thought. Wherever 'Zidan' went,
until he made his peace with Galen he would always be
alone.

'In my country,' Faulk concluded, 'the men of the
mountains still speak of Zidan, but none of them have seen
him since he left his home. To this day he is wandering
still, searching for a way to atone for what he did.'

And I'm supposed to lead him to the place where he can
do that, Terrel remembered, finding that another burden
had settled upon his overloaded shoulders.

When it was clear that Faulk had finished, there was a
brief and slightly awkward round of applause from the
actors, which the soldier did not acknowledge.

'For someone who professes no skill with words,' Laevo
commented, 'you make a fine storyteller.'

Faulk did not respond.

'But if I were to turn this tale into a play,' Laevo added,
'I would need a better ending.'

Terrel wondered if the actors' leader suspected the truth
behind the story – and Zidan's identity – but when Faulk
remained silent Laevo did not pursue the matter.

Faulk would still not meet Terrel's gaze, and the healer
knew better than to try to talk to him now.

CHAPTER FORTY-FOUR

The next few days passed uneventfully, except that each day brought Terrel closer to the time and place of his goal. The company were working their way down the western side of Vadanis, and the central range of mountains that included Tindaya was now occasionally visible to the east. Terrel knew that sooner or later he would have to tell Laevo where he was going, and that this would probably mark the parting of their ways. Compared to the coastal plain there were few settlements in the uplands, and the trails there were difficult to follow, so the troupe was unlikely to accompany the healer inland. However, Terrel wanted to delay that moment for as long as possible. The Red Moon was already waxing again, the White was about to turn and the Amber would do so a few days later – all of them then growing in strength as the day of the confluence approached. Every time the healer thought of what might happen then, it was as though a knife was being twisted in his stomach, but he forced himself to act normally. Even so, he felt the presence of the Dark Moon inside him. It still had a full cycle to go before it caught up with the others, but its changes had always been the quickest of all, even though they were invisible, and Terrel knew that time was running out. His one consolation was knowing that whatever destiny awaited him, it would be over soon. And in the meantime he tried to distract himself as best he could with the people and the small unimportant events all around him.

Terrel kept waiting for Faulk to refer to his story again, but he did not. The healer was certain his friend had wanted him to know the truth, but having revealed so much Faulk obviously didn't want to talk about it any more, and Terrel did not feel he had the right to force the issue. What the soldier had done had been hard enough; anything more was clearly beyond his strength.

However, there were others with whom it was much easier to strike up a conversation. Laevo was always happy to talk, although Terrel generally got the feeling that the actor was either trying out new material, using him as a sounding board, or absorbing new ideas with the intention of incorporating them into a later work. Nevertheless, he was always entertaining company, and Terrel did not resent being used in either capacity.

Taryn was also a constant source of interest. Ever since his conversation with Elam, Terrel had wanted to talk to the boy about his experiences, his memories and dreams, but he didn't want to do so in a way that might burden the child with responsibilities he would not be able to bear. The healer wasn't even sure that Taryn knew what he was doing with his pictures – that they represented a unique form of protection without which Terrel's own quest might well have failed some time ago. Equally, he did not want Taryn to bear the guilt of all the suffering that had been necessary to produce his talent – assuming Elam's theory was correct – so he avoided any mention of the boy's mother or any of those who might have gone before her. The one thing Terrel could do with a reasonably clear conscience was probe the boy's connection with Tindaya. He asked to be shown the picture of the temple again, and Taryn was happy to oblige. This time Terrel looked at the scene with new eyes, trying to see the link between the ruins he had visited and the magnificent building of Taryn's dream. In that he failed – if it was the same place then it had been changed beyond recognition by some unimaginably violent event – but at the same time he could see similarities between the two mountains, their slopes and crags, the views of the other mountains, and the plain with the river snaking across it. Nothing was quite as he remembered it, but even the shape of mountains might have been altered by such an upheaval. In itself that was a frightening thought.

'I wish it was real,' Taryn said when the connection was broken and the image had vanished.

Maybe we'll *make* it real, Terrel thought, but he said nothing to the boy, not wanting to raise his hopes too high.

Naturally enough, the other person Terrel spent most time with was Sarafia. Although they had caught up with much of what they'd been doing since the time of their earlier friendship, they hadn't touched on the events that had led to his departure from the farm. For some reason they both shied away from the subject, until one morning when they were sitting on the tailboard of the last wagon in the caravan, out of earshot of the rest of the company.

'Are you still in love with Alyssa?'

The question came out of the blue, and Terrel paused before answering.

'You don't have to tell me if you don't want to,' Sarafia went on, mistaking the reason for his hesitation.

'I'm just surprised you remember her name,' he said.

'It's hard to forget someone who can turn herself into an owl,' she remarked. 'I'm still not sure it really happened.'

'It happened.' Terrel could have explained that Alyssa had only borrowed the bird's body, rather than transforming herself, but it seemed too complicated a task, too subtle a distinction.

'Does she still change her shape like that?'

'Sometimes. It's the only way I've been able to see her for the last ten years.'

'Really?' Sarafia was horrified. 'That's like a curse in a children's tale.'

'It's better than not seeing her at all.'

'I suppose so,' she conceded. 'But you'll see her again properly one day, won't you?'

'Yes.' I have to keep believing that, he told himself. 'I'm going to make sure this tale has a happy ending.'

'Laevo would approve.'

Terrel nodded, smiling faintly.

'Is that where you're going now?' she asked hopefully.

'No. There's something I have to do first.' He waited, knowing curiosity would eventually outweigh her reluctance to pry.

'What's that?' she asked on cue.

'I'm sorry, I can't tell you.'

'Can't or won't?' Sarafia didn't sound aggrieved, just a little disappointed.

'I wouldn't even know where to begin. I'm sorry,' he repeated.

They rode in silence for a while, watching the countryside slide away behind them.

'Did you get into trouble when you helped me escape?' Terrel asked eventually.

'Not really. Jehar was angry, but he calmed down once he knew you'd gone, and my parents were just glad I was safe.'

'They must have known I'd never hurt you.'

'No one was thinking straight just then,' she replied, but a shadow had passed over her face at the mention of her parents.

'You still miss them, don't you?' he said quietly.

'Sometimes,' she admitted. 'Especially my mother. In the end she actually helped me run away. I'd seen the chance and she knew I'd never be happy unless I took it. I just hope Dad's forgiven her by now.' She paused, then added, 'I'll go back one day, but just to visit. This is my life now.'

'What made you decide to go?'

'I think when you kissed me I knew I had to get away one day.'

'But—' Until that moment Terrel had not even remembered the chaste farewell touch of his lips upon her cheek. He was astonished that it could have had such a far-reaching effect.

'I thought I was in love with you,' Sarafia explained, smiling at his confusion. 'I was young and foolish – and I couldn't compete with an enchantress, could I? So I got over that, but when I saw you run off, with all your adventures ahead of you, I decided I couldn't stay on the farm my whole life. So it's your fault I'm here with this band of reprobates,' she concluded with a grin.

'I'm glad we met up again,' Terrel said, pleased to see her happiness.

'So am I,' she agreed. 'I knew you were special as soon as you saved that calf.'

That had been the unwitting start of Terrel's career as a healer, but he'd made little use of his talent of late, in part because the actors were healthy enough but mainly because he no longer trusted his own gift.

'And everything you've done since has proved me right,' she added. 'I can't believe you've seen and done so much.'

'I find it hard to believe myself sometimes,' he admitted.

'And you haven't finished yet,' Sarafia stated confidently. 'I can see that. I hope you succeed in whatever it is you want to do, Terrel. You deserve a happy ending.'

The next evening Elam fulfilled his promise to return. Unfortunately, he appeared while the actors were in the middle of their latest performance and Terrel was in the prompter's position at the side of the stage. The healer glanced round at the faintly luminous figure, delighted by his arrival, but he knew he would not be able to talk to him and concentrate on the play at the same time. He also knew that whatever Elam had to say must take precedence over following the script, but for a few moments his friend seemed more interested in what was going on on stage than anything else.

I used to enjoy the travelling players, he murmured wistfully.

I'm glad you could come, Terrel said. *Is there any news?*

Not really, but this is probably the last chance I'll get to see you.

Terrel had already noted that a wind he could not feel was ruffling the ghost's hair and clothes. They were obviously on the edge of the area affected by the elemental's unknown powers, and as the troupe went closer, the strength of the wind would reach hurricane force for the ghosts even though it remained undetectable in the healer's world.

You ought to be turning east soon, Elam said. *It's not so long now until you have to be at Tindaya.*

Sixteen days, Terrel replied. The White Moon would be new that night.

Plenty of time, his friend said, nodding. *But you don't want to take any chances.*

How's Alyssa?

The same. She told me to tell you she still has your ring, even if she can't use it at the moment. And she's still waiting. She also said, and I'm quoting word for word here, that remembering is only the first stage. I don't know what that means, and she wouldn't tell me. You know what she's like.

Terrel thought about that for a moment, but couldn't make any sense of it.

Tell her she won't have to wait much longer, he said. *What about Muzeni and Shahan?*

They're still busy, but they're holding their own, Elam replied. *Don't worry about us.*

Easier said than done, Terrel thought, but he saw no point in pressing for more information about the ghosts.

Do you know if Jax is heading for Tindaya? he asked instead.

We know he left Makhaya some time ago, heading in that direction. But the route's taken him close to Betancuria, so we haven't been able to follow his progress.

I'm going to have to face him sometime, I suppose, Terrel said, trying to remain calm at the thought.

I take it you haven't had any trouble with the soldiers recently? Elam inquired.

We haven't seen much of them lately, Terrel confirmed. *And those we have seen don't seem so interested in the players any more.*

That's good.

Do you think— the healer began, then broke off as he was distracted by increasingly frantic signals from one of the actors on stage. He had obviously forgotten his line and wanted a prompt, but Terrel had no idea where they'd got to in the script. He shifted through the pages as Laevo began to extemporize, and eventually found the place and fed the forgetful actor his line. But when he turned back to the ghost, Elam had gone.

That night Terrel talked to Laevo about his need to go east, fully expecting to be told that this would mean they'd have to part company. To his surprise the actors' leader readily agreed to head towards the mountains, claiming it would give them the chance to visit places they only went to every three or four years, where even their oldest material would not have been seen before. If Laevo was curious about Terrel's reasons for wanting to go in that direction, he made a point of not asking, and the healer was grateful for that.

Over the next few days, the central mountain range grew to dominate the eastern horizon. Terrel constantly scanned the various peaks, trying to make out the ruined temple that would identify the one he was looking for, but he met with no success. Either he was still too far away to see such detail or Tindaya had not yet chosen to reveal itself.

As the caravan made its slow but steady progress over terrain that was becoming more rugged and sparsely populated with each mile, Terrel found himself thinking about the fact that mountains had played an important role in all his travels. In a sense, everything had begun when the ghosts had spirited him to the summit of Tindaya and he'd claimed the amulet, but since then there had been the forbidding black mountain above Fenduca, Makranash in the arid heart of the Binhemma-Ghar, and the volcano which had been one of the Lonely Peaks rising above Myvatan's central glacier. And now he was returning to Tindaya, completing the circle.

At last Terrel spotted a jagged, unnatural outline that he recognized. It was still some miles away, and there were several ridges in between, but his goal was finally in sight. Being so close filled him with a mixture of relief and dread. The weather was warm now, as spring turned to summer, and even if he had to go the rest of the way on foot there was nothing to stop him reaching the mountaintop in time. It was the thought of what might happen when he got there that made his skin feel so cold he might have been back in the snow fields of Myvatan.

'Are you sure you want to go this way?' Laevo queried as their cart jolted along a narrow and rutted trail.

Terrel nodded.

'If it gets much worse we may have to turn back,' the actor went on.

'You can go back any time,' the healer replied. 'I told you that earlier. We can carry on on our own from here if we need to.'

Laevo just grunted in response, and the horses plodded on, finally reaching the top of the latest pass. Ahead of them the trail wound down into a broad valley. On the far side Tindaya rose majestically, unmistakable now, but for once it was not the summit Terrel was looking at.

'What's going on there?' Laevo muttered, seeing the same thing the healer had.

Terrel did not answer. His way ahead no longer seemed so straightforward, and it was clear now why the actors had not been so closely observed in recent days. At the base of Mount Tindaya was a vast military encampment.

CHAPTER FORTY-FIVE

'We're not interested in the mountain,' one of the villagers complained, 'but they won't even let us cross the river. A third of our land's over there.'

'There's so many of them they've trampled half the crops into the ground,' another grumbled. 'And they've stolen most of what's left – though you won't get them to admit it.'

'We still don't know what they're supposed to be doing here. They won't tell us anything.'

'They should have stayed in Makhaya, where they belong. There's no place for generals or seers here.'

'Seers?' Terrel queried. 'I thought it was just the army.'

'Half the court's come as well, so they say. I heard the Empress herself is there.'

Terrel was both alarmed and confused by this unexpected piece of news. The realization that the mother who had cast him aside at birth might be only a short distance away was unsettling to say the least. He'd never met either of his parents – and the possibility of ever doing so had not entered his thoughts until now.

'And the Emperor?' Laevo queried.

'No. Dheran's still in his sickbed back at the capital, but his son's here, Prince Jax. Up to no good as usual, I reckon.'

'It must have something to do with the way the moons

are coming together,' Jonath said. He was the nearest thing the villagers had to an underseer, and it was he who watched the lunar cycles that helped determine the farmers' routines. 'It's only a few days away now.'

'But they won't tell us anything,' one of the others repeated. 'Maybe you'll have better luck.'

'Well, we won't be going across,' Laevo said. The river was too deep to ford, and the only way over was either on a narrow footbridge or in one of the villagers' boats – neither of which were big enough to carry the troupe's wagons. 'I've no fondness for soldiers myself.' He glanced at Terrel, but the healer didn't say anything.

The entire company had come down into the valley and made for the village that was the only settlement in the area. The arrival of travelling players would normally have caused much excitement in such a remote place, but for once the troupe had already been upstaged. The recent arrival of what seemed like the entire imperial army, and the establishment of their camp on the far side of the valley, was the most momentous event the villagers had ever known. As a result there had been no suggestion of a performance that night. Instead everyone had gathered to talk – the visitors hoping to learn what was going on, and the locals taking the opportunity to gossip and air their grievances. They had come together in the open air because there was no building big enough to house them all. Luckily the evening was dry and mild.

As usual Terrel's appearance had caused some initial unease, but the fact that he came as part of an actors' troupe – the home of many eccentrics – had reassured their hosts, and the strangeness of his eyes was soon forgotten. Before they'd even reached the village, the healer had finally admitted to Laevo where he was headed. The actor had been surprised and had asked several questions, most of which received evasive answers. Terrel had simply repeated that he must get to the summit of Tindaya, and eventually Laevo had realized he wasn't going to learn any more. Now, after having heard what the villagers had to say, the actor was clearly still mystified.

'I'll have a better look tomorrow,' Faulk said later that night, 'but I've already seen enough to know we're not going to be able to sneak past them, unless you can make us invisible.'

Terrel wondered briefly whether he could employ Cobo's trick and do just that, but he rejected the idea. Even if he could pull it off, such use of the glamour would certainly alert Jax to their presence – and that was the last thing he wanted.

'The cordon's too tight,' Faulk went on. 'They've got too many men.'

Terrel nodded. The three travellers were sitting together next to one of the wagons, discussing their plans. Faulk had simply accepted the healer's need to get to the top of the mountain, and Taryn had assumed he would be going with them. This had caused Terrel a few qualms, but in truth he knew he would be glad of the boy's company – and the protection he might provide.

'I'm good,' Faulk added with a rare grin, 'but even I can't fight my way through an entire army.'

'Why would they want to stop us?' Taryn asked innocently.

He has a point, Terrel thought, especially if Jax really does want me to join him on the summit.

'I'm not certain they do,' he told the boy, 'but we have to consider all the possibilities. I have a job to do up there, and not everyone wants me to succeed.'

'Why not?'

'Because they don't really understand what I need to do.'

'Then why don't you explain it to them?' Taryn asked.

'It's a good question,' Laevo said, strolling up and sitting down next to the trio. 'Why don't you?'

Faulk frowned and glanced at Terrel, as if waiting for instructions to get rid of the intruder.

'I may just do that,' the healer said.

'You think you can talk your way through?' Faulk was obviously surprised. 'An army doesn't usually put up a guard like that unless they want to keep people out. I don't know what this is all about, but—'

'You don't?' Laevo exclaimed. 'I know Terrel isn't keen on telling anyone what he's up to, but surely he must have told *you*?'

The soldier's silence gave him his answer.

'What about you, boy? I've seen you looking at the mountain. Do you know what's going on, or is he keeping you in the dark too?' The actor sounded indignant now, but because he *was* an actor, Terrel knew he might simply be pretending. 'Don't you trust them, Terrel?'

'I would trust them both with my life,' the healer replied evenly, 'but in the end this is my task, and mine alone.'

'And there's no need to shout at Terrel,' Taryn said, indignant in his turn. The boy had swelled with pride when the healer had declared his trust in him. 'He's just doing what's right.'

Laevo smiled.

'Your followers are loyal,' he commented. 'Even if you keep your secrets to yourself.'

'That's because they trust me in return.'

'Exactly,' Taryn declared emphatically.

'I almost wish I was coming with you,' the actor said, shaking his head in exaggerated bewilderment. 'There's got to be something special up there if you and the army are both interested, not to mention all the seers and the imperial family. I get the feeling there'd be a good play in this.'

'In what?' Sarafia asked as she joined them.

Laevo gestured in the general direction of the mountain and the lights of the camp around it.

'Are you really going up there?' she asked Terrel.

'Yes.'

'What for? The temple at the top is just a ruin, you know.'

'I know.'

'Does it have anything to do with the confluence everyone's talking about?'

'The moons are important, yes.'

'So you've got some time yet,' Laevo deduced. 'Keep going, my dear. You're clearly better at extracting information from this curmudgeon than I am.'

'What's a—' Taryn began suspiciously.

'A grumpy old man,' Laevo replied, anticipating the question. 'Someone who doesn't talk too much – even to his friends, it seems.'

'I've had enough of this,' Faulk muttered, glaring at the actor. 'If Terrel doesn't choose to tell you something, that's his privilege. So keep your snide comments to yourself.'

Laevo merely grinned.

'A hundred pardons, General,' he said. 'Or have I mistaken your rank?'

'You've promoted me,' Faulk replied, his expression softening a little. 'And the only man I command now is myself.'

'No more arguing,' Terrel decreed. He did not want to

part on bad terms. 'I'm doing what I think is best. It's all I can do.'

'So you'll be leaving us?' Sarafia sounded sad but not surprised.

'Yes. I'm grateful for your help – it would have been much harder to get here without all of you. And a lot less fun.'

'We can take some credit for that, then,' Laevo said mildly.

'We've played a small part in a much bigger production,' Sarafia surmised, 'but we played it well.'

'And now it's time to make my exit,' Laevo added as he got to his feet. 'Good luck with the third act, Terrel.'

'He can't help being nosy,' Sarafia said as the actor wandered off. 'It's part of what makes him so good at his job. I'm the same way myself, sometimes.' She stood up, then knelt to kiss Faulk, Taryn and Terrel in turn. 'That's just in case I don't get to say goodbye properly,' she explained.

Both Faulk and Taryn were obviously surprised and a little embarrassed, but Terrel was smiling.

'You should be careful,' he warned her. 'Remember what happened the last time we kissed?'

'That worked out all right in the end,' she told him. 'So will this.'

'I hope so. Thank you, Sara.'

'Will I ever see you again?' she asked softly, echoing her words from a decade earlier.

'I don't know,' Terrel replied, repeating his own line.

'We haven't gone yet,' Taryn said earnestly. 'We'll still be here in the morning.' He looked puzzled when they laughed.

Early the next day Faulk disappeared on a solo reconnaissance mission while the company prepared for a show that

night. In anticipation of their departure, Laevo had chosen
not to involve either Terrel or Taryn in the play and so
the two were left to their own devices. Terrel had been
waiting for the opportunity to talk to the boy alone, and
suggested that they go for a walk along the river bank.
They chatted about inconsequential matters for a while
and then, when they were some distance from the village,
Terrel stopped and looked up at the mountain. Prompted
by Laevo's remark the previous evening, he had begun to
wonder about Taryn's reaction to seeing Tindaya properly
for the first time. The boy had said nothing about recognizing the mountain, but Terrel had caught him staring up
at it on several occasions. From where they stood now only
a few fragments of the ruined temple were visible, and
they looked nothing like the boy's vision, but Taryn
frowned as he followed the line of the healer's gaze.

'What are you thinking?' Terrel asked.

'Nothing, really.'

'Tell me.'

'It's just odd,' Taryn said, after a slight hesitation. 'I
know I've never been here before, but there's something . . .' He paused, searching for the right word.

'Familiar?' Terrel suggested.

'Yes. That's silly, isn't it?'

'Not necessarily. Everyone gets feelings like that now
and then.'

'Do you?'

'Oh, yes.'

'Is that why we're going up there?'

Terrel nodded.

'Have you been here before?' Taryn asked.

'Yes, but only in a kind of dream,' the healer replied,
wondering whether this would prompt the boy to think
about his own experiences.

'My father had dreams like that,' Taryn said. 'Where he went to different places. But most of them were horrible, and he wouldn't let me see them.'

'There were a lot of bad things in your father's life,' Terrel stated soberly, 'but there were good things too. And the best of them was having you. He would be proud of everything you're doing now.'

'You think so?'

'I'm sure of it.'

The sorrow in the boy's eyes lifted a little at this, but Terrel knew it would take more than a few words to dispel it altogether.

'Come on,' he said, not wanting to dwell on serious matters any more. 'Let's go and see what a mess Laevo's making of the rehearsals without us to help him.'

Faulk was away for most of the day, and when he returned his news was much as expected. There was no way past the military lines, which stretched as far round the mountain as he'd been able to see – and probably encircled it completely.

'There are places where there's no permanent encampment,' he said. 'Mostly on the ridges and spurs, but even there they've posted a lot of sentries. We'd have trouble just trying to climb in places like that, and even at night I don't think we'd make it through without being spotted. Whatever's going on up there, they're making sure no one gets in without them knowing about it.'

'So we'll have to talk our way in,' Terrel concluded.

Faulk shrugged.

'For all I know they may just let us walk through,' he said. 'All I'm saying is, they'll certainly be able to stop us if they want to.' He paused, perhaps waiting for Terrel to explain the situation further, but when the healer remained silent he added, 'But if you *do* want to talk, you may have a choice about who you talk to.'

'What do you mean?'

'I spotted several command tents among all the rest. That'll be where the generals are based. There were also tents that looked like quarters for more important members of the party, including one with a royal standard flying above it.'

'The Empress?' Taryn guessed, wide-eyed at the idea.

'Could be,' the soldier replied. 'And one of the other tents seemed to have a lot of old men going in and out. They weren't in uniform.'

'The seers,' Terrel murmured, wondering what Shahan's former colleagues were making of the current situation.

'So if you want to make contact,' Faulk concluded, 'the question becomes who would you rather speak to? The generals, the Empress or the seers?'

Terrel didn't really like any of these options, but one of them was a more attractive proposition than the other two.

'The seers,' he said. 'I'll have a better chance of convincing them.'

'Do you want me to take them a message first?' Faulk asked. 'See how the land lies?'

'I'm not sure.'

'I've acted as a courier between armies before. I know the drill.'

'Or I could go if you like,' Taryn said brightly. 'No one's going to worry about a boy, are they?'

'A message may not do any good, whoever takes it,' Terrel said. 'There's no reason to think they'll know my name.'

'But if they don't know you,' Faulk argued, 'will going in person be any better?'

'They might not recognize my name,' the healer replied, 'but they'll recognize *me*.'

Faulk took a while to consider the implications of this statement.

'Prophecy?' he hazarded eventually.

'That, and the fact that at least some of them will have seen me when I was a baby. The rest of me may have changed, but my eyes haven't.'

'Fair enough. I hope you know what you're doing.'

It was the first time Faulk had revealed any hint of doubt about Terrel's decisions, and it made the healer feel even more guilty. Faulk and Taryn had both made considerable sacrifices for his sake, and Laevo had made a good point — he did owe them some explanation.

'Listen,' he said, looking around to make sure they could not be overheard. 'I can tell you why I need to get up there, but it's going to take some time, and at the end you may wish I hadn't said anything. So, are you ready for the whole story?'

'Yes,' Taryn replied eagerly.

'Go ahead,' Faulk said more soberly.

By the time Terrel finished talking he was growing hoarse and weary, but his heart felt lighter for having shared his secrets and his burdens. He had told them about the late discovery of his own royal lineage, and the fact that he had been discarded at birth at the time of the last four-moon conjunction. He had described his seemingly endless search for the Ancients, and the way in which various ghosts and sleepers had helped and hindered him along the way. And he had told them about the Tindaya Code, and the catastrophic upheaval it predicted if the Guardian and the Mentor did not combine to prevent it.

Throughout his monologue Faulk and Taryn had

remained silent, engrossed. Both seemed to accept the truth of what the healer was saying, despite the fact that so much of it was incredible, but as Taryn grew more and more excited and awe-struck, Faulk's expression became ever more grim. While the child was lost in wonder at the tale, the soldier seemed to be seeing the wider implications for Nydus, taking in the true gravity of the situation. But when Terrel finished at last and waited for the reactions of his two companions, the response from Faulk was surprisingly personal.

'So you have a twin brother too,' he said quietly.

CHAPTER FORTY-SIX

'Is it that one?' Terrel asked, looking across the river.

'Yes,' Faulk replied. 'Their commander always reports to the seers' tent first. There's no way we can get there ourselves without the soldiers intercepting us, but if we allow that patrol to take us in, there's a chance you'll be able to persuade them to go to the seers rather than the generals. There are divided loyalties in this army, it seems.'

'Which way do they go?'

'If they follow the same route as before, they'll cross over the lower slopes to the lookout station above that scarp there, then down and back across the fields over here. That's where we can intercept them.'

'So when should we go?'

'As soon as you're ready,' Faulk answered. 'The earlier in their route we make contact, the less likely it is we'll run into anyone else.'

Terrel nodded, then turned to Taryn.

'Ready?'

The boy had already shouldered his small pack.

'I'm ready,' he said.

'Then let's go,' Terrel said, and led the way across the footbridge.

'They came from the village, Seer, but they're not locals. I think you ought to see them.'

'All right. But you'd better not be wasting my time, Captain.'

Terrel and his two companions listened to the voices drifting from the inner section of the large tent. When they'd been taken there Terrel had assumed there would be several seers inside, but the outer room had been empty and there was apparently only one occupant within. But at least he now seemed willing to grant them an audience.

The captain who had escorted the travellers to the camp emerged and beckoned them forward, signalling to the armed guards to stay where they were. Faulk had already surrendered his sword without protest and the captain clearly did not consider the other two any threat. Terrel chose to go in after his companions, his heart beating fast as he wondered what sort of reception he was likely to get. When he stepped out from behind Faulk's bulk, his answer came in an instant. The seer – who had been sitting at a trestle table with several documents strewn across its surface – stood up so quickly that his stool clattered to the floor behind him. The man stared at Terrel in shocked disbelief, ignoring the other newcomers completely.

'Moon's teeth!' he gasped, then made a visible effort to control himself and turned to the escorting officer. 'Captain, send a message to all the seers. *All* of them. Tell them the council will meet here precisely at noon.'

'Yes, Seer.' The soldier had reacted with some alarm to the seer's astonishment, and was relieved to see that his master seemed to be in control once more.

'You will not tell them about our visitors,' the seer went on, 'and you will not report any of this to your superiors until I give you permission to do so. Is that understood?'

'Yes, Seer.'

'And make sure your men say nothing either. To anyone. Post guards inside and outside this tent *now*. I do not wish to be disturbed until midday. No one is to come in without express permission from me. Is that clear?'

'Yes, Seer.'

'Good. Remain in the outer chamber yourself so I can send further messages if necessary.'

As the captain saluted and left, the seer turned his attention back to the newcomers, inspecting Taryn and Faulk briefly before staring at the healer again.

'I expect this means you know who I am,' Terrel said.

Terrel sat between Faulk and Taryn behind a screen that hid them from the main room of the tent where Chief Seer Kamin and his colleagues were gathering. The room was crowded now and the rising buzz of conversation – much of it sounding argumentative – was almost deafening. Over the last few hours Terrel had been forced to relive his travels once more – and now he faced the prospect of doing so yet again, this time in front of the entire Council of Seers. Ironically enough, his fate would soon be decided by the same group of men who – by the admission of their own leader – had been responsible for his exile from the imperial court.

'Gentlemen,' Kamin said, rapping on the table and waiting until the noise subsided. 'Now that we're all here I have a very important matter to discuss with you. But first there's someone I want you to meet. Come out, please, Terrel.'

'Good luck,' Faulk whispered as the healer got to his feet.

Taryn just smiled, apparently quite confident, and continued to swing his feet below the bench.

Terrel walked out into instant pandemonium.

'Let me get this straight,' Fauria stated. 'Are you claiming to be the Guardian or not?'

'No,' Terrel answered patiently. 'I believe the elementals make up the Guardian. That's why the Tindaya Code seems to contradict itself so often when describing him.'

'That's absurd,' the seer muttered.

In telling his story, Terrel had left out any mention of ghosts and sleepers – just as he had done when talking to Kamin – concentrating instead on the Ancients and the prophecies of the Code. While he had been speaking, it was noticeable that some of the seers seemed more friendly than others. He knew that they all thought Adina's second son had died a long time ago. Indeed, several of them had accused him of being an impostor, and insisted on examining his eyes closely, as well as his twisted limbs. He had been exhaustively cross-examined over his tale, including the details of his meetings with Shahan when he had still been an inmate of Havenmoon.

'Before he died, Shahan told me he believed I was the Mentor,' Terrel said. Actually it had been *after* Shahan died, but revealing that would just confuse the issue further. 'And everything I've done since seems to bear that out. I've been the go-between for the Ancients and the rest of Nydus.'

'We only have your word for it that there are more than one of the creatures,' another seer said.

'Look for references in the Code,' Terrel suggested. 'There are clues enough there if you have an open mind. And you all know the prophecy often speaks of landscapes that simply don't exist on Vadanis. *I* know because I've seen them for myself.'

'Jax is the Guardian,' Fauria declared angrily. 'That has always been the council's belief. Are we to change all this on the word of an interloper?'

'It hasn't been the belief of all the council,' Kamin said quietly. 'I've been aware of a group calling themselves

"Alakor" – the disaffected – for some time. They seem to believe that the missing twin . . .' he waved a hand towards Terrel, '. . . was significant to the prophecy. And I must say, now that I've met him I'm inclined to agree with them.'

'This is treason!' Fauria shouted, jumping to his feet.

'Sit down,' Kamin snapped. 'I've been Chief Seer for more than a decade now, since the murder of my predecessor, and I've spent a lot of time with Prince Jax. But for the timing of his birth, I would not have said he was anything like the hero described in the Code.'

'And he *is*?' Fauria exclaimed, pointing at Terrel.

'No. But Terrel's achievements speak for themselves.'

'If they're true,' the sceptic muttered.

'He too shares the crucial time of birth,' Kamin pointed out, 'and you don't have to agree with Shahan's theory to realize that this young man has an important role to play in the events soon to be upon us. There are several other possibilities.'

'Such as?' another seer demanded, making it sound like a challenge.

'One is that Jax *is* the Guardian, just as we have long believed, but that he needs the help of his twin brother to fulfil his destiny. Terrel's role could be that of the Mentor, or even as the other half of the Guardian.'

'A team!' Batou exclaimed in a frail yet piercing voice. He was the oldest of the seers. Having lived to his eighties was a considerable achievement in itself, and yet he had not only insisted on coming with the rest of the council to Tindaya but had also survived the journey – in defiance of several dire predictions by his colleagues. What was more, he was eager to add his two phinars-worth to any debate. 'They're twins, after all. It makes sense that they should be the two halves of a whole.'

'This is gibberish,' Fauria declared.

'On the contrary,' Kamin replied. 'It's an idea many of us had years ago, but abandoned when we believed the second twin to be dead. There is also the intriguing possibility that together Jax and Terrel make up the Mentor, not the Guardian. In some sections of the Code the text does seem to imply there are more than one of them.'

'You're twisting facts,' an elderly seer objected. 'If—'

'There are few *facts* in prophecy,' Kamin cut in. 'It's all a matter of interpretation. At the very least, what we've learnt today means that we should go back to the text and reinterpret it in the light of this new knowledge. I suggest we meet again in full council two days from now to discuss our findings.'

'Whatever happens, you have to let me go to the temple for the confluence,' Terrel said quickly. He was alarmed by the thought of delaying any decision for so long.

'We don't *have* to do anything,' someone informed him.

'Jax isn't going to like this,' another seer commented.

'The prince is some distance away,' Kamin said calmly. 'On the opposite side of Tindaya, in fact.'

This was welcome news to Terrel, who had been wondering just how soon his brother would become involved.

'I think, for the moment, there is no need to be in any rush to alert him to Terrel's presence,' the Chief Seer went on. 'That way, by the time he gets here we'll have a better idea of what we're going to do. That's it, gentlemen. We have work to do.'

'So now what happens?' Faulk queried. 'Do we just sit here for two days?'

The three travellers had been billeted in one of the seers' personal tents. The guards outside were from the same patrol that had brought them in in the first place, and although Kamin had assured them that they were under his personal protection, Terrel knew it was going to be impossible to keep the news of their arrival from spreading through the camp – and eventually to Jax.

'I don't see we have much choice,' he said. 'Even if we could get away undetected, we'd have to survive on the mountain for six days before the night of the confluence. That wouldn't be easy, especially if we're on the run at the same time. Our best hope for the moment is to wait and hope the council comes to the right conclusion.'

'I'm not sure I'd want to put much faith in that lot,' Faulk muttered.

Terrel knew what he meant. The seers had seemed like a gang of quarrelsome children. All they could hope for was that the wiser, calmer voices would prevail.

'Kamin strikes me as a reasonable man,' the healer said. 'And he wields a lot of power.'

'He's a politician,' Faulk said contemptuously.

'Yes, but he's a seer too. He'll know how important all of this is.'

'You didn't tell them everything, though, did you?' Taryn said.

'No,' Terrel admitted. 'It would have made it even harder for some of them to believe me. The important thing was to get them to agree to me climbing the mountain, so I left a few things out.'

'Isn't that like lying?'

'No. I didn't tell them anything that wasn't true.' Well, not much anyway, he added to himself. 'Sometimes it's just better not to say *everything*.'

Taryn nodded solemnly, and Terrel felt a little sadness as another part of the child's innocence was stripped away.

'And you didn't tell them Jax was your enemy either,' Faulk said quietly.

'I know. They may decide the two of us need to work as a team, and I didn't want to discourage that idea. It may be the only way they'll let me go up there.'

'Do you think it might be true?' Taryn asked. 'About the team, I mean.'

'I hope not,' the healer replied. 'I'd rather Jax had nothing to do with the future of Vadanis. But I can't rule it out. He must be part of the prophecy somehow.'

'And what about us?' Taryn asked, indicating himself and Faulk. 'What are we here for?'

'We're here to protect Terrel,' the big man replied. 'Me with this,' he patted his sword, which had been returned to him earlier, 'and you with this.' The soldier tapped the side of the boy's head.

'What?' Taryn looked confused. 'What do you mean?'

Too late, Faulk saw his error and gave Terrel an apologetic glance.

'Your pictures have been helping all of us,' the healer explained reluctantly. 'Shielding us from our enemy's minds.'

'They have?' There was pleasure mixed with the boy's bewilderment now.

'That's why Araguz wasn't able to control us,' Terrel added. 'And why Jax hasn't been able to find me recently, even in my dreams. But you don't have to change anything,' he went on quickly. 'Just keep doing whatever you've been doing.'

'I didn't know I *was* doing anything.'

'Then don't worry about it.'

'Does it have something to do with the temple from my dream?' Taryn asked, his face lighting up. 'Is it the same as the one on top of the mountain here?'

'I think it is, yes,' Terrel replied. 'But you saw the temple as it was long ago, before a great earthquake turned it into the ruins that are there now.'

'How could I do that?'

'I don't know. I think maybe there are ghosts who help you as well as some who help me.' It was as close to the truth as he was prepared to go.

'Really?' Taryn whispered, his eyes wide. 'But I've never seen a ghost.'

'Maybe you have,' Terrel said, 'but only in your dreams.'

That seemed to satisfy the boy for the moment, and Terrel could only hope that the revelation would not affect the way the shield worked. He needed to hide from Jax now more than ever.

In the next moment they were distracted by a commotion outside the tent. Angry voices, one of them very shrill, were raised in an argument they could not follow, until a single voice rose above the rest.

'If you stand in my way a moment longer I'll have you skinned alive!'

Faulk rose to his feet, his hand instinctively going to the hilt of his sword as the tent flap was thrown back. The woman who came in was in her forties, richly dressed and with a beauty that was striking rather than subtle. Ignoring the other occupants of the tent, she fixed her amber-coloured gaze upon Terrel.

He stared back, feeling his mind beginning to tear loose from its moorings. For the first time since the moments after his birth, Terrel was looking into his mother's eyes.

CHAPTER FORTY-SEVEN

For a few moments no one moved or made a sound. Taryn and Faulk were mere spectators. They might as well have not been there, such was the tension between the Empress and Terrel. A fury of emotions seemed to fill the air around them, so that when the lamplight flickered it appeared as though it too was being affected by the invisible turmoil. Flecks of gold glittered in Adina's eyes, making her seem even more intimidating.

'Do you know who I am?' she asked, her voice deceptively quiet.

Terrel could only nod.

'Then why aren't you standing?' she shrieked, her sudden vehemence making Taryn jump, and even startling Faulk. They had both got to their feet when the Empress came in, but Terrel had been too stunned to move. He stood up now, feeling his legs shake beneath him.

'You may well tremble,' Adina remarked caustically. 'How dare you come here? It's an insult.'

Terrel could think of nothing to say. He wasn't even sure he could make his tongue work.

'You won't get away with this,' she hissed. 'I will see to that. *My son* will see to that.'

'I am your son,' Terrel said, finding his voice at last.

'You're no son of mine.' She spat out the words as if she had swallowed something venomous. 'You—' The

Empress broke off then and put a hand to her brow, which had creased in a sudden frown. She shot a suspicious glance at Taryn, then turned back to Terrel, even though she had clearly lost her train of thought.

In the silence the healer heard more voices outside the tent.

'It's not only the moons that are waxing,' Adina murmured. 'No one sings any more.' She seemed almost pensive now, her rage quenched by her strange words. 'Even the bells are silent.'

Terrel was completely at a loss. Her peculiar statements made no sense in the context of their meeting, whether taken together or in isolation. They sounded almost like something Alyssa might say. He had no idea how to respond, but he noticed that both Faulk and Taryn were regarding the Empress as if she were quite mad.

The tent flap opened again and Kamin entered, calmly assessing the scene before him.

'Your Majesty,' he said formally. 'What brings you here?'

Adina rounded on him, her anger reasserting itself in an instant.

'Why didn't you tell me?' she demanded.

'We needed time to assess Terrel's story before bothering you with such matters,' he replied smoothly.

'Terrel?' she muttered, as if weighing up the name. Then her momentary distraction ended. 'There's no need to assess anything. He's an impostor.'

'No, Ma'am, he is not. There can be no other eyes like these in the world. I saw the baby for myself, and they have not changed. And Terrel's tale has passed the council's fiercest scrutiny. I have no doubt—'

'You're a traitor!' the Empress screamed. 'You've always conspired against me, ever since you murdered Mirival.'

'No, I—'

Adina brushed aside his protests.

'You're only doing this to discredit Jax,' she accused him. 'You're in this together.' She glanced again at Terrel.

'I have no wish to displace Jax,' he said.

'I should think not!' she exclaimed. 'He is the Guardian and I am the Mentor. I have guided the prince all his life.'

Terrel could have told her a lot about Jax that she almost certainly did not know, but he held his tongue, knowing it would be a pointless exercise.

'All we are doing,' Kamin said with exaggerated patience, 'is following the tenets of the Tindaya Code in order to avoid a terrible disaster.'

'By accepting this . . . this *thing*?' She waved a contemptuous hand at the healer. 'It never came from my body. It's simply not possible.'

'Ma'am, the facts—'

'He is not. My. Son,' Adina repeated, emphasizing each word heavily. 'There were no twins. Only Jax.' Having made this flat denial, she then chose to contradict herself. 'Whatever happened after he was born means nothing. It was rejected. Dead.' She turned mad, malevolent eyes upon Terrel. 'Dead.'

By now even Kamin could see no point in arguing with her, and he called to someone who was evidently waiting outside the tent. A handsome young man came in and bowed courteously to the Empress. At the sight of him all the spite seemed to drain out of Adina, and she gazed at him with an almost pleading look on her face. He whispered a few words in her ear, then offered her his arm. She took it gratefully and allowed herself to be led out of the tent.

'I'm sorry,' Kamin said when they had gone. 'The Empress' health has suffered recently. I'll see to it that you aren't disturbed again.' With that the Chief Seer made his own exit, leaving the three travellers alone again.

So much for my family reunion, Terrel thought bleakly. He had always dreaded any possible meeting with his parents, but the actual event had been much worse than anything he could have imagined.

Kamin was as good as his word, and they spent the next day and a half in virtual isolation. They spoke to no one, apart from a few words exchanged with the soldiers who brought their meals or guided them to the camp latrines. Even among themselves there was little conversation. Terrel had retreated into his shell after the traumatic confrontation with the Empress, and neither Faulk nor Taryn knew quite what to say to him. As a result the hours dragged by with an agonizing slowness, so that as the time of the council meeting approached Terrel's anxiety reached fever pitch.

'It must be noon by now,' he muttered, pacing up and down. 'Where's Kamin?'

A little later, when he could stand the suspense no longer, Terrel went out and asked the guards what was going on.

'The council's already in session.'

'Without me?' he cried in dismay.

'They'll send for you when they're ready,' the soldier replied.

Terrel found his exclusion hard to understand, but there didn't seem to be much he could do about it. He was about to go back inside when something else occurred to him.

'Has Prince Jax arrived yet?' he asked.

'Not as far as I know,' the guard answered. 'What's it to you?'

'Just curious,' Terrel replied, and then rejoined his friends.

In the end the healer was not called to the council at all, leaving him stunned and furiously angry. Faulk and Taryn tried their best to calm him down, though they were mystified too.

Kamin came to see them once the meeting was over, and was quick to reassure Terrel that nothing was wrong.

'We just need more time,' he explained. 'The developments in the reading of certain sections of the Code have been remarkable, but they're far from definitive.'

'So I'm supposed to just sit here?' Terrel demanded. 'Surely it's obvious you've got to let me go up there.'

'To me, perhaps,' the seer conceded. 'Others are not so sure. And the Empress' opposition complicates matters. But I'm confident that all these concerns can be resolved. There is time yet.'

Four days, Terrel thought, his anger temporarily swamped by fear. Time enough perhaps, but that didn't make the waiting any easier.

'Is Jax here?' he asked abruptly.

'I have no word of his whereabouts or his plans,' Kamin replied, sounding exasperated but resigned – as if he had expected nothing more.

'Can you at least tell me what the new findings in the Code indicate?' Terrel asked.

'All in good time,' the seer replied with infuriating calm. 'I wouldn't want to burden you with any premature or misconceived ideas.'

'This is ridiculous!' Terrel shouted. 'Aren't you going to tell me *anything*?' He was on the point of losing his temper completely, and Faulk quickly sought to deflect the healer's rage by returning the conversation to practical matters.

'How long will it take us to climb to the summit?' he asked.

'The distance is not great,' Kamin told him, 'but it isn't an easy climb. Eight or nine hours should suffice, but we'll allow a good deal more than that, in case of any mishap or delay and to allow time for rest before the confluence itself.'

'Who else will be coming with us?'

'Exactly who should make the climb is one of the issues under discussion at the moment,' the Chief Seer replied. He refused to elaborate on this statement and his evasiveness worried Terrel, in case the council might consider leaving Faulk or Taryn behind. The thought of losing either of his shields was horrifying.

'Be patient, Terrel,' Kamin concluded as he made to leave. 'We won't let you down.'

Two agonizing days later, Kamin arrived with the news they'd all been waiting for.

'The council's deliberations are complete,' he said. 'Not everything is clear, but the one matter on which we're all agreed is that both the Guardian and the Mentor are supposed to be present, so whichever role you are to fulfil, you'll need to be there.'

Terrel breathed a sigh of relief, then warned himself not to assume too much.

'And my friends?' he asked.

'They can go too, if they choose to do so. We've found references to not one but two shields, each in a different realm, which are to protect the principals. From what you've told us, Faulk and Taryn fit the description better than anyone else we can think of.'

'Good. Who else?'

'A single guide, Captain Igard, and he will accompany

you only part of the way. After that you'll have to make your own way to the summit.'

'No one else?' Terrel queried in surprise. 'What about Jax?'

'The prince cannot be found,' Kamin informed him, his disgust plain. 'And the Code makes it clear that anyone else who ventures on to the mountain during the night of the confluence will not only be in great peril but could also put the entire venture at risk.' He turned to Faulk and Taryn. 'You need to consider this carefully. If you're not meant to be there, there's little chance of you returning alive. And you may put Terrel at risk.'

'We're going,' Taryn declared.

'We are indeed,' Faulk said, smiling faintly at the boy's determined expression.

'If Terrel wants us to, that is,' Taryn added less confidently.

'We've come this far together,' the healer said. 'We'll finish it together.'

'Good.' Kamin's satisfaction at this outcome was plain. 'Now, I need to tell you something about the reinterpretation of the Code. There are several things you must remember. I'm going to assume that you're right about the Ancients being the Guardian and you being the Mentor, or at least part of him. One of the things we've learnt is that "the disparate parts" of the Mentor need to be "healed". We hope this means the reunion of you and your brother – if Jax ever deigns to make an appearance, that is – but in his absence the meaning is unclear. In any case, the Guardian has three main tasks on the night of the confluence if he is to avert disaster. He must make sure that the pendulum, of which the temple forms the top, does not stop completely. Or if it does, he must make sure that it – and the Floating Islands – begin to move again at once. At the same time, two worlds are described as colliding. There are several possible interpretations of this, but the only relevant detail is that the Guardian has to keep them apart. And, of course, he must choose between good and evil. In all these things the Mentor is to be his guide, so you must advise the elementals in the obvious ways. And if all goes well, the night will witness the birth of four new moons. This will be the signal that Nydus will survive. Have you got all that?'

'I think so,' Terrel replied, trying to put this new information together with everything the ghosts had told him earlier. Now more than ever he wished that Muzeni and Shahan could be there to advise him about the Code's enigmatic clues.

'Quite how the Ancients are supposed to arrive is still a mystery,' Kamin added, 'but for beings of such power anything is possible.'

Terrel nodded, feeling numb and weighed down by responsibilities he had not asked for and did not understand. Then Faulk asked the most important question.

'When do we leave?'

'Tomorrow morning,' Kamin replied.

Captain Igard called at the tent early the next day to find the three travellers already awake and ready to begin the ascent. Their packs had been augmented by clothing and equipment for the trek and for the night they would have to spend on the mountain before the final climb up to the ruined temple. Faulk had shouldered most of the extra weight.

As they left, they were acutely aware of everyone watching them, but Terrel could not look anyone in the eye. However, just before they passed beyond the perimeter of the camp, where most of the seers and senior officers had

gathered to bid them farewell, there was one spectator he
was unable to avoid.

The Empress Adina stepped forward until she was
immediately in front of her disowned son.

'I have a message for you,' she murmured, her eyes
glowing with triumph. 'From Prince Jax. He said to tell
you that he will meet you at the top.'

CHAPTER FORTY-EIGHT

'There's only one safe route from here to the top,' Igard told them. 'But the trail's easy enough to follow.' He pointed to a distant outcrop of dark grey rock. 'Keep going until you reach that crag. The path swings round there and heads directly to the summit.'

At dusk, the climbing party had pitched their tents on a small area of level ground on the southwest flank of the mountain. Taryn had fallen asleep quickly, but Igard had been keen to give Terrel and Faulk their final instructions before they tried to get some rest.

'From there the route couldn't be more obvious,' he went on. 'It runs along the top of that ridge all the way to the top. It's a knife edge, with steep drops on either side. For the most part the path's wide enough for three men to walk abreast, but there are stretches where it's narrow and the footing is sometimes treacherous. It can be tricky, but if you watch your step you shouldn't have any problems.'

Unless we meet someone up there, Terrel thought. There had been no sign of Jax yet, but it would be easy enough for him to intercept them on such a restricted approach.

'And that's the only way up?' Faulk asked. He was assessing the terrain as he always did, perhaps anticipating the healer's worry.

'Yes,' Igard confirmed. 'The ridge has its dangers, but

you don't have any choice. The summit is a plateau, like a table top, and apart from the trail it's surrounded by sheer cliffs. To my knowledge no one's ever scaled them.'

Faulk nodded.

'What about the plateau itself?' he asked. 'Any problems there?'

'Not really. It's relatively flat. There are places where the ruins mean you have to scramble, but generally it's solid underfoot. The plateau itself is shaped like a giant teardrop – a bit like Vadanis itself if you believe the map makers. You'll be approaching from due south, which will lead you to the flat bottom of the tear, if you see what I mean. The cliffs curve round to the narrow point to the north. Most of the ruins are clustered around the central area, though there are some buildings near the edges.'

'Where's the dark star?' Terrel asked.

'At the centre of the plateau, near the highest point,' Igard replied, giving the healer a measuring look. 'It's surrounded by a floor maze, but that's broken in places, and parts of it are hidden by stones that have fallen from elsewhere. It was at the heart of the ancient temple. If you want to reach it all you have to do is keep going straight ahead once you leave the trail.'

'How long should it take us from here?' Faulk asked.

'Three hours. Four at the most, even with the boy. My advice is to wait for full daylight before you set off. You'll still have plenty of time, and you don't want to risk any accidents at this stage.' The captain's nervousness was becoming more obvious now. Terrel could see that he was looking forward to making his way down the mountain again the next day and leaving the travellers to their own devices.

'What do you think of the place?' he asked curiously.

'I've been up there several times and never liked it

much,' Igard replied. 'It's one of the eeriest places I've ever seen, even in daylight. I don't envy you having to wait for night.'

When Terrel woke the next morning, he felt sick at the thought of what lay ahead. He was surprised that he had managed to sleep at all – and even more surprised to find that he couldn't remember any of his dreams. Surely, on this of all nights, they should have been significant. He glanced over at Taryn but the boy was still sound asleep – and so, not wanting to deprive him of some much needed rest, Terrel crawled out of the tent as carefully and quietly as he could. Even though the sun had barely risen, and the slope they'd camped on was still shadowed by the ridge above, the two soldiers had already packed up the tent they'd shared and Igard was nowhere to be seen.

'He was keen to get on his way,' Faulk said in answer to Terrel's questioning glance. 'And I didn't see any reason for him to stay. He wished us good luck, by the way, but he obviously wanted to get back to somewhere a bit safer as soon as he could.'

'If we don't get things right up there,' Terrel said, 'I don't think it'll be any safer down in the valley.' I don't think it will be safe *anywhere*, he added to himself.

They reached the plateau by mid afternoon. The last section of the trail had been steep, and the strenuous climb had left both Terrel and Taryn struggling for breath. The knife-edged ridge had provided them with spectacular views as the scree-strewn slopes dropped away to either side, but they'd been concentrating so hard on each footstep and on the way ahead – waiting for their first glimpse of the ruined temple – that they had taken little notice of the mountainous landscape. However, now that they'd reached the summit at last, they were able to forget their tired legs and aching lungs and look around. Even the biting wind, which was much colder now, did not bother them.

Together they explored the ruins, marvelling at the scale and complexity of the original construction, and at all the fascinating details that seemed to mark each fallen stone, each crumbling tower and cracked pavement. There were inscriptions on almost every exposed surface, and even though Terrel could not read the writing or decipher many of the pictures and diagrams, he knew he was looking at the original version of the Tindaya Code. Even a brief inspection of the site was enough for him to realize what a vast and time-consuming undertaking its construction must have been. He could feel the presence of those long-ago scholars and stonemasons, who must have dedicated their whole lives to their single-minded pursuit and who had then had their achievements ruined by a catastrophe they had been powerless to prevent. The only way Terrel could repay all that effort was to make use of the clues they had bequeathed him, and to try to ensure that such a tragedy did not happen again.

When they reached the dark star mosaic, surrounded by the broken maze, Taryn began to follow the pattern as best he could, but Terrel and Faulk hung back and the boy soon hesitated. He had simply been playing, but he realized that his companions did not feel this was the moment for any light-heartedness. Walking slowly back to the others, he stood in silence, one of his uniquely solemn expressions on his face.

'Well,' Faulk said. 'We're the only ones up here so far, and even if Jax does come there's only one way in, so it should be easy enough to stop him from interfering.'

Terrel nodded absently, lost in memories of his previous

visit. He had already picked out the five distant peaks where lights had flared and where he knew the star would form. But if his premonition had been accurate, he had to remember to take the human element into account as well. Where would he need to be? In that earlier time he'd been to the north of the mosaic, close to the highest point of the ruins, and he'd looked across the maze to his future self. So he should be somewhere to the south, between the ruins and the head of the trail. But that, of course, was also where Jax had been.

What if I make sure I'm somewhere else? he wondered. Would that break the pattern of events? The possibility of saving his own life by such a simple expedient was very attractive, but he rejected it almost immediately. Instinct told him that in changing the present he might also change the past. The first thing he had to do was make sure his younger self reached the amulet in time. Without that the Ancients would never have accepted him, and nothing that had happened since would have been possible. He would just have to take his chances with Jax. After all, he knew this time that the prince was coming, so perhaps he could avoid his attack. He had not actually seen the death blow fall, but it had seemed inevitable. He had been defenceless. Terrel shivered. It was one thing to see a vision, quite another to face the imminent prospect of it coming true.

It occurred to him then that neither Taryn nor Faulk had been in his earlier vision. So where were they supposed to be? Should he send them away? With Kamin's warning still sounding in his ears, the last thing he wanted was to be responsible for their deaths. Then again, it could be that it was their presence that would make the difference in his struggle with Jax. They were supposed to be his shields, after all. Could his premonition have been incomplete? Or simply wrong? And if that were the case, what had been the point of the ghosts going to so much trouble and effort to make sure he'd seen it?

Terrel shook his head, trying to clear his mind, and noticed that his companions had withdrawn a little, obviously recognizing his need to think. Faulk had taken up a position where he could watch both the maze and the point on the rim of the plateau where the trail emerged. Taryn was shivering, despite several layers of warm clothing, and he looked frightened – though he tried to hide this with a brave smile when he saw Terrel looking at him. Fresh doubts assailed the healer, but he knew he had to concentrate on his own tasks.

He decided that he had to assume his vision had been accurate, in which case he would at least have a good idea of when it would all happen. It had been night-time. The three visible moons had already risen and had been moving towards the point in the sky where they would join together. The Dark Moon had just appeared over the eastern horizon. All those events were still some hours away, so he would just have to wait. He wasn't sure what else he was supposed to do – except worry about the two questions preying constantly on his mind.

Where was Jax? And when would he arrive?

The sun set, and in the deepening twilight Terrel felt the tension inside him build to such a pitch he could hardly breathe.

'What should we do?' Faulk asked.

The trio had chosen their position carefully, placing Terrel as close as possible to the spot where he had seen himself, but also allowing Faulk to keep watch.

'I don't know.' A sense of helplessness was threatening to overwhelm the healer. He felt totally unprepared for what was coming. His whole life had been leading up to this moment, and yet now everything was in place he could only think about all the unanswered questions. He had almost begun to wish that Jax *would* arrive, so that at least they would be one step closer to resolving some of the conundrums.

The three friends were all watching the maze, the end of the path and the eastern horizon, glancing back and forth almost continuously.

At last the Red Moon rose, gliding purposefully into the night sky and bathing the mountaintop in its warm glow. Violence, fire and love, Terrel thought. Which of those would they witness tonight?

'It's beautiful,' Taryn whispered. 'Like your crystal.'

A little while later it was the White Moon's turn to illuminate the scene, and if the earlier arrival had presaged a rush of emotions this one at least helped to cool Terrel's fevered thoughts a little. The White's spheres of influence were logic, destiny and the precision of mathematical calculation, but in purely practical terms its serene presence made the night much brighter, easing some of their worries about missing what might be going on around them. Faulk in particular seemed to relax a little.

In due course the Amber Moon followed its sisters into the sky, adding a third, more ambivalent hue to their joint radiance. This was the moon that ruled the spirit realm, intuition and dreams, and Terrel had always thought it was the most beautiful of all. On this occasion, however, he greeted its appearance with a deep sense of foreboding. All they could do now was wait for the Dark Moon, and for the shadow play to begin.

'Listen,' Terrel said quietly. 'Some very strange things are going to start happening soon. I want—'

'The confluence won't be for a while yet,' Faulk pointed out.

'I know that, but before then we have to go back into the past and make sure some things happen the same as before. Otherwise we won't even *be* here.'

'But we are here,' Faulk objected, looking bemused.

'Just trust me on this,' Terrel pleaded, knowing it would be impossible to explain properly.

'This is where you get the amulet,' Taryn said knowledgeably.

Faulk gave the boy an envious look.

'I'm glad *you* understand it,' he muttered, then turned back to watch the spot where the ridge joined the plateau.

'I don't know how all this is going to turn out,' Terrel said, 'but I couldn't have done it without you two, and I just wanted to say thank you before—'

'Thank us afterwards,' Faulk cut in quickly. 'You'll be fine. Taryn and I will see to that, won't we?'

The boy nodded.

'I wish I could've seen the temple before it fell down,' he said. 'Dreams are all right, but the real thing must have been amazing. Just being here is . . .' He fell silent, lacking the words to express his feelings properly.

But Terrel was no longer listening. He had just seen a star above the eastern horizon blink out of existence. The Dark Moon – *his* moon – was rising, bringing with it thoughts of all the shadowed mysteries of life and death, of the invisible forces that ruled their world.

Terrel stared, remembering the words he'd read in Muzeni's journal all those years ago. 'The Dark Moon is a bird of prey, black wings stooped in a hunter's silent flight, black eyes fixed upon her target, talons outstretched, slicing the sky above her unsuspecting victims. No rules confine her; no defences can turn her away. When she strikes, her speed and savagery will be unmatched, unmatchable. We will not even feel the death blow.'

The sky-shadow was taking flight, and when it hid the other moons from the sight of men the darkness would be the most profound that any of them had ever seen. And perhaps the last thing most of them would *ever* see.

Terrel swallowed nervously, every fibre of his being thrumming with terror, then tore his gaze away and glanced round in a sudden moment of alarm. Even though he hadn't heard or seen any movement, both Faulk and Taryn had disappeared. He couldn't see them anywhere. As far as he could tell, he was now alone among the ruins of Tindaya.

CHAPTER FORTY-NINE

Terrel was given no time to panic because in the next moment the second, overlapping world appeared, super-imposed upon his own. In that world the Dark Moon was in the western sky, blocking the light of the sun. In the artificial darkness of the eclipse, five earthbound stars burned like beacons on the surrounding mountaintops. Terrel stared across the mosaic floor and saw the gangling, awkward boy that he had been. Nearby stood a man, whom Terrel took a moment to recognize. Lathan had been one of the seers from the imperial court, and had become a sleeper. Terrel had met him some months later in the shape of a kestrel. Both he and the young Terrel appeared now as ghostly figures in a shadow-world.

Within the superimposed realm, five beams of light sped towards Tindaya, meeting in a silent collision of light that spread out into a swirling, mesmerizing pattern above the stones of the mosaic. Both the boy he had once been and Lathan were clearly spellbound, and Terrel silently urged his earlier self to look up. Instead the boy turned to glance at the seer, then back at the shifting mass of firefly sparks. And then, at last, he did look up – and for the first time Terrel found himself staring into his own eyes.

'Hello, brother.'

Terrel had been so preoccupied that he'd forgotten that at this point he had seen not only his future self but also his twin. The prince had come up behind him unnoticed – and neither of Terrel's shields were anywhere to be seen.

'I knew you'd have to come here eventually,' Jax went on. 'It's about time you stopped hiding.'

'There's no point now, is there?' the healer replied, trying to conceal his fear.

'True enough. This was supposed to be *my* night, but you couldn't even leave that alone, could you? How am I supposed to be a hero when you're always hanging around and getting in the way?'

'Do you *want* to be a hero, Jax?' Terrel asked. This was not the attitude he had expected.

'When did I ever get to be what *I* wanted?' Jax snarled. 'If it wasn't the seers bleating on or my stupid mother whining, it was *you*, pushing me this way and that.'

'If you truly want to be a hero,' Terrel persisted, 'then you can help me.' He was keeping half an eye on his younger self, assessing his progress, and Jax realized that his twin's attention was divided.

'You see?' he complained. 'I could be just about to agree, or I could be about to kill you, and you'd still be thinking about something else. No one's ever thought about *me*.'

Such self-pity was hard to take coming from the prince, who had spent most of his life indulging his own whims and ignoring the consequences to others.

'This is more important than either of us,' Terrel pleaded. 'We have to work as a team or everyone will suffer. The whole *planet* will suffer.'

'Oh, so *now* you think we make a good team!' Jax exclaimed sarcastically. 'Too late, *brother*. It's time to end this.' He drew his sword from the scabbard that hung from his belt, and took a step forward. Terrel backed away a little, but dared not move too far. The vision of his death was about to be played out – only this time it would be for real.

A strangled yelp came to their ears from far away, but Terrel had no time to listen now. His eyes were fixed on Jax's blade. But the noise distracted the prince for an instant, and gave Terrel the chance to glance up into the sky, where he saw a grey bird above them, circling.

Alyssa? he tried hopefully, but there was no response.

Jax was very close now, almost within striking range, but Terrel was rooted to the spot, his legs unable to move. He knew he lacked the strength or agility to match his twin, and he had nothing with which to oppose his murderous intent.

'Don't do this, Jax,' he begged. 'We can still—'

'Shut up,' the prince growled, something close to madness in his eyes.

It was then that Terrel turned instinctively to the only weapon he had left – his mind. Using the telepathic link that had connected them since they'd dreamed together in Adina's womb, he spoke not in words but thoughts.

Why do you hate me so much? he asked. *What have I ever done to you?*

'Don't do that!' the prince screamed. 'Keep out of my mind.'

Like you kept out of mine? Terrel queried. *Doesn't feel so nice the other way round, does it?*

The connection was there now, a stronger bond than either of them would ever have expected – and Terrel saw the chance to save himself. Far from withdrawing, he let his consciousness slide deeper into his brother's malevolent mind – until he realized that he was effectively within Jax's waking dream. He saw the jealousy, the cruelty and malice, as cankers, diseases within the prince's internal world. And until recently he had known how to deal with illness.

Instinct took over and Terrel became a healer again – at least in intent. He didn't know if it would work, but he knew he had to try. Even as he worked, he remembered Kamin saying that the disparate parts of the Mentor needed to be 'healed'. If he and the prince really were a team, then this could be exactly what the Code had prophesied. However, the effect upon his twin was not what he had expected.

Jax screamed, writhing in agonized convulsions that made his limbs twitch and his face contort horribly. His eyes stared wildly and his mouth was stretched into a grotesque grimace.

'What are you doing?' he gasped. 'What have you done to me?'

Belatedly, Terrel realized what was happening. In 'curing' the selfish core of Jax's being, he was exposing the hidden parts of the prince's mind to the true nature of his evil – to the terrible effects on others of his past callousness. And without his thick, protective skin, such dreadful knowledge was becoming impossible to bear. Terrel had reawoken his twin's dormant conscience – and it had plunged him into torment. It was hardly healing, but at least it was keeping Terrel alive for a while longer. Jax was too busy fighting his own internal battles to worry about his brother.

At that moment they were both distracted by a distant rumbling, a noise so vast that even though it originated in another world it echoed loudly in their own. The first deep note was soon joined by a second, less cavernous note, just as Terrel had known it would be. In the earlier world, his younger self had been thrown to the ground by the immense vibration, and Lathan had collapsed too. At the same time, the shimmering swirls of light above the dark star had coalesced into a maze of sparks – and at its centre a tiny new star had been born. The fourteen-year-old

Terrel was now looking at his adult counterpart, who knew this was his cue to intervene.

Go to the centre, he implored, feeding all his energy into the psinoma in order to send it back in time to the boy he had been.

He was rewarded by the sight of his younger self scrambling to his feet and running towards the star-maze, only to be violently repulsed by the walls of light. Then, as the boy recovered his wits, he saw what he had to do and, with the older Terrel silently cheering him on, he began the circuitous route through the maze to its centre. But when he reached his goal he hesitated, obviously afraid.

Take it! Terrel urged him, desperate now. He could see that in the nether world the eclipse was almost over, and in a few moments the chance would be lost.

At last the boy stretched out a trembling hand and caught the miniature sun in his fist. He shuddered as his hand shone blood red, lit from within – but he had gained the prize. He looked up and Terrel smiled back at him, knowing that the first stage of his own task was complete. He could feel the amulet within his own hand now.

A look of horror passed over the boy's face then and he cried out an inarticulate warning, just before he – and the star-maze and everything else in the phantom world – vanished.

Too late, Terrel realized that this was the moment he had been dreading. In his preoccupation with the talisman, he had forgotten about Jax. Freed from the healer's attentions, the prince had reverted to his malevolent self – with the added fury caused by Terrel's meddling making him even more dangerous.

As Terrel turned to face his brother, he saw the raised sword begin to fall.

CHAPTER FIFTY

In the moment before his death, Terrel glimpsed the grey bird again and this time he hoped it *wasn't* Alyssa. He didn't want her to see him die, to witness the failure of his promise to return to her. And in the same moment he wondered if he would still be able to fulfil his role as Mentor as a ghost. But then there was only a vast, engulfing pain and a flickering darkness that blurred his vision. He felt himself falling, heard a series of incomprehensible noises and smelt the stench of blood. Moons whirled before his eyes. He realized that this was how it felt to die – this boundless disorientation mixed with torment.

It was only when he hit solid ground with a thud that shook every bone in his body that his perceptions began to change. Through a haze of pain and shock his memory reasserted itself, and began to show him what had really happened.

A second blade had appeared above him, flashing in the moonlight as it rose to crash against Jax's sword. The blow that would have split Terrel's skull had been deflected so that it glanced off the side of his head and then his shoulder. It had been enough to knock him senseless for a while, but not to kill him.

I'm not dead, Terrel told himself in disbelief. I'm not dead!

The excruciating pain should have been enough to tell

him that. He couldn't move his left arm, and when he reached round with his other hand he winced as he discovered that the prince's blade had sliced off the top part of his left ear. The side of his head and his shoulder were slick with blood.

But he was *alive*.

Even after that simple fact had finally registered, it took Terrel a few moments to put together the other pieces of the puzzle. There was only one person who could have saved him. One of his shields had returned – and only just in time. Faulk had appeared out of nowhere, just as he had vanished earlier, and saved the healer's life. With that realization came the understanding that Faulk had still been following the teachings of his own oracle. He had finally been able to atone for the 'murder' of his own brother by preventing the deadly conclusion of another conflict between twins. By averting Terrel's death, the soldier had begun to earn the forgiveness he so craved.

And Faulk was not done yet. The fight between him and Jax continued, with the prince screaming insults and swinging his blade wildly. But he was no match for the warrior's battle-hardened skills. Faulk parried each blow easily, at the same time driving his opponent further from the place where Terrel sat on the ground. In fact, as the healer soon realized, Faulk was simply intent on defending himself and his fallen comrade, and had no thought of attacking Jax. There had already been several openings and if the soldier had wanted to kill the prince he could certainly have done so by now. But that would have led to the twins being separated after all – and Faulk was not prepared to be responsible for that.

Terrel wasn't sure whether Jax realized what was going on, but his efforts were becoming wilder and more desperate as the fight continued, his frustration driving him mad. He was tiring now, and even his oaths were losing some of their vehemence.

Put the sword down, Jax, Terrel said wearily, fighting through his own pain. *He's not going to hurt you, but he won't let you hurt me either.*

'Shut up!' Jax screamed. 'Keep out of this.'

'I don't know what you did to me, warlock,' Faulk replied, under the mistaken impression that the prince had been speaking to him. 'But it's not working any more. You're no match for me without your magic.' He fended off the latest headlong assault with almost nonchalant ease, waiting for Jax to wear himself out.

The soldier's earlier disappearance made sense to Terrel now. Jax had evidently used his powers as an enchanter to lure him away from his post – which meant that the prince had been able to find one of the gaps in Taryn's protective shield. However, the shield was obviously back in place – so where was Taryn?

Stop fighting, Jax, Terrel tried again. *There's no point.*

'Perhaps not with this,' the prince said abruptly, and flung his sword aside.

Faulk regarded him calmly, still ready in case he tried another means of attack. The look in Jax's eyes was chilling, seeming to catch the light of the Red Moon, and Terrel remembered suddenly that his twin's magic did not lie solely in his skills as an enchanter. He was also a fire-starter.

No, Jax, no! he cried, even as he felt the first tentative intimations of power and heat. *Not here. The shield will turn it back on—*

Be quiet! Jax snapped. He was intent now, and determined, seeking out the lines that would kill his target. *Or I'll burn you too.*

It's not going to work. You'll just kill yourself!

But Jax only laughed, his fire-bright eyes now locked upon Faulk.

Terrel steeled himself to oppose his brother's sorcery. He believed that Taryn's shield would protect Faulk, but if there was any doubt then he would find the strength and the will to enter the conflict himself. In the event his intervention was unnecessary, because at that moment something happened that was so extraordinary, so numbingly awe-inspiring, that all petty human disputes were instantly forgotten. Even Jax turned to stare in open-mouthed wonder.

The Dark Moon was dark no longer. Its entire surface was ablaze with light, making the other three moons seem dull and turning night into day. But it was not just the transformation from invisible shadow to vivid brightness that was so remarkable; it was the actual nature of that brightness. The moon seemed to be composed of a million shifting prisms, each turning the light of the distant sun into swirling patterns of colour, like countless rainbows being woven into an ever-changing tapestry. Terrel knew that the same thing happened deep within his eyes, that his moon was now mirroring his own appearance in a manner that defied all explanation. But his eyes were like the Dark Moon now only in the sense that a single drop of water was like an ocean. What they were seeing was so enormous, so incomprehensible, that all comparisons were pointless.

The spectacle was also incredibly beautiful. For some time, all they could do was stare. Thought was almost impossible, but one memory did surface in Terrel's astonished mind. Kalkara, the strange, mute girl he'd befriended in Misrah, had once completed a mosaic depicting the Dark Moon – not with black pebbles but with the multi-coloured crystals of the desert, creating a swirling pattern that had mimicked with uncanny accuracy what he was seeing now. Terrel had had no way of knowing it at the time, but she had evidently gone 'beyond the winds' and seen into the future – to this very moment.

Thinking of her reminded the healer of the child who was currently playing a part in his life. Looking round, he was not surprised to see that Taryn had reappeared and was now standing beside him, gazing up at the sky in rapt silence. Both Terrel's shields had returned, but he still didn't know what he was supposed to do.

Although the healer had no idea what the Dark Moon's transformation signified, he knew that the confluence could be no more than an hour away. The other three moons were already moving closer together, and the fourth would soon catch up with them. Whether Jax co-operated or not Terrel would do his best as the Mentor, but unless the Guardian arrived all his efforts would be in vain. Where were the Ancients? he wondered helplessly. They should be here.

The healer's head was already swimming from pain and loss of blood, but he knew he had to do *something*.

'Jax?' he called, eschewing psinoma in the hope of not alienating his twin still further. 'This is the beginning. By the time it ends, all of Nydus will have changed, one way or another. You can—'

The prince glanced round then, and the look on his face silenced Terrel. He had never before seen eyes so empty, so lost – and for a moment he felt pity stir within him. Then Jax turned away again, gazing up at the sky, and the healer knew there was no point in trying to enlist his brother's help. He also knew that Taryn and Faulk had done their part. He was on his own now.

When the noise came again it was just as vast, but now it was in *their* world, and the effect was devastating. A thunderous wave of sound crashed over them, making the mountain shake and almost tearing the breath from their lungs. Taryn screamed and clapped his hands over his ears, then fell to the ground. Jax and even Faulk were also knocked down by the impact of the deafening roar, and they too were trying to block their ears, the prince writhing as if in agony. Terrel felt the same surge of inexplicable and contradictory emotions he'd experienced eleven years earlier. When a second note was added to the gigantic rumbling he heard echoes of that first unearthly conversation, but then two more 'voices' were added to the avalanche of sound, building it into a kind of massive, almost musical chord. However, when the fifth and final element was added to the mix, the sense of discord, of *wrongness*, was immediately apparent. Its combination with the others produced a lacerating, inhuman scream that seemed to shake the entire planet. At the same time Terrel felt a surge of warmth from the red crystal he'd carried with him from Myvatan and that, as much as anything else, made him realize what had happened. The Ancients might not be actually coming to Tindaya, but it was their voices he was hearing. The Guardian had made his entrance at last – and the healer felt a little hope rise within him.

But there was still a huge problem to be faced. Terrel was certain that his efforts to persuade the elementals to help him would be doomed to failure while the last of their number was insane. Regardless of his internal doubts, he *had* to become a healer again and restore the balance of the group. He knew this would be the last thing asked of him, the final seal on a bargain he had first made more than a decade ago, unwittingly condemning himself to so many years in exile. If he failed, everything that had gone before would have been for nothing, and there would be no way of stopping the unthinkable devastation predicted by the Tindaya Code. But what drove him even closer to despair was the knowledge that he had tried to heal the sick elemental before, when he'd been much closer to its lair – and he had failed. What chance could he have now, when he was thousands of miles away?

Distance means nothing to the Ancients, he told himself. And you're the Mentor. *Do* something!

The boundless noise was still roaring in his ears, making normal conversation impossible, but he had no need to use his voice to contact the person he needed most now.

Jax? Listen to me. I need your help. And this is your chance to be a hero. We have to heal the sick elemental or it'll be the end of everything. He knew his twin could hear him, but there was no response, just a stubborn mental silence and a sense of cold, malevolent anger. *Please, Jax. You and I are the Mentor. Together. We are a team.* It cost Terrel a great deal to make this admission, but there was still no response.

The healer saw then that starlight was flooding from his left hand as the amulet – which the elementals called the spiral – woke from its hibernation. He still couldn't move that arm, but the talisman's rebirth was confirmation that contact with the Ancients really had been established, and it gave Terrel a second jolt of hope. It was even possible that the healthy creatures would help him in his efforts to heal their brother, just as they had seemed to guide the healer to Myvatan earlier.

Instead of trying to shut it out, Terrel now chose to immerse himself in the vast recesses of the noise all around him. In a sense, it was the closest he could come to sinking into the waking dream of the Ancients – and it was a bewildering process. He had been inside the creatures before, several times, but on each occasion he had been dealing with only a single entity. This time they were *all* there — and there was another presence beyond that, one he did not recognize. But the one he *was* seeking was easy to find. The deranged elemental was just as powerful as any of the others, just as intelligent, but it was full of hatred and an unreasoning appetite for destruction. Its immense energy pulsed in fractured, chaotic patterns that defied analysis. Terrel couldn't think of how to even begin to adjust them in order to return it to sanity and health. The task was utterly beyond him.

CHAPTER FIFTY-ONE

The unconscious realization that he needed help led Terrel to seek it in his own past, and the memories soon became an unstoppable flood. He was helpless, engulfed by the images that showed him once more all the events and emotions, all the people and places, every sensation of his life. He had no real idea what purpose it was serving, but he was aware that the Ancients saw every fragmentary recollection as he did.

The first thing he saw clearly was Alyssa's hand as he put the makeshift ring on her finger, but even now, even in his memory, he could not see her face. Elam, on the other hand, grinned back at him as their friendship grew. Terrel relived the moments when they found Muzeni's journal and the pipe belonging to the long-dead heretic — the pipe he carried with him still — and experienced once more the surprise of Shahan's visit to the asylum, which had been frightening at the time but had marked the beginning of a valuable friendship. He felt renewed gratitude to Ahmeza and her brother Jon when they helped him escape from Havenmoon, and was comforted by a dream on the haunted island in the lake.

Sarafia became the first real friend he made in the outside world, and he felt the glow of achievement when he brought a dying calf back to life. Then he was talking to an owl, lost in the wonder of that first visit from Alyssa in the course of her long sleep. He heard Babak's voice as the old swindler taught him how to use the glamour, and took pleasure in the company of Laevo and his actors as they travelled towards Betancuria. His capture of the talisman flashed by, and he moved forward to the time when his bargain with the elementals had first been struck – the bargain that had saved the Floating Islands from destruction.

As the dream moved on to the next stage of his life, and he felt thankful for the kindness of strangers in a place called Fenduca, Terrel's first qualms began. When he saw himself healing one of the villager's babies and rejoicing in blind Talker's unexpected gifts and then Ysatel's even more unexpected pregnancy, the doubts grew deeper. Even his remembered delight at the reconciliation between Kerin, the ghost of his first wife and their sons did not assuage his growing fears. Something was not right.

When the next thing he saw was Esera's smiling face, as the success of his plan to lift the curse from the fog valley became clear, Terrel realized what was wrong. His memories were being carefully selected, showing him only the good moments, friends and events that had added to his store of happiness. But that was not the help he needed now. These memories might make him feel stronger, but he was also the product of all the bad things that had happened to him. His enemies had often had just as profound an effect upon his development as his allies. To regain his true strength he needed *all* the influences – for good or ill – that had led him to where he was now, that had made him *what* he was now. And yet that was somehow being denied him, as if there was a barrier between his mind and anything unpleasant. Understanding came with that thought.

Taryn? he called. There was no response, but then he had not expected any. *Taryn, I want you to take the shield away. I don't need it any more, and it's getting in the way of something I have to do. Will you do that for me?*

Still lost in his dream-world, Terrel was oblivious to his surroundings and could not see the boy, so he was unable to tell if he was reacting to his plea. The last time he had seen Taryn, the boy had been lying on the ground, apparently unconscious, and it was possible that his mind was out of reach.

Taryn? Can you understand me? I don't know how to put this in pictures. Terrel felt a flicker of recognition then, and clung to it tenaciously. *Take it away. Please. Take the shield away.*

An image appeared then, not from memory but from outside the dream. It was Tindaya's temple in all its glory, but as Terrel watched it faded into shadowy outlines and then disappeared altogether. His protection had gone.

This time his story began even before he was born, within the thunderous pulse of the red ocean that was filled with unseen terrors and pain when it should have been a haven of safety and warmth. It swept on through his years as a lonely and bewildered young orphan, growing up among the madmen of Havenmoon. Together with the incidents he had relived earlier, he now heard his own voice saying 'Sometimes I hate the world so much I wish I could destroy it all.' He saw Shahan's death from afar, and heard Alyssa's scream as she avoided death only by becoming a sleeper. Then it was his own voice screaming as Elam was murdered in front of him. He woke in Tiscamanita's gaol, faced tornadoes in Betancuria and shared the elemental's primeval fear as water spilled towards its underground retreat. And he knew again the despair that had shredded his heart when he was sent into exile.

And this time his sojourn among the 'barbarians' of

Macul included the unpleasant aspects of life in Fenduca and the fog valley. He saw mudslides and grinding poverty, witnessed the cruelty of the soldiers and the superiority of the sharaken, as well as the dreadful time when Ysatel became a sleeper, setting in train a series of events that split her family apart. He learnt of the curse that killed the newborn children in the fog valley, and felt himself a prisoner in that sunless realm until he was able to find a solution to the problem.

He was swept on through time, seeing everything that had happened to him as he went in search of the sharaken's fortress stronghold. He witnessed their dreaming, and suffered through the time when Jax usurped his body on a second occasion and killed the fox that had been Alyssa's host. The stews outside Talazoria horrified him, and when he was able to get inside the city he witnessed barbaric executions and was paralyzed for several days by a misuse of magic. Then came the sharaken's treachery and the destruction of the depraved king's palace, when Terrel had thought he was going to die – only to be rescued by Ysatel in the form of a caroc, a giant mythical bird. After that his renewed hope for Macul's future was counterbalanced by his distress at the unforeseen consequences of his bargain with the Ancients.

His story went on, moving to the desert land of Misrah – where the satisfactions of friendships, healing and the final restoration of peace and a degree of prosperity to the land were set against massacres, plague and tribal wars. He experienced once more the extremes of inhumanity and kindness, loyalty and betrayal, bravery and deceit, as well as the realization of how he had come to know the unforgiving yet entrancing nature of the place itself. He saw legends and ancient history spring back to life and was accepted as a member of the Toma, whose gift of a clay emblem he still wore around his neck. He came to love and respect many of the nomads, saw some of them die, and used his particular talents to aid them in their struggles before moving on again.

Myvatan provided even more contrasts, right from the moment he had first stepped ashore and sensed the madness that imbued the very fabric of the island – and which drove the pitiless war that had been raging there for centuries. He learnt the vile ways to which wizardry had been turned, culminating in fire-starters – the ultimate perversion of magic – but at the same time he witnessed great heroism and courage amid the pointless violence, and recalled how the greatest courage of all had been shown by those who fought for peace, not victory. He saw the misery of wraiths convert an ancient sword to a weapon not of blood but of truth and mercy. And he left knowing he had failed in the last and most important task of his visit there.

The final part of his long journey went by in moments, the years blurred together, but that was all Terrel needed. He now had access to *all* his formative memories, to everything that had made him a healer. What was more, he understood the reason for his failing powers. In protecting him from malign powers without, Taryn had also locked most of his own magic within. But the shield had been lifted. Terrel was a healer once more, his faith reaffirmed – and he was ready to try again, to rectify his failure.

He understood now that there would be no direct help from the Ancients themselves. They had all been infected by the illness in one way or another, and it had made them hostile and suspicious. Their waking dream was still there, but Terrel was going to need help to try to set it to rights. He was about to call out to Jax, to make one last effort to enlist his brother's help, when – without knowing how it had happened – he realized he was no longer alone. Other dreams had joined his own. He saw the sharaken, sitting cross-legged in their communal trance, their tattooed eyelids staring blindly as they shared the dream that entranced them all. Then came the bizarre visions that the nomads called desert dreams, the images the Toma's shamen used to empower their healing magic. And then there were the dark dreams of the people of Myvatan during their annual winter hibernations. But that was just the beginning. All of Nydus seemed to be sharing Terrel's dream. Only one vital piece was missing.

Jax? Jax! We have to heal the mad one. Or the whole planet will be destroyed and we'll all die. Everyone's ready. You can feel them, can't you? We can succeed if you'll join us.

At first there was no response, and Terrel felt only his twin's frustrated malice as he fought against the debilitating noise that was still shaking the entire island, and against his own fear. But then he realized that Jax had at least accepted the truth about the Ancients.

Do this for me and I'll let you take all the credit, just as I did at Betancuria, Terrel offered, hoping that if self-preservation was not enough to persuade his brother then the prospect of glory might be. *If we can survive this night, I don't care what happens afterwards.* That was a lie. Terrel cared a great deal, because he still had to fulfil his promise to Alyssa — and to himself.

Make it stop, Jax whined. *Make the noise stop.*

It will, Terrel promised quickly, hoping this wasn't true. *As soon as we heal them. It's the Ancients who are making the noise.* He could sense Jax wavering, and knew enough to keep quiet now. If he tried to push too hard it would only make the prince belligerent and spiteful.

What do I have to do? Jax grated eventually.

Nothing. Just let me guide your thoughts.

But you—

I won't hurt you, Terrel cut in, wondering how much time might be left before his chance was gone. *All I want is to be a healer again.*

Jax's reluctance was obvious, but as Terrel felt the last of his brother's defences go down, he let himself sink even deeper into the waking dream that was now enveloping the entire planet. His twin's presence made an extraordinary difference. In the past the prince had been at best a nuisance, at worst a positive danger, but now – as his dream combined with Terrel's – the healer felt truly complete for the first time in his life. It was a shocking and not entirely comfortable transition, but he had no time to dwell on its philosophical implications. He was too busy taking advantage of the situation.

The immense complexity of the task he had set himself left Terrel breathless and terrified by his own audacity. How could he possibly hope to achieve anything within this colossal maze of alien energy? He tried to identify patterns within the healthy part of the dream and work out how he could fit the rest of it into a similar mould, but there were so many invisible forces here, and many of them were so *remote*, that he couldn't see how to do it. Now that he had all the power of his many allies available to him, strength of will was not a problem – but direction was. It was like trying to sculpt seawater with his bare hands.

Just relax, he told himself. Let your instincts guide you.

His first tentative efforts to readjust some of the strands within the labyrinth met with resistance, but he persevered, probing and nudging at one of the smaller areas of chaos until a semblance of order began to appear. He sensed surprise and confusion within the entity as a whole, together with some relief. Moving on, he set to work on a neighbouring region and this time it was a little easier and quicker. The creatures' trust grew.

Terrel was making progress now – and a kind of incredulous elation began to take hold of him as he methodically set fractures and soothed the cuts and bruises that marked that unimaginably huge, alien body. All his manipulations were subtle, each one making the next more immediate, using a combination of logic, love, intuition and luck – the healing aspects of all four moons. Whenever he grew tired, Terrel received help from another unseen source, which renewed his resolve and his hope. He kept believing.

In the real world, far away from the centre of his struggles, the physical repercussions of his work became apparent. In and around the volcano where Myvatan's elemental had its lair, the effects of meltwater were being excised, as if the inundation that had driven the creature mad had never happened. Its home became a sanctuary of fire and rock once more, devoid of the hated magical substance that had spilled out of the glacier. But that was only part of the process. Once the first objective had been achieved, it was still necessary to restore the hideously distorted energy patterns to their original state of health, and to correct the effects of the earlier changes that had spread out from the core of the original illness. This was what Terrel was engaged in now, a piecemeal war of attrition that seemed to go on for ever.

It took every last scrap of his skill as a healer, every last scrap of energy bequeathed to him by all those who shared his dream, but eventually he knew he was going to succeed. And once he was sure that the final goal was in sight, he had no thoughts of rest or even the possibility of failure. The patterns as *they ought to be* glowed in his mind and he moved the Ancients' dream towards them, impatient now but careful still, wary of any mistake at this late stage. By the end he was not even conscious of what he was doing; it was as though some higher power had taken over, directing his mind, his thoughts and the progress of his efforts. And when it was over, he knew it was the greatest achievement of his life – of any healer's life – and he withdrew with a sigh that echoed through history.

He opened his eyes to find the scene around him unchanged – except for the fact that the four moons had almost come together. The Ancient on Myvatan was whole and healthy once more and so, by inference, were all the others. The Guardian was there, ready and waiting, the massive chord of his voice now in harmony. Terrel knew that all he had to do was persuade the elementals to 'choose good', and the disaster they had long feared would be averted. Exhausted though he was, he knew they would listen to him now.

Looking up into the sky, and marvelling again at the new beauty of the Dark Moon, he could see that the conjunction was almost upon them, the moons beginning to overlap. And then, just as he was preparing to renew his contact with the Ancients and plead his case, two things happened almost simultaneously. The first was that Jax began crawling towards his discarded sword, glancing up at Terrel with loathing burning once again in his eyes. Even as the healer tried to make sense of this development, wondering if he could somehow get Taryn to restore the shield and free Faulk to protect him again, the second occurrence set Terrel's mind reeling.

The thunderous noise stopped. In one moment all of Vadanis was vibrating with its resonance; in the next there was only ringing silence. The elementals – and the Guardian – had gone.

CHAPTER FIFTY-TWO

For a few moments Terrel was too stunned to react at all, but as Jax's fingers closed around the hilt of his sword the healer recognized his most immediate danger and glanced quickly at his allies. Taryn was still unconscious, and although Faulk was sitting up he looked dazed, as if he didn't know where he was. In any case, now that the shield was gone the soldier would presumably be vulnerable to the enchanter's spells again. Terrel himself did not feel capable of moving. His damaged ear was extremely painful, and the injury to his shoulder meant he still could not lift his left arm. Even if he had been able to stand up he wasn't sure his legs would support him; his entire body felt weak and drained of energy. Physically he had never felt more vulnerable, and although his mind was racing he couldn't see a way out of his predicament. Triumph had turned to disaster so swiftly that he could hardly take it all in.

As Jax dragged himself to his feet, sword in hand now, Terrel saw that the prince was also weary and in pain, and this gave him a little hope. But that didn't last long as Jax began to advance upon him, his intentions plain.

'You tricked me,' the prince rasped hoarsely. 'You're always trying to trick me.'

'No. All I was doing—'

'Well, it won't work this time,' Jax declared, already savouring his victory.

Taryn? Terrel called. *Can you hear me? I need—*

The grey bird Terrel had seen earlier flew down between the brothers, making Jax hesitate, and landed near the healer.

What do you want? the bird asked in Taryn's voice.

'What's going on?' Jax shouted.

As Terrel glanced at the boy's unmoving form, he realized what had happened. Taryn had become a sleeper, and now he'd returned. The grey bird had not been Alyssa, as Terrel had hoped, but it had been waiting for another wandering spirit to make use of its wings.

The shield, he said quickly. *We need it back.*

All right, Taryn replied, *but she says there has to be a gap or your friends can't reach you.*

She says? Terrel wondered hopefully.

It means your enemies may get in too if they find the opening, the boy went on.

This sounded better than nothing to Terrel.

Go ahead, he told the boy.

'You're doing it again, aren't you?' Jax exclaimed. 'I thought you might try something like this, so I arranged for a few reinforcements. They'll be here very soon,' he added smugly.

Faulk was getting to his feet now, his eyes fixed on the prince.

'Tell that ugly brute to stay where he is,' Jax said without looking round. 'I can kill you before he gets close.'

'Stay where you are, Faulk,' Terrel said obediently. 'I'll take care of this.' He was trying to sound more confident than he felt. 'What reinforcements, Jax? You can't bring people up here. It'll ruin everything.'

'Too late,' the prince replied with a malicious grin.

The sound of marching feet could now be heard from the trail at the edge of the plateau. Terrel and Faulk realized simultaneously what it meant.

'The Imperial Guard,' Jax confirmed. 'And don't try any more tricks. They're loyal to me.'

'Can you hold them off?' Terrel asked Faulk.

'Yes, but . . . what about you?' The soldier was obviously reluctant to leave the healer alone with Jax.

'I can defend myself now.' When Jax had been inside the dream, Terrel had gained new insights and knowledge – and he knew they would help him face his brother.

'Are you sure?' Faulk queried, still doubtful.

'Yes. Go!' The approaching force was getting closer.

The soldier ran off, jumping nimbly over the tumbled stones of the ruins. Jax smiled.

'Do you really think you're a match for me?' he asked.

'I know I am.' The healer's mind was a better weapon than any sword.

'Really?' Jax took a step sideways, so that his blade now hovered over Taryn's prostrate figure. 'Even if I slit the boy's throat?'

Terrel's heart lurched, but he had no option but to trust his instincts now.

'He's protected,' he said. 'You can't harm him.'

'You're a liar. You were never going to give me any credit for this night – and you're lying about this too.'

The sound of fighting came from the head of the path but Terrel didn't dare look round to see how Faulk was faring.

'Then try it,' he challenged his twin, praying that he was right to take such a terrible gamble with Taryn's life.

Jax hesitated, obviously wondering if this was another trick.

Is he going to – Taryn asked nervously.

The prince screamed then – a wordless battle cry – and raised his sword. He swung it down in a vicious arc, aiming for the boy's neck, but the blow never reached its target. Instead, the blade was repulsed by an invisible force so violent it almost wrenched the weapon from the prince's grasp as it flew up into the air again. Jax staggered back, looking first bewildered, then furious. He started to advance on Terrel, then saw the look in his brother's crystalline eyes and thought better of it.

'It's no use, Jax,' the healer said quietly. 'Whether you like it or not, you're part of this now. Call off the guards. We have to contact the elementals again.'

'You can't fool me.' The prince's eyes were wild now. 'You're trying to trap me again.'

'I've no reason to do that. Call the guards off.'

'No!' Jax shouted.

Faulk needs your help! Taryn cried urgently, but Terrel somehow had the feeling that he wasn't talking to him. The bird took off and flew towards the site of the battle.

Turning his back on Jax with a deliberate show of disdain, Terrel looked over to where the soldier had placed himself. The narrowness of the path meant that he had been able to hold his position against a large number of men. Several bodies were already piled up below him and, as Terrel watched, two more soldiers were dispatched, screaming as they fell down the precipitous slopes to either side of the ridge. Faulk showed no signs of tiring, and his deadly expertise was both horrifying and mesmeric – but he seemed to be shouting something the healer couldn't hear properly, but whose tone indicated an uncharacteristic degree of panic.

As the grey bird swooped down over the soldier's head Terrel blinked, no longer trusting his own eyes. There were now *two* Faulks at the top of the trail, each wielding a sword with devastating precision. The only difference between them was that one was outlined in a faint aura of blue light. At the same time, Terrel saw that there were now two armies attempting to storm the plateau from below – but only one was composed of living men. Faulk was dealing with them, but he'd needed help with the other force. And he had got it from his own brother.

Faulk and his twin were each defending the gap in Taryn's shield – the living brother matching himself against the guards while the ghost fended off the wraiths of the fallen when they rose again to continue the attack. Galen and Zidan were together once more, fighting side by side as they had always done, and Terrel could sense their joy at the reunion. Now perhaps they could write a different ending to the legend, just as Laevo had wanted.

The healer turned away, knowing he could trust the brothers to do the job fate had assigned to them, and found that Jax was still standing where he had been. But he was no longer alone. Next to his own twin was a figure Terrel had hoped never to see again.

So now the confluence comes, Araguz said, seeming to bask in the new light of the Dark Moon. *And I am here to see that the will of the Dark Star is done.*

Even as the horror of this development swept over him, a small part of Terrel's brain was considering another puzzle. Ghosts? he thought. Here? Had healing the Ancients ended the effect of the invisible wind? And did this mean that his own allies might be able to join him after all? Would they be able to find the gap in the shield, as Araguz had done?

'Not all my reinforcements are stupid soldiers,' Jax gloated. 'You know the prophet, I think. He's going to save me.'

'He's not going to save anyone,' Terrel replied, seeing

the true depths of his brother's madness for the first time. 'If he gets his way he'll kill us all.'

It was the will of the Dark Star that I be here to welcome you all into the next world, Araguz claimed, *when this one is destroyed by the righteous fire.*

The prophet's words brought the urgency of the situation back into focus again. Glancing up at the sky, Terrel saw that the other three moons were overlapping, awaiting only the arrival of the shimmering bulk of the Dark Moon. The confluence was just a short time away – and there was no sign of the Ancients returning. He couldn't afford to concentrate on Araguz, but to ignore his presence would be insane. Indecision threatened to paralyze him completely.

The grey bird returned, chattering angrily as it alighted next to Taryn's human form. A moment later another ghost appeared. Nomar gave his son a brief glance full of yearning and regret, then turned his attention to the prophet.

You can't push me to my death this time, Araguz laughed. *Have you come to ask for my forgiveness?*

Killing you was a mistake, Nomar replied, moving towards his nemesis without apparent fear. *My first instincts were right. I'm going to heal you.*

From somewhere far away, Terrel heard the faint drift of music and knew that another of his former companions was playing his part in enabling Nomar to act. For the first time, Araguz began to look concerned.

Keep back, he muttered, holding out a spectral hand in warning.

Far from retreating, Nomar reached forward and grasped the prophet's arm, pulling Araguz towards him in a single, irresistible movement until the two ghosts seemed to merge – becoming enmeshed in the same space as if

they had stepped into each other's bodies. Araguz
screamed then, writhing as he tried to escape the intimate
embrace – but his efforts were in vain. Nomar held him
fast, and the prophet's image gradually faded from sight.
When he finally disappeared, Nomar seemed vaguely surprised.

Is it over? Taryn asked quietly.

It's over, his father confirmed. *This time for good. I'm a
healer again.* His smile was weary but contented.

Araguz has gone?

When the evil in him was gone, there was nothing left,
Nomar replied. *And it means I can move on now too.
Farewell, Taryn. You're all the son I'd hoped for, and more.
Thank you for the ring.*

Farewell, Father, the boy answered, his voice small but
brave.

Nomar glanced at Terrel, who silently renewed his
promise to look after the child. That seemed to satisfy the
other healer and, after a final look at his son, he vanished.

Jax was left staring at empty space, looking rather forlorn.

Making an effort to shrug off his exhaustion, Terrel was
about to turn his thoughts back to the problem of the elementals when a second bird – a falcon – swooped down
from the sky and a familiar voice sounded in his head.

Haven't you realized what's happening yet? Alyssa cried
urgently. *The Ancients are going to be born soon!*

CHAPTER FIFTY-THREE

Born? Terrel echoed, wondering what she was talking about even as he rejoiced at her arrival. Her voice sounded whole and healthy again.

Yes, she replied. *Nydus has been acting as a womb for them.*

But—

What you've seen and felt is them dreaming, Alyssa told him impatiently. *Just as you remember dreaming before you were born, or like the frightened babies in the fog valley. They've been moving up towards the surface for a while. Their time is due.*

The name Terrel had given the creatures seemed even more ironic now. He had known that in their own terms they were very young, even though they were indeed ancient by human standards – but he had not understood until this moment that their real lives hadn't even begun.

The confluence is their signal too, Alyssa went on. *The end of our time of change and the beginning of theirs.*

So is it their emergence that's going to cause the upheaval here? Terrel asked, trying to come to terms with this new information.

No. They may use it, perhaps, and in doing so make things worse for us, but the long cycle's coming to an end anyway.

What will they do when they reach the surface? Where will they go then?

Back to where they came from. They're not of this world.

The Dark Moon, Terrel breathed, seeing the connection at last.

That isn't their home either, Alyssa said, *but it has played host to one of their kind. The moon never really changed size, but the presence of the elemental made it seem as if it had.*

It bends light, he murmured, remembering her dismissive assessment of Muzeni's ancient telescope.

It also altered the unseen forces that guide its path, Alyssa added.

So that was the fifth voice, Terrel concluded, remembering the giant chord.

Yes, but it's much bigger and more powerful than the ones we've been dealing with – and it's been here before.

To lay her eggs, Jax said unexpectedly.

And now she's come back to see them hatch, Alyssa confirmed.

Terrel turned to look again at the swirling beauty of the light in the sky, knowing now that it represented *life*.

'They're a family,' he breathed aloud. 'A family.'

The Ancient's splendour was beginning to hide the other moons, which seemed almost dull in comparison.

But they can't leave now*! Terrel exclaimed as he finally caught up with the implications of what Alyssa had been telling him. *They're the Guardian.*

No, they're not, she replied, her voice filled with wonder. *You are.*

For a few moments all Terrel could hear was the sudden pounding of blood in his own ears, but then another sound registered. Jax was laughing.

'Oh, this is priceless!' the prince gasped. 'My deformed little brother's a hero!'

Ignore him, Alyssa said earnestly. *You* are *the Guardian, Terrel. The clues have been there the whole time if you think about it. It's just that we've all been too stupid or too preoccupied to see them. There isn't time to explain, but* you're *the one who has to act now, or there'll be nothing left of either palace.*

I can't . . . Terrel had been prepared to guide the elementals so that they might save Nydus, but the idea that he could achieve anything like that himself seemed preposterous. He didn't have that kind of power.

You're a healer, Alyssa told him. *You've healed animals, people, unborn babies, ghosts – even the elementals now. In a way you've actually healed whole countries. Now you have to do the same for the planet.* Although she sounded matter-of-fact, that didn't make what she was saying any less absurd. Part of Terrel wanted to laugh hysterically along with Jax; the rest of him wanted to crawl into a hole and hide.

But I'm supposed to be the Mentor, he objected feebly.

No, Alyssa replied. *That's me. And all the other sleepers. We'll help you as much as we can. Just call for us.*

All the sleepers?

We had to leave our bodies behind in order to stay with you, she explained. *I've simply been the go-between for the rest, for any joint wisdom we could gather. We're all here now, one way or another,* she added, glancing at Taryn.

But—

The great cycle is about to end, she cut in. *We don't have the time to argue.*

Terrel's mind filled with all the apocalyptic imagery of the Tindaya Code, and he shuddered at the thought of it coming true.

'This is what you've always wanted, isn't it?' Jax said. 'To destroy the world. Well, here's your chance.'

The healer instantly recalled the remark he'd made when he was much younger – in spirit as well as in years – and felt ashamed of himself. He knew he was a different person now, and he wasn't even tempted to accept Jax's suggestion. The prince was the destructive, malicious half of their team. Terrel was a healer, and if he didn't try to prevent the threatened disaster, what would have been the point of all his earlier efforts?

'You're mad, Jax,' he said. 'Why would I want to condemn us all?'

'Not all,' his twin replied. 'We'd be safe here. This is the hub, isn't it, the tip of the pendulum? Tindaya is meant to survive. That's why they built the temple here. And when it's over we'll be able to rule the world.'

'What's left of it.'

'Who needs the rest?' Jax argued. 'What has the world ever given you except pain and suffering?'

Terrel was silent for a while, expecting Alyssa to intervene. But she said nothing, and he realized he was being left to fight the last of his inner demons alone.

Although he had spent his whole life trying to suppress his anger at the hand fate had dealt him – solitude, disfigurement, pain and exile – he was suddenly filled with a burning rage. Why him? Why was *he* the one who had to do everything? Why hadn't he been born into a loving family? Why had he been forced to spend so many years separated from Alyssa? Terrel felt sick at the thought of what his life had been, and his frustration almost choked him. He longed for someone to take the responsibility from him.

Even his healing, his saving grace, had made him capable of inflicting pain as well as salving it. He could still remember the agony Elise and Ethilie had experienced at their final separation – and the sudden loathing he had felt at the time for all mankind. He could almost taste it again now. As disgust and cynicism threatened to overwhelm him, he wondered if perhaps Jax was right after all.

Terrel?

Alyssa's voice, her presence, was all he needed. She said nothing else but, suddenly, his life made sense again. Although she had been guiding him all along, this was one choice – the choice between good and evil – that the Guardian must make for himself.

'The world has given me a chance,' he replied finally.

'For what?' Jax asked sarcastically.

'For love, for peace of mind. For self-respect. For a life that means something. And you can have the same thing. All you have to do is choose your own path, as I have chosen mine.'

Jax said nothing.

'You know it's true,' Terrel went on. 'Why else did you help us heal the Ancient?' After holding his brother's gaze for a heartbeat, he turned back to Alyssa. *How am I supposed to do this?*

Left to itself, the surface of Nydus will buckle and shift so violently that almost nothing will survive, she replied. *You've controlled earthquakes before. This will be the same thing, only on a much bigger scale.*

Terrel was almost overwhelmed by dread and disbelief. It was a task beyond imagining.

I can't stop that from happening, he said bleakly.

You mustn't even try, she told him. *The Ancients will leave and the cycle will end, no matter what we do. Your job is to control the effects.*

But how?

Just as you did with the volcanic crevasses in Myvatan. We'll all be with you, so you won't be doing it alone, but you're the only one who can control such forces.

Terrel's thoughts sank into a well of terror so deep and dark he could not believe he would ever get out into the light again. But he knew that – for Alyssa's sake if nothing else – he must at least make one last despairing attempt to do as she said. Even as he made the decision, the ground beneath him shook and growled ominously. The pendulum had come to a stop.

Looking up, he saw that the Dark Moon ruled the skies unchallenged. The confluence had finally arrived.

CHAPTER FIFTY-FOUR

Terrel was blind from the moment the first tremor struck. This was the earthquake he had seen coming eleven years ago. It was already terrifying, making the mountain shake and groan like the timbers of a ship in a stormy sea, but he knew this was just the beginning, a foretaste of what was to come. He felt helpless, sensing no patterns that he could even attempt to manipulate. What was going on around him was bad enough, but he couldn't even be certain of what was happening on the rest of Vadanis, let alone all the other lands and oceans of Nydus – and without that rudimentary knowledge he had no way of trying to do something about quelling the worst effects of the upheaval. Another world had claimed him, but he was lost within it, and – in spite of Alyssa's claims – entirely alone. He couldn't think, he couldn't see or speak. And yet from somewhere came the memory of a piece of advice he'd been given. *Remembering is only the first stage.* And then another voice told him, *Remember us.*

He *did* remember then, seeing once more all the sleepers whose bodies littered the central square in Vergos. Kaeryss' appeal had lodged in his mind, but until that moment he'd forgotten the bargain he had struck with the prophetess. And he still wasn't sure what use it had been to either of them.

Remembering is only the first stage.

So what was the second? The answer came in the memory of another piece of Alyssa's advice, this time delivered in her own voice. Just call for us.

Will you help me? he tried tentatively.

We're here, Alyssa responded instantly, her voice filled with relief.

She was the first, of course, but Taryn was not far behind, and after that it became an enormous, bewildering procession. There were so many voices he could only recognize a few, but he was immediately aware of Lathan and Ysatel, each pledging their support. Then there were all the people he had seen but had never been able to communicate with – the comatose miners in a cave near Fenduca, the ranks of unconscious soldiers on Myvatan, Karn and the entire population of Vergos. He heard Kalmira's voice again, and glimpsed Vilheyuna's face. But the assembly went far beyond the realms of his own personal experience. There were sleepers everywhere on Nydus, all waiting until now to discover the purpose of their enforced absence from the living world. Their network spread far and wide, encircling the globe, but all the links, all the wandering dreams, went through one mind. Terrel felt overwhelmed by the responsibility that had been placed upon his shoulders – but he was no longer alone. When the Tindaya Code had talked of the disparate parts of the Mentor needing to be 'healed', it had not been referring to a possible reconciliation between Terrel and his brother; it had meant this coming together of the sleepers, under the healer's guidance.

Terrel gathered his allies around him, seeing the world through ten thousand pairs of eyes, all of them airborne on borrowed wings. He had no idea how he was going to make sense of everything he was being shown, but at least now he had the information he needed in order to begin. The trouble was, he didn't know *where* to begin.

Everywhere he looked, something terrible was happening. The entire surface of the planet was being rocked by a multitude of earthquakes, shock wave after shock wave pulsing across land and sea. Volcanoes exploded, hurling flame and ash into the atmosphere; tsunami towered into the sky, racing across the oceans to drown the coastal regions at their shores; and mountains shifted and crumbled as whole continents began to pull free of their foundations. And against the sort of power that could smash such eternal monuments of the natural world, the puny works of humankind were of no more consequence than a few grains of sand before an incoming tide. Terrel knew that thousands of people must be dying with every moment that passed, but he was still paralyzed by the scale of the disaster and the impossibility of doing anything about it.

In the end it was only desperation that lent him the strength to begin. Heedful of Alyssa's warning – that he should not try to prevent any of the upheavals – he attempted to find a more subtle approach. Instead of outright opposition he tried to shape the forces being unleashed, changing their patterns so that he could minimize the damage – or at least spare as many lives as possible. Separate the things you need from those you don't, he told himself, remembering his time on Myvatan. But he was also acutely aware that the volcanic conflagration then had been created by an elemental – and he'd had Tegan to help him make sense of its apparently random assault. Unthinkable though it was, this was infinitely bigger, its primeval forces born of the fabric of the planet itself. He told himself that the principle was the same nonetheless, and that by accepting information from the sleepers and feeding his instructions back via the network, he ought to be able to do some good.

You're a healer.

He had to treat the planet like a patient, its convulsion like a disease. Ease the pain; allow it to heal itself where possible; separate those things that were warring against each other and creating even greater imbalances; cauterize the wounds and reset broken bones. All this was fine in theory, and – in part – he did recapture an understanding of what he had achieved on Myvatan. But his piecemeal efforts met with only partial success, and every time he concentrated on one particular area, he was aware of a hundred other places that suffered because of it. What was more, the process was gradually becoming more violent, building up to what he knew would be a catastrophic climax. Unless he could find another way of combating Nydus's illness before then, all would be lost.

Terrel also realized that all the sleepers, all his willing allies, seemed to believe that he knew what he was doing, that he would eventually be able to solve the problem. As his efforts became increasingly desperate, their contributions remained as swift and reliable as he could have wished for. Yet sooner or later they would sense his inadequacy, and would then surely begin to lose faith – and when that happened the battle would be lost. Without the aid of the sleepers he would have been truly helpless. Even with them, he needed more.

Inspiration came to him when one of the sleepers showed him a city he recognized even from the air. It was Talazoria, the capital of Macul, and the place where he'd encountered the second Ancient. Looking down on the ruined fort, Terrel saw that the creature had left its lair and risen up to the surface, creating a miniature earthquake of its own as it did so. The elemental was a swirling vortex of darkness, a being of pure energy, without weight or substance – and now it was free above the city, and beginning to rise.

You gained the friendship and trust of the Ancients, Ysatel told him. *That's something no one else has ever achieved. Perhaps they'll help you now.*

Terrel stared through the eyes of the caroc, and wondered.

I don't know how to contact them, he said. He could sense no part of the creature's waking dream.

Then let's try this, she said.

Immediately, the great bird swooped down towards the amorphous shadow. Her intention was plain and Terrel could only admire the bravery of such an act. Even as a remote passenger he was terrified. As the caroc plunged into the elemental all his senses rebelled – but he didn't really care. What he saw or felt was irrelevant; all he wanted was a chance to communicate with the creature.

Will you help me? Please. I—

He met with a wall of complete indifference. The Ancient was not even moved to anger by the intrusion. His presence – and that of the bird – was utterly insignificant. The elemental – *all* the elementals – were too concerned with their own birth struggles to pay any attention to the planet or its inhabitants. The caroc was expelled effortlessly, spat out into the sky, and Terrel lost his fleeting contact with the mind of the alien entity.

Shall I try again? Ysatel asked, though she was obviously shaken by the experience.

No, Terrel replied. *They're not interested. I don't want to antagonize them.* His bargain with the creatures was obviously not a two-way deal.

The healer returned to his increasingly frantic efforts to

keep the worst ravages of the convulsion under control —
but knew he was running out of time.

This is hopeless, Jax said, his voice filled with panic. *It's
all your fault.*

Then help me. Tell me what I'm doing wrong. Terrel
could hardly believe he was asking his brother for advice.

I'm already helping you, Jax replied, *but you have to do
something about the pendulum. The Floating Islands have
stopped. You've got to get them moving again.*

Terrel had forgotten that piece of Kamin's parting
instructions, and was grateful to his twin for reminding
him. Concentrating on the area immediately around
Vadanis, he soon discovered that the islands had indeed
run aground and were now held fast upon the continental
shelf. However, it would only take the redirection of some
of the many tremors running through the region to lift
them off again. He began feverish preparations to put his
ideas into effect, only for another voice to interrupt his
efforts almost before they'd begun.

What are you doing? Shahan exclaimed. *Terrel? This is the
last thing—*

I have to start the pendulum up again. Kamin said—

What rubbish has that idiot been telling you? Muzeni cut
in. Even though Terrel couldn't see them, his ghostly
allies were there somehow.

You can't do that, Shahan said quickly. *The pendulum
must stop. For ever. Otherwise we'll have no chance of breaking the cycle.*

It counts down the time to the next upheaval, Muzeni
added. *So don't let any other islands start moving either.*

*I'd have thought the fact that Jax reminded you of it
would've been enough to let you know it was a bad idea,* Elam
commented. *Leave Vadanis just where it is.*

Cursing his own gullibility, the healer attempted to

reverse the changes he had already made, trying to ensure that the empire became lodged even more firmly on the ocean floor. His reversal confused some of the sleepers helping him, and resulted in a series of violent tremors that ran the length of Vadanis. Almost at once, to Terrel's astonishment, he found himself in contact with another of the elementals – the one in his homeland, in the mines below Betancuria. The unexpected shifts caused by Terrel's mistake had affected the area badly and, to his horror, he saw that the creature – who had not yet reached the surface – was now under threat from an underground river that had burst out of its normal tunnels. The Ancient was on the verge of panic, just as it had been more than a decade earlier. It was as if it had learnt nothing from that experience.

Acting instinctively, Terrel directed the elemental's path, keeping it calm enough for the relatively easy task of avoiding the deluge and reaching the open air. Once it was safe, the contact vanished before he had the chance to ask for help again. The elemental had accepted his assistance as if it was its due, without any thought of repaying the favour.

Feeling utterly dejected, Terrel went back to the thankless task of trying to preserve what was left of Nydus, only to become aware of a new presence within the complex realm he now inhabited. There seemed to be an argument going on, but he couldn't tell what it was about or who was involved – until a strident voice overrode the others.

Just let me speak to him. Let him *decide.*

Kaeryss? Terrel queried, recognizing her from her nocturnal visit to his bedroom in the palace in Vergos.

Yes. Can you hear me?

Yes, I can. But you're not a sleeper, are you?

No, but I'm speaking on behalf of everyone here, the prophetess replied. *All of us.*

The entire city's coming to my aid after all, Terrel thought.

Your friends aren't sure whether to trust me or not, Kaeryss went on, *so I'm going to let you decide.*

Be careful, Terrel, Shahan warned. *We know nothing of this Raven Cypher, and it seems to contradict the Code.*

I told you, Kaeryss snapped impatiently, *Tindaya was once part of Kenda. We're talking about two parts of the same thing.*

That's a dangerous conclusion, Muzeni said.

Just let me hear what she has to say, Terrel decided. He felt he owed the prophetess that much. *What is it, Kaeryss?*

Roskin and I came across part of the cypher that had never made sense before, she told him. *It talks about what's happening now, all around us, but says the only way to survive it is to counter the upheaval as a whole, not piece by piece. In your terms, you need to treat the underlying cause of the disease, not just the symptoms.*

I'd love to do that, Terrel responded. *But how?*

It has something to do with the centre of a great arc.

The arc of a pendulum? Terrel wondered.

And the house of the talisman, Kaeryss went on. *Does that make any sense?*

Yes. Go on.

It has to be rebuilt, she told him.

Rebuilt? The temple here was destroyed long ago. It would take centuries to rebuild.

You can read the text another way, Kaeryss said doubtfully. *What you may need to do is make sure it was never destroyed in the first place. Rebuild it in that sense. If the house of the talisman had survived, the cycle would have been broken then and none of this would be happening now.*

That's impossible.

Not according to the cypher. It has something to do with—

Pictures? Terrel guessed.

Yes. Kaeryss was beginning to sound excited now. *But you'd better be quick. The sky's on fire here, and I'm not sure how long we can survive.*

Taryn? Terrel called. *Are you there?*

I'm here, the boy replied nervously.

Can you show everyone the picture of the temple as it was?
I can try.

As Tindaya grew around them, a vast and intricate palace dedicated to the future, Terrel made sure that everyone saw it – in all its glorious detail. But, marvellous though it was, it remained just an image, as insubstantial as a dream.

We need to make it real, Terrel told the network. *Let's make it survive!*

He felt a rush of energy, the focus of all their beliefs and faith, and for a moment the temple *seemed* real, but it was still no more than a mirage. Like that it meant nothing.

Meanwhile, all round them Nydus was tearing itself apart.

Their failure left Terrel on the point of giving up, and it was only when he heard Alyssa's voice again that he forced himself to continue the unequal battle.

All of us, she was saying. *They protected all of us. Why would they have done that if it was going to end like this?*

The Dark Moon flickered into Terrel's consciousness and then, with a suddenness that shook him and the entire network to the core, a new voice was added. But this was no ordinary voice. It was the overpowering roar that marked the presence of the largest of the elementals, and it was soon joined by the other four. Without knowing what had prompted the end to their indifference, Terrel found that the Ancients were feeding him and his allies all the power they needed.

He could only think that the creatures' 'mother' had finally accepted his friendship, and – in gratitude for his care and healing of her 'children' – was upholding her end of the bargain. His interaction with them had been the only thing that could possibly have made them concerned about the fate of mankind. At the end of his long journey, Terrel's efforts made sense at last. For a short time, the Ancients became part of him, part of the Guardian.

Time, Muzeni muttered. *We didn't have enough power before.*

Now we do, Kaeryss declared. *Do you know what to do, Taryn?*

Yes, the boy replied, sounding as if he was almost dancing with glee. *Yes, yes, yes!*

This time the picture was subtly different. It was a blur of overlapping images, most of them identical, and Terrel knew they were travelling back down through the line of Taryn's female ancestors, each of them giving way to the one before. They travelled further and further into the past, from one bequeathed dream to the next, until they reached the time when it was no longer a dream. The temple on the mountaintop was real again. Solid, whole and incredibly beautiful. All the worlds and all the times came together. The power to see and do such things was beyond mere humans, but Terrel's network had been granted superhuman strength by the Ancients. As Yllen had predicted, the healer had finally done the impossible.

The infinite number of worlds collided at the moment when the great cycle had begun, and Terrel had no intention of keeping them apart as Kamin had suggested. The seer had been wrong about that too, but Terrel needed no advice to see the error this time. His task was to ensure that they came together in one accord, to allow Tindaya to survive. And when that extraordinary moment passed,

Terrel was back in the present, in his own time – and he could see the whole world as a single entity. His patient.

The gigantic waking dream was set out before him, and because he had just witnessed its evolution he found he could control its progress to some degree. What was more, it was working with him now, as if it *wanted* to be healed, knowing for the first time that such a thing was not only possible but desirable. The planetary fever that had become the upheaval was finally seen as unnatural, and although it was still going on, the dream was prepared to fight against it – and to be guided by Terrel. What had already happened could not be undone, but the future was suddenly full of different possibilities. There was no need to bow to the inevitable any more.

The healer's task was far from over, but although his instincts and his talents were stretched to the limit, he was able to keep the devastation to a minimum. The convulsion subsided as the gigantic sections of the planet's crust became truly stable for the first time in history. Nowhere on Nydus would life be the same – but life would go on.

CHAPTER FIFTY-FIVE

When Terrel opened his eyes, it was to daylight. Faulk and Taryn were sitting nearby, talking quietly, but as soon as they saw the healer stir they came over to join him.

'We're still here,' Terrel said, hardly daring to believe it. The confluence was over and the mountain beneath them was unmoving and silent.

'We are,' Faulk replied. 'And from what Taryn tells me, we're likely to stay for a long time now.'

'The long cycle is over,' the boy confirmed. 'It won't happen again.'

Terrel looked around him. The temple was still in ruins, exactly as it had been before.

'I thought . . .' he began, then fell silent.

'It was real,' Taryn explained. 'Then. What it is now doesn't matter.'

'So it's truly over?'

'Thanks to you,' Faulk said, nodding. 'How are you feeling?'

Terrel realized that his head was wrapped in a bandage and his left arm was supported by a makeshift sling. But his pain seemed irrelevant now.

'I'm fine,' he said. He took a little more time to let the events of the night sink in. Had he really healed a *planet*?

'Hard to believe, isn't it?' Faulk remarked.

Terrel nodded. 'Where are the others?' he asked.

'They've gone,' Taryn replied.

'Even the birds?'

'We're the only ones here now,' the boy confirmed.

'What about Jax?'

Faulk and Taryn exchanged glances.

'I'm sorry,' the big man said. 'He's dead.'

Terrel realized he had known it all along. There were hollow spaces inside his head and heart.

'I know . . . he wasn't the brother you would have wanted,' Faulk said awkwardly, 'but no one should have to lose a twin. I found my brother again, and I'm sure you will one day too.'

Terrel wasn't certain he even wanted such a reunion, but while his brain told him he should be rejoicing at his brother's demise, his heart felt nothing but a rather sad emptiness. If he hadn't been able to take care of his own twin, what right did he have to call himself a healer?

'What happened?' he asked, needing to know how Jax had died.

'I only know what Taryn's told me,' Faulk said, glancing at the boy.

'After it was over and you were asleep,' Taryn said, 'Jax seemed very upset. I don't know why. He kept crying and saying things I couldn't understand. He was shouting something about a baby and someone called Mela. I don't know who she is.'

I do, Terrel thought. Mela had been a minor princess in Makhaya, who had been pregnant with Jax's child when he forced her to commit suicide by jumping from the top of one of the towers of the imperial palace. Maybe I did heal him in a way, Terrel thought, recalling the earlier awakening of the prince's dormant conscience.

'Anyway, I was more concerned about you,' the boy went on, 'so when Jax wandered off I wasn't sure where he was going. Then I heard him scream Mela's name. I turned round to look and he was standing over there, by the cliff. Before I could call out or do anything, he stepped over the edge.'

Some time later, when Terrel had had something to eat and was feeling a little of his depleted strength returning, Faulk asked whether he wanted to make his way to the valley or stay on the summit for another night.

'If we go now,' the soldier added, 'we won't get there today, but we ought to get most of the way down.'

'We should probably go,' Terrel replied. 'But there's something I have to do here first.'

Faulk nodded, and helped the healer to his feet. Terrel walked stiffly to the outer edge of the maze and then, as his two companions watched from a distance, he followed the intricate pattern of broken stones as best he could, retracing the steps of his younger self until he reached the dark star at its centre. By then the amulet was glowing in the palm of his left hand, where the sling held it close to his chest. For a moment it hovered there, then the miniature star floated away and gradually faded from sight.

Turning round to return to his friends, Terrel saw three ghosts standing at the edge of the maze, watching the ceremony in silence. When he limped across to them, their solemn expressions were replaced with smiles.

I told you we'd get through this, Elam said with a broad grin on his face.

It was rather more complicated than we thought, Muzeni admitted, but even in making such an admission the old heretic seemed cheerful enough.

I take it your world has survived too? Terrel said.

Yes, Shahan replied. *And now that Vadanis is no longer*

moving, there's no chance of the cycle threatening us again either. You did well, Terrel. The pride in the seer's voice was almost paternal.

I had a lot of help, the healer said.

But you were the one who had to pull it all together, Muzeni pointed out. *I think I'm going to go now. Don't forget my pipe.* With that the old man vanished, and Terrel knew he would never see him again.

We can move on, Shahan affirmed. *Thanks to you. Enjoy your life, Terrel. I hope we don't meet again for a very long time.* The seer disappeared, leaving another gap in Terrel's heart.

Moons! I hate goodbyes, Elam remarked.

Me too, Terrel said, knowing that this last one was going to be the hardest of all.

I was right, wasn't I? Elam said. *We did have some more adventures.* He grinned again, but there was sadness in his eyes too. *But they're over now, I reckon.*

For now, Terrel conceded.

It'll feel good to move on, Elam said determinedly. *I should have done it ages ago, but there always seemed to be a reason to stick around for just a bit longer.*

Do you have *to go?* Terrel asked forlornly.

Yes. You'll understand when you're dead.

Terrel nodded. *You've been my true brother,* he said, almost choking on the words.

Elam did not reply. Instead he held out his hand as he had done before, and Terrel – moving awkwardly with his twisted right arm – reached out and clasped it as best he could. The faint sensation as they touched meant more to the two friends than either of them could put into words.

Goodbye, Terrel, Elam said. *Don't waste any more of your time here.*

I won't, the healer said, knowing what he meant. *Goodbye, Elam.*

A moment later he was alone again.

That night, as they watched the sky from their camp halfway down the mountain, the Dark Moon was the first to rise. It was still glowing with the shifting colours of a thousand rainbows, but now there seemed to be four new stars orbiting its surface.

Moonlight and movement, Terrel thought, watching as the four smaller lights moved towards their mother until they seemed to kiss the surface of the moon and were then absorbed into it. He remembered the Ancient in Makranash, the Toma's sacred mountain, and the fact that it had seemed interested in kissing – and realized now that this was because it had seen in that intimate contact some vestige of the merging he had just witnessed. Ghadira and Jax, who had been in control of Terrel's body at the time, would never know what their embrace had meant to the Ancients. The thought made him smile.

After a little while the elementals simply left, returning the moon to its former shadowed self. As Terrel watched their glorious light dwindling away into the darkness of space, he knew he would never see their like again.

CHAPTER FIFTY-SIX

'So this is where you leave us for a while?' Faulk asked. He had brought their horses to a halt at the fork in the trail.

'Yes,' Terrel replied, climbing down from the cart. 'I'll join you soon in Cotillo. You know who to ask for there?'

'We ask for Jon,' Taryn recited obediently. 'Ahmeza's brother.'

Several days had passed since the three friends had left Tindaya. They had been travelling continuously, but they'd almost come to the end of their journey now – and Terrel knew he had to do this last part on his own.

'Will she still be there?' Taryn asked quietly.

On the way north, Terrel had often found himself looking at various animals and birds, wondering whether they might be Alyssa – until he'd realized that if everything had turned out as he believed it had, she would no longer be a sleeper and her spirit would not be able to wander like that. She had to be awake. He had no way of telling how her re-emergence would have been received by the wardens or the other inmates of Havenmoon, but he knew one thing for certain. She had said that she would wait for him – just as he'd promised to come back for her.

'She'll be there,' he said.

Terrel and his companions had arrived at the army camp

below Tindaya to be greeted by a surprisingly muted reception. The healer had not expected – or wanted – a hero's welcome, but the sombre mood had seemed strange nonetheless. However, the reasons for the subdued atmosphere had soon become apparent.

While it was obvious to everyone that the worst predictions of the Tindaya Code had been avoided, the nature of the earthquakes that had affected the valley had convinced many of the seers that the islands had come to a permanent halt. Even when Terrel tried to persuade them that this was a good thing, the huge adjustment to their way of thinking about the world and their place within it was causing great difficulties. Prejudices that had been ingrained for many centuries could not be set aside overnight. There was also a growing conviction among the soldiers – and even some of the seers – that there had never really been any danger of the worldwide cataclysm they had so feared. Now that the dreaded confluence had come and gone – with the valley escaping relatively unscathed – it was easy for the onlookers to suppose that the prophecy had simply been the result of over-fertile imaginations. Although Terrel had known the truth, he'd seen no point in insisting on its acceptance. To his credit, Kamin had accepted the healer's version of events, but he knew too much about human nature to think it was worth the effort of publicly announcing his beliefs.

The other event that had served to curb any thought of celebration had been Jax's death. When the prince's body had been discovered it had sent the Empress into a downward spiral of depression, until her grief became indistinguishable from madness. Terrel had felt glad when he was advised not to go and see her, even though he knew this was cowardice on his part. The mother

who had been no mother to him at all had no part in his
life now.

There were already several rumours in circulation about
the manner of Jax's death. Although no one had stated this
directly, it was obvious that some people suspected either
Terrel or Faulk of murdering him. Officially, Taryn's
story of what had really happened had been accepted –
though Kamin decided to suppress any mention of the
prince's references to his half-sister – but that had not
stopped the tongues from wagging. One of the other
rumours that had reached Terrel before he left had been
that the soldiers who'd found the prince's body had
noticed some strange marks on his chest, as if his clothes
and skin had been scorched from within. Some even said
that his heart had been burnt to ash.

Once things had settled down a little, Kamin told Terrel
that he and his senior advisers had discussed the possibility of taking Adina's other son to Makhaya, to restore the
imperial line, but that they had decided this would be
much too awkward politically. Not only would it have
meant admitting to the mistake they'd made twenty-five
years ago, but with Dheran close to death, Adina insane
and Jax dead, it had been decided that it would be better
to make a fresh start. A new imperial line would be established with one of Dheran's sons from an earlier marriage.
The fact that this would in effect deprive Terrel of his
rightful heritage had seemed to concern the seer, but the
healer could not have cared less. He wanted nothing to do
with the court. There was only one thing left on his mind
now.

In return for Terrel's agreement to make no claim on
the imperial throne, Kamin had promised to give him
whatever help he needed – both now and in the future.
Terrel had asked only for a cart, two horses, supplies for

himself and his friends, and a little money to speed them on their way. Then they had headed north.

As soon as Terrel came in sight of the estate, he knew that a great deal had changed. The iron-clad gates stood open, hanging crookedly on broken hinges, and parts of the surrounding wall had fallen into disrepair. As he went inside the grounds, he saw that the inner moat was overgrown with weeds and the gatekeeper's cottage was dilapidated and obviously unused, its doors and windows gaping open.

As Terrel continued along the road, misgivings built up inside him. Everywhere he looked there were signs of neglect and decay – and when he caught his first glimpse of the great house that had been his home for the first fourteen years of his life he gasped in dismay. Part of the south wing, where he, Alyssa and Elam had each had their cells, had collapsed, exposing some of the inner rooms. That in itself was not an immediate concern, because the dungeon where Alyssa had lain during her long sleep was at the far end of the building. But if the mansion was all as unstable as the south wing, then it was possible she might have been trapped there – or even crushed by falling masonry during the recent tremors.

As he hurried on, certain now that the haven had been abandoned, and terrified by the implications for Alyssa, Terrel saw other indications that the estate was going to rack and ruin. The stable roofs had fallen in, the lawns and courtyard near the main house were littered with fallen roof tiles and other debris, and several stone balustrades had broken away and tumbled to the ground. However, the northern end of the building seemed to be relatively unscathed, and that gave him a little hope.

As he came round to the main entrance, the setting sun was behind Havenmoon, spreading a halo of orange light across the sky all around it. Some brightness shone from windows that had previously been dark, so that it seemed as if lamps had been lit within – but Terrel knew the promise of warmth and welcome was just an illusion. In reality his former home was cold and dark and empty – and his apprehension became even more acute. The place he had been longing to see for the past eleven years now had a melancholy air, as if only ghosts could live there. All he could do was hope that outward impressions were wrong and that it was not *entirely* empty.

He went in the main entrance and turned right at once, following the corridor that led to the north wing. He moved carefully, even though he longed to hurry, because there seemed to be dangers everywhere. Ceilings sagged ominously, floorboards had sprung up in places and one interior wall was now just a pile of rubble. There was an all-pervading musty smell of damp, and everything was covered with a layer of either dust or mould. Havenmoon had been old when he had lived there, but it was hard to believe that it could have deteriorated so much in such a short time. However, none of that would matter at all if only he could find Alyssa.

At last he found the stairs that led to the dungeons, and made his way down into an even gloomier realm. Her cell was at the far end of the passageway, and as he hurried towards the door Terrel's heart was beating so hard he thought it might burst out of his chest. Lifting the latch, he had to wrench the wood free and the hinges squealed in protest – but nothing as flimsy as a warped door was going to stop him now. He flung it back – only to see that the room was completely empty.

He almost screamed with frustration and sheer disbelief. At first he wondered if he'd got the wrong cell but he knew deep down that he had not. Then he took a step forward and looked around stupidly, as if he expected her to be hiding in a corner somewhere, but the orange light from the small barred window was enough to tell him that no one was there. Alyssa had gone.

It can't end like this, he told himself despairingly. It *can't*. All sorts of possible explanations occurred to him. The wardens might have taken her with them when they'd left the haven. They might have moved her somewhere else within the building. Or she might have woken up and left of her own accord. But he didn't believe any of them. She had said she would wait for him.

'Looking for someone?'

At the sound of her voice he spun round to find Alyssa standing in the doorway.

Seeing her in her own shape filled him with such a welter of emotions that it seemed to him there was no way a single human heart could contain it all. Tears filled his eyes and he could not speak. She was even more beautiful than he remembered. She was still thin, but she did not appear as frail or insubstantial as she had once done. Her straw-coloured hair was cropped short in uneven clumps, as it always had been, and he wondered idiotically if she had cut it herself. Her deep brown eyes were still the most striking feature of her fine-boned face, but there was less of the child in them now. During her long sleep she had obviously grown a little with the years – and through her wanderings she had seen a great deal. And yet she was still Alyssa, and the bond between them was as strong as ever.

Alyssa held out her hands and he moved towards her in a dream, hardly daring to believe that his own happy ending – the one Sarafia had predicted – had finally arrived. As their hands met, they both looked down at Alyssa's ring – the ring that had for so long been the only link between them.

Then they looked up at each other, and Terrel saw the whole world reflected in her eyes.

'I came back,' he said, finding his voice at last.

'And I waited for you,' she responded softly.

Their promises were fulfilled.

Terrel thought of all the things they had to tell each other, of everything he wanted to say – but only one phrase made any sense at that moment.

'I love you.'

'I love you too,' she replied, with the smile that he'd longed to see for eleven years.

In the next moment Terrel was locked within Alyssa's arms. And now, finally, he was home.

EPILOGUE

'You still miss them sometimes, don't you?' Alyssa said.

'Who?' Terrel asked.

They were sitting in the small rooftop garden of their home in Tiscamanita, watching the sun set over the Movaghassi Ocean.

'The ghosts,' she replied. 'You dreamt about them again last night.'

'Did I?' He still found it odd that his wife could often remember his dreams when he could not.

'I miss them too,' Alyssa admitted, 'but it's better for them that they've moved on.'

'They were our friends,' Terrel said. 'It's not surprising we miss them, especially after all we went through together.'

Alyssa nodded, and stretched like a cat basking in the warmth of the summer evening. Watching her, Terrel felt a contentment he had never thought to find in his lifetime.

'It's a shame about Muzeni's journal, though,' she added.

Before they had left Havenmoon for the last time, they'd made a pilgrimage up the hill to the estate's graveyard, where Terrel and Elam had hidden the chest containing the many volumes of the old heretic's writings. But when they located the tomb where the two boys had left the chest, they found that the books were damp and mildewed, with most of their pages stuck together and the rest so smudged and discoloured that they were unreadable. However, the trip had not been a complete waste of time and effort. Having forced their way through the jungle-like undergrowth to reach the disused observatory, Terrel had found the small pile of bones that were the last of Muzeni's remains and placed his pipe among them, honouring another promise.

'I'm sure there were a lot of interesting things in them,' Alyssa went on now, still talking about the journals, 'but I suppose in a way they've moved on too.'

'So has the world,' Terrel said.

In the year that had passed since the events at Tindaya had settled their fate, the people of the Floating Islands had had to get used to a number of changes in their way of life. The most dramatic of these was the fact that their islands no longer moved but were now firmly anchored to the sea bed. Because of this – and for the first time ever – the coastline of Vadanis was now affected by the rise and fall of the tides. But this was a minor change compared to the adjustments that had been necessary to the population's way of thinking. The belief that land ought to move was so deeply ingrained that many thought coming to a halt would cause a catastrophe, but as time passed and life in most respects went on as usual, their fears were eased. And the fact that the orbits of all four moons had at last reverted to normal helped reassure them even further.

The second major change was the way in which increasing contact with the outside world was starting to dispel some of the xenophobic attitudes prevalent during the empire's centuries of isolation. Vadanis was now no more than two or three days' sail away from the nearest point on the Kendan coast, and – after a tentative beginning – trade between the two countries was expanding rapidly. What was more, under the guidance of the new Emperor, envoys had been dispatched to other lands further afield in the hope of promoting greater communication and co-operation. It would no doubt take some time to overcome mutual suspicion, but the fact that such efforts were being made at all gave Terrel great hope for the future.

For the healer himself, the alterations to his life during the last year had been even more profound. From being a wanderer on an unknown road, he now had a permanent home and a family of his own. The house he shared with his wife and their adopted son had been bought with a gift granted to him by the Seers' Council in recognition of his services. He lived quietly for the most part, making a modest living as a healer, and despite their eccentricities and his odd appearance, Terrel and his wife had made many friends in the town.

Alyssa and the outside world were still coming to terms with each other. When people looked at her, they saw first her ethereal beauty and her youth. She in turn delighted in telling them that she was actually older than her husband – though few believed her. However, those who got to know her well soon realized there was more to her than just a pretty face. Although, because of her long sleep, she appeared to be no more than eighteen years old, she was much older than that in terms of emotional and mental development. Although she never spoke with strangers about her experiences as a sleeper, the contrast between the two facets of her personality were usually obvious to all but the most casual acquaintances. And what was obvious to everybody was that she and Terrel were utterly devoted to each other.

The third member of their household was also revelling

in his new-found security. Taryn had been given his child-hood back again, and for the most part seemed to have put his sorrows behind him. He too had made several friends and, to Terrel's delight, was showing signs of developing his own talent as a healer.

The choice of Tiscamanita for their home had come about by chance. Given his personal history there Terrel had been nervous of the idea at first, but one of Kamin's last acts before standing down as Chief Seer had been to contact Seneschal Cadrez about the healer. Terrel never discovered exactly what passed between the two men, but since that time his welcome had never been in doubt. The seneschal was now numbered among Terrel's friends, as well as occasionally being one of his patients. Underseer Hacon had also given the newcomers his tacit seal of approval, which meant that even if the events of Terrel's first visit to the town hadn't been forgotten, they had long since been forgiven.

No one in the town outside his own family — with the possible exception of Cadrez — knew anything of Terrel's connection to the imperial court, or to the events at Tindaya. Those events were still the subject of a huge number of rumours — most of them erroneous — and the healer had no wish to complicate his life with such things now. He was perfectly happy just as he was.

Rapid footsteps sounded on the steps leading to the roof, and Terrel and Alyssa both turned to see what Taryn wanted.

'We've got a visitor!' the boy reported, breathless as much from excitement as exertion.

'A patient?' Terrel queried.

'I don't think so. Shall I ask him up?'

Terrel glanced at Alyssa. He had been enjoying their

quiet time together, and wished it had not been disturbed, but Taryn was obviously eager to bring the newcomer to him. He nodded and the boy ran off, returning with a man Terrel and Alyssa both recognized at once.

'Seer Lathan,' the healer said, standing up to greet his guest. 'What brings you here?'

'If you want to be formal,' their visitor replied, 'it's Chief Seer now, but I'd rather you just called me Lathan. I'm here because I've been wanting to talk to the two of you for some time, and this is the first chance I've had.'

After they had sat down, and Taryn had been asked to bring them some refreshments, the seer smiled.

'This feels good,' he said. 'You were wise not to think of living in Makhaya. The place is a madhouse. Since I was confirmed as Chief Seer I haven't had a moment to myself. Until now – and that's only because I insisted on some privacy for this visit. You wouldn't have wanted my entourage descending on you, believe me.'

Taryn returned with the drinks and passed them round, then sat on the floor in front of his adopted parents.

'I owe you a great debt, young man,' Lathan told the boy.

'Me? Really?'

'It had always been one of my greatest desires to see the temple at Tindaya in its heyday. You granted me that wish.'

'You were part of it too,' Taryn said. 'We needed all the sleepers to make it real.'

'But none of us would have had the chance without you three.'

'And Faulk,' Taryn added loyally.

'Indeed.' Lathan took a sip of his drink and sighed with pleasure, apparently relaxing more with every moment.

Terrel had only met Lathan on three previous occasions,

and two of those had been under rather unusual circumstances. Their initial meeting had been on the summit of Tindaya – the first time Terrel had ever been there – when he had been in spirit form and Lathan had become a sleeper. The second had been in Betancuria, when Terrel had been accompanied by Alyssa in the shape of a stonechat, and Lathan – after instruction from Elam – had taken the form of a kestrel. The third occasion had been earlier that year, in Makhaya. It was the only time Terrel and his family had left Tiscamanita since they'd settled there, and he would not have gone at all if it had not been for a specific request from the Emperor's deathbed. Dheran had expressed a wish to see his other son, and although Terrel's initial reaction had been to refuse, Alyssa had persuaded him to go. Afterwards he'd been glad she had done so, but their visit to the capital had been a difficult and solemn occasion.

When he'd been ushered into the dying Emperor's bedchamber, Terrel hadn't known what to expect. At first he had not even been sure Dheran was aware that anyone was there, and he hadn't been able to bring himself to speak. Eventually his father had opened his eyes and seen him, then held out an unsteady hand. In taking it, Terrel had known instinctively that there was nothing he could do to reverse the old man's decline.

'I'm sorry,' Dheran had whispered. 'It was a mistake. I should have . . .'

Then he'd fallen asleep again and after a while Terrel had left, his emotions in turmoil. Two days later the Emperor had died.

On the same trip, the healer had also seen his mother – but only from a distance. The Seventh Empress was now quite insane, living in a make-believe world of her own, and had effectively been committed to secure quarters within the palace – her own private Havenmoon. Terrel had declined the offer of talking to her, and not even Alyssa had tried to change his mind.

He had also decided not to stay in Makhaya for the coronation of the new Emperor, a decision met by the court with some relief. He represented a potential embarrassment should his real ancestry become widely known. Kamin had still been Chief Seer then, though elections were under way to choose his successor, and Terrel had had little time to speak to any of the other seers – including Lathan.

'What was it you wanted to talk about?' he asked now.

'With all the stories you could tell, I could give you a hundred answers to that,' the seer replied, 'but what I most want to ask is a question only Alyssa can answer.'

Alyssa smiled.

'You want to know how I was so sure Terrel was the Guardian,' she said.

Lathan glanced at Terrel.

'Is your wife always this perceptive?' he asked.

'Absolutely. All the time,' the healer replied with a straight face. 'It makes her almost impossible to live with.'

Alyssa punched his shoulder as the seer laughed.

'Well, how *were* you so sure?'

'I wasn't.'

'What?' Terrel exclaimed. 'You never told me that!'

'I don't have to tell you everything.'

'I'm confused,' Lathan said.

'So was everybody,' Alyssa said. 'That was the whole point. Look, no one's ever accused me of being a perfectly logical thinker. I just knew that someone had to do something – and nothing else made any sense. Call it a madwoman's intuition, if you like. And as soon as the words were out of my mouth, I kept seeing all the reasons why it was right.'

'Such as?' Lathan prompted.

'When Terrel was born, for a start. And everything he'd achieved since then. To me they seemed like the deeds of a hero, not a go-between, but there were specific things too. A lot of the confusion in the Tindaya Code stemmed from the fact that when it referred to the Mentor and the things Terrel did, I was with him – like on the journey to Talazoria. And do you remember the reference to the double-headed man and the hero being the same person at Makranash?' she asked Terrel. 'That meant it was the Guardian and not the Mentor who split in two there. The Ancient certainly didn't, did it?'

'And there were already two Mentors there,' Terrel added. 'You and Vilheyuna. And he died later.'

'That's right,' she said. 'It's no wonder it was impossible to interpret. And it was you the wizard helped in Myvatan when the ice exploded.'

'Yarek,' Terrel said, remembering.

'And it was supposed to be the Guardian who was helped. None of the wizards there helped the elemental, did they?'

'The reverse, if anything,' Terrel agreed.

'And the ice-worms protected *you*, not the Ancient,' Alyssa went on. 'Then, more recently, the Guardian was supposed to fight against himself in Vergos. That couldn't be the elementals, but it could have been you and Jax. And it was one of the Guardian's allies who was supposed to sacrifice himself there.'

'Nomar,' the healer said, nodding, and put a hand on Taryn's shoulder.

'And the Code said the Mentor needed the help of the entire city of Vergos.'

'But I did need them,' he said.

'No, *we* needed them. The sleepers. Without them the

network wouldn't have been possible. Once they were with us, we were *all* able to help you. The Guardian.'

'I suspect,' Lathan said, 'that a lot of the confusion about the Ancients came about because of how they joined you at the end. They actually *did* become part of the Guardian for a time.'

'So did the sleepers in a way,' Alyssa said. 'And that's all reflected in the Code. So it was obvious, really,' she concluded with an innocent grin.

'But you only thought of all this *after* you told me I was the Guardian?' Terrel queried incredulously.

'Well, it worked, didn't it?' she replied.

A few days after Lathan's visit, another traveller came to the healer's home, and once again Taryn was the one to announce his arrival.

'Faulk's home!' he exclaimed as he rushed into the kitchen where Terrel and Alyssa were preparing the evening meal.

The soldier's periodic arrivals were always an occasion for celebration. There was a room in the house set aside for him, but he was far from being a permanent resident. Terrel doubted whether Faulk would ever be able to settle in one place for long, unless – as Alyssa had pointed out – he found someone like Eden again. As it was, he was still very much part of their family, with Taryn regarding him as a much-loved uncle. He had already taken several trips around Vadanis and some of the other islands, always returning to Tiscamanita with new tales to tell, but his most recent – and longest – expedition had been to the mainland, and they were all hoping he would be bringing news of their former travelling companions.

After the big man came in and dropped his pack on the floor, he exchanged traditional greetings with his friends.

This involved picking Taryn up and swinging him round, complaining all the while about the boy getting too big and heavy for this sort of thing, then enfolding Alyssa in a bear hug. Terrel always worried that Faulk was going to crush her when he did this, but she never seemed to mind. Finally Faulk came over to inspect Terrel, especially his truncated ear, before embracing him too.

'No more injuries?' the soldier asked, completing the ritual. 'I suppose you two must be looking after him all right then.'

A little while later they were all sitting round the table, listening to Faulk's account of his latest exploits. Once so taciturn, he had become a good storyteller now – especially after a cup or two of wine.

'So, did you find them?' Taryn demanded when the tale didn't move fast enough for his liking.

'Who?' Faulk teased.

'Yllen and Lawren of course,' Taryn stated indignantly. 'You *know* who!'

'Yes, I found them,' he admitted, relenting. 'They're still together in Leganza, and they're both well and happy. They were lucky. The place they were staying in was destroyed during the quakes, but they weren't there at the time. Like a lot of people they'd gone up into the nearby hills to watch the confluence. There's much more damage there than there was here, and it's the same all over Kenda, but it could have been much worse. There's rebuilding going on all over the country.'

'So where are they living now?' Alyssa asked.

'In a tavern. They're both working there at the moment, but give them a few years and my bet is they'll own the place. The landlord's half besotted with Yllen, even though he knows she's spoken for.'

'That sounds like her,' Terrel said, smiling.

'They're glad that everything worked out well for you,' Faulk added, 'and told me to say that if you're ever in Leganza, there'll always be a room for you at The Flounder.'

'Sounds delightful,' Terrel said, laughing. 'What about the sailors? Did you see them?'

Faulk shook his head.

'The *Musician* was away on a trading expedition,' he said. 'I wouldn't be surprised if they turned up here one day. I'll tell you who I did see, though. Daimon's back to his old ways, only now he has some new stories to tell in The Caltrop. The funny thing is, the cat chose to stay with him rather than on the ship. Paws goes to the inn with Daimon every day, and even has his own dish in the bar. He looks well on it too – he's a lot fatter than he used to be.'

Terrel smiled as he pictured the scene.

'Any news from Vergos?' he asked.

'I didn't go that far myself, but I heard some of the gossip. Apparently it was chaos there for a while after everyone woke up, but it seems Karn is making a good king even though he's so young. He's got his mother and Kaeryss to advise him, so I should think he'll be all right. The city itself took a lot of damage, mainly from fires. No one's sure how they started. But at least the place wasn't completely wiped out by a fire-scythe. That's what most people were afraid of.'

'What about Roskin? Did you hear anything of him?'

'No. Not a word.'

The healer wasn't sure whether to be glad or disappointed about that.

'Did you ever think of going back to the mountains?' Terrel asked, a little later in the evening. 'Back to your own country?'

'Maybe next time,' Faulk said.

'You're going to stay here for a bit first though, aren't you?' Taryn asked anxiously.

'Of course,' the soldier replied. 'You've got to tell me about what I've missed while I've been away, and show me all the new places you've discovered.'

'Good.' Taryn was happy now.

'But not tonight,' Alyssa decreed. 'It's past your bed-time, young man.'

'Do I have to?' he moaned.

'Yes,' Terrel said. 'Get going.'

Faulk waited until the boy had kissed them all good-night and gone to bed.

'You two make good parents,' he observed solemnly.

Over the next couple of days Terrel felt a few stirrings of mild dissatisfaction, not with his life but with his lack of knowledge. Having received news of his recent compan-ions, he found that he was thinking more and more about everyone who had been important to him earlier in his travels – and who were now impossibly far away. Although he had no intention of setting out on any long journeys, he wished he could find out what was happening in other parts of Nydus. When Alyssa noticed his preoccupation and coaxed him into telling her the reason for it, she became thoughtful for a while, then spent some time talk-ing to Taryn. That night, as she and Terrel were going to bed, she broached the subject again.

'If you're serious about this, there's a chance – and it's *only* a chance – that we may be able to do something about it.'

'How?'

'Taryn says there are pictures in the things you brought home with you. The pendant and the red crystal, for example. I've often felt that when I've touched them, but nothing was ever clear to me – and I can't show you my dreams anyway. But Taryn can.'

Terrel was surprised.

'But even if it works,' he said, 'wouldn't it just be pictures from when I was actually there? I want to know about what's happening now.'

'Taryn thinks the links are to the present, but you're the only one who'll be able to tell for certain. You're the one who forged the links in the first place.'

Terrel thought about the idea for a while, hardly daring to believe such a thing was possible.

'We could try when the Amber Moon's next full,' Alyssa suggested, 'when dreams are strongest.'

Terrel shook his head. 'I've got a better idea,' he said. 'When I was in Misrah it was the White Moon that was dominant. We should try when *it's* full.'

'Tomorrow, then,' Alyssa said.

'Which should I try first?' Taryn asked, looking at the objects laid out before them. The boy was both excited and a little nervous – as was Terrel.

'The pendant,' the healer told him.

They were sitting cross-legged in the roof garden, with Alyssa and Faulk watching nearby. Above them, the White Moon was a perfect bright disc amid the stars. Taryn held on to Terrel's good hand, then picked up the clay tablet. This was inscribed with the symbol the nomads called 'the river in the sky' – two wavy lines and a star – and had been presented to the healer in recognition of his tribal name, 'the voice of rain'. Taryn closed his eyes. Terrel did the same, and felt a surge of emotion as he sensed the links spring into life.

The first thing he saw was Medrano talking in front of

a large group. Although he couldn't hear what was being said, it was obvious that the artist's audience was spell-bound by his words. Initially Terrel assumed that this was one of the Toma's frequent storytelling sessions, but then he realized that the gathering was made up of people, most of them children, from many different desert tribes. That in itself was a good sign, but better still was the fact that everyone there seemed to be smiling and enjoying themselves immensely. Then Terrel saw that Medrano was being assisted by a young woman, who was evidently acting out the events he was describing. Her manner was both expressive and engaging, and she switched from drama to comedy with graceful ease. At first he did not realize who she was, but then he noticed Mlicki in the audience. The boy Terrel had known had grown into a man, and he wore the many-eyed head-dress of a shaman. Like his mother beside him, he was watching the performance with a degree of pride. Terrel's attention was drawn back to the young woman – and for a moment she seemed to look directly at him, her bright blue eyes widening in surprise. He saw her mouth form the words 'the voice of rain', and then Kalkara smiled in a way she had rarely done when Terrel had known her. The troubled child was now a woman of stunning, if unorthodox, beauty, and the happiness he saw in her face was a long way from the sadness that had been ever-present then.

The dream-image faded, and that would have been enough for Terrel, but Taryn had other ideas. He put down the pendant and picked up the curved dagger in its decorated scabbard. Immediately Terrel saw Zahir, his wife Chiara and their children at his side, as he welcomed leaders of visiting tribes to a feast in one of the nomads' largest tents. The healer recognized several other faces – and although the atmosphere seemed rather formal, and it was clear that important matters were to be discussed during the coming meal, it was also clear that there was no animosity between any of the participants. Misrah, it seemed, was still at peace.

The final picture came when Taryn picked up the woven belt – and it came as something of a surprise. Terrel would have known Ghadira anywhere. Even though she had been a girl of sixteen when he'd first known her, and was now a woman of twenty-four, her oval face, dark brown eyes and lustrous black curls had not changed a great deal – and there was still an air of mischief about her that made the healer smile. The surprise came not from Ghadira herself but from her surroundings. Terrel saw mountains around her rather than desert, and it was obvious that she had left the Toma behind. The reason for that soon became clear. A tall young man appeared beside her, took her head in his hands and kissed her with both tenderness and passion – as Terrel had done several years earlier, on the day before they'd parted for ever. As the embrace ended, Ghadira opened her eyes and – like Kalkara before her – seemed to catch the healer's gaze. In that moment he knew she was reliving the same memory and that, like him, she had no regrets about what might have been.

Four nights later, when the Red Moon was full and Faulk had left on another of his expeditions, they repeated the experiment using the crystal from Myvatan. With the nomad's artefacts Terrel had been connected to the people who had given them to him, but Jarvik – the person who had given him the crystal – was dead, so the healer didn't know quite what to expect. In the event it was Tegan's face he saw, and he remembered that she had been with him when he'd first touched the red stone. It was immediately obvious that she was still the Priestess of Akurvellir, and that the ancient site was still a place of pilgrimage. Myrdal was at her side, of course, but it was the couple with them who caught Terrel's attention.

Latira had come to show the magian her baby, and the new mother's eyes were full of joy and wonder. Beside her, looking both proud and possessive, was Pjorsa, the grizzled veteran who had been part of the company that had accompanied Terrel. He was in civilian clothes now, though, and the doting look in his eyes spoke of a man who found peace to his liking after so many years of war. Latira had found someone worthy of loving her, just as Terrel had predicted, even though at the time she had thought it just wishful thinking. It was Latira Terrel watched most carefully, hoping she would look up as Kalkara and Ghadira had done. But her gaze remained fixed on her child – and that had to be enough for the healer.

As the image faded and both he and Taryn opened their eyes, Terrel found that Alyssa was looking at him with a wry smile.

'Is that all your old sweethearts taken care of?' she asked.

'They weren't my sweethearts,' he replied patiently.

'You could've fooled me,' she said, but then she grinned and made it obvious that she was teasing him.

'They could have been,' Terrel claimed, teasing her in return, 'but I always knew I was coming back for you.'

'It's true,' Taryn said earnestly, obviously not quite sure how to take their exchange. 'He always said that.'

'I'm glad to hear it,' Alyssa commented.

'Actually, there are some we've missed,' Terrel said, 'but I don't have anything from Macul.' The only gifts he'd been given there had been a fire-opal, which he'd had to sell, and the sharaken's staff, which had been destroyed in Talazoria.

Alyssa pulled him to his feet and kissed him.

'Oh well,' she said. 'You'll just have to make do with me then.'

Later that summer, when Terrel had stopped thinking about the past so much and was simply enjoying the present, the missing part of his history came to him. When he saw the people on his doorstep he was speechless, and could hardly believe the evidence of his own eyes. Kerin Mirana was over fifty now, though he looked younger and was clearly still fit, but Ysatel was just as Terrel remembered her. She had been a sleeper for most of the intervening years, and so had aged little.

Alyssa and Ysatel greeted each other like long-lost friends, which in a sense they were, having each spent more than a decade with their spirit wandering in the mysterious realm of the sleepers. Over the following days the two women spent a lot of time together, comparing experiences and finding that they had much in common. Ysatel, of course, had been pregnant for the entire time of her long sleep – 'the longest pregnancy in history!' as she put it – but had finally given birth last winter. In spite of the unusual circumstances, the baby had been born safe and well. As soon as it had been feasible for them to travel, Ysatel had insisted on making the voyage all the way across the Movaghassi Ocean in search of Terrel, and of the place she'd seen on the night of the confluence. Always an explorer at heart, Kerin had set his misgivings aside and agreed, and they had set out with their new daughter to find Vadanis.

'Kerin never gave up on me,' Ysatel told them one evening when they were all sitting round the kitchen table. 'Even after so many years. It made me realize all over again why I love him so.'

'I couldn't believe it when she finally woke up,' her husband added. 'And when Cara was born, and she was all right, it was just incredible.'

The baby gave a squeal of delight, as if agreeing with her father's sentiments, and they all laughed.

'We'd already left Fenduca by then,' Kerin went on, 'which was just as well, because the place was all but destroyed in the earthquakes. The black mountain had been free to all miners for a long time, so there was no need to scrabble in the river any more.'

This development was only one among the many changes in Macul that the travellers had already described. The end of the corrupt monarchy had ushered in a chaotic but generally beneficial period of adjustment as the people had taken control of their own destiny. Aylen, one of Kerin's two sons from his first marriage, had been one of the leaders of the democratic movement and was still heavily involved in the country's government. Even the sharaken, the dream-traders who were Macul's spiritual leaders, had played their part in the transformation, becoming less aloof and giving the general population rather more practical and benevolent advice than before.

'You haven't told us about Olandis,' Terrel said a little later, naming Kerin's other son. 'What's he up to now?'

'We haven't seen much of him these last few years,' Kerin replied. 'He's become a wanderer, like me when I was younger.'

'He does visit occasionally,' Ysatel added, 'and he told us something that might interest you.'

'Moons! Yes, I'd forgotten,' Kerin said. 'He met some people in a really odd valley which was under a permanent bank of fog. They said they knew you. And there was a message from one of them . . . what was it?' He glanced at his wife.

'It was from Esera,' Ysatel said. 'She wanted to tell you that her daughter is well. She'd be about ten now, I suppose. And that she called her Terrella.'

Terrel glanced at Alyssa, who was grinning.

'So now you really *do* know about all your sweethearts,' she remarked.

'I haven't spoken out of turn, have I?' Kerin said, looking worried.

'No, silly,' Ysatel told him. 'Esera was pregnant before Terrel got there.'

'He just made quite an impression on her, obviously,' Alyssa said, still teasing.

'He does that,' Ysatel said fondly. 'But there was never any doubt where his heart lay. Aylen said he was distraught when he found out he couldn't go home straightaway.'

The visitors stayed in Tiscamanita for more than a long month, but eventually left to visit Tindaya and then return to Macul. The house seemed awfully quiet without them.

'You look very thoughtful,' Alyssa said that night as they lay in bed. 'Is everything all right?'

'As long as I have you, everything will always be all right,' Terrel replied as he took her in his arms. 'It just seems a bit quiet now they've gone. And it's strange not having a baby in the house any more.'

'That may change soon,' his wife told him quietly.

It took Terrel a few moments to realize the significance of what she'd said.

'Really?' he exclaimed, his eyes wide with joy and amazement.

Alyssa nodded.

'That's wonderful! Do you want me to look at you . . . as a healer, I mean. Make sure—'

'Everything's fine,' she assured him. 'I've got my own way of checking. I've been watching their dreams.'

For a few moments Terrel was too stunned to speak.

'*Their* dreams?' he said eventually.

Alyssa just smiled.